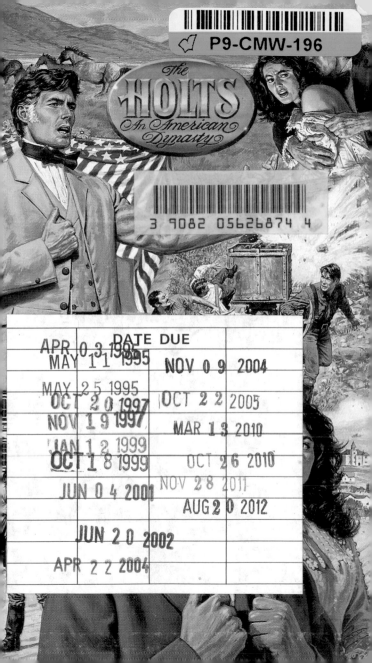

A NEW SERIES OF ORIGINAL ADVENTURES
FROM THE AUTHOR OF *WAGONS WEST*

BEGINS! CAUGHT BY THE TREACHERY OF
BOTH MAN AND NATURE, THE HOLT
FAMILY RETURNS TO ITS OREGON HOME-
STEAD AND MAKES IT THE SEAT OF A
DYNASTY WHOSE POWER WILL FORGE
THE FUTURE OF THE AMERICAN WEST
. . . WHOSE VISION WILL SHAPE THE
IDEALS OF A VIBRANT, PASSIONATE
GENERATION! COME THEN, MEET THE
HOLTS. . . .

(please turn the page)

THE HOLTS: AN AMERICAN DYNASTY

OREGON LEGACY

THE HOLTS MUST SINK THEIR ROOTS DEEP INTO THE OREGON SOIL TO WEATHER THE COMING STORMS—BUT NO FOE CAN DESTROY THEIR HUNGRY DESIRES, THEIR UNQUENCHABLE AMBITIONS . . . THEIR FIERY COURAGE.

TOBY HOLT—

A man to be feared and revered, he has lost his vast financial empire in the roaring snowstorms of a cruel western winter. He vows to begin again, but will it cost him a son . . . or a wife . . . or everything?

ALEXANDRA HOLT—

A gorgeous, passionate woman, she envisions her rugged husband transformed into a Washington senator . . . and clings so tightly to her sickly son that she may kill the very thing she loves.

JANESSA HOLT—

The illegitimate, half-breed daughter of Toby Holt, she fights back as her hopes of becoming a doctor slowly die, determined to face the world's prejudice . . . and to conquer her own fears.

TIM HOLT—

His father's spitting image but twice as rebellious, twice as hotheaded, he is seduced by dreams of quick money in a silver-mining town, but he may be headed for disappointment . . . and sudden death.

SAM BRENTWOOD—

Twenty-one, handsome, and a rogue, he fills Tim Holt's head with foolish illusions, but his dreams of easy money aren't from silver . . . but from schemes of a more shady and scandalous kind.

ANNIE MALONE—

A pretty, wealthy widow, her desire for a younger man in her bed blinds her to the difference between a brief fling and a lasting love.

ISABELLA ORMOND—

A coquette of seventeen, she's pretty enough to turn Tim Holt's head, and her kisses are sweet enough to capture his heart . . . but is love just a cruel game she's playing?

JOHN ORMOND—

A powerful and unscrupulous mine owner, he views Tim Holt as a potential son-in-law until Holt's support of the miners turns the young man into an enemy who may just have to die.

WHITE ELK—

The Shoshone Indian raised by Toby Holt believes he can be a cowboy, marry the girl he loves, and manage the Holt ranch—until racial prejudice teaches him a cruel lesson in the real world. . . .

MAI LI—

The delicately lovely Chinese American girl who sees in the tall, copper-skinned White Elk a soul mate, a cherished friend . . . and the lover she may never touch . . . never kiss . . . never possess.

AMERICAN DYNASTY #1

OREGON LEGACY

DANA FULLER ROSS

Created by the producers of
Wagons West, White Indian,
and **The First Americans.**

Book Creations Inc., Canaan, NY · Lyle Kenyon Engel, Founder

BANTAM BOOKS
NEW YORK · TORONTO · LONDON · SYDNEY · AUCKLAND

This is a work of fiction. While the general outlines of history have been faithfully followed, certain details involving setting, characters, and events may have been simplified.

OREGON LEGACY
*A Bantam Book / published by arrangement with
Book Creations, Inc.*

*Produced by Book Creations, Inc.
Lyle Kenyon Engel, Founder*
Bantam edition / November 1989

ISBN 0-553-28248-4

Published simultaneously in the United States and Canada

*Bantam Books are published by Bantam Books, a division of Bantam Doubleday
Dell Publishing Group, Inc. Its trademark, consisting of the words "Bantam
Books" and the portrayal of a rooster, is Registered in U.S. Patent and
Trademark Office and in other countries. Marca Registrada. Bantam Books,
666 Fifth Avenue, New York, New York 10103.*

PRINTED IN THE UNITED STATES OF AMERICA

O   0 9 8 7 6 5 4 3 2 1

Tim glanced up to see his father looking like a personal representative of the Day of Wrath.

"What are you doing home?" Toby demanded. "Of all the asinine stunts, this takes the cake."

"I thought I should rally round, sir," Tim protested. "I can't expect you to pay my tuition in these bad times."

"I am not yet in such dire straits that I cannot afford college tuition," Toby said. "And at such a time as I wish you to 'rally round,' I will mention it. In the meantime you are going back. Tomorrow. On the first train. With a humble note of apology for the dean."

© BOOK CREATIONS INC 1989

RON TOELKE '89

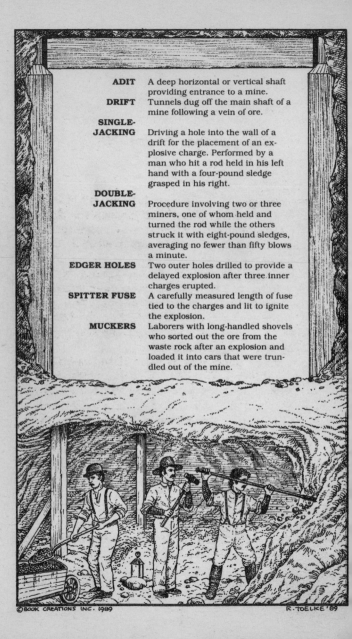

ADIT	A deep horizontal or vertical shaft providing entrance to a mine.
DRIFT	Tunnels dug off the main shaft of a mine following a vein of ore.
SINGLE-JACKING	Driving a hole into the wall of a drift for the placement of an explosive charge. Performed by a man who hit a rod held in his left hand with a four-pound sledge grasped in his right.
DOUBLE-JACKING	Procedure involving two or three miners, one of whom held and turned the rod while the others struck it with eight-pound sledges, averaging no fewer than fifty blows a minute.
EDGER HOLES	Two outer holes drilled to provide a delayed explosion after three inner charges erupted.
SPITTER FUSE	A carefully measured length of fuse tied to the charges and lit to ignite the explosion.
MUCKERS	Laborers with long-handled shovels who sorted out the ore from the waste rock after an explosion and loaded it into cars that were trundled out of the mine.

R. TOELKE '89

I

Dakota Territory, February 1887

The cow bawled, a hopeless bovine wail of terror. Her red eyes glared at Toby Holt through the driving snow. He could see that her lashes were encrusted with rime. The calf by her side was nearly dead, floundering in snow up past its belly.

"Move!" Toby shoved at the cow's flank, his head hunched into the turned-up collar of his sheepskin jacket. The cow swung her head, horns sweeping through the snow, a futile gesture of defense against the blizzard. Toby lurched against her flank again, and she began to move. The calf struggled after her.

Toby didn't know why it seemed so important to him to save this cow, this one out of thousands. Maybe it was because she was so close to the barn, maybe because she had the calf with her. Maybe she was a symbol—some living thing snatched out of the endless frozen white death that blew around them.

The blizzard had been howling through the Dakota Badlands for ten days, piling up drifts forty feet high, filling the air with blinding snow so thick a man could choke on it, and burying everything in its path. Toby's hat, eyebrows, eyelashes, and the scarf over his mouth were encrusted with snow. His hands, in thick leather work gloves, were numb. If he flexed his fingers, he had to look down to see whether or not they had moved.

Ahead, he could hear voices faintly, snatched away by the howling wind and snow. The dim glow of a lantern showed like a phantom ahead of him in the storm. Toby picked up the calf and staggered toward the light, the cow bawling desperately behind him. He staggered through the drifts, eyes on the yellow glow that shone erratically through the snow. He tripped, fell, and landed on the calf. The snow felt warm to him and soft. It would be so pleasant just to lie down in it. . . .

The calf bawled and struggled feebly under him, and Toby's mind snapped back to reality. That was how you felt when you were about to freeze to death—warm, peaceful. You just lay down and let it have you. *Like hell I will*, he thought.

Toby stood and dragged the calf up, too. Its mother was a blurred shape in the snow. Her head hung, and she looked as if her knees might buckle. "Come on," Toby said. "Hee-yup. This baby's not going to make it if you don't." Now he was talking to cows, he thought. But at least he wasn't lying down flat and waiting to die.

The lantern looked a little closer. Toby had set it in the barn window—hoping the wind wouldn't blow it over and set the barn on fire—when White Elk, who was the ranch foreman, and he and the ranch hands had gone out during a lull in the storm to see if they could bring in any more stock. As many of the cow ponies as they had been able to round up at the start of the storm had been penned in the horse barn, and the men had saddled the least weary looking of them for one more try. There wasn't room in the barn for more than a fraction of the Antelope Horn Ranch's cattle, but Toby hadn't supposed they were going to find more than that.

"What are you going to feed them if we find them?" White Elk had asked Toby as they stood inside the bunkhouse a few hours earlier. What feed there was in the barns would barely last the cow ponies another day or two.

Toby had shaken his head. "I don't know, but we've got to try."

White Elk nodded. He turned his coat collar up, pulled his hat brim down, and tied his bandanna around his mouth. It made him look like an outlaw and older than his twenty-five years. He motioned to the cowboys huddled in the far corner of the bunkhouse, where the wind didn't blow under the door so fiercely. "Come on," White Elk said. "We're going to make one more sweep."

The sky had held clear for two hours, with the horses leaping like porpoises through belly-deep snow. And then as quickly as a hand drawing a shade across a lantern, the snow had come. They had seen it, rolling in a black cloud from the horizon to darken the land beneath, and had turned and raced for the shelter of the Antelope Horn's barns and bunkhouse. Toby had been the farthest out.

The rest of the men had made it, he thought. He hoped so, knowing that if they hadn't, it would be his fault for trusting to a lull in a Badlands wind.

As his pony came staggering down the slope toward the barns, herding the cow and calf ahead, it had stepped on something, maybe only an icy patch, and gone down suddenly with a scream. Toby had jumped, landing face first and choking in the snow, while the pony floundered and tried in vain to get up. Its foreleg was broken, and Toby Holt, grim faced, had taken out his pistol and shot it. He had had to shoot horses before, and he never had liked it, but there wasn't any other option. . . .

Now, eyes on the light, he half carried, half dragged the calf, deliberately jostling it so it would bawl and bring its mother along. Another howling gust whipped snow into his eyes and ears. Then, in a half second of stillness, before the wind began to shriek again, he heard the cow bawl. Her voice had a different note this time—anger and panic—and Toby turned to see the gaunt shape of a wolf, almost as white as the snow and as thin as the bitter wind, crouched just beyond reach of the swaying horns, awaiting its chance.

Toby dropped the calf and grabbed for the knife in his belt as the wolf lunged away from the cow. A longhorn, even half dead, was dangerous. The calf was more vulnerable—and so was Toby. It sprang at him, and they rolled into the choking drift together, the wolf snarling at Toby's throat as he flailed desperately with the knife.

Toby put up his arm to shield his throat, but he felt the wolf's teeth sink through his heavy sheepskin jacket and into his shoulder. Its breath felt hot in Toby's face, and he knew that the wolf was starving and beyond fear of man. Frantically, he beat at it with his gloved fist while his frozen fingers tried to keep their grip on the knife. The wolf straddled him, blood-flecked spittle running down its jaws, and Toby brought the knife up and sank the blade into the fur above the breastbone. The wolf hung on the knife, snapping at Toby, and then with a shudder it went limp.

Toby crawled from under it and stood shakily. Blood was pooling under the body of the wolf, freezing as it touched the snow. Toby staggered a few paces and saw that the blood followed him—it was his own blood.

The snow around him seemed to grow very pale, bright enough to hurt his eyes, and then he could no longer see the cow or the calf or even the wolf at his feet. He began to feel warm again, and as he sank into the snow, he knew that this time he wasn't going to get up.

He tried to force his mind back to reality, but he couldn't move. He could hear voices in his head, but he knew they were only a dream. And then a brighter light came out of the brightness of the snow, moving toward him, and the snatches of voices became clearer through the shrieking wind.

"There he is!"

"I see him!"

"Watch that light!"

"Don't let go of that rope, or we won't see you till spring!"

Hands reached out of the snow and grasped his arms. A face, looming out of the blowing powder, was unrecognizable—brows and lashes caked in white, mouth and nose muffled in a scarf.

"Grab the rope!" White Elk yelled at him. "I've got the calf."

"I can't," Toby managed to say.

"He's hurt!" White Elk shouted

Someone else grabbed the calf, and White Elk got his arms under Toby's shoulders. Toby could see a rope tied around the young man's waist. The other end disappeared into the swirling white wind. White Elk, clutching Toby, felt his way along it. In a moment, hands reached out from the barn door and hauled them through.

Ben Jenkins, one of the workers, came in after them, with the calf under one arm. The cow stood bawling in the doorway, her horns looming at them out of the snow. One of the cowhands tossed a rope around the horns and pulled her in, and another slammed and barred the door behind her. He took the lantern from the window and barred that, too. The cowboys began brushing snow from their coats and faces. The cow stood looking numbly at them, her head low.

"Go on, git!" Ben Jenkins smacked the rope against her backside, and the cow lumbered toward the far end of the barn, where a dozen other longhorns stood, steam rising from their gaunt flanks. The calf staggered after her and began to nurse.

"You've got blood all over," White Elk said. "Let me see that." He peeled Toby's coat back and cleaned his shoulder with the snow that was on his own jacket. "What got you?"

"Wolf," Toby said. His head was beginning to clear, and he realized he had come close to dying.

"We thought we lost you, boss," Miguel Santos said. "That kind of storm, it eats a man up."

"It nearly did."

As White Elk bandaged the wound, it began to ache, a good sign that circulation was coming back. The bite would heal, Toby thought. It was the storm that had nearly killed him. He could see his breath hanging in puffs in the cold air. It wasn't a whole lot warmer in the barn than it was outside, but in this wind Toby knew they wouldn't make it across the yard to the bunkhouse. After White Elk had buttoned Toby's coat again, Toby staggered up and cracked the shutter a half inch and looked out. He couldn't even see the bunkhouse.

The cow ponies stamped and snorted. Toby sat on a bale of hay. He ached from head to toe, nearly as badly as in his shoulder, and was regretfully aware that what a man might do with impunity at twenty-five could make him very sick indeed at forty-six. He leaned his head against the barn wall. Funny how fast the time went by, he thought. He didn't feel any older than he had back then, not inside his head anyway. But the rest of him was sure starting to feel the years. He supposed he must look older, but a man never really saw change in his own mirror. When Toby looked into his, he saw the same sandy hair and light blue eyes, the same square-jawed face: "that determined-looking Holt face," his wife, Alexandra, called it. It was a little more weathered now, with lines around the eyes and the sandy mustache, but still pretty much the same face he'd always had. It wasn't on the same body, though; he had to admit that.

It was time to settle down, Alexandra had said. Time to quit gallivanting across the country, time to let the younger men chase Indians and do the government's work; time for Toby Holt to tend to his home ranch and his family and act his age. So he had sold off the Wisconsin timberland to Frank Woods, an old friend and business associate whose parents' estate had made the purchase possible. The sawmills and foundry he owned in Chicago had gone to Dieter Schumann, a close and trusted friend. Then Toby had put all his money, and then some, into this new operation in the Dakota Badlands and into improvements on the Holt homestead in Oregon.

The ranch, heretofore called simply the Holt ranch, had been renamed the Madrona by Alexandra for the evergreen trees, native to Oregon. They seemed to her to embody the sum and spirit of the place. Their graceful red-barked branches bore shiny dark-green leaves and pyramidal clusters of white flowers that turned to red berries in the autumn.

Alexandra had approved of Toby's buying the Badlands ranch. He could leave White Elk, the assistant foreman from the Madrona, to run it, and it would give the Holts financial diversity. The Antelope Horn was a cattle ranch, whereas the Madrona raised horses, cavalry remounts mostly. In any given year, one if not both of them was bound to turn a profit—unless, of course, it sank under forty feet of snow.

Toby sighed as he sat thinking about the ranch. He had wanted it badly, having caught cattle fever from Theodore Roosevelt, whose spread was just west of the Antelope Horn.

Theodore was a young New Yorker who had the light of a prophet in his eyes. Steers fattened on Dakota grasslands brought as much as fifteen dollars a head more than Texas steers, Theodore had told Toby. The young man loved the West; he had been a sickly child who built his strength up here, and now the area had an unshakable place in his heart. The Dakotas were the plains of heaven, Theodore had said. Toby sighed. He supposed Theodore's spread had been wiped out, too. There wasn't much hope of anything else—which was not the best news to get on your honeymoon.

Toby supposed his friend and the second Mrs. Roosevelt must be halfway to Europe about now. Theodore's first wife had died a few years back. Toby shifted uncomfortably on his hay bale and closed his eyes. All the same, he thought, he imagined he would just as soon get the news with a glass of champagne and a woman for company as six wet cowhands and a herd of longhorns.

Toby's head was starting to ache, too, and his nose to run, now that it had warmed up enough to do so. Besides a wolf bite, Toby thought with disgust, he was going to catch a cold. He hated having a cold.

One of the ponies stamped its feet and tossed its head, bit jingling. Toby opened his eyes. The ponies, still saddled, stood miserably in the center of the barn. He got up and touched White Elk on the shoulder. The two of them prodded the cowhands until they, too, stood, stiffly, their breath coming in puffs of steam. Slowly the seven men began to pull the saddles from the sodden ponies and to rub them dry with the saddle blankets. Toby worked one-handed until White Elk persuaded him forcibly to sit down.

They stayed in the barn for thirty-six hours, huddled together for warmth in much the same fashion as the cow ponies and the straggling band of longhorns. When the wind finally died and the sky cleared, White Elk had to climb through a window and shovel snow from the barn door before they could open it. Toby stood in the doorway and looked out on desolation.

There was nothing but endless snow, sometimes with the tops of fence posts just visible above the surface. Drifts were piled against the bunkhouse walls across the yard—or what had been the yard. It looked like the rest of the land now. The ranch house, no more than a cabin really, was just beyond, making three sides of a square with the barn and bunkhouse. The single cottonwood beside it had frozen and split, and its top branches lay across the cabin roof.

"God Almighty," Miguel Santos said under his breath.

"I don't reckon He had much to do with this," Steve McInnes, another ranch hand, said from behind Toby. "What're we going to do, boss?"

They all looked at their employer. White Elk was

the only one of the men who had worked for Toby before. The rest were local men, hired on a year ago in North Platte. White Elk had been running the ranch, but now that Toby was here, he had taken charge.

"We're going to shovel a walk to the bunkhouse," Toby decided, "and settle in for a while." He flexed his shoulder and winced. "*You're* going to shovel the walk. And nobody rides out again until we're sure there's not another storm coming."

"We ain't got but a dozen cans of beans left, and some tomatoes," Steve said.

The rest of them groaned. Steve was the bunkhouse cook, but his culinary skills didn't extend beyond managing to get a substance hot. Other than that, it generally remained in its natural state.

"We've got them." Toby jerked his thumb at the penned longhorns.

"I never thought I'd get sick of beefsteak," Ben Jenkins grumbled. He looked without enthusiasm at the congealed lump of meat and fat on his tin plate. The potbellied stove didn't put out much heat, so meat turned cold again within minutes of being cooked. The men were wrapped in blankets and two or three wool shirts apiece.

"First thing I'm going to do," Steve said dreamily, "is go down to Topeka and have me a dinner at the Harvey House there. Oysters on the half shell, and pork roast and applesauce, and lobster salad, with one of those nice little waitresses in her sassy little uniform to bring me a cup of real hot coffee that don't taste like it's been brewed up in an old pot full of beetles."

Toby looked at him sympathetically. The men had been stuck with one another in the bunkhouse for a week now. It was a wonder that there hadn't been any fistfights born out of boredom. The weather had held clear, and two days ago they had reluctantly turned the rest of the longhorns loose to forage for themselves if they could. The horses had eaten nearly the last of the feed.

Toby cracked the shutter and looked out. "Tomorrow. Tomorrow we ought to be able to get through. White Elk and I will catch the railroad in North Platte. If you want work, I expect I can find it for you on the Madrona." No ranches would be hiring on in the Dakotas this year.

Ben shook his head. "Naw, I figure I'll ride down Topeka way. Or maybe Cheyenne. Try to catch the spring roundups."

"Guess I'm kind of used to these plains," Steve said. "I've rid back and forth across them most of my life. They'll eat me up one of these days, I reckon, but if I made it through this, they'll have to go some."

The others nodded, murmuring the names of towns, of men they knew who had gone to work on this ranch or that.

Oregon was too far for them, Toby thought, as if it had been in a valley on the moon. It must have seemed that way to the first settlers, his father and mother among them. His father, now dead, had been a frontier scout, an explorer who had loved the solitude of the Northwest long before he had led the first wagon train there. Toby's mother; remarried, drove a fancy carriage and spent most of her time now instilling culture into the city of Portland; but she could remember the days when she had crossed the Rockies in a Conestoga wagon and arrived with nothing more to live on but what she and Whip Holt could make of their land grants—the government's reward for having survived the journey: six hundred acres apiece in the Willamette Valley, plus another six hundred they received as a wedding present.

Toby realized with a grimace that White Elk and he would be arriving home in much the same financial condition. There was money owed on the Antelope Horn and on the new barns he had built and the brood mares he had bought for the Madrona. It would have to be paid somehow, no question of that. Debts weren't something you tried to get out from under. Nobody in his right mind would buy the Antelope Horn now, but the Willamette Valley land, where the Madrona was situated, would bring something. He wouldn't sell the original acreage—he'd hire on to lay track on the railroad before he parted with those. But he could sell off some of the land that had been bought later.

Those tracts, beautiful, lush country where you could grow anything, totaled nearly one thousand acres more. As Portland had grown, expanded, sprawling from a frontier outpost into a city, Toby had had plenty of offers for that land. But he had held onto it stubbornly, determined not to part with an inch of it, even through a bad Oregon winter in 1885. Being rich had its privileges: You could hold onto land that wasn't paying, just because it was a buffer between you and encroaching civilization.

Maybe I've gotten too big for my britches, Toby thought. Maybe he wasn't allowed to hold back change. He had tried, but his money froze to death in the Badlands blizzard.

Toby closed the shutter and bolted it. No use repining, he thought, using one of his mother's favorite phrases. The Holts always just picked up and went on. He just wished he weren't so tired. And he wished he didn't have to tell Alexandra.

Cambridge, Massachusetts, April 1887

"Here, Holt, open your eyes. Here's the post!" Shepherd Loudon bounced into their chamber in Stoughton Hall, overlooking Harvard Yard, then slowed his pace to take on an expression of immense weariness and disdain, suitable for a Harvard man.

On the bed nearer the window, Tim Holt opened

one eye. "I've been swotting for a chemistry exam," he explained balefully. "I've got to sleep."

"Well, wake up," Loudon said. "It's nearly dinnertime. And besides, you have a letter." He passed the envelope under his nose, inhaling extravagantly. "I believe it's a billet-doux. Smells of attar of roses. My poor boy, you should have told me. Is it serious? Is it fatal?" He held the envelope just out of reach as Tim swung his feet onto the floor.

Tim looked at the feminine handwriting adorning the envelope. "It's from my sister, you idiot. Give it to me."

"Your sister? Oh, what a bouncer." Loudon sniffed the envelope again dreamily. "Is she really your sister? I'll give it to you if you'll introduce me."

"You're incorrigible." Tim snatched the envelope. "She's twenty-six. Far too old for you. You wouldn't last a minute."

"It's nearly dinnertime. Aren't you coming?"

"What are we having?"

"Fricassee of superannuated hen," Loudon said. "I call it cruel to kill an animal that's so near to dying of old age." The cuisine in Memorial Hall was notorious, but no number of complaints ever changed it, for the administration held firmly to the theory that the average college-age male was always hungry enough to eat anything.

"You go on," Tim said. "I want to read this." He settled back onto the collection of souvenir pillows on his bed and pulled the quilt up to his chin. The room was cold even with a coal fire burning on the grate, and the water in the pitcher on the washstand was generally frozen in the morning. The walls were adorned with a pair of steer horns, a Harvard banner, and a music-hall poster of a dancer in spangled tights. A derby hat hung precariously from a nail holding the mirror over Loudon's washstand, and stuck into the crack between the glass and the frame were photographs of girls. The mirror over Tim's washstand held a picture of his mother and a horse. So far, feminine charms held no fascination for Tim. In any case, he considered Alexandra at thirty-two to be just as pretty as the Boston debutantes who cluttered up Shep Loudon's mirror.

. Alexandra Woodling Holt was his stepmother, but Tim had long ceased to make that distinction. His was an odd family, put together of strangely disparate parts and somehow functioning as a whole. Tim's father Toby had been married three times, the first unhappily. That union had produced no children, but out of unhappiness or just general restiveness, Tim supposed, Toby had fathered Tim's sister Janessa with a nurse in an army field hospital during the Civil War. Mary White Owl had been Cherokee.

After Toby's first wife died, he had married Tim's mother, and then she had died, too. Not long after, Janessa had surfaced—Toby hadn't known anything about her until then. When Toby married Alexandra, she inherited Tim and Janessa, but it hadn't seemed to faze her any. Alexandra had had two children of her own, Michael and Sally, and loved the four of them indiscriminately, ruling them all with the same humor and resiliency with which Alexandra faced nearly anything in her path. Alexandra was petite, with hazel eyes and auburn hair fluffed up into a fashionable fringe above her brow, and she was a lot tougher than she looked.

Tim looked just like his father and, he was told, like his grandfather Whip Holt before him. And Janessa looked like their father but with faint overtones of Cherokee, like a photograph twice exposed. She had light brown hair, darker than Tim's dishwater blond, and her face was more defined than that of the other Holts, who had square, determined-looking jaws. An aggressive face, a face with opinions, Tim thought, although she was certainly pretty enough, especially when she smiled.

Right now Tim didn't think Janessa was very happy. At fifteen she had gone east to college because the family had decided that Janessa was a bit young to hurdle all the obstacles that would likely be put in the path of a female wishful of studying medicine. Janessa had reluctantly agreed to postpone her doctor's training, and Grandmama Eulalia was thrilled, thinking that an eastern education would give the girl some polish. (Tim was supposed to be getting polish at Harvard, too, but he didn't think it was going to take with him.) There, Janessa had been snubbed by the other students because word got around that the illustrious Toby Holt's daughter was part Indian and her mother and father hadn't been married. Janessa had stuck it out and gone through four years with top marks, but she hadn't applied to medical school as she had planned. Most women didn't feel as if they needed any education beyond high school, if that, but Janessa had been determined to be a doctor ever since she was little, even though most places thought that training was unsuitable for females and did their best to keep women out.

Janessa had graduated from college the summer that Michael got rheumatic fever and nearly died, and naturally she'd stayed around to help Alexandra nurse him. But that was almost seven years ago. Michael still had something wrong with his heart from the fever and had to be careful what he did, but he didn't need a full-time nursemaid to follow him around.

It was Tim's opinion that Janessa had been made so miserable by her almost total social ostracism at college, she was too scared now to take any more chances. She hadn't gotten married, either. And since Janessa was not the sort who liked to admit to being defeated by anything, it sometimes made her difficult to be around.

She wrote to him all the time, though. Janessa was the family correspondent, filling her letters with all the facts and details that nobody else ever thought to mention and keeping her sometimes far-flung family in touch with one another.

Tim settled back on the pillows and took out four folded sheets.

Dear Tim,

Dad is home finally. We have all been fussing over him since he got here. The situation in the Dakotas was worse than we had feared, and he and White Elk were caught in the worst of it and nearly froze to death. Dad actually had to fight off a wolf that was starving and desperate enough to attack him. (They didn't starve, Dad says, because they killed a longhorn and ate it. Dad says there is more meat than you would ever expect on a longhorn, and you can get sicker of it than you would ever dream.) He doesn't say so, but I think we were lucky to get him back. He looks thin, and the skin on his face and hands is still chapped raw. His face is just tired. White Elk looks a little better, but not good, either. He sends his regards and says if you don't like Harvard, you should try spending eight days in a cabin with the boss and six cowboys and a raw steer carcass.

Tim, people froze and starved to death in that storm. We read in the newspapers that several women in outlying cabins shot themselves rather than starve slowly. And people got lost just trying to go across their own yards. No one will find their bodies, some of them, until spring, probably. Everything is dead out there. As you can guess, there aren't any cattle left on the Antelope Horn. They are all either frozen or starved or killed by the wolves. Dad called it a desolation. Poor Mr. Roosevelt's ranch is wiped out, too, I'm afraid.

Dad and White Elk and the cowboys finally got out by following the telegraph poles. Dad said that was about all that was sticking up above the snow. The men rode clear across our land, heading for the depot at North Platte, and never saw a single living thing. Now Dad says he's going to have to sell off some land here to pay the bills. I think he feels worse about it than we do. Alexandra says eighteen hundred acres are enough for anyone, and wanting more is just greedy. This, mind you, is the same Alexandra who wanted to buy the tract along Cold Spring to stop that man she didn't like from building cheap houses on it, but that was when we could afford to. Now she's so determined to keep Dad from feeling worse than he does, you wouldn't think she minded a bit. Abby's baked his favorite pie three nights running and offered to work for half wages. Dad assured her we aren't that destitute yet. And Amy filled White Elk a big tub full of hot water and Epsom salts so he wouldn't get rheumatism, and made him get in it, which embarrassed him half to death.

Sam Brentwood is here now, too. He arrived about a week ago, just after Dad, and following a telegram from his father to say that Sam had been thrown out of Washington and Lee, his third college, and would we please keep him for a while. Uncle Andy wants Dad to "give him responsibility and make a man of him." I don't know why everyone always lays their reprobate offspring and unsolvable problems at Dad's feet.

Everyone else is fine. Michael is restive, poor boy, and wants so badly to be doing something. He wants to go places, do dangerous things, and ride into blizzards with Dad—all the things you can't do with a bad heart. But he is doing his exercises, and if he will just be patient (never easy for any of us) I think he can strengthen his heart. In fact, I do think the murmur sounds a little better, or rather, the heart itself sounds stronger. I had Dr. Martin listen to him, and he thought so, too. (Dr. Bright said Michael oughtn't to exercise at all, very dangerous; worst possible thing, harrumph, harrumph, ought to resign himself to invalid status. Will of God. Fixed me with an awful eye and said females had no business fooling with matters not their concern, experimental treatments, harrumph, harrumph. Old fool.)

Dr. Martin is doing as well as he could be, considering that he's nearly ninety. Your friend

Rufus Gooch has devised a bicycle that will also operate a butter churn, driven by the motion of the wheels. He rode it through town, with the churn on a platform behind, and had butter when he reached his destination.

Sally can write her own name now and is convinced that this feat entitles her to do anything she pleases. "You can't tell me what to do," she informed me in a queenly fashion yesterday as I was scooping her out of a mud puddle. "I can write my name."

Grandmama Eulalia and Grandpa Lee are well. They came to have dinner with us when Dad came home. Grandpa looks so frail. I hate it so when people I love get old. Stalking Horse is getting old, too. I'm so relieved that White Elk is back! This winter here was hard on Stalking Horse without him. I asked Stalking Horse how old he was, and he said he didn't really know, but he's probably as old as Grandfather Whip would have been, which is nearly eighty. Most of the new brood mares are in foal, and he watches over them like a nanny. We should have a good crop of foals in the spring, and if we can limit ourselves to absolute necessities for a couple of years, I think we will have our feet back on the ground.

Now you mind your studies, darling, and have a good term. We all miss you terribly, but Abby has baked you a mountainous batch of cookies, and another of taffy, which we are sending with our love.

Your loving sister,
Janessa

Tim folded Janessa's letter and stuck it back in the envelope. He knew the winter had been bad in the Dakotas. Accounts of the blizzard had been in all the newspapers, stories with headlines such as "Prairie

Tragedy" and "Heroic Schoolteacher." But the Antelope Horn, wiped out! He hadn't expected that.

They still had the Madrona, Tim thought. That was their home, the place they loved. Nothing else mattered.

Tim kicked the quilt back and stood up. A Holt always took advantage of opportunity—and an opportunity had definitely presented itself. Whistling, Tim stuck Janessa's letter in his pocket, then lifted the Indian blanket and china lamp that disguised his steamer trunk as a table. He opened the trunk, took his shirts out of the chest of drawers, and tossed them in, followed by long underwear, trousers, socks, handkerchiefs, collars, ties, and waistcoats. He took the picture of Alexandra out of the mirror frame and tucked it in the top pocket of the trunk.

He collected the souvenir pillows—one from the Centennial Exposition in Philadelphia, one from the Statue of Liberty in New York, and one on which Janessa had stitched his profile when she was learning to embroider—and pitched them in, followed by ice skates and a football. The Harvard banner was Shep Loudon's, as was the dancer in the spangled tights. He was scooping up his hairbrush and shaving mug from the washstand when the bell in Memorial Hall began to toll and Shep stuck his head through the doorway.

"You coming?" He spotted the open trunk. "I say, Holt, what are you doing?"

"Packing," Tim answered. "I've got to go home."

Shep looked shocked. "They haven't given you the gate? Don't tell me old Eliot found out about the bullfrog in his privy."

"Of course not," Tim said scornfully. "And they wouldn't give me the gate for that if he had. You have to do a lot worse than that to get expelled. My cousin Sam—well, courtesy cousin—has been thrown out of three colleges, and believe me, it wasn't for bullfrogs in the privy." Tim slicked down his hair with the brush and then tossed it into the trunk, along with the shaving mug and his razor.

"Well, why are you going then?" Shep demanded. "Term's not even over."

"Financial reverses," Tim said solemnly. "Our cattle operation's been pretty nearly wiped out." He took down the steer horns from the wall.

"Oh, Holt. I am sorry." Shep looked somber. "And they've sent for you to come home?"

"Well, not exactly," Tim admitted. He reached under the bed and pulled out a dusty Latin text. "But I can't expect my dad to go on paying my tuition when he's in such a bind. And I'm needed at home."

"Oh, Holt. I think that's absolutely noble of you."

Tim dropped the steer horns in the trunk and closed the lid. "It's the only honorable thing to do."

II

And four hundred thirty-seven dollars for patent feed racks . . .

Toby Holt laid the pen down and ran his hands through his hair. The pigeonholes above his desk held unpaid bills on the left, paid ones on the right. Slowly the stack was transferring itself from left to right. He had sold off nearly one thousand acres, including the Cold Spring tract, and was silently grateful for the price he'd gotten for it. The money would stretch to cover nearly all the obligations, and some draconian penny-pinching would take care of the rest.

We still have Madrona, he thought. It was what everybody had been saying: *We still have Madrona,* as if it were a litany. There had been Holts on the Madrona since the early 1840s—not so very long as Easterners counted tenure on the land, but longer than nearly any other white man in Oregon.

Toby had been born here, in this house. It had been a log house then, successively enlarged and improved over the years by Toby's mother, Eulalia, then Tim's mother, and finally by Alexandra—the last revision a result of the place having been set fire to by Tim. Not that he had meant to. Toby reflected that Tim as a child had never meant to produce most of the disasters for which he was responsible. This one was the result of an outing in an old road locomotive that Toby had gotten for Tim to tinker with, never thinking that his son and Calvin Rogers, a former hot-air balloonist who

20

lived on the farm and did odd jobs, would get the
locomotive in running condition. Calvin had put a whistle on it, however, in the event that Tim tried to start it
up. But late one night when everyone was asleep, Tim
had snuck into the barn, removed the whistle, and
started the road locomotive. Predictably it had gotten
away from him and taken its own wayward path through
the barn wall and bunkhouse porch before coming to
rest in the kitchen of the house, which then caught fire.
The resulting damage had provided Alexandra with ex-
tensive opportunities to redecorate.

The house that had been built around the remains
of the original one was a tall red and white structure of
brick and clapboard with a round tower on the east
side, bay windows, and elaborate gingerbread adorning
porches and eaves. The first-floor porch ran around
three sides of the house and widened on the west side
into a pavilion. A winding avenue of Madrona trees led
from the house to the road, and a grove of them shaded
the house.

Even in its new incarnation, the house looked lived
in. Despite the existence of an elegantly furnished nursery, dolls, trains, or books were always scattered in the
parlor. Alexandra's embroidery and Janessa's knitting
overflowed from their baskets by the fireside. The bay
window in the parlor, Sally's vantage point to see what
was coming down the drive, was always smudged with
fingerprints. There was generally a cat or two asleep
somewhere, curled into a ball in a pool of sunlight. The
floors were polished oak, with Indian rugs. It was the
fashion just now to fill a room with as many objects as
possible, and the piano and parlor tables were adorned
with Indians pots, wax flowers, a stereopticon and book
of slides, china figurines, vases of dried pampas grass,
photographs of the family and such sights as Niagara
Falls, the Grand Canyon, and the Devil's Chimney,
fringed shawls, cutwork mats, hand-painted china, and
bowls of polished agate pieces.

Above the desk in Toby's office were the mounted
head of an elk and the rifle that had belonged to his

frontier-scout father, Whip Holt. The original log walls could be seen as a faint pattern beneath the buff plaster, and old log beams still supported the ceiling. One wall was lined with bookcases, and another was decorated with Toby's oddly chosen assortment of art. He hung up the things that suited him, and never mind if they suited the rest of the house or even anyone else's idea of what they would want to look at all day. There was an engraving of a medieval damsel who Toby thought looked like Janessa. Flanking that were a lithograph print of a Western landscape done by his sister, Cindy, and a picture of the house, painted by Michael at seven, as well as a framed citation from the President, presented to Toby on the occasion of his retirement from government service.

It was a chilly morning at the end of April, and a log fire burned on the grate, with a basket of pine cones beside it for kindling. Above the fireplace was a bull's-eye mirror between a pair of photographs: Toby's mother, Eulalia, and his father, Whip, in a buckskin jacket, his hair curling over his collar. There was a faraway expression in his eyes. Newspapers had always referred to him as "legendary frontier scout Michael 'Whip' Holt." Toby wondered what his father would make of Portland now.

He sighed and leaned forward in the oak swivel chair to tally up the next account. *Seventy-six dollars for pine planking and three bolts of sisal rope. Eighty dollars for fencing—*

He stopped and cocked an ear at the window, then got up and lifted the sash. Whooping and cheering from behind the barn cut through the misty April air. As he watched, his four-year-old daughter, Sally, rounded the corner of the house and went tearing across the yard, trailing a doll by one arm. Her rose-gold hair streamed out behind her, and there was a large splotch on the backside of her blue dress. If there was anything messy to be sat in, Sally sat in it. She raced for the excitement behind the barn—whatever it was—and Toby pulled out his pocket watch, then leaned his arms on the windowsill, waiting. As expected, Alexandra's personal maid, Juanita, who doubled as Sally's nurse, puffed around the corner five seconds later.

"*Niña, niña!* You come back here. Put your shoes on!"

Sally didn't stop, and Juanita slowed, gasping and clutching her side. She trudged toward the barn with determination.

Two stable hands came out of the barn, dropping their shovels as they went, and disappeared around behind it. Another, swinging an empty oat bucket, followed them.

Driven by curiosity, Toby closed the window and went into the kitchen, down the back steps, and toward the barn. Toby bent to pick up his daughter's doll, apparently abandoned in her flight from Juanita. Dangling it from one hand, he rounded the corner of the barn and looked with interest at the paddock, which seemed to be the source of the commotion.

In the center of the enclosure a horse spun in furious circles, back legs kicking in an effort to unseat its rider. The corral fence was lined with stable hands, wranglers, members of the haying crew, and a lot of other people who were supposed to be at work. White Elk was perched on the top rail with Sally in his lap and ten-year-old Michael beside him. The unbroken horse gave a convulsive leap and nearly flipped over backward. White Elk gripped Sally firmly with one arm and cupped his other hand to his mouth.

"Ride him!"

The rider stuck to the saddle and came up still in it. The crowd on the fence cheered and offered encouraging advice.

"Try glue!"

"Look him in the eye—that always tames 'em!"

"Whisper in his ear!"

The horse bounced across the corral in stiff-legged hops, ears flattened.

"A dollar says he rides 'im!"

"Hell, two dollars!"

"Two dollars on the horse!"

"Keep going, he's getting winded!"

Toby Holt eyed the animal with interest: a three-year-old colt gelded too late and generally held to be incorrigible. Its steel-blue hide twisted wildly in a cloud of dust. The rider's face was turned away, but there was something ominously familiar about that dusty-blond hair and the lanky torso jolting in the saddle.

The horse gave one last outraged flip, then stood, head hanging.

"Hee-yup." The rider kicked the animal into a reluctant trot. At the paddock gate he dismounted and handed the reins with a flourish to the elderly foreman, Stalking Horse, whom Toby noticed for the first time, leaning silently inside the enclosure's fence.

"I told you I could ride him."

"Maybe he was having an off day," Stalking Horse said, but the dark eyes under white brows were amused.

A few of the wranglers on the fence jumped down as if to offer congratulations and then backtracked. The rider looked up to see what had caused their retreat and discovered his father, looking like a personal representative of the Day of Wrath and holding a blond doll in one hand.

Tim grinned at him cheerily. "I knew I could do it this time. I finally figured him out. Did you see me?" He hooked his thumbs in his belt, pleased with himself. No one had ever ridden Trout to a standstill.

"What in the hell are you doing home?"

"Janessa wrote me the news," Tim explained. "About the Antelope Horn. Lord, I'm glad you made it out all right. I had to come home. I couldn't have it on my conscience to be lolling around at Harvard when—"

"You come with me." Toby started to take Tim by the arm and discovered he still had Sally's doll. "Here." Toby thrust the doll at White Elk, who was studiously attempting to give the impression of a man not listening to a conversation between his boss and his boss's son, as were all the other men on the paddock fence. White Elk grinned and tossed the doll to Juanita, who had finally caught up with Sally and was panting by the gate. The once lithe Juanita was growing steadily stouter, and with each ten pounds she added another brace to her corset until, as Sam Brentwood had said, the entire structure might have supported the new bridge Portland was building across the Willamette River.

Toby pulled Tim a few paces from the gate. "Of all the asinine stunts, this takes the cake."

"I thought I should rally round, sir," Tim protested. "I can't expect you to go on paying my tuition in these bad times. And I figured you'd need a hand."

"I have more hands than I need," Toby said with asperity. "I have Sam Brentwood lolling around the place, picking up a hayfork every now and then when I look at him."

"You know I work!" Tim said, stung.

"I also know you're supposed to be at Harvard getting an education, not here starring on the rodeo circuit."

"But what about the tuition?"

"I am not yet in such dire straits that I cannot afford college tuition," Toby said. "And at such time as I wish you to 'rally round,' I will mention it. In the meantime, you are going back. Tomorrow. On the first train. With a note of humble apology for the dean."

"But, Dad—"

"Tim!" A feminine voice called to him over the sound of flying feet, and Alexandra hurled herself into his arms. "Tim, darling! Why didn't you tell us you were here? Sneaking off to the stable without a word—"

"Well, I meant to," Tim said, "but I rented a horse in Portland, and when I went to put him in the barn, I saw that Stalking Horse had Trout out, and—"

"And you couldn't resist trying to ride that devil," Alexandra said.

"I did it, too."

"You didn't!" Alexandra looked up at him, plainly impressed.

"You ought to put a plaque up in the barn," Sam Brentwood said, coming up and shaking Tim's hand.

"For the only survivor." Sam had dark hair, nearly black, and deep blue eyes in a handsome, roguish face. He slapped Tim on the back. "Term end early?"

"Not exactly," Tim said.

Toby Holt watched, arms folded.

His older daughter, Janessa, came out of the house, saw Tim, and ran toward him.

"Have you brought me something?" Sally hung on Tim's sleeve, dancing up and down in her bare feet.

"Of course I have. Not on me. I left my trunk in Portland at the station." He smiled at Sally's crestfallen expression. "But I paid someone to deliver it this afternoon. You know we can't come home without presents. That's the rule. I have something for everyone."

"What? What what what?"

Juanita detached Sally from Tim's arm. "That's not good manners."

"A chemistry set," Tim said. He didn't care whether Sally had manners or not.

"A chemistry set! Tim, how could you?" Alexandra looked horrified. "She's only four!"

"And dangerous enough," Juanita said.

"A beginners' chemistry set," Tim qualified. "I was planning to do the experiments with her." He looked balefully at his father.

The crowd of onlookers had begun to surge around him again, offering congratulations and speculating on whether or not he could ride Trout a second time. The betting was running two to one that he could. By this time, Janessa and Michael had pushed their way through the crowd and were hugging Tim, too. Michael, a slim, red-haired boy, wore knickers and black stockings. Janessa's light brown hair was pinned in a knot on her head in a fashion similar to Alexandra's, and she wore a dark-blue grosgrain skirt and a prim white shirtwaist. She kissed Tim in a motherly fashion on his cheek.

"What are you doing here?" she whispered. "How are your studies?"

Tim gave his sister a look of appraisal that took in her outfit. "You aren't an old-maid schoolteacher yet," he informed her. "That's an awful getup. And my studies aren't any of your business."

Janessa grinned at him suddenly, and her expression was transformed from brooding solemnity to glowing beauty. "Uppity, aren't you?" she whispered. "What have you done? Dad looks mad enough to chew nails."

"He came home from Harvard because we don't have any money," Michael whispered to her. "But Dad says we have enough money for Harvard, and he has to go back." He looked at Tim wistfully. "I wish I could go for you. I've never been anywhere. Probably never will go anywhere," he added moodily.

Tim looked at him with sympathy.

"You aren't old enough to go anywhere," Janessa told him. "By the time you are, you may be strong enough, if you'll do those exercises I gave you, and not cheat." She turned to Tim. "Cheat means trying to do too much," she explained.

Toby put a hand on Michael's shoulder. "As for you right now, young man, you belong in the house, where you're supposed to be taking your afternoon nap." He hugged the boy to be sure that Michael understood he wasn't annoyed with him. Toby gave the rest of the crowd a look that held no such assurance, followed by a pointed glance at his watch. "Day's not over yet, boys."

The crowd melted off into the landscape. Sam Brentwood put his arm around Tim's shoulders. "Come and tell me the news."

A hand tapped Sam's shoulder. "Haying crew," Toby said. His eye rested on Tim in turn. "You, too, as long as you've come to 'rally round.' "

Sally slipped under the pasture fence and trotted along the side of the south hay field. In the kitchen Abby Givens, the cook, had put Sally's black stockings and high-button boots back on. Then she had given the little girl some cookies, which were now tied up in the corner of her pinafore, and a pickle jar full of cold milk.

Juanita was asleep. It was Sally's nap time, but

usually Juanita was the only one who did any sleeping. Generally Sally would wait ten minutes and then slip up to Juanita's room on the third floor to be sure she could hear her snoring. Next she would go to the kitchen to see what Abby was fixing, then go exploring until someone caught her. With the excitement of Tim's homecoming behind her, Juanita would probably sleep until dinnertime, at least.

Sally walked toward the meadow where the haying crew was working. They put in several crops a year in the mild climate of the Willamette Valley, and by late April the first grass was ready to cut. Sally skirted the edge of the hay field until she came to the cleared strip where the mowing machine had already passed. For a few minutes she watched the mules pulling the mowing machine, with the crew following. Then she sat on the freshly cut grass and took off the lid of her pickle jar. The milk smelled faintly of pickles. As Sally drank it, she looked up at the sky, where a meadowlark was swooping. It lit on a fence post and began singing. The child looked down and found a small green beetle crawling up her black high-button boot. She peered at it intently, and it whirred away into the sunshine. Sally had discovered that there was always something to look at that you hadn't seen before.

Farther down the meadow, the haying crew was raking the mowing machine's cut into swathes to dry. Sally could hear them singing, with Tim a little off-key and louder than the others: "The old gray mare she ain't what she used to be, ain't what she used to be, ain't what she used to be . . ."

Tim saw her sitting in the mown grass and waved, wiping his face with his bandanna. The grass seed and pollen churned up by the mowing machine made him sneeze, but it smelled good to him, and he took a deep, appreciative breath. No other place smelled this good, he thought, certainly not Harvard, where he was supposed to be learning to be an engineer. He had always displayed a natural mechanical bent, had always been a tinkerer; but at Harvard they were long on theory and short on action. Tim didn't care what the ancient Greeks had had to say about the principles of the construction of an arch. He didn't want to build a bridge anyway. He wanted to go down to Rufus Gooch's workshop and fiddle around with his internal combustion engine and invent something amazing.

Sam looked at him and shook his head. "You ever thought of just telling your old man to go to hell?" he asked.

"No," Tim said shortly.

"For the love of heaven, you're twenty years old," Sam said. "Are you going to be daddy's little angel all your life? Tell him to go to hell. That's what I do when my dad pushes me too far."

"Yeah. Worked out just great for you, hasn't it?" Tim pointed out. "Here you are, sweating behind a mowing machine, raking hay. Pure paradise."

"This is just till I get something else going," Sam said, jabbing the rake irritably at the cut hay.

As far back as Tim could remember, Sam had always had "something going," which was why he had been thrown out of West Point, Dartmouth, and most recently from Washington and Lee. The last expulsion had been for gambling with marked cards in an attempt to win back money lost to a land speculator who had proved to be wilier than Sam. He remained convinced that it was possible to get rich without doing any work, and he was annoyed with life for not making him rich to start with.

Tim didn't see why Sam's father cared whether his son got expelled or not. Tim had overheard conversations between his own father and his grandmother Eulalia, and according to them, Andrew Brentwood hadn't given any other signs of caring much what Sam did, or Sam's younger half sister, Eden, either. Andrew and his second wife, Lydia, were more interested in stewing over a kid who had died years before, at age seven. A big, black-draped portrait of the sainted Franz, when he was a year old hung in the parlor. According to

Eulalia, the place was practically a cathedral to his memory. It didn't leave much room for anybody else.

"Hey, shake a leg!" the head of the haying crew shouted, and Sam and Tim redoubled their efforts. It was monotonous, methodical work. The mowing machine creaked, the hay fell under the blade. Grasshoppers shot forward ahead of them, spring loaded, triggered by the mules' feet. Sam surveyed the acres of waving hay before him with loathing. Tim read his cousin's expression: Sam wasn't going to spend the summer out here following a mowing machine just on Toby Holt's say-so.

Sally finished her milk and cookies as the haying crew passed into the next field. When, in the stillness, she heard the jingle of another harness, she stood and shaded her eyes to see where it came from. The farm wagon, with Stalking Horse on the seat, was just turning into the avenue of trees that led from the ranch house to the main road into Portland. Maybe he would take her with him, Sally thought. Going into Portland was more interesting than anything.

Sally sprinted along the edge of the field, the empty jar in her hand, and arrived breathless at the edge of the road just as the wagon came abreast of her. Stalking Horse tugged on the reins and looked down, amused.

"Can I go with you?"

Stalking Horse leaned down and scooped her up. "Where's Juanita?"

Sally settled down on the seat beside him. "Sleeping."

Stalking Horse backed the mules to turn the wagon around in the narrow road. "First we have to tell your mama. And you shouldn't run away from Juanita like that," he added. "It is not good for fat ladies to chase little girls."

A few minutes later, he drew rein in front of the house. "Now you go in and tell your mama I'll take you if it's all right with her."

Sally scooted down off the buckboard seat and pulled the heavy front door open. "Mama!"

"Mercy, don't bellow like that," Amy Givens said. Amy was the maid, and she was dusting the front parlor. "Your mama's in the pantry."

Sally found Alexandra reviewing three headless chickens with Amy's sister, Abby. "No, I don't think so, either," Alexandra was saying. "That rooster had a few years on him. You can fry the hens, but send Bill out to catch us a good fish. We can have a salad and some early peas, and a cobbler for dessert. Yes, what is it, dear?"

"Can I go with Stalking Horse? He's going to Portland and says he'll take me if you say."

Alexandra looked at her daughter. Her curling rose-gold hair had completely escaped the ribbon that it started out with in the morning, to spill over her blue dress and black pinafore. One black stocking was bagging around her ankle, and the other had a long run in it. Alexandra sighed. "You look like a ragpicker's child, but all right. You're to stick like glue to Stalking Horse everywhere he goes, mind."

"Yes, ma'am!" Sally whisked out into the hall and through the front parlor again. Amy Givens, perched on a step stool to dust the high window sashes, clutched her feather duster to her chest. Loud noises made her jump, and Sally was a perpetual loud noise. The door banged shut behind her.

The child happily held out her hand to Stalking Horse, and he pulled her up into the seat beside him. To Sally, Portland was an adventure, equal to the kingdoms in her fairy-tale books. The houses rising from the riverbank into terraced hillsides were of brick or clapboard or board and batten, laced with curlicues of multicolored gingerbread. At the wharves, river steamers docked, ferryboats tooted back and forth across the Willamette, and tugs towed the great ocean steamers. Along the riverfront were the canneries and sawmills, their chimneys puffing steam and the overpowering smells of sawdust and salmon into the air. In Chinatown the wooden sidewalks were lined with circular mats drying strange and wonderful things—shark fins, small devilfish, oysters, and shrimp. In the shop windows you could see plucked ducks, and dried turtles tied together in pairs, like fans. The Chinese bulletin board was a long wall on Pine Street, plastered with notices in black Chinese characters on flame-colored paper.

Along Front Avenue were the St. Charles Hotel and the Esmond. Hotel weddings were the fashion, and Sally had been to two weddings in the Esmond's green plush parlors.

Stalking Horse tied the mules in front of the Callahan Emporium, which sold everything that anyone could think of: feed, seed, plow blades, harness, dress goods, boots, coffee, tea, sugar, pickles, red-checked tablecloths, straw hats, window shades, and cake pans. Inside, Sally stared around her, delighted, clutching Stalking Horse's hand. On the counter was a coffee grinder with a long handle and penny candy in glass jars.

"I got Mr. Holt's order right here," Donny Callahan said. His father had bought the store from Horace Biddle and promptly changed its name. Donny wore a starched collar, a red bow tie, and red garters on his sleeves. He hefted a hundred-pound sack of flour onto his shoulder. "I'll just carry it for you, Pops."

Stalking Horse took the flour from Donny and slung it over his own shoulder. "I'll load the wagon," he said. "You just add up the order."

There was a hoot from the contingent of the otherwise unoccupied who could usually be found playing checkers at the back of the store, and Donny flushed.

Making several trips Stalking Horse loaded the flour and another sack of coffee beans, two cans of tea, three long bars of soap, which Amy would cut into smaller cakes, then a dozen wool saddle blankets, a pitchfork, and some dress goods for Alexandra, ordered from San Francisco and just arrived on the coastal steamer.

Stalking Horse bought a nickel's worth of butterscotch drops for Sally, then lifted her into the seat again. He climbed up beside her, but he didn't pick up the reins for a moment. His breath sounded loud to her.

"Hoo," he said after a moment, shaking out the reins, "that flour is heavy. Donny Callahan is too big for his britches, but I think maybe I am too old to show off."

The mules clopped down the road, weaving around the wagons and carriages and foot traffic. A fish wagon went by with the afternoon catch, heading up the hillside to Council Crest. The driver would stop in the middle of each terraced block, calling "Fresh fish, nice fat salmon!" and the cooks would come out with baskets on their arms, to buy for dinner.

Stalking Horse stopped next at the post-office building on Morrison Street. After he had tied the mules, he and Sally crossed the square in a throng of government workers and lawyers in frock coats. The post-office building housed the federal district court as well as other federal offices. Inside, as they made their way to the post office, the halls were crowded with witnesses, litigants, jurors, spectators, and more lawyers. Sally clung to Stalking Horse's hand, her eyes wide as they passed the courtroom where two city policemen were ushering in the defendant. He had curly brown hair and blue eyes, and his hands were handcuffed behind him. He didn't look much older than her brother Tim.

"Bank robber," someone muttered as the policemen escorted him inside.

Stalking Horse pushed through the double glass doors into the post office, and the hum of legal activity faded to a buzz outside. The post office was huge, cavernous, with a high beamed ceiling and a long oak counter behind which the postmaster presided. Big brass spittoons and potted palm trees sat at either end. The air smelled of cigar smoke. Behind the counter were rack upon rack of wooden pigeonholes with letters in them. The postmaster was an imposing and portly figure with blue suspenders that showed under the bottom of his vest, and his brown hair was parted in the middle and slicked down. He had a gold watch chain across his middle.

"Madrona Ranch," the postman acknowledged. "I'll have it in a jiffy."

Stalking Horse waited, leaning on the counter, ignoring the fact that everyone else in the office was looking at him. The last Indian war in Oregon hadn't been more than ten years before, so Stalking Horse made some people nervous, despite the fact that he had lived among white men for over fifty years and was a Cherokee from Tennessee. He dressed like a white man, in woolen work pants and a collarless red flannel shirt, mule-ear boots, and a pointed crowned Montana peak hat.

He didn't look like a white man, though. His skin was a dark-copper color, startling against his white hair, which he wore short, for convenience. He was growing thin, and his dark eyes were deeply sunken in his lined face; but he was still plainly a force to be reckoned with. Enough of a force to aggravate the prejudiced and, in this case, the unwary.

A beefy man in lumberjack's boots spat a stream of tobacco juice and glared at Stalking Horse. "Can't even pick up the mail without falling over a damn Injun," he said. "Hey, you, what are you doing with that little white girl?"

Sally gasped, startled, and clutched Stalking Horse's hand again.

Stalking Horse looked the man up and down and didn't bother to answer.

"I asked you, Injun—"

"That's Toby Holt's daughter," the postmaster said. "He's Holt's foreman."

The logger ignored the postmaster. He looked a little drunk, and stubborn. "You answer me, Injun. Little girl, you get away from him. He ain't got no business with a white girl!" He made a lunge for Sally, and Sally screamed.

Stalking Horse's hand shot out, and the short whip that had been coiled at his belt wrapped itself around the logger's arm. The logger found himself facing the nose of a pistol, cradled in Stalking Horse's other hand. Stalking Horse still didn't say anything. He just flicked the whip free and pointed with it at the door. Sally clung to Stalking Horse's belt with both hands.

"You better get out of here," the postmaster said to the man. He took a shotgun from behind his counter and leaned it on the polished oak.

"I don't like Injuns," the logger announced, but he retreated anyway.

"They don't like you, either," Stalking Horse remarked. When the man had gone, he bent down to Sally. "You all right?"

Sally nodded.

"He wasn't dangerous," Stalking Horse said soothingly. "Just mean and dumb."

"I'm sorry about that," the postmaster said. "Some of those fools from up in the logging camps haven't got any sense."

Stalking Horse nodded. It wasn't the first time this kind of thing had happened to him.

Sometimes he thought about going to whatever miserable piece of ground the United States government had run his people onto now and dying as an Indian. But he had been here since 1839. He had known Toby Holt since the day he was born, been his daddy's best friend back in the days when the two of them had run together in the mountains, trapping and surveying for the government. He had helped Whip rope the wild horses that were the origin of the Holt ranch. He wasn't sure he would know how to live as a Cherokee.

The postmaster handed him a packet of letters off the morning train and a burlap sack with a tag from an Ohio nursery.

"Your mama's roses," Stalking Horse told Sally. "Think you can carry them? They feel spiky inside."

Sally nodded and took the burlap sack gingerly by the top. They set off again through the lawyers and the crowd in the halls. Halfway down the corridor, Stalking Horse traded the letters for the roses.

"You're going to trip somebody if you drag them along like that. I should have known. They're bigger than you are." He tucked the roses under his arm and took her hand.

So here he was, he thought as he boosted Sally into the wagon seat, being nursemaid to a four-year-old girl and delivering roses. Sally snuggled up against him when he sat beside her. She yawned. "You lean on me," Stalking Horse told her. Maybe it wasn't such a bad way to get old, he thought.

Alexandra sat at her rosewood dressing table in the bedroom she shared with Toby on the second floor, brushing out her long hair preparatory to pinning it up again for dinner. She was in her chemise and petticoat, and her black-stockinged feet were shoeless. Toby leaned against the four-poster bed and watched her. He was dressed—clean shirt and waistcoat and black tailcoat, hair newly combed, a process that had taken him no more than five minutes. It took him even less time when he was getting ready to go out to the barns in the morning.

Alexandra looked at him in the mirror. "Men's clothes are so easy," she said, vexed.

Toby chuckled. "You could always go back to wearing them. You had on boy's clothes the first time I saw you."

"Maybe I will," Alexandra threatened. "It would be a nine-days' wonder in Portland." She finished brushing her hair and began to coil its length into a knot and pin it to the top of her head. She fluffed up the short front curls with a comb. Beyond the dressing table was an open window, which looked down on the avenue of trees that led to the house. The farm wagon rumbled down it, and she saw Juanita come out and collect Sally, and Janessa come out and collect the mail. "Toby, what are we going to do about Tim?"

"We're going to ship him right back to Cambridge,"

Toby said, surprised. "You don't expect me to let him stay here?"

"I suppose not," Alexandra conceded. "But he's so happy to be home." She shook out her petticoats.

Toby handed her her dress. "The way things stand, Tim will need some profession besides this land. There isn't enough to split now, and you know that Michael has to be the one to inherit it. He may never be strong enough to do anything else."

"Managing the ranch isn't exactly a leisurely occupation," Alexandra pointed out. "You're in the saddle most of the day." She bit her lip unhappily. Michael was her firstborn, her own son, and she lived in daily terror that she was going to lose him. But she loved Tim, too, and just now she felt so dreadfully sorry for him.

"If Michael grows up learning about the ranch and has a good foreman, he can manage Madrona more easily than he can do anything else," Toby said. "Here, put your arms up." He dropped the heavy green faille dress over her head and began to hook it up the back. Juanita would have come to help her, but this had become their evening routine, their chance to sort out the day before dinner.

"All the same, don't you think you were hard on him?" Alexandra asked.

Toby sighed. He put his arms around her and leaned his face into her hair. "Tim hasn't exactly been banished to the salt mines. He's going to Harvard and pursuing a course of study for which he is eminently suited. Nor is the work beyond him. He was capable of making far better marks in high school than he did."

"He gets bored," Alexandra said.

"The results of being bored are difficult to distinguish from the results of being lazy," Toby told her. "Tim is going to stay in Harvard. I am not going to raise another Sam Brentwood."

"Well, if you ask me," Alexandra said tartly, "Sam is Lydia and Andy's fault. Andy was hardly ever around, and when he returned with Lydia from Europe, they never paid enough attention to Sam. The years they spent trying to get that child home—"

While Andrew Brentwood was stationed with the army in Europe, Sam had lived with his grandmother in Independence, Missouri. The widowed Andrew had fallen in love with Lydia von Hofstetten, the young widow of an Austrian count. Andrew married her and brought her home, leaving behind Lydia's baby boy, Franz. The count's family had demanded Franz be raised in the Hapsburg court, in preparation for eventual assumption of his hereditary title and responsibilities.

Andrew and Lydia spent the next six years trying to get custody of the child. To make it easier for them to travel, they sent Sam to a boarding school, and even little Eden, once she had been weaned, had been left with a nurse. Eventually they had received the news—a short, curt letter in German—that Franz had died of scarlet fever.

"And they've been mourning him ever since," Alexandra said, "because Lydia feels guilty."

"Lydia's not the only one," Toby said. "Franz was Andy's child."

"Mercy!" Alexandra said.

"Well, it's not generally known, obviously, but Andy told me. He fell in love with Lydia while she was still married, and the blasted fool let himself be maneuvered into having an affair with her by some old duke who masterminded the whole thing. The family needed an heir for the title, and Lydia's husband wasn't up to it."

"Toby, no!" Alexandra's eyes had a wicked gleam. "And dear Lydia has always acted like butter wouldn't melt in her mouth."

"She was tricked into it, just like Andy," Toby said. "Then when her husband died, she and Andy tried to sneak the baby out and got caught. The duke could have had them thrown into prison for kidnapping. Instead, he threw them out of the country. I honestly thought she was going to kill herself the winter after she married Andy."

"Oh, poor thing," Alexandra said. She thought of losing one of her own children, and her heart clenched. "But still, they should have paid more attention to Sam. And poor little Eden—"

"I know, Alex," Toby said. "But Lydia's always been obsessed with that child, even to the exclusion of Eden, and Andy's obsessed with Lydia."

"Well, I only hope you never do anything that awful for my sake," Alexandra said.

"Certainly not," Toby said. "You aren't Lydia, thank God." He buttoned the last ivory button. "There. You're dressed." Toby kissed the nape of her neck. "And stop worrying about Tim. He'll do fine."

"I know," Alexandra said. "He isn't anything like Sam. But he just doesn't seem to fit into the pattern at Harvard." She waved her hands, trying to pinpoint just what it was that she thought ailed Tim. "Or it doesn't fit into his pattern."

"Nevertheless," Toby said, "back he goes."

III

Janessa took the mail from Stalking Horse and went into the house, sorting the envelopes as she went. There was a letter from her aunt Cindy in Washington, addressed to Toby, which might take some of the sting out of the bills that she also added to his pile. Three of the letters were for various ranch hands on the Madrona, including one from the Patent Hair Restorer Company for Bill Eddings, who pinned his hopes anew on each advertisement he saw in the paper. And there was a letter for Janessa from Charley Lawrence, postmarked Virginia City, Nevada.

She put her father's letters in the blue and white Chinese bowl on the hall table, where family correspondence was always left, and the others beside it to go out to the bunkhouse. Then she ran up the stairs with Charley's letter.

Charley was an old friend from her miserable college days; he was the brother of Nan Lawrence, the only classmate Janessa had felt affection for. Nan and Charley were from Fincastle, Virginia, ten miles from Hollins Institute, the college that Janessa and Nan had attended. Charley had wanted to be a doctor, too, but the Lawrences hadn't had any money since the war, and his undergraduate tuition at the University of Virginia had been all his mother had been able to manage. Charley knew if he was going to medical school, he would have to earn the fees himself. The last time Janessa had heard from Nan, Charley had been trying

to make money in a silver mine in Nevada. Judging
from the postmark, he was still trying.

In her bedroom Janessa settled into the cushioned
window seat, with her back against the wall and her
knees tucked up. She eagerly tore the envelope open.
Charley's letters always made her laugh. This one, however, proved more serious.

Dear Janessa,

You will no doubt be stunned to read that I
have actually found silver. Not much silver, mind
you, and I have a deep suspicion that the vein is
about to peter out at any moment, but enough
silver to bring me $2,000. Having reached that
magical figure, I have sold the claim to the owners
of the Consolidated California Mining Company,
the octopoid entity that owns the major mining
concern here. The proceeds from the sale will improve my bank account a little and buy me a horse
and some decent clothing in which to make my
appearance at the University of Southern California, which is young and hungry and therefore willing to take me on, despite the rather lengthy gap
in my academic career. This venture has been
greeted with hoots of laughter from my fellow prospectors, who find the idea of making $2,000 and
going home again hilarious.

But I never wanted to be rich; I only wanted
to be a doctor (the two of which are not likely to be
synonymous), and it has been my experience that
all silver mines, like all lucky streaks at poker, run
dry just about the time you have bought champagne all around and ordered a new carriage.

The odds are not with the single prospector
now. The time of major, new strikes here is gone,
and all the big veins have been found. What remains are small veins, such as the one that I stumbled upon, and low-grade ore passed over in the
first boom days in favor of the high-grade rock.
Low-grade ore may be profitably extracted, given

the right equipment, a sizable crew, and a good transport system to the stamping mills some seven miles away on the Carson River. Virginia City will last awhile yet, but its boom days are behind it.

Oddly enough, now that I am preparing to quit this city, I feel a certain affection for it. Not for the bottom of a mine, certainly, which is as dark as the inside of a billy goat and prone to flooding with scalding water, but for the town itself. There is a certain charm about Virginia City, where the nabobs are newly rich miners vying to outdo each other in ostentation. The all-night saloons are cheek by jowl with the opera house, and the most famous gravestone is that of a lady of less than sterling virtue.

Virginia City has more saloons than I can count, and several ornate churches built with the silver of the newly rich and thankful. It has no water aboveground (all is brought by flume and water pipe more than twenty miles from Marlette Lake) and far too much below. Huge quantities of hot water are to be found at the lower levels, generally unexpectedly. No surprise is quite like having scalding water suddenly erupt from a drill hole. The problem is somewhat worse now than it was in the boom days. Since so many mine shafts have been sunk in and around the city, all are virtually interconnected. When one mine shuts down, the loss of its pumps places an additional burden on the others. The Combination Mine was the last to operate a big pump, and when it shut down last year, deep mining was just about brought to a stop.

In the winter it is freezing cold here, with much snow. In the summer it is as dry as tinder and as hot as an oven. The surrounding hillsides are green only in April, the rainy season. For the rest, they are brown, with stunted grass and a few pitiful pine trees trying valiantly to cling to the upper slopes. Altogether not a garden spot, but life here has a boisterous and unruly quality that is invigorating in its way. I expect I'll look back on it fondly, given sufficient time to forget how much I hated mining.

Tomorrow I leave for Reno, and from there, home via the Southern Pacific until fall. The University of Southern California, incidentally, accepts female students in its medical college, which is even younger than the rest of the school. And what, the learned doctors will ask me, has become of Janessa Holt, who displayed such promise? Or maybe they won't, but *I* am asking you. Janessa, you ought to be a doctor by now. What have you been doing? And don't think I don't know why you didn't go, because I do. But the world is full of nasty people, and you can't hide from life forever.

Nan, by the way, is thriving. I know she writes to you and would be happy to see you again. She will have told you she is getting married in the fall, to a good egg from Richmond. I like him, and I think he'll take good care of her. He owns a carriage works and has political ambitions and isn't the stuffed shirt that that sounds like.

It's now or never, Janessa. The older you get, the harder it will be. I think my profits from the sale of the Nancy Belle Mine will stretch to a steak dinner in Los Angeles if you will pack up your bags and your nerve and show up. I am dead serious. If I don't find a telegram waiting for me when I get home, you aren't the woman I took you for.

> Fondly,
> Charley

Janessa dropped the letter in her lap and leaned her head back against the wall. How like Charley. Most men would have gotten silver fever and stayed in Virginia City, trying to make another strike, to pull more silver out of the claim, to get rich.

Janessa remembered meeting him for the first time: Charley had come down to Hollins from the University of Virginia to see Nan and had gotten Miss Matty's permission to drive his sister into Roanoke for dinner. Miss Matty was the founder's daughter and served variously as registrar, social dean, and confidante of the hundred or so girls in residence at Hollins. Nan had suggested bringing Janessa, who was huddling miserably in her room after a particularly trying week, and together they had dragged her forth, put her hat upon her head, and bundled her into the buggy.

Janessa had looked at Charley curiously. She had known that Nan had a brother, older by a year, who went to the university, but she had never met him. He had nondescript brown hair, not quite straight, so that it never stayed down when he combed it, gray eyes, a long friendly mouth that quirked easily up or down according to his moods, and a compact muscular build that made him look somehow solid, a friend one could depend on.

When she had looked down at him querulously from the buggy seat, knowing her hair to be a mess and herself to be in a foul temper, her irritation had nonetheless melted. She had liked Charley instantly. He had seemed to be able to look through her, to puncture her balloon of misery when she was feeling sorry for herself, and to share in the joke without being told when she was laughing.

He had treated them all to an enormous dinner of steak and oysters at the Hotel Roanoke, which, knowing Nan's circumstances, Janessa had been fairly sure he couldn't really afford, and had taken them for a mad, midnight ride on the little incline railroad that went to the top of Mill Mountain. He had brought a bottle of champagne with him, and they had been in disgrace when they got back to school.

After that, when he came to see Nan, they had always made a threesome. Charley had told Janessa more of their family's history—the tobacco plantation and the father both lost in the war—and hadn't seemed to care that her own father had fought on the other side. It was all water under the bridge, Charley had said; you couldn't turn time around. He hadn't cared either that Janessa's mother hadn't been married to her father or that she herself was part Indian. Cherokee blood was strong, resilient stock, Charley had said, no matter how you came by it.

He had been fascinated by Janessa's life, her early years with her mother, who had been a medicine woman among the Cherokee, the long journey across America when her mother was dying, to bring Janessa to the father she had never seen, and her life on the Madrona as Toby Holt's daughter. When he found out that she had trained at the hospital in Portland with Dr. Martin and had even been allowed to help him in surgery, he had made her tell him everything, every word, every detail. Charley was going to be a good doctor, too. He had wanted nothing else since he was eight years old.

He didn't care for "those knock-kneed hens"—that had been Charley's phrase—who made a social pariah of Janessa and sniped at each other. He had liked Miss Matty, though. Miss Matty was very outspoken and had said that Janessa would have to learn to live with what she was and turn it to good use. Charley had considered that to be good advice.

When Janessa had fallen in love for the first time, disastrously, Charley had helped her through that, too. Brice Amos had been the son of a visiting professor of biology, and Brice had spent a glorious year at Hollins as nearly the only young male on campus and consequently the center of attention for a hundred adoring young ladies who fell victim to his charm and dashing blond looks. He had courted Janessa assiduously until just about the time that she fell in love with him and one of the other girls told him about her mother.

She still cringed every time she recalled her last meeting with Brice. They had been promenading on the Quadrangle Bridge, the accepted spot to show off beaux and new dresses. They hadn't strolled for very long, just until they were out of earshot of two girls at the bridge's far end. Then, to Janessa's surprise, Brice had turned on her.

"I would like to think that you would not deliberately keep your situation from me!"

"I didn't keep anything from you," she had faltered. "I thought you already knew. I thought you didn't mind."

"You presume too much," Brice snapped. "I knew only that you were the daughter of Toby Holt. Unaware as I was that you were trading upon that name without bona fides—"

"Without—" Janessa's eyes had overflowed, and to her own horror, she began to cry.

"You're making a spectacle of yourself," Brice said stiffly.

At the end of the bridge, the two girls, in their pale spring dresses, parasols over their shoulders, turned to stare.

Janessa put her hands over her face, feeling as if she had been kicked.

"For God's sake, pull yourself together!" Brice hissed. He strode off in the opposite direction, hands in his pockets.

She turned and fled down the bridge. As she passed the girls, they laughed at her disgrace.

That had been Janessa's most brutal lesson in the fact that the standing she enjoyed in Portland was accorded her out of respect for Toby Holt and was not transferable to other places. At home she never felt herself anything but a Holt. Away from the ranch, who was she? Hollins had admitted her because she was Toby Holt's daughter. But the administration, with the best will in the world, could not force her fellow students to treat her as anything other than Toby Holt's half-Indian bastard.

Only Nan Lawrence had made a friend of her from the start, for reasons Janessa could not fathom. Nan was a cheerful, freckled girl with sunny brown eyes and a round, pretty face. When Janessa's roommate, recoiling in horror, demanded another room assignment from the dean, Nan, who had arrived late and was rooming alone, had offered to trade. When Brice Amos abandoned

Janessa, Nan had held her in her arms while Janessa cried out her bewilderment and fury.

Charley Lawrence had volunteered to punch Brice in the nose for her. She had refused that offer, but she had been grateful to Charley just for his support. Charley had always been a friend; except for her father and brothers, he was the only man she could be sure was not going to court her for Toby Holt's money, throw her over for who her mother had been, or both. Charley and Nan had made Janessa's life bearable—but just barely.

Miss Matty had also done her best. She had refused to write to Alexandra and suggest that Janessa be taken home, because she said that Janessa would have to learn to deal with life sometime. And Janessa had not written to Alexandra because she was too proud. But four years had been all she could stand up to. The idea of another three years, in medical school, where her tormentors would be men, was unbearable. With Brice as an example, men seemed to her to be even more vicious than women.

Janessa got up out of the window seat now, leaving Charley's letter on the cushions. She went to her mirror and stared into it. Her image always looked strange to her, and she found it difficult to assess her heart-shaped face. She had blue-gray eyes; straight, determined brows; high, angular cheekbones; and a narrow chin. Her hair was light brown with a slight wave in it, less than that of the rest of the Holts. Even though everyone said she resembled her aunt Cindy, Janessa knew that she had inherited her high cheekbones and narrow chin from her mother. She could remember her mother—she had been ten when Mary White Owl had died—but the memory was fading, overlaid too heavily with the Madrona and its people. Mary White Owl had had no place on the ranch. She was buried here in the family graveyard, but she had held that place only with her dying.

Janessa turned from the mirror and paced restlessly. In keeping with current fashion, the walls of her room were cluttered with pictures of all descriptions and draped with fans and shawls. On her cherrywood bed was a hand-pieced quilt. The washstand and dresser were marble topped. Janessa stopped, staring at each item as if viewing it for the first time. She sank into her rocking chair and stared at the rug. She was twenty-six, and she felt paralyzed.

How easy it would be to spend her life in this room, slowly turning into Tim's "old-maid schoolteacher," safe and comfortable. Slowly running down, she thought, like some mechanical contraption, until finally she just stopped and they stood her up in the hall, like a stuffed elk. *That's Janessa. She just quit moving one day, so we stuck her in here. Lifelike, isn't she?*

Janessa shot a glance at Charley's letter in the window seat. She picked it up and took it slowly across the room to her desk, where she scrabbled urgently for a fountain pen in the drawer before she lost her nerve.

"Oooh, Mama! Look, I can make magic!" Sally peered in wonderment into the wooden box. It held glass jars of things in wonderful colors: ruby-colored powders, aquamarine rock, emerald water. Across the front in red and black letters it said: McKinnon's Junior Chemist's Set.

Alexandra gave Tim a look that stated with no words necessary that she considered him to have taken leave of his senses.

"Janessa can help her with it," Tim said. "There isn't anything in there that'll explode. I asked."

"Prudent of you," Toby said.

Sally looked disappointed.

"And where is Janessa?" Alexandra inquired. The rest of the family had gathered in the parlor to open their presents before dinner.

"She's upstairs," Tim said. "There's a light in her room. I knocked, but she wouldn't come out."

"Well, what's she doing?"

"I don't know," Tim replied. "Baying at the moon. You know Janessa. She'll come out when she's ready."

Tim handed a box to Michael, and others to his father, Alexandra, and Sam. He kept Janessa's in his lap.

"Stereopticon slides!" Michael shouted when he had pulled off the wrapper. "Oh, boy!" He held one up and squinted at it.

"Scenes of Egypt," Tim said. "The tombs of the pharaohs and mysterious veiled women."

"This one's a camel," Michael said.

"Well, you've got to take a few camels with your mysterious veiled women," Tim said. "Keeps your feet on the ground."

Michael got the stereopticon viewer from the table and put a slide in it. He sat still, gazing through the eyepieces, lost in whatever distant world he viewed. "It's almost as if they could move," he breathed.

Toby looked at Tim. "I trust those women are wearing something more than veils?"

"Caftans down to their toes," Tim assured him. "Open your present."

Toby pulled the paper off the box and took out a small porcelain horse. It was glazed in an improbable chartreuse, and its mane and tail were blue. It looked at him over one shoulder, and it had a cork stopper in its stomach.

"It's Chinese," Tim said. "I think it's supposed to hold opium."

"I may take up the habit at any moment," Toby said, but he grinned. He liked the little horse. It was just odd enough to suit him.

Sam, looking a little embarrassed, opened his. It was a box of Havana cigars.

"I didn't know what you'd like," Tim admitted. "But I thought cigars were safe."

"They're top-notch," Sam said. "Thank you. We'll try them after dinner."

"Outside," Alexandra said firmly. She looked at Tim. Cigars. Was he getting that old? She supposed he must be, but where had the time gone?

"Mama," Tim said. He pointed at the little box in her lap.

Alexandra opened it. It held an oval scrimshaw brooch, carved from whalebone, with a sailing ship engraved on it. She pinned it to the front of her gown and smiled at him affectionately.

"I brought Janessa one, too," Tim said.

"It's lovely."

"You brought Janessa one what?" She came through the doors, bent over, and kissed his cheek. She had changed for dinner and wore a bright blue taffeta gown with a gray velvet overskirt gathered up at the sides. She had a bow in her hair. "Do I look better?" she whispered in his ear.

"Beautiful," Tim said. He held out the box to her.

Janessa's brooch was round, and engraved on it was a walrus, perched majestically on a rock. She burst out laughing.

"I thought you liked animals," Tim said. "What's so funny?"

Janessa put her hand over her mouth. "It looks just like the general!" she spluttered.

Alexandra looked over. "Heavens, so it does." The general was General Leland Blake, Grandpa Lee, Toby's mother's second husband.

"I adore it," Janessa said. "I'll wear it always."

"Possibly not around your grandfather," Alexandra murmured.

A crystal tinkling from beyond the parlor announced that dinner was ready. They rose and made their way into the dining room, with Sally pattering along behind. Ordinarily she ate in the breakfast room with Juanita and was in bed by the time her elders sat down at the table. Her presence tonight was in Tim's honor, and she bounced excitedly. Tim grinned when he saw the table.

Abby Givens adored Tim, and she had laid the long mahogany dining table with Alexandra's best Haviland china and the silver that had been the general's wedding present. The dubious rooster was nowhere to be seen, but the hens, fried, made an imposing golden mound in a blue and white Chinese platter. At the center of the table, on another platter, was a salmon, whole, with a sprig of parsley in its mouth and a crock of lemon butter beside it. Crowded into every other spare inch of space on the table were dishes of vegetables, pickles, gingered peaches, corn muffins, biscuits, hot bread, olives, and eggs in hollandaise sauce.

"Bring hither the fatted calf and kill it," Tim said.

"There wouldn't be room," Janessa replied. She peered at the table. "What, no oysters?"

"On the sideboard," Abby said indignantly, wiping her hands on her apron. "Of course there are oysters."

"I was joking," Janessa said faintly. She cocked an eye at Tim. He was smiling happily, enjoying the fuss.

"Let us sit down and eat," Alexandra said firmly, "since Abby has gone to such trouble."

They sat dutifully, heads bowed while Toby said grace. "Oh, Lord, bless this food to our use, and us to Thy service. Amen."

They began with the oysters while Toby filleted the salmon. One flat, gelatinous eye looked back at him. "I wish Abby wouldn't be so fancy," he muttered. "I prefer my dinner cut into steaks, not glaring at me accusingly."

Sally inspected the oysters. "I don't like those," she announced. "They look like—"

"Shhh!" Michael put a finger over her mouth.

"Give her a muffin, Mike," Janessa suggested.

"I went to town today," Sally said importantly. "With Stalking Horse."

"Did you see anything fun, sweetheart?" Alexandra asked.

"I saw a bad man," Sally answered. "And I saw Chinese people. I like the way they sound, and they have turtles in their windows."

"Turtles?" Alexandra asked.

"In the Chinese pharmacy, I expect," Janessa said. "They're dried. The Chinese boil them and drink the soup for rheumatism."

Honestly, Alexandra thought, Janessa knew the oddest things.

"Does it work?" Tim asked.

"Heaven only knows," Janessa said. "Probably as well as anything. But turtles *are* very nutritious."

"I think I'd just as soon you all stayed out of Chinatown for a while," Toby told them. "I meant to mention that to Stalking Horse."

"The Chinese don't do any harm, sir," Tim said.

"No, I'm afraid it's our people who may make trouble, the damn fools," Toby said. "Excuse me." He glanced at Alexandra, who had definite ideas about how a gentleman should conduct himself at the dinner table.

"What sort of trouble, sir?" Sam asked, perking up with interest.

"It's a problem that's surfaced before in Portland," Toby explained. "It seems to be getting up a head of steam again, from what Willis Larken was saying at the bank yesterday."

"What did Willis have to say?" Alexandra asked him. Toby's visits to the bank generally included the genteel poker game that went on in the back room on Friday afternoons. The National Bank poker game formed a sort of Portland gentleman's club, and as a source of information, it was better than the newspaper.

"He was all worked up about the Chinese labor question," Toby said. "Willis owns a cannery, and he depends on the Chinese to keep him in operation."

"Is there a shortage of them?" Sam asked. "Looked to me like the place was overflowing with them."

"That's the problem," Toby said. "When half the men in Portland went off to California to dig gold thirty-five years ago, employers brought Chinese in to fill the void. They brought more to build the railroad. Now the railroad is built, and the unions want to throw the Chinese out again because they'll work for less than half of what a white man calls a living wage. Naturally the factory owners want to keep them. Willis had a lot of pious talk about responsibility to our yellow brothers, but what he really means is he can mistreat a Chinese in a way a white man wouldn't stand for."

"What about the Chinese?" Janessa asked. "Isn't anybody for them?"

"Unfortunately, no," Toby said. "I'm afraid each side has its own ax to grind in this. That's why I want you all to stay out of Chinatown for the time being. When the bosses and the unions start fighting over the Chinese, they generally do it on the Chinaman's ground."

"Will there be riots again?" Janessa asked him.

"Probably," Toby said. "Human nature being what it is. I sometimes ask myself what the good Lord had in mind when He set out to create us. I don't think the Lord had His full attention on us that day, or maybe there's a plan beyond our knowing. But I have too much experience of human nature to have any confidence in it."

Alexandra looked worried. A year ago the "good" citizens of Oregon had attacked the Chinese. The governor had called out the state militia, but the militia had refused to act.

"I had a letter from Charley Lawrence today," Janessa said, changing the subject. "Would you believe he's actually found silver?"

"In Nevada?" Toby asked, diverted. "I thought the Comstock Lode was just about petered out."

"Charley says they've come up with a system for profitably extracting silver from low-grade ore," Janessa said. "But what he found was a high-grade strike."

"A new one?" Sam turned to her, interested.

"Well, I don't think it was very big," Janessa said. "Charley took two thousand dollars out of it and sold the claim to a mining company, so I don't know."

"Sold out?" Sam asked, incredulous.

Janessa laughed. "He got what he came for. All he wanted was medical-school tuition." When she saw her father's eye on her, she looked down at her plate.

"Do you mean to tell me this fellow could have been rich, but he sold out his claim to go to school?" Sam rolled his eyes heavenward in disgust.

"Well, he might not have been rich, too," Michael pointed out. He pushed his beans expertly under a strip of fish skin and ate his salmon, smiling beatifically at his mother when she looked at him suspiciously. "I mean," he continued, trying to divert any thoughts from the beans, "you never know where a vein's going to end. I think this guy did the right thing. It's better to go after what you know you want than hang around because you might get rich. Isn't it?" Mike looked at his father for corroboration.

"Unless, of course, what you want is to get rich," Toby said, eyeing Sam.

"Charley says the mines fill up with scalding water at the lower levels," Janessa said.

"That sounds a little too close to the devil for my taste," Alexandra said. "I admire Mr. Lawrence's tenacity."

"It's his main character trait," Janessa said cheerfully. "He's as stubborn as a pig. It's probably why nobody's ever married him."

Alexandra looked at her thoughtfully. It wouldn't surprise her if that was why nobody had ever married Janessa, either. Or rather, why Janessa had never married anybody. She was old enough to be considered an old maid, except that she didn't look like one. She just didn't trust any man to want her for something more than Toby Holt's money. Didn't trust them not to look down on her. *Maybe now that there isn't much money,* Alexandra thought, *a man who loves Janessa for herself will surface, and she'll believe in him.*

"What's a mine?" Sally asked. She had been listening with rapt attention.

"It's a hole in the ground, honey," Toby explained. "Out of which you hope to extract money."

"That gooseberry tart Abby made for dessert was good. Too bad it didn't quite make up for an afternoon on a haying crew." Sam leaned back in his chair and put his boots on the porch railing. A cloud of cigar smoke wreathed his head. He turned to look at Tim through the haze. "The trouble with you is, you never take advantage of opportunity."

"Well, I tried," Tim said. "It just didn't strike my dad the same way." He lit one of Sam's cigars and contemplated the cool dusk. The air smelled wet and verdant, and the tree leaves rustled in a little breeze. Tim felt mistreated, and he poured a splash of liquor into a brandy glass from the bottle beside him.

"Hell, that's no opportunity," Sam said. "Coming home to work your ass off in a hay field."

"I like haying," Tim said stubbornly, although he didn't, much. He just liked being home.

"Horse apples," Sam said. "You really want to leave Harvard?"

"Lord, yes," Tim said. "It's not just Harvard; it's the whole landscape out there. It feels different, wrong, like I had on a collar that was too tight, and I was stuffed into one of those rickety little gold chairs listening to some long-haired jackass in a silk neckerchief play the cello for three hours. I feel like I'm going to strangle."

"Like I said, you're not thinking about your opportunities." Sam blew a cloud of smoke out and grinned at Tim through it. "Virginia City, for instance. My mother lived there. She started a paper—the *Journal.* Sounds to me like there's a new boom there, although this friend of Janessa's was too dumb to see it."

"Virginia City?" Tim sat up. "You mean go prospecting?"

"I'd say it was more certain than that," Sam said. "With this new low-grade ore process, we could get in on the ground floor."

"You know anything about mining?" Tim asked suspiciously.

"Sure," Sam assured him. "And you studied engineering. I don't see how we can go wrong. Most prospectors are uneducated old coots who've been out in the desert so long it's fried their brains. You and me, now—that's different. Brains are what it takes, and some education. Being able to see the big picture."

Tim wondered fleetingly how much education Sam had acquired in the course of being thrown out of three universities, but Sam was persuasive, and the picture he painted alluring.

"Virginia City's a coming town," Sam said. "Not some hole-in-the-ground mining camp. Lots of opportunity. You can't be your daddy's little boy all your life."

"I'm not my daddy's little boy!" Tim half got up from his chair and glared at Sam.

"Simmer down," Sam said placatingly. He picked up his brandy glass and looked at Tim over the rim. His dark blue eyes were sincere and compelling. "I'm just trying to help you. You don't want to go back to Harvard, and you can't stay here. Virginia City's a chance to prove to your old man that you can be a success in your own way. He's just too used to thinking of you as a kid. He treats you like he treats Michael, and you haven't even got a gimpy heart. Toby's used to running the whole show, and he just can't see you're getting too old for that."

Tim thought about Virginia City. He had heard it was a hell-raising town, full of new money and flamboyance and a transient, shifting population that moved with the flow of the silver. He imagined it as a distant glow in the night sky somewhere to the south beyond the mountains, lit by its own energy. It seemed to him to represent an attainable dream.

"I'm not going to lie to Dad," Tim said. He knew he was waiting for Sam to show him how to do it without lying.

Sam watched him through the shifting cloud of smoke. The cigar was clenched between his teeth, and his mouth curved into a reckless, confident grin. "Plenty of trains heading out of Portland. No one's likely to ask which one you're catching. You just leave it to me."

Tim knew, guiltily, that he was going to let Sam do the lying for both of them.

IV

The next morning, Alexandra was pulling on her gloves by the front door at eight o'clock and calling up the staircase, her usual Sunday-morning ritual.

"You all are going to be late! Juanita! Where's Sally?"

The buggy, with Stalking Horse in the driver's seat, crunched to a stop in the oyster-shell circle in front of the house as Sally came flying down the stairs with Juanita behind her, trying to tie on her bonnet as she went. Janessa followed them at a more sedate pace, prayer book in hand. In the hall they were joined by Amy and Abby Givens, in their Sunday best of stiff black bombazine and sensible black bonnets pinned firmly to their heads.

Alexandra waited by the door, counting heads, as Toby emerged, with Tim and Sam on his heels. The gentlemen wore dark cutaway coats and sober four-in-hand neckties. Their garb and blond hair made Tim and Toby appear as alike as two peas in a pod, while Sam seemed a dark and night-blooming flower that had crept into a row of marigolds by mistake. Michael came last, buttoning the front of his jacket.

Alexandra surveyed her household. Outside, Stalking Horse and White Elk awaited them, accompanied by whichever ranch hands were inclined toward church-going. Alexandra climbed into the buggy with Janessa, Sally, Abby, and Amy. The men accompanied them on horseback, and the little cavalcade set out down the road toward Portland.

When they arrived, the yard of Trinity Church was full of carriages and buggies and rows of tethered horses. Alexandra swept her brood inside and into the Holt family pew. She liked going to church; it gave her a sense of the solidity and endurance of things. As she looked up at the stained-glass panel of the risen Christ above the altar—it had been shipped by boat around the Horn—she wondered what it had all been like in the early days, when the church was a hand-hewn log house and the pews were packing crates. Exciting, probably: The first pastor was reputed to have personally broken up a fistfight in the aisle between two drunken laborers. But the church must have given the settlers the same sense of permanence; the conviction that Portland was going to succeed. Churches and schools were always the first buildings constructed when people were planning to stay.

"Let us pray."

The congregation knelt. Alexandra opened her prayer book and made herself concentrate on the service. One of the difficulties with so much peace and serenity was that it allowed her mind to wander.

After the service, when they emerged through the brass-bound red doors, they found that there had been a rainfall, leaving the trees misty and ethereally lovely as the sun shone through them again.

Alexandra smiled. The cessation of rain and the following sunlight always made her feel that here was the chance to begin things again, to correct past mistakes, to scale new heights—even to take new chances without the baggage of past doubts. She glanced at Tim and Janessa, standing side by side and breathing in the new, rainwashed air. They looked, she thought, as if they felt the same way.

Maybe Tim had resigned himself to Harvard? . . . Alexandra cocked her head at him doubtfully. He didn't look like it, she decided. He seemed to have a new look altogether. His trunk had been sent on to the railway depot, and he would ride there from church, with Sam to bring his horse home. Tim had been quite firm that he did not wish to be seen off at the depot. It was, he had said, a little too much like being put on the train by the warden. She watched him kiss Janessa, then stride over, long-legged, cheerful, and not particularly repentant looking.

"You behave yourself now," she said. "Have you told your father good-bye?"

"I'm just about to," he answered.

"You mustn't be angry with his making you go back. He's never had anything but your good at heart."

Tim looked embarrassed. "Yeah, I know."

Toby came over and put his arm around Tim's shoulders. "Stick it out till summer, Son. College won't look so bad in the fall. Sophomore year is always the hardest."

"Right," Tim muttered. He saw Sam waiting for him under the trees, already mounted. "Listen, I've got to get going. I'll, uh, write." As he moved off, his horse fidgeted at the end of its rein, as if it had absorbed Tim's restlessness.

"Something's bothering him," Alexandra said. "He looks—" She stopped. What he had looked was guilty, she thought. "Are you sure this is a good idea? Making him go back when he doesn't want to?"

"We've been over this," Toby said, taking her arm and leading her toward the yard. "It's the best idea I've got." He pulled out his watch and glanced at it. "I have to stay in town. Willis Larken asked me to stop by. I'll see you after dinner."

"What does Willis want?" Alexandra asked.

"I don't know," Toby answered, mounting his horse. "But he insisted I have dinner with him at the Esmond. I'll tell you at supper."

"You do that." It had been Alexandra's experience that when men discussed business at a gentlemen-only dinner, it was usually because there was something they didn't want women to know about until it was too late. Toby wasn't like that, but Willis Larken was. If Alexandra had been married to Willis, she thought, she would have killed him with a shovel long since, but his wife prefaced every sentence with "Willis says" and seemed quite happy with him.

As Toby made his way toward Front Avenue, he grinned, having divined his wife's thoughts accurately. The Esmond was a fair distance from the church. He preferred the St. Charles Hotel, but the Esmond was newer and more stylish, fitted out with dazzling conveniences. The Esmond had a plush bellpull in every room.

He tied his horse outside the hotel and was directed by an assistant manager to one of the private dining rooms; Toby raised his eyebrows as he walked in: Willis was entertaining three other guests, as well. They were all known to Toby, but he was not what he would have called chummy with any of them: Ephraim Bender, president of the Portland Land and Auction Company; Donald McCallum, who was the Union Pacific Railroad chairman in Portland; and Noell Simpson, who was Portland's congressman.

"Afternoon, Holt."

"Glad you could join us."

"Have a seat."

They escorted him to a chair, then pressed a cigar into his hand. Willis Larken poured him a shot of whiskey.

"Tell the boy he can bring dinner in twenty minutes," Willis told the assistant manager. Then he turned to Toby. "Good of you to join us. I hope you'll give my regards to Mrs. Holt."

"Certainly," Toby murmured.

"I heard you had a good crop of horseflesh at the last sale," Ephraim Bender said. "Sorry to hear about your troubles in Dakota."

"An act of God, gentlemen." Toby shrugged. "I was one of the lucky ones. None of my workers died."

"Oh, aye," McCallum said. He bent his head. They all looked solemn.

Toby eyed them all warily. "Willis, what the hell do you want?"

"We were, er, hoping you could advise us on the senatorial election," Larken said.

Toby looked blank. "Why me?"

"No point in pussyfooting," McCallum said. "We want you to run."

Toby sighed. "I haven't got the money to run. You know that."

"We'll undertake to provide financial backing," Willis said. "Commitments have been made."

Toby leaned back in his chair. "Supposing you tell me why you're so eager to have me run. We don't usually see eye to eye, Willis." He looked at Noell Simpson. "I didn't even vote for you last time."

"Politics is the art of the practical," Simpson said. He didn't look annoyed. "The practical consideration is that the party gets its man in."

"Can't think of anyone else," Bender muttered.

Toby grinned. "A high recommendation."

"I meant to say, can't think of anyone else who's got a chance of squeaking through the legislature. Senators are elected by a vote of the state legislature, and everyone in there's got some ax to grind. Can't please 'em all. So we thought, give 'em a man they know'll vote his conscience. Times are changing, Holt. Sympathies aren't with the deal makers anymore. Folks want an honest man to represent them."

"I'm flattered." Toby studied the whiskey in his glass. "The fact remains, this isn't a good time for me to take on something like this. I wasn't counting on spending much time in Washington."

"Think about what's best for Oregon, Holt," Bender urged.

Toby glared at the man. "My father gave the better part of his life for Oregon, Bender, and I've given a fair share of mine, too. Don't preach patriotism at me."

A waiter arrived with a tray of covered dishes, and Toby was quiet while the boy laid them on the table, uncovering each with a flourish. A monstrous standing rib roast was at the center, and the waiter carved it while Toby counted the side dishes and grinned. If the expense of the dinner was a measure of sincerity, they were courting him seriously.

"No question of your patriotism, Toby," Willis said when they were all seated and had been served. "It's one of the things that makes you a good candidate. If ever there was a man who could run on his reputation, it's Toby Holt."

"That's right," McCallum agreed. "Even folks who don't agree with your politics say you're an honest man."

"Nearly everybody hasn't agreed with my politics at one time or another," Toby pointed out. He had the ability to look at a question from multiple viewpoints, which often set him against prevailing opinion on both sides.

"We recognize that," Simpson said. "We may not like your stance all the time, either. But we need a man who can bring together all the factions in Oregon. It's a young land. Change and uncertainty are natural. We need a candidate who commands universal respect to make this state a cohesive force."

Toby thought about that. A senator represented the entire state, not just his district. The Cascade Range divided Oregon into two halves that had always been unlikely partners. West of the range, the humid winds and warm rains of the coast gave the land a lush prosperity that bred lumbermen, dairymen, fishermen, and farmers. And politicians. East of the Cascades, walled off by the mountains' height from the life-giving water, eastern Oregon was a land of drought and distance, of high desert that would grow only juniper and sage, and of tortured mountains flung skyward in jagged, awesome crests. The land had a certain stark beauty, but the cattlemen, sheepmen, and miners who inhabited it had little in common with the farmers of the west. Toby had the feeling, however, that the divisions that Simpson had in mind were more local. Portland's troubles could easily become Oregon's troubles just by virtue of Portland's population.

"Maybe we ought to discuss just exactly the changes and uncertainties that are worrying you," Toby suggested.

"Either we settle these unions down or the Portland business community's going to go belly up in six months," Willis said.

"No, it isn't," McCallum told him. "But it isn't going to do it any good, either. We need those coolies."

"The unions want to run them out," Bender said. "If we don't watch our step, we're going to have riots again. Won't do Portland any good when that sort of thing gets reported in the eastern papers."

"I'm no union buster," Toby warned. "You fellows know that."

"We aren't looking for a union buster," Bender said. "We're looking for a fellow the union men will like. And someone who the businessman doesn't have to worry will round up all his coolies and ship them back to China." He made a wry face. "Repatriate them, isn't that what they call it? Stuff them in a ship made to hold half that many and send them off. About like one of the old slave ships, I expect."

"Your social conscience is admirable," Toby said dryly. "For a land developer."

Bender snorted. "No social conscience about it. I just like to keep us looking good for the easterners. Progress, Holt. That's what Portland is built on. It doesn't look good to be bringing these Chinamen over here to work and then throwing them out again."

"Whereas probably no one will notice that you're paying them starvation wages while they're here," Toby observed. "And if you don't think I'm for repatriating the Chinese, what makes you think the union sympathizers will vote for me?"

"Because in everything else, you've always been on the unions' side," Willis said with a look of mild disgust.

"I'm for America, Willis," Toby said. "Not for the Chinese laborers, not for the union, not for the land developers, and not for your pocketbook. Not even for my pocketbok. I'm for the whole country. I've got a loyalty to Oregon, but I've got a bigger one to the United States. Maybe you boys better keep that in mind." He looked thoughtfully at Noell Simpson. "And what do you want, Congressman? And don't tell me about cohesiveness and all pulling together again."

"I want our party to get a man in the Senate," Simpson said. "I want the man who can win."

Willis hooted. "The Democrats would support a Madagascar monkey if they thought the legislature would elect him."

Toby cut, chewed, and swallowed the last few bites of his roast, and ate a salmon cake thoughtfully, aware that they were all watching him. He smiled slightly and sipped his wine. Politics did not breed selfless honesty, and it amused him to have pinned these four down far enough to make them admit it. Now he was enjoying making them wait for his decision. It was, he thought ruefully, the most fun he might have for a while—because he knew that he was going to say yes. The fancy talk about bringing the state together and finding an honest man might be so much hogwash to these four, but it meant something to Toby. Oregon did need a man who could unite its widely distanced factions, who could see both sides of a question. And God knew the Chinese needed someone to protect them from their employers, as well as from mindless, prejudiced mobs.

The waiter removed their plates and presented chocolate mousse in a liqueur sauce, and a brandy bottle.

Toby poured a splash of brandy in his glass. "You may not like me much better than the monkey," he suggested.

"We'll take our chances," McCallum said. "I meant it when I said you were honest. At least we know you won't sell us down the river."

Toby sighed. "All right. I'll run. But you remember you said that when you want me to sell someone else down the river for you and I won't do it."

"Absolutely."

The men surged around him, slapping his back, congratulating themselves as well as him, and giving him another cigar. They assured him that he was senatorial material, that they admired his honesty, and that they would be stoic, even admiring, if he should vote his conscience and not their pocketbooks.

They'll squeal like stuck pigs, Toby thought, riding home, *the first time I vote against their interests.* But surely they realized that, and he guessed they wanted him badly enough to back him anyway. Whether he should have taken them up on it was another matter. As his horse clip-clopped along Front Avenue, Toby shook his head and wondered if he was losing his mind or entering into a premature senility, doomed in three or four years to be drooling and vacant eyed, bound to his wheelchair. He grinned. That ought to make him just about fit in on Capitol Hill.

He mulled it over on the ride home and decided that his major problem at the moment was finding the right way to inform Alexandra of his decision. Toby was not a man ordinarily given to rearranging his family's lives without first consulting his wife.

He found Alexandra in the lower ring beyond the barn, putting one of her hunters through its paces. They were big animals, towering above the working stock that was the Madrona's bread and butter. She sold them one or two at a time through auction houses in the East to men who could afford to ride the best horseflesh available. The hunters were not advertised in the auction ring as ladies' mounts, and the gentlemen who bought them would have been considerably startled if they had known the sex of the trainer. Alexandra wouldn't have been caught dead on a "ladies' mount."

Toby watched the big bay fly around the ring, muscles bunched as it lifted to take the jump with a flip of its heels and a quick toss of its head. Toby thought he had never seen a horse that looked quite so pleased with itself as the bay after the successful jump.

Alexandra sat perfectly erect on its back, crop in her hand, her auburn hair coming out of its pins and flying behind her. Her hat was on the ground, a tall silk hat, much like his own, but with a dark veil tied around the crown. Toby dismounted to pick it up and handed it to her as she sailed past. Alexandra smiled at him, dropped the reins on the bay's neck, and replaced the hat with no apparent effort. She was riding astride, he noted, in a split skirt. That was not an endeavor that she could have gotten away with in Portland, but Alexandra maintained that what she did on the Madrona was her own business. Nevertheless, everyone in Portland knew that Mrs. Holt rode astride at home, and they had had a fine time discussing it.

The bay sailed over another jump, four feet of post and rail. Toby rested his arms on the paddock fence. From the first day he had met her in Kentucky, he had liked to watch Alexandra ride. It was like watching someone unrestricted by the laws of gravity.

After a few more minutes, Alexandra drew rein and smiled down at him. "I was going to ride him cross-country. Why don't you come with me?"

"Could it wait, Alex? I need to talk to you."

"We could talk while we ride."

"This isn't something I want to bellow at you while you jump a ditch," Toby said.

"Oh-ho." Alexandra looked at him with interest. "Willis?"

"Willis," Toby said.

"Johnny!" Alexandra swung off the horse and gave the reins to the stable hand who came running. She linked her arm through Toby's as they strolled toward the house.

Toby admired her riding skirt as they walked. "That's a scandalous outfit, Mrs. Holt. Somebody might think you actually had legs."

"We all do," she whispered. "But it's a secret."

*   *   *

In Toby's study Alexandra settled herself in one of the brown leather armchairs and looked up at him. "What is Willis up to?"

"He wants me to run for the Senate," Toby said.

"The Senate? You? Willis is a Republican."

Toby chuckled. "He's afraid the unions have too much influence to let a Republican in, and he's terrified of what the Democrats will elect if they don't elect me. I'm the middle-of-the-road choice."

"How flattering," Alexandra observed.

"It was pretty funny," Toby admitted. "He had Noell Simpson with him, and Donald McCallum and that old reprobate Ephraim Bender. They've all agreed to support me."

"Toby, those four agree with each other about as often as a nest of weasels."

"Yep. But they agreed on me. Simpson wants a Democrat—any Democrat. Willis wants someone who won't ship all the coolies back to China. McCallum wants pretty much the same thing. Bender wants somebody who'll keep the peace and not let Portland get in the eastern newspapers as a place where we have race riots."

"Makes it harder to sell his swampland," Alexandra said.

"You're a cynic."

"Maybe if I could vote, I'd have more faith that the government wouldn't let people like Ephraim Bender ruin this state with cheap houses that'll be shantytowns in ten years." Alexandra narrowed her eyes at Toby. "When you're elected I expect you to vote for women's suffrage."

"Well, I would anyway," Toby said mildly. "I think you've got as good a right to gum things up as the men do. You really think I ought to run?"

"Didn't you already tell them you would?"

"Yes, but I'll back out if you're flat against it."

Alexandra got up and paced in front of the mantel, thinking. "No, I think you ought to do it," she decided. "I think Oregon needs someone who's not beholden to one faction. I think those poor Chinese need someone on their side—Willis Larken hardly pays his workers enough to live on. And I think you'd be good at it. You always have had a flair for getting things accomplished without having to punch anyone in the nose. Mostly. And I think you're getting restless out here without the Antelope Horn to manage. Maybe we pulled back too much, Toby."

"Maybe," he allowed.

"I'd like to see Washington," she continued. "Do you know, I've never been there."

"I don't think it's that impressive," Toby said. "It's hotter than the hinges of hell in the summer and full of mosquitoes. It's a fine place if you like statues."

"We wouldn't be there in the summer, would we?"

"No, if Congress sat in the summer, I expect they'd all kill each other. But are you sure you want to uproot the family? There's Sally and Mike to think of. Sounds mighty unwieldy for just a few months of the year, which is all I'd be gone. And there won't be much money to spend—not for a few years, at least."

Alexandra turned to look at her husband. He was leaning back in his chair, long legs stretched out in front of him, boots on an Indian rug. Even in a cutaway coat, with his tall silk hat on the table beside him, he looked as if he belonged on a horse. There was something feral, not quite domesticated about him. Women loved it.

"I'm absolutely positive," she said sweetly. If she wanted to add up all the women in Toby's past, she would have had enough for two tables of whist. It wasn't, she knew, that he was naturally unfaithful; there had been no other women since he had married her. It was just that he wasn't immune, either. He seemed to fall into entanglements while he had something else on his mind. Alexandra intended to see that he didn't fall into anything in Washington, where she had heard that the women were worldly and elegant and had time on their hands.

She bent over and kissed his cheek. "I'm dying to

go to Washington. Think of the theater and the music. And I have cousins I haven't seen since I left Kentucky."

"Kentucky's not exactly next door to Washington," Toby observed.

"It's closer than Oregon," Alexandra replied.

"Well, we can decide when the time comes," Toby said. "When I win. If I win."

"Certainly." Alexandra never believed in putting her foot down until it was necessary. If it came to that, he might lose, although she doubted it. Toby's reputation in Oregon was just slightly lower than George Washington's. He could win on his name alone. Willis Larken and Noell Simpson and the rest knew it, the wily old devils.

"I'm going to bathe and see about supper," she said. "There's cold ham from dinner and some chicken from last night. I might make a custard." Sunday night and Thursday were the household staff's time off.

Toby nodded absently.

Alexandra looked at him with affectionate exasperation. He always ate whatever was put in front of him and never understood why she spent hours each week worrying about what people were going to eat. One of these days she was going to ignore supper and see what happened. Men didn't realize that somebody had to worry about it. Or maybe they didn't see it that way. Maybe if she ignored supper, Toby would just go in the pantry and find a piece of cold chicken and an apple and eat them standing up while he was thinking about something else. Maybe men and women just didn't see the world the same way. Well, that would certainly explain it, she thought. Alexandra kissed Toby's cheek again, cheerfully, and went to see if there was still any hot water in the kitchen boiler.

Toby put the Washington question out of his mind. He had a habit of compartmentalizing things, to work on the matter at hand without being distracted by concerns in the future. Right now he needed to concentrate on the stable records. He was shipping a load of two-year-olds to the auction ring in San Francisco, where the army did its buying. Madrona stock mostly went for cavalry remounts or to be used as cow ponies for the western ranches. He had the bill of lading to write out and instructions for the ranch hand who was going to deliver them.

Toby opened the top of his rolltop desk, and an envelope fell to the floor. He picked it up and started to stuff it back in its proper pigeonhole but saw how it was addressed: *Dad*. Toby tore it open with the strong suspicion that he wasn't going to like the contents.

Dear Dad,

This is just to let you know that I am all right but have decided that Harvard is not for me. I have to make my own decisions now, although I respect your judgment. I want to make my own way, and I do see that staying at Madrona isn't the way to accomplish that, so I have hit on a plan. I am going to Virginia City with Sam.

You're what? Toby strode out of his study and toward the front door, as if to grab the fleeing Tim by the collar. He flung open the door and stood glowering at the pleasant Sunday dusk. Tim was long gone, a fact brought home to him by the sight of a young boy on a mule, clip-clopping up the madrona-shaded avenue with Tim's and Sam's horses on a lead.

"Man gave me fifty cents to bring these here, mister," the boy said.

Toby's fingers closed around the sheet of paper. "Put them in the barn," he growled. He stalked back into his office, uncrumpled Tim's letter, and read the rest of it:

We're going to stake a claim like Charley Lawrence's. Sam says Virginia City is a coming town, and I hope it won't be long until I can send money home. I expect you are going to be angry at first,

but I have every confidence that we will make our
pile soon, and I'll write again then. With all respect,

Your loving son,
Tim

Toby ground his teeth. *Of all the harebrained*—
He knew who was at the bottom of this. *Sam says.* He
just bet Sam did. Sam hadn't ever done a lick of honest
work in his life, and it would be just like Sam to decide
he could get rich quick in a Nevada silver mine. And he
knew who was responsible for that. If Andrew Brentwood
had ever paid any attention to his son—

Toby threw the letter down on his desk and stalked
out again, heading for the barn this time.

"Here, give me that horse." He took the reins
away from the stable boy who was starting to unsaddle
Tim's horse and flung himself up in the saddle. *I haven't
had supper, either,* he thought irritably as he kicked
the horse into a gallop, but he had something to say to
Andrew Brentwood before his stomach would be in any
state to digest food.

Toby rode at a gallop most of the way back into
Portland and tied the lathered horse up outside the
telegraph office. The door was locked. A little sign
stuck over the latch proclaimed that the office would
open for business at eight in the morning. Toby pounded
on the door anyway until the telegrapher, who lived in
a room on the second floor, came down and let him in
just to shut him up.

"Can't you read?" The telegrapher was in his undershirt, his pants held up with red suspenders.

"I want to send a telegram."

"Lots of folks do," the telegrapher said. "Eight in
the morning." He had a red face and a shock of gray
hair. "I got my supper to eat, same as other folks."

"Let me in, or I'll bust the door down and send it
myself," Toby threatened.

The telegrapher inspected him. Toby, still in his

church clothes, was dust covered and seething. "Cost you double," he said.

"Fine." Toby stalked in, pulled a pad off the counter, and started to write. "There. I want it delivered, and I want an answer, and I'm going to wait for it. You tell them that at the other end."

The telegrapher looked at the message. "Reckon you'll get one," he murmured.

ANDREW BRENTWOOD, HOLCOMB STREET, INDEPEN-
DENCE, MISSOURI

TIM AND SAM GONE VIRGINIA CITY STOP DAMFOOL IDEA
TO MINE SILVER STOP SAM AT BOTTOM OF THIS STOP
DON'T TELL ME HE'S NOT STOP DOUBT HE HAS ANY
CHARACTER LEFT TO SALVAGE BUT IF YOU WANT HIM
BACK YOU GO GET HIM STOP IF I DO I WILL PROBABLY
SHOOT HIM STOP TOBY HOLT, PORTLAND, OREGON

"This is going to be expensive," the telegrapher warned. "I can't put no cusswords in, neither."

"Just send it," Toby said. "He can imagine the cusswords." He was not a man given to profanity, but he could not remember having been so angry as he was now. Fuming, he sat down. The only available reading material was the *Police Gazette*, so he read "Ax Fiend Loose in Chicago Red Light District" while he waited to see what Andy Brentwood had to say for himself.

Andy, dragged from his own Sunday supper table, had quite a lot to say, but his response had been softened because the Independence telegraph office would not transmit profanities, either:

TOBY HOLT, PORTLAND, OREGON
WHY THE HECK DID YOU LET HIM GO STOP I DON'T LIKE
YOUR TONE STOP I PUT SAM IN YOUR CHARGE STOP WHY
ISN'T TIM IN HARVARD NOT GOING OFF TO NEVADA STOP
HOLD HIM TO BLAME STOP SAM NEEDS FIRM HAND
NOT BAD INFLUENCE STOP LYDIA VERY UPSET STOP
ANDREW BRENTWOOD, INDEPENDENCE, MISSOURI

"Give me that." Toby grabbed the pad again.

ANDREW BRENTWOOD, INDEPENDENCE, MISSOURI
LYDIA'S UPSET QUESTION MARK STOP I'M UPSET STOP
THAT BOY IS WORTHLESS LAYABOUT STOP DUE TO FA-
THER NEVER PAYING OUNCE OF ATTENTION TO HIM STOP
ALL YOU CAN THINK ABOUT IS FRANZ STOP YOU OUGHT
TO HAVE FUNERAL AND GET MIND OFF HIM STOP PAY
SOME ATTENTION TO LIVE CHILDREN STOP I DIDN'T LET
HIM GO YOU GODDAMNED IDIOT STOP

"I told you—"

"Just change it," Toby said. "I can't write in hecks
and durns."

TOBY HOLT, PORTLAND, OREGON
GOSH DARN IT DON'T YOU GET PIOUS WITH ME STOP
WHEN WERE YOU EVER AT HOME WITH CHILDREN STOP
LYDIA NOT WELL STOP NERVES UPSET STOP EXPECT
YOU GO VIRGINIA CITY IMMEDIATELY STOP HOLD YOU
RESPONSIBLE STOP

The wire quit clicking, and Toby glared at the
message.

"Who's Franz?" the telegrapher asked. He was
getting interested.

"Of all the goddamned gall!" Toby kicked his boot
against the counter, furious.

The telegrapher shook his head sympathetically.
"Kids need a firm hand," he volunteered. "Need their
old man around, that's what I always say. Knock them
one upside the head when they get out of line. That's
what I always say."

"Well, I didn't ask you." Toby paced back and
forth across the dusty little room, peered irritably at the
Wanted posters and the train schedule hanging on the
wall. He was *not* going to go to Virginia City. Andrew
Brentwood could fry his head before Toby bailed Sam
out of this one. He was aware that some of his irritation
was due to the fact that Andy had scored a hit with his

comment about Toby's time with his children. He hadn't spent much with them, and that was a fact, although it wasn't from lack of desire. Toby sighed. If he went to Washington, he would take Alex and the young ones with him. Janessa, too, if she wanted.

Toby picked up the message pad. He wasn't going to tell Andy Brentwood that. He had plenty of other things to say to Andy Brentwood.

> ANDREW BRENTWOOD, INDEPENDENCE, MISSOURI
> NO INTENTION GOING VIRGINIA CITY STOP INTEND LET
> TIM TAKE RESPONSIBILITY FOR ACTIONS STOP IF YOU
> WANT SAM GO GET HIM STOP BUY LYDIA SOME NERVE
> TONIC STOP

"I dunno." The telegrapher shook his head. "Virginia City's pretty wild, from what I hear. You sure you're doing the right thing?"

"It'll give him an appreciation for Harvard," Toby muttered. He looked at the counterman. "Why am I discussing this with you? Just send the telegram!"

The man sat down and began clicking the button. A few minutes later it clicked back at him in reply. Toby thought he could detect a faint aura of smoke rising from it.

> TOBY HOLT, PORTLAND, OREGON
> WILL NOT ALLOW YOU INSULT MY WIFE STOP YOU ARE
> INSENSITIVE CAD STOP IF YOU MENTION FRANZ TO LYDIA
> I WILL BEAT YOU TO BLOODY PULP STOP ARE YOU GOING
> TO GOSH DARNED VIRGINIA CITY GET MY SON OR NOT
> QUESTION MARK STOP

"He's mad," the telegrapher said. "Who's Franz?"

"His son," Toby said. "He's dead."

"Oh. I thought he was in Virginia City."

"That's the other son. Will you stay out of this?"

"Anything you say. You know, this is getting expensive."

"Yeah," Toby said. Andy was going to be annoyed about it, too, when he got his bill.

"You going to answer?"

"Sure," Toby said. He scribbled on the pad again.

ANDREW BRENTWOOD, INDEPENDENCE, MISSOURI
NO YOU TACKHEAD I AM NOT GOING VIRGINIA CITY
STOP GOING HOME AND EATING DINNER STOP

Toby handed the pad to the telegrapher. "I don't think I'll wait for an answer."

The telegrapher looked at it. "I wouldn't bother," he agreed. By the time the operator in Independence took out the cusswords, there probably wouldn't be enough answer left to send.

V

Nevada, April 1887

The Southern Pacific from San Francisco screeched and hissed to a halt under the canopy of the Reno, Nevada, depot. Tim Holt awoke, got up, stretched with a cracking sound as if knuckles were popping, and prodded Sam.

"Reno!" the conductor shouted.

Tim grabbed the carpetbags from the overhead shelf and handed Sam's to him. They looked around curiously as they came down the steps. Reno was a new town, less than twenty years old, but it was already the seat of a thriving community and a state university. It had an opera house and a gold coast of saloons and gambling dens, a Civic Betterment Society and a thriving red-light district. It owed its existence to the transcontinental railroad and Comstock silver.

The depot platform was thronging with people: miners in faded clothes, bankers in frock coats, ladies in tan and teal traveling suits, and less ladylike females in cerise satin with birds in their hats. Porters criss-crossed among them, pushing handcarts or carrying bags on their shoulders.

A preacher in a faded black coat was standing on an apple crate beside the engine, Bible in hand, exhorting the crowd to repent for whatever evil they might be about to embark upon in the sinful fields of silver. No one paid any attention to him except for three small boys in knickers who peered up at him, enthralled by his side-whiskers and fury. The engine hissed out a

76

cloud of steam, which rolled up around the preacher's knees so that he looked as if he himself were emerging from the fiery pit.

"Carson City! Virginia City!" a conductor shouted farther down the platform.

"That's us!" Tim said. "Come on. They said we wouldn't have much time to change."

"I'm hungry," Sam protested. There was a grill in the depot.

"We can eat when we get there." Tim hustled him along, eager to travel, to be moving again. "If we miss this train, there won't be another till tomorrow."

They swung aboard one of the cars of the Virginia & Truckee Line as the engine spurted steam and its heavy drive wheel began to turn.

"All aboard!"

The steam whistle shrieked, the silver bell mounted beside the boiler clanged, and the passenger car vibrated as the engine picked up speed. Tim and Sam slung their carpetbags overhead and staggered into seats, looking out the window as the train steamed out of Reno toward the state capital of Carson City. The windows had flaps that could be lowered to keep out the soot and hot embers, but the boys were more interested in seeing where they were going than in staying clean. It was impossible to stay clean on a train anyway. Everyone's skin was pale gray with soot after only a few miles.

The landscape before them looked bleak and forbidding. The craggy angles of the Sierras were pale red-brown with stunted shrubs and a few windblown pines grasping dismally onto their sides. An occasional patch of yellow wildflowers flashed luminously in the bright sunlight, which seemed to swallow up the whole landscape, train and all.

The conductor called out the names of the silver towns that clung to the slopes along the way: Ophir and Franktown. Ophir, built as a milling town, stood ghostly and abandoned in dusty sunshine now that all business had gone south to the Carson River mills. A fox stuck his nose out of a cabin door as the train passed.

They stopped briefly in Carson City to take on passengers and freight bound for Virginia City and wood to make the head of steam needed to pull them up the grade. Beyond the Carson City wood yard, the tracks followed close on the banks of the river past the stamping mills. On the return trip, the train would unload ore cars at these mills and load up silver ingots bound for Reno and Sacramento. The thunder of the ore-reduction works seemed to shake the whole river valley, even over the rumble of the rail cars.

At a bend in the river, the tracks swung abruptly northward, up the steep switchback grade to Virginia City. A series of trestles and tunnels and zigzag rail bed clinging to the mountain's edge took the train upward in a cloud of soot and steam. It swayed over a high wooden trestle above an arid gorge, then plunged into the mountain, its light glowing ahead and the wail of the steam whistle filling the tunnel. Then they shot out into daylight, and soon Tim could see the hills of Virginia City, with the elaborate houses of the rich built along the slopes, and everywhere the dark squares of the adits—low, horizontal mine entrances—among them.

In the city the railroad dived into another tunnel beneath the streets and came up again at the Virginia & Truckee passenger depot. It was late afternoon, and the sun hung above the mountains, illuminating the white and gilt façades of the business district and the red and white spire of a church.

Tim and Sam took their carpetbags and looked around them eagerly. It was as if the railroad had dropped them suddenly into some entirely new world, where possibilities were endless.

On the advice of the ticket seller in the depot, they headed for the Silver Dollar Hotel on C Street. Their route took them along Union Street, past what was plainly the red-light district, where the doors stood open a little too invitingly and the flash of white petticoats could be seen behind the windows. The boys did find a room at the Silver Dollar, which was not grand by any means—Tim thought a prudent man would probably sleep with his pistol under his pillow—but was reasonably clean, and the bed was big enough to hold them both. What money they had would have to last until they got rich. With that goal in mind, Tim suggested they have dinner in the hotel dining room and turn in early, before Sam could decide to investigate the row of small white houses they had passed on Union.

In the morning, with two horses and a pack mule bought with their carefully hoarded funds, Tim and Sam set out to get rich.

"How do you know this is the place?" Tim looked with some reservation at the patch of sandy scrub in the lee of one of Sun Mountain's bleak outcroppings.

"There've been three strikes on this slope this year," Sam answered. "I asked around. You don't think all these men are here because they like dirt, do you?" He indicated the canvas tents of other prospectors dotting the slope in the distance. "All the signs are right. Money in the ground. All we have to do is dig it up."

They dug industriously for days, lured on by faint hints of silver, traces of bluish black against the ocher earth. Where there was some, there must be, had to be, more.

It was cold in the mountains at night, even as the days grew progressively hotter. In the evening, wrapped in blankets around the campfire, listening to some miner in the distance playing a harmonica—"My Old Kentucky Home" seemed to be all he knew—they would watch the lights of the big houses on the hillside below, and Sam would tell Tim again the kind of house he was going to build when he got rich.

"Big, three stories with a cupola, with marble fireplaces and Chinese rugs. Silver doorknobs. They say Sandy Bowers put solid-silver doorknobs in his house."

Tim snorted. "And where is Sandy Bowers now? Dead, that's where he is. After all the money he made on silver, he was nearly penniless at the end. His wife lost the rest and is making a living as a fortune-teller. The Washoe seeress. I'll get you a crystal ball to go with the rocks in your head."

"I don't care," Sam said stubbornly. "Sandy Bowers was an uneducated lout, and he threw away all his money." He stared at that glowing hillside, entranced. "I'll do better, that's all. I'm going to have a carriage with a matched team of bays, and any woman I turn my eye on is going to give her soul to ride in it."

Tim chuckled. "I wondered when you were going to get to women."

Sam grinned at him. "If I don't get to women pretty soon, I'm going to go crazy. You aren't exactly what I had in mind to share a bed with for a year."

"Then you can just dig a little harder in the morning," Tim suggested. "In the meantime, you want some more beans? We made exactly enough today for a second helping."

Sam scooped what was left in the pot onto his plate with loathing. "Put some tomatoes in next time," he muttered. "It makes a change."

"Sam, why are you so desperate to get rich?" Tim had been wondering about that. The Brentwoods had never been poor. They weren't rolling in money, either, but they had enough for anything within reason. "I know why I'm out here, but why are you? You don't like the West. You don't even like to work."

"Because I don't ever want to have to go home again," Sam said fiercely. He wouldn't say any more.

Tim stood up and wrapped his blanket around him. "I'm going to bed." He crawled into the tent and lay so that he could see the night sky through the flap, inky black and spangled with stars. They looked infinitely distant. *Poor old Sam,* he thought. It would be awful not to want to go home. Where did you have to go, if you didn't have home?

"We've got to shore up that tunnel," Sam said, "or we can't go any deeper."

Tim groaned. That meant another trip down the mountain with the mule, to lug timbers back up. The will-o'-the-wisp silver flitted in front of them as they dug, surfacing, running out, amounting to nothing. The most promising vein ran straight into the depths of the mountain. They had to go deeper. "I'll go." He glared at Sam. Sam would go, but he wouldn't come back for the rest of the day.

Sam tossed him a canvas sack that landed with a thud in the dust. "Get that assayed. Then we'll know if we're on the right track."

"Not bad," the clerk in the assayer's office said. "About fifteen hundred dollars a ton. You got any more?"

Tim shook his head. "Not yet. But we think we know where it goes. We're trying to go deeper."

The clerk shook his head. He had a round head, nearly bald, that rocked from side to side like a ball. "That's what they all think. You still ain't got high-grade ore. High-grade ore's played out in these mountains."

"What about the strikes last year?" Tim asked indignantly. "What about Charley Lawrence's mine?"

"Charley Lawrence's mine played out two weeks after he sold it to the Consolidated," the clerk said. "Charley was a smart young man. Nothing left in that shaft but low grade. Consolidated can take low grade out—they got the equipment and the men. Ain't no single miner gonna make a dime out of low-grade ore. It's like trying to shovel up a beach with a spoon."

"Well, I'm going to keep on shoveling awhile," Tim said. "If you get so you can see through solid rock, let me know, and I'll listen to you."

As Tim banged the door behind him, he could hear the clerk laughing. "Hope you get lucky!" the man called. "Poor bastards, you all think you're going to get lucky. The whole world thinks it's going to get lucky!"

Tim stood on the boardwalk outside the assay office, feeling restless. The last thing he wanted to do was drag those timbers back up Sun Mountain and shovel some more sand with a spoon. He watched the traffic in

the street. Virginia City was still the biggest town between San Francisco and Denver, and its streets were
full of buggies and delivery wagons and riders on horses
and mules. He watched a woman go by in a buggy with
a fringed canopy. She had reddish-blond hair and a
pretty face with a determined look. She wore a black-
and white-striped dress with yellow ribbons down the
front, and her hat was yellow straw with an enormous
blackbird on it. The bird, Tim noticed as she went by,
had orange glass eyes, bright and inquisitive. They
seemed to look back at him over the edge of her hat.

He knew who she was: Annie Malone, widow of
Joe Malone, who had taken more silver out of the
Washoe region than any man ever. Like Sandy Bowers,
he had died young, but unlike Bowers's widow, Annie
Malone made up in shrewdness what she lacked in
education. Not only had she hung onto her money, but
she also had invested it well. She lived in the fanciest
house in Virginia City, and the only reason she didn't
have silver doorknobs was that the minister's wife had
told her they were in poor taste.

Annie's buggy moved on up the street, followed by
a snarl of drays unloading beer at the Washoe Club and
bales of blankets at Hooper's Dry Goods. The drays
wedged themselves nose to nose across the street, their
drivers shouting curses while the traffic became tangled
around them. A young girl in a pony cart drew rein
apprehensively, her pony snorting and jiggling his head.
She looked to be about seventeen, very pretty, with
dark ringlets pinned in a knot on her head. One of the
dray drivers offered to punch the other one in the nose,
and as he tried to do so, his mules backed up, bumping
the pony's nose. The pony reared.

Tim dodged out into the street and grabbed its
bridle. He ran a hand down the pony's neck, gentling
it, reassuring it, until it stood still, and then he led it
around the stalled wagons. The drivers, oblivious, were
rolling in the street trying to gouge out each other's
eyes, and quite a crowd had collected to cheer them
on.

"Thank you," the girl said when they were clear of the scuffle. "Thank you so much." She beamed at him, and Tim nodded, tongue-tied now, aware of his filthy trousers and leather vest, and the dusty felt hat on his unkempt hair. With a dazzling smile, she shook out the reins and was gone.

Oh, you sure made a good impression, Tim thought. *What with your sparkling wit and dapper appearance and all. You look as if you've been cleaning out a sewer, and you couldn't even think of anything to say. She probably thinks you're illiterate, too. Aw, damn.*

He turned into the American Saloon, feeling a little guilty because he had come down for the timber himself to keep Sam from spending the afternoon in a saloon. Not guilty enough to keep him out, though. Just guilty enough, he thought, to make the whiskey taste a little better.

He put a quarter on the bar. "Double whiskey."

"Hey, Holt!" A face he recognized peered at him through a cloud of cigar smoke from the other end of the bar. "You rich yet?" Waldo Howard joined Tim just as the bartender put a pair of shot glasses in front of him. Waldo owned the *Virginia City Beacon*, rival paper to the *Territorial Enterprise*. The *Enterprise* could claim the distinction of once having had Mark Twain on its staff. The *Beacon* could only claim Waldo and a press that probably qualified as an antique. "How's the diggings?"

"Poor," Tim answered. "I'm playing hookey."

"All work and no play makes Jack a dull boy," Waldo said. "If you get desperate, I hear the Consolidated and the Ninevah are hiring."

"Lord, Waldo, that's more work than I'm doing now."

"With the advantage of regular pay," Waldo observed.

"You're the college boy with diggings up the mountain, aren't you?" a miner next to them asked in the accent of Cornwall.

Tim sighed. He wondered if he was ever going to look any older. "Yeah."

"You'll break your heart in the mines, lad." The miner looked about thirty-five and had rock-roughened hands and black hair. "Mining used to pay a decent wage in Virginia City, but now the Consolidated and John Ormond are paying two dollars a day. We used to get four."

"That was in the boom days when you Cousin Jacks got a premium for knowledge of hard-rock mining," Waldo said. "There ain't no more deep mining now."

"My name's Yellan," the miner said, with a look at Waldo. Cousin Jack was the local name for Cornishmen, some of whom had been fourth- and fifth-generation miners in Cornwall. "That was when the miner's union had some guts to it, and men like John Ormond couldn't get by with starvation wages."

"Who's John Ormond?" Tim asked.

"He owns the Ninevah Mine," Waldo answered. "It's the only one operating on any scale now, besides the Consolidated."

"The Con's just as bad," Yellan said. "A man can't even tell who's in charge there. Stockholders and banks." He frowned and drank the rest of his whiskey.

"Can't the union do anything?" Tim's natural inclination was for the underdog.

"Too many miners and not enough work," Waldo said. "There's always another man wanting the job." He grinned. "Or I'd try it myself, the price of paper being what it is and all."

"You can't buck the mine owners, either," Yellan said darkly. "Since they bought the *Enterprise,* the paper's been sucking hind tit like the rest of us. If the *Beacon* would support the union, we'd make some headway."

"If I supported the union," Waldo said, "I'd go under. My sympathies are with you, but I'm too old to starve."

"Sure," Yellan said. "We're all too old to starve."

He looked at Tim. "Take my advice, lad, and stick to your own diggings."

Waldo shrugged. "Make up your own mind, Holt. You've got engineering training. That pays better. You know it does, Yellan."

"Maybe," Yellan allowed. "But if I had it to do again, I wouldn't go down in another man's mine. It's too far up to daylight." He looked at Tim again, his face angry and, Tim thought, somehow secretive. "I'll tell you this, lad: Don't sign on unless you're ready to be in a fight, because there's going to be one." He set his glass on the bar and left, hands in his pockets, his back stiff.

Tim saw that the eyes of the other miners followed Yellan to the door. He looked around the room and saw that a trio of businessmen, impressive in whiskers and gold watch chains, were sitting at a table in the corner. They were watching Yellan, too.

"That's John Ormond," Waldo murmured. "The stout party with the fancy waistcoat. Joe Yellan ought to watch where he shoots off his mouth."

Tim finished his second drink, then stepped back from the bar. The miner's union was the least of his worries right now. He had a load of timber to haul up the mountain and probably Sam to wake up and bully into helping him start to set it. He lifted a hand to Waldo, who appeared to have settled in for the day, and headed for the door. As he laid his hand on the saloon door, a voice behind him stopped him.

"Holt? Is that your name, son?"

Tim turned back. "Yes, sir."

John Ormond looked him over. "Did I hear you had some engineering expertise, Mr. Holt?"

"Some," Tim said. "Two years at Harvard." Well, almost two years. It wouldn't hurt to fudge a little.

"Hmm. You wouldn't be any relation to Toby Holt, would you?"

"He's my father," Tim replied. "Do you know him?"

"I used to," Ormond said. He was a round, barrel-chested man with black hair and a well-kept black beard.

"I knew him in the army, during the war. He's made quite a name for himself since. I thought you had a look of him."

"Thank you, sir."

"That was my daughter you rescued from difficulties out there, Mr. Holt." John Ormond smiled. "I was going to her aid when I saw that you had matters in hand. If you want an engineering job, I am able to help you."

"Thank you, sir, but I think I've got good prospects in my own diggings."

"Well, keep it in mind." Ormond gave him a friendly nod. "And I wouldn't hang around with Joe Yellan, if I were you. He's a troublemaker without much to say for himself."

Tim nodded. "I'll remember that." He thought Joe Yellan had had quite a lot to say, but he didn't expect Ormond would see it that way.

California, September 1887

Janessa's train swayed with a monotonous click and rumble that would have been hypnotic if the air hadn't been so hot. The inside of the Pullman car, behind the curtains of her lower berth, was stifling. She opened the curtains a little. Everyone else seemed to be asleep, she thought, until the bare legs of the gentleman in the berth above her descended past her nose; he was on his way to the convenience at the end of the car. Janessa ducked back in as his nightshirted form lurched down the aisle.

Janessa turned on her side and stared out the window, into the dark countryside sliding by. It was a moonlit night, and she could see the silvered flow of bean fields and sometimes the dark bulk of a silo or a barn. There was one light in a farmhouse window. Janessa looked at her watch by moonlight. Four in the morning. The wife would be starting breakfast. It was odd to be awake and passing through other people's lives at this hour, looking through their windows.

What would they think if they could look back at her, she wondered. *That Holt female? Did you hear, she actually intends to be a doctor. Well, I myself feel that it is indelicate. Women haven't the temperament for medicine. Prone to hysteria, you know, and of course their cranial capacity is smaller. And to examine a patient—well, you can say what you like but no nice woman would do it.*

Janessa wriggled her bare toes in the moonlight. She had heard it all before. She was going to be one of two females in the second class at the new University of Southern California Medical College. There had been two the previous year, too, but only one of them was still enrolled. The other's nerves hadn't been up to it, the dean had told Toby. Janessa knew what he meant— the woman's nerves hadn't been up to the constant battle to prove she was entitled to be there. Toby had assured the dean that Janessa's nerves were fine.

She hoped so. Toby had been a bit taken aback when she said she was going, but he had not been displeased. "I knew you'd get around to it if you wanted it," he had said, and then sat down to write a firm letter to the dean, with whom he happened to be acquainted. Praise God, Janessa thought, for a father who found ordinary women boring—and whose own checkered career had left him acquainted with people all over the country. She knew she wouldn't have even considered medical school if it hadn't been for her father and her mentor, Dr. Martin. Never, not once, had her father ever told her she couldn't do something because she was female. And the good doctor had been single-minded in his plans for her.

The train rattled into the outskirts of a town. First a few lighted windows flashed by, then the windows of a shantytown. Beyond were the factories and their loading docks, then an underpass with a humpbacked bridge above it, lit by gas lamps. The train slid into the depot, into a bright flare of light. Janessa saw a load of milk cans waiting and a lone drummer, sleepily sitting on his sample case. She pulled her shade down and buried her face in her lumpy Pullman pillow as the train lurched forward again.

The train pulled up under the brick arches of the Los Angeles depot, and Janessa sat up sluggishly. The air was as hot as an oven's, almost dry enough to crackle. She fanned herself with the paper fan that had lain in her lap as she dozed. Not having slept much the night before, she had spent the day in a sort of half-waking trance from which she emerged now and then to see where they were. Janessa had drifted in and out of slumber as Salinas, Santa Barbara, and Ventura rushed away behind her. Los Angeles had looked big but sprawling, like an overgrown farm town, as it slid past the train windows.

She tried to smooth the wrinkles from her brown serge skirt. It was hopeless. Two days on the train had left her feeling wrinkled clear down to the bone. She took a silver-backed mirror out of her carpetbag and peered into it. The face that looked back had dark circles under the eyes and a lock of brown hair rakishly askew above one eye. Janessa pushed the offending strands back under the brim of her hat and anchored the hat more firmly with its long silver hatpin.

She looked out the window. The depot was full of people. She put the mirror back in her carpetbag and scanned the crowd. She saw Charley waiting for her, two cars down the platform. Janessa opened the window and leaned out, and Charley saw her. He took his hat off and waved it at her.

He was waiting at the steps to help her down. She hugged him, oblivious to the fact that they were creating a bottleneck at the foot of the steps.

He grinned, his gray eyes crinkling. "I knew you'd do it."

"Well, I sent you a telegram," Janessa said.

"No, I knew you'd do it when I wrote you from Virginia City."

"Where my idiot little brother has now gone to dig

up a fortune in silver. So he thinks. You are really a dreadful influence."

"Not on my say-so!" Charley said, horrified.

"No, but it caused the most awful row. I'll tell you later." She stood back to look at him. Charley was not very tall but was compact and muscular, and he looked tougher to her than he had five years ago. "You're older," she said.

"Of course I'm older," Charley replied. "You're older, too. Very dashing, though. I hate that hat." He replaced his own, a hard panama straw, and offered her his arm. He picked up her carpetbag in the other hand. "Steak dinner first. Then the boardinghouse. I've picked one out for you, near the medical school. We'll have your trunk sent along later if the accommodations suit you."

In the restaurant he slid her carpetbag under the table and regarded her with satisfaction. "I can't tell you how glad I am you're here. All these other twerps are going to be seven years younger than I am and know everything there is to know, or at least I feel that they are."

"I wouldn't be here if it weren't for you," Janessa admitted. "You don't know what it took me to screw up my courage to come."

"Yeah, I do," he said gently. The waiter appeared and hovered attentively at Charley's elbow. "The New York steak for both of us. Cooked rare, please. And champagne."

"Certainly." The waiter whisked away.

"Can you afford this?" Janessa demanded.

"Once," Charley answered. "Special contingency fund."

The waiter poured their champagne with a flourish, and Janessa sipped hers, staring at Charley while they waited for the steak.

"Is my toupee on crooked?" he inquired finally.

She smiled. "No, I'm just trying to figure out why you look older without really looking different. It doesn't seem as if it's been this long. Tell me about Nan's wedding plans."

"Well, she's disappointed you can't be a bridesmaid. She charged me to deliver her love and to tell you that she'll write you a letter as soon as there's a pause in the whirlwind. Planning a wedding seems to plunge every female member of the family into advanced stages of hysteria."

Janessa chuckled. "I remember when my dad married Alexandra. You would have thought my grandmother was planning a coronation. Is her fiancé nice? Nan waited a long time."

"Very nice. When you get settled in, I'll tell you all the gossip."

Janessa frowned. "Where *am* I going to settle?"

"You're all taken care of," Charley said. "For tonight, at least. If you like the landlady, you can stay." He grinned. "I think you will. She's a corker."

After dinner, Charley hailed a hansom cab, put Janessa and the carpetbag into it, got in himself, and told the driver, "Alameda Street." It was cold now. The heat had vanished with the setting sun.

"This is old Los Angeles," Charley explained as the cab rattled down a street of graceful houses, many of them adobe, with wide porches shaded by bougainvillea and wisteria. "Very historic, very Spanish. Very down at the heels. It looks better at night. But the board is reasonable."

"It's lovely," Janessa murmured. It looked tropical to her, and exotic. The street lamps cast inviting pools of yellow light on the brick street and palm-shaded lawns. A light wind rustled the palms. Charley leaned forward and tapped the driver on the shoulder. "Stop here."

They got out, Charley carrying Janessa's bag, and went up the walk to a slender three-story house with gabled windows and a wide porch with a swing on it. A marmalade-colored cat was asleep on the welcome mat. The shades were only half-drawn, and Janessa could see a parlor full of overstuffed chairs and ottomans, with an ancient upright piano in the corner. Charley rang the bell, and after a moment the door was opened by a small woman who might have been sixty or seventy, in a black dress with a gingham apron over it.

"This is Janessa Holt, Mrs. Burnside."

"So I imagined," the old lady said. "Well, come inside before all the insects come in with you."

The front hall was furnished with an elaborate coat tree and a chipped table on which stood framed daguerreotypes of a young man with the sort of side-whiskers that had been fashionable in the forties, and a baby in a white christening robe. "I understand you are planning to enter the medical college, Miss Holt." Behind the hall tree, Janessa could see a row of interested faces peering through the parlor doorway.

"Yes, ma'am," she replied. "I trust you don't disapprove of that."

"Certainly not," Mrs. Burnside said. "I believe women need every advantage they can get, just to stay even." She had a headful of tight white curls, which bobbed vigorously under a lace house cap as she spoke. "Not that you won't have your troubles anyway." She gave Charley a withering look, which appeared to be directed not so much at him as at men in general.

"I'm on Janessa's side, ma'am," Charley protested.

"Gentlemen callers are to be entertained in the parlor only," she informed Janessa. "I trust you do not object to animals."

"Why, no," Janessa said.

Mrs. Burnside whistled, and something that Janessa thought at first might be a bear, and then, possibly, a dog, lumbered through the swinging door at the other end of the hall.

"This is Fifi," Mrs. Burnside said. Fifi sat down and leaned against Mrs. Burnside, and the woman staggered slightly. "She doesn't go outdoors much until fall, except at night. Newfoundlands are cold-weather dogs."

Janessa held out a hand, and Fifi came over and drooled happily on her skirt. "How do you do?" Janessa said gravely, scratching the big black head.

Mrs. Burnside seemed to come to some decision. "Room and board are twenty dollars a month with no reduction for meals taken elsewhere. You will be expected to make your own bed except on Saturdays, when Clarice changes the linens. Do you go to church?"

"Yes," Janessa said.

"You may ride with me if you are an Episcopalian. Otherwise, you will have to make your own arrangements."

"Yes, ma'am." Janessa felt herself unable to argue, even if she had wanted to. In any case, Mrs. Burnside didn't give her the opportunity.

"Breakfast is at eight, lunch at noon, and dinner at six." Mrs. Burnside's expression softened slightly as Fifi flopped down across Janessa's feet, panting contentedly. "She likes you. If lunch is not convenient for you, I can pack a cold lunch to take to the college. Do you wish to see the room?"

"Yes, please."

"You may wait here, Mr. Lawrence," Mrs. Burnside informed Charley.

Janessa followed, feeling herself carried on some irresistible tide, with Fifi galumphing up the stairs behind them.

The hooked rug was old, and the crazy quilt on the cherry-wood bed was faded, but the small room was spotlessly clean, and the lace curtains at the windows were freshly starched. There were a stand with a flowered pitcher and bowl, a chest of drawers topped with a starched dresser scarf, and a tall oak wardrobe. A velvet armchair by the window had a small oak table beside it, with a reading lamp, and another lamp sat on an old school desk in the corner.

"I had that brought down from the attic," Mrs. Burnside said. "I thought you might want it."

Janessa smiled at her. "You are thoughtful."

The old woman smiled back suddenly. "My dear girl, you are doing exactly what I have always wished that I had done. Of course I married at eighteen instead," she added tartly. "The more fool I."

There didn't seem to be any answer to make to that, so Janessa didn't. Instead she said, "I think the room is just right. I would be happy to stay here if you are agreeable." She took a twenty-dollar bill out of her purse and gave it to Mrs. Burnside.

The old woman tucked it into her apron pocket. "Very well. Come downstairs and meet my other boarders. They're all dying to get a look at you, of course. You'll be a nine-days' wonder for a while, so you'll just have to put up with it. Begin as you mean to go on," she added as they went downstairs.

Three men and two women awaited her in the parlor, with Charley, who gave her a look of amusement over Mrs. Burnside's shoulder. *A corker indeed,* Janessa thought.

"Mrs. Bellow," Mrs. Burnside said, presenting a middle-aged woman with a severe fringe of gray curls and a starched white shirtwaist.

"How do you do?"

"Mr. Pepperdine." He was a tall, cadaverous man in a frock coat and a string tie.

"Miss Gillette." A thirtyish woman with faded blond hair and a soft, pleasant-looking face inclined her head.

"Mr. Anderson and Colonel Hapgood." Mr. Anderson was clerkish looking, and Colonel Hapgood was elderly and frail. He leaned on a cane.

They stood in a semicircle inspecting Janessa. She felt rather like a housemaid applying for a post.

"I understand, Miss Holt, that you intend to indulge in the practice of medicine."

"I wouldn't call it an indulgence exactly, Mr. Pepperdine. It is my chosen profession."

"Woman's chosen profession ought to be being some fellow's wife." Mr. Anderson scowled. "That's what I would tell you if'n you were my daughter."

"Then we both must be grateful that I'm not," Janessa said nicely. *Begin as you mean to go on. . . .*

An amused snort erupted from Mr. Pepperdine.

"I didn't bring her in here to answer her catechism," Mrs. Burnside said. "Miss Holt has had a long journey on the train and needs her rest."

"Of course," Miss Gillette said. "And you must pardon everybody for their—curiosity." She gave Mr. Anderson a reproving glance and took Janessa's hands. "We are so glad to have you with us."

Mrs. Burnside picked up the carpetbag that Charley had carried. "I don't encourage callers after ten o'clock," she informed him. "You may come back tomorrow, Mr. Lawrence." She started up the stairs with the carpetbag.

VI

Janessa awoke at seven with the sun streaming through her window and the sound of the ice wagon in the street. It was going to be hot again. She washed her face and hands with the tepid water from her pitcher, brushed her teeth, and pulled on her drawers and shimmy. She hooked her corset as loosely as possible and brought a light-blue cotton day dress out of the wardrobe. It hadn't been improved by being rolled up in her carpetbag for two days, Janessa thought, but her trunk would arrive that afternoon, and perhaps she could pay Clarice to iron the dresses in it. Janessa hooked her stockings, buttoned up white kid shoes, and slipped down the stairs and out into the backyard to the privy.

Janessa met Mr. Pepperdine coming along the brick walk that led behind the tactful screen of shrubbery, no doubt returning from the same errand on which she was bent. He pantomimed the tipping of a hat to her.

Returning to the house, Janessa saw that the other boarders were gathered around the dining table. Apparently no one wished to be late for breakfast. She took her place at the table as Mrs. Burnside joined them.

"You all get earlier every morning," a black woman in a white apron announced, coming through the kitchen door, a serving bowl in each hand. When she was introduced as Clarice, she gave Janessa a smile of welcome.

Sniffing the aroma of ham and eggs and hot coffee, Janessa could understand why everyone was prompt at the breakfast table. She was certain that it smelled even better because her last breakfast had consisted of mysterious congealed substances eaten at a depot counter. Clarice disappeared and came back with a basketful of hot biscuits and a bowl of fresh butter. Fifi, Janessa noted, was under the table.

Mr. Pepperdine said grace, and then the boarders fell on the food like starving wolves. *Goodness,* Janessa thought, *no wonder she charges twenty dollars a month. I'd ask more than that.*

Mr. Anderson appeared to be stoking up for the day, but everyone else, after a few mouthfuls, seemed inclined to chat. Janessa discovered that Miss Gillette worked at the Los Angeles County Library; that Mrs. Bellow was a widow of moderate circumstances who spent a great deal of her time knitting mufflers for the poor with her crony Mrs. Endicott across the street; Mr. Pepperdine was a lawyer; Mr. Anderson was a clerk for the railroad; and Colonel Hapgood was retired. He also had been a lawyer, but his health had never really been good since the war, and he walked with a limp.

"Something irreparable to the thigh bone," he explained. "The traditional cavalryman's wound. It actually fared me rather well in my career," he added with a mild smile at Janessa. "Folks trust a man with a war wound." He shook his head. "The average man isn't very intelligent, I fear."

"That can hardly be construed as news, Colonel," Mrs. Burnside remarked.

"I fear not," Mr. Pepperdine said. "We tried a case last week in which my client claimed to have been on another man's back porch in order to warn the other man's wife that there had been malicious rumors spread about her, when he was accidentally shot by her husband as being the featured element in those rumors. The jury believed him, largely, I think, because the wife in question is ethereal and blond, with a demure demeanor. They didn't quite credit my client, but they couldn't help believing her. It would have been different, I daresay, if she had had red hair."

"Mr. Pepperdine, I do not consider that a suitable topic for breakfast-table discussion," Mrs. Bellow admonished.

"Which?" Mr. Pepperdine asked. "Human gullibility or the question of illicit relations?"

"Neither," Mrs. Bellow answered.

"Mrs. Bellow, if we don't take an interest in the affairs of the world," Miss Gillette said, "how can we expect men to give us the vote?"

"I don't expect it," Mrs. Bellow responded.

"Quite right," Mr. Anderson said in a pause between eating his eggs and ham. "Woman's proper sphere is the household. Politics and business are men's sphere. Stepping into the wrong sphere is unnatural."

"You make it sound as if we were all encased in little glass balls," Janessa said, unable to resist the conversation any longer. "Little bubbles with doors on them."

"One of these days someone's going to stick a pin in all those little bubbles," Miss Gillette said quickly, with a fairly dark look at Mr. Anderson.

"And then you'll all fall out of them," Mr. Pepperdine portended. "Hundreds of ladies, arms and legs waving in the air, dropping through space, eyes bugging out. Think of the confusion when you all land on top of each other."

"Mr. Pepperdine!" Mrs. Bellow said.

Janessa tried to suppress a giggle.

"A purely hypothetical theory," Mr. Pepperdine said.

The doorbell rang, and Janessa stood. "I'll go. It's probably Charley. Mr. Lawrence."

"Miss Holt," Mrs. Bellow inquired, "are you engaged to be married to that young man?"

"Good heavens, no," Janessa replied.

"Is he any relation to you?"

Begin as you mean to go on, Janessa thought again,

eyeing Mrs. Bellow. "No, ma'am. Mr. Lawrence is an old friend. If you require any further information, I am afraid you will have to ask him." She dashed into the front hall to answer the door, leaving what she was sure was an irate Mrs. Bellow behind her. "I am not going to answer every single question just because people are rude enough to ask," she muttered as she pulled open the door.

"I didn't ask anything," Charley said mildly.

"Mrs. Bellow," Janessa whispered. "She inquired about your bona fides."

"I look like an ax murderer," Charley declared. "It always makes people suspicious."

Janessa giggled. "You look very respectable." She eyed his sober, blue serge suit and bowler hat. "Maybe I should have worn something more—"

"Ugly?" Charley suggested.

"No, more doctorish. But it's so hot."

"Wear what you feel like," Charley encouraged. "You worry more than anybody I ever knew. In a couple of days you'll really have something to sink your teeth into, so forget about your clothes."

Janessa picked up her handbag, which she had left lying on the hall table between the daguerreotypes of the young man and the baby. She wondered if they were Mrs. Burnside's husband and child. Except for her unenthusiastic reference to marriage the night before, the old woman had so far mentioned neither.

"Cable car or shank's mare?" Charley inquired as she joined him.

Janessa looked at the sun. "Cable car," she said firmly. "And I'll pay since I'm the lazy one." She knew Charley had walked here to meet her.

The cable car ran just around the corner, down Aliso Street, and they caught a car headed for the medical school. "They tested an electric trolley in Richmond last spring," Charley said. "Amazing idea. It broke down on a hill, though, and had to be hauled away with mules, so maybe its time hasn't quite come."

"My brother says electricity and the internal-combustion engine will power all sorts of things in a few years," Janessa said. "Horseless carriages and who knows what all."

"That's what Frank Sprague says," Charley replied. "He invented the trolley. Lee Cochran, who's going to marry Nan, knows Sprague. Says he's a coming man."

"All this change," Janessa said. "Everything in the world is changing. You'd think they could make a little more room for women in it."

"That's your department," Charley said.

"Well, I'm petrified," she whispered as the cable car lurched to a stop and deposited them in front of the medical school. It proved to be a single building, two storied, with a wide porch around three sides. Beyond it was a vineyard, and across the street, the Los Angeles Cracker Company and a brewery.

An hour later, having registered for her courses, Janessa was no less petrified but considerably more indignant. The registrar had seemed at first unable to convince himself of Janessa's existence, a performance he reserved for women students. The male students proved to be more demonstrative. One of them spat on her skirt as she left the building.

"No!" Janessa grabbed Charley by the arm as he turned back with the obvious intention of punching the young man in his offending mouth. "You aren't going to start out getting in a brawl for my sake. I have to fight my own battles, Charley."

"Only up to a point," he said grimly.

The following morning, entering the lecture hall for her first anatomy class, Janessa found twenty pairs of eyes turned upon her in a collective, icy stare. Charley had saved a seat for her next to his, and she slid into it gratefully, trying to make as little stir as possible.

Professor Osterman at first registered little impression on Janessa except as a frock coat and a formidable high-domed head of white hair. Then he faced the class, hands clasped behind his back, and said, "Gentlemen, we have with us today two representatives of the fair sex who feel that they are strong enough to survive a course that will send many of you whimpering home to Mama in the next few months."

Janessa spotted another woman, with black hair and straight dark brows, sitting defiantly in the far corner.

"Whatever my opinions of the appropriateness of female physicians," Professor Osterman continued, "let me assure you of two things: One, the ladies will be given no quarter in this course in deference to their gender. Since they have chosen to force their way into a male profession, they will be expected to prove their competence and fitness for it. Two, every gentleman in this room will conduct himself as such. Whatever his opinions on the subject, he will keep them to himself, in the confines of this lecture hall at least. This course will not degenerate into a circus, whatever the provocation. Now then . . ."

"And now, Mr. Jurgen, if you will relate to us the primary layers of the musculature of the body . . ."

"Miss Holt, the layers of the skin and their specific qualities . . ."

"Mr. Felts, the reproductive organs of the male . . ."

Mr. Felts looked at Professor Osterman with alarm. "In front of them, sir?" His eyes glanced at Janessa and Eliza Thoms.

"Are you embarrassed, Mr. Felts?"

"No, sir, but it's—well, it's indecent!"

"Since the ladies have chosen to join us, they will have to put up with that!" Professor Osterman snapped. "Miss Thoms, are you embarrassed?"

"No, sir."

"Miss Holt, are you?"

"No, sir," she replied. She knew he was hoping she was. "Would you like me to answer your question?"

"I would not! Mr. Felts, you may continue."

"Felts was the little pig who spat on your skirt,"

Charley said indignantly as they left the lecture hall. "Pretending to be concerned about your sensibilities!"

"Well, Osterman jumped on him pretty hard," Janessa said. "He mixed the urethra up with the vas deferens."

"I hope he's never *my* physician," Charley murmured.

"He won't last long enough," she said.

They were three weeks into the term, and Professor Osterman's predictions regarding the attrition rate had proved accurate. Among the terrors of anatomy, physiology, histology, obstetrics, materia medica, and dissection, the class had lost three students already.

"I may not last long," Janessa said. "I am so tired. That devilish man called on me three times today in class."

"Well, you got the answer right every time."

"I have to," she said wearily, "because he's hoping I won't."

They came to the corner where their paths parted, and she waved a hand at him. She couldn't expect him to escort her home every day. She sank wearily into a seat on the cable car, feeling as worn out from the constant strain of proving her right to exist as from her studying—although there was plenty of that. The sound of the cable seemed to hum the names of the bones of the hand to her, her current memorization project: lunate, navicular, triangular, pisiform, hamate, capitate . . .

Janessa opened her eyes with a jerk to find that she had somehow gone home and sat down at the dinner table without, apparently, ever being really conscious. She stared at the fork lying in her plate, beside untouched chops and mashed potatoes.

"Don't worry," Mr. Pepperdine soothed gravely. "If you had actually started to snore, we would have awakened you."

Janessa looked at him, horrified.

"What were you thinking about?" Mr. Pepperdine asked her gently.

"Bones," she replied. "Dissections." Mr. Pepperdine looked a candidate for that himself, with his long, bony face and figure, all knobs and bumps.

Mrs. Bellow's fork clattered in her plate.

"I'm sorry," Janessa said. "I wasn't thinking."

"I shall be ill," Mrs. Bellow threatened, but she didn't move. If she left the table, there might not be another pork chop when she got back.

Mrs. Burnside spoke to Janessa while glaring at Mrs. Bellow. "You stick with it, dear. I'll have Clarice bring you some cookies and tea later on tonight, to give you something to keep on with." She fixed small, bright eyes on the rest of the boarders. "If more of us women had done what Miss Holt's doing, we might not be in the fix we are now, taking in boarders or working for starvation wages or wasting our days with a pair of knitting needles and a cupful of gossip." She got up and began to clear the table without waiting for Clarice.

Janessa looked after her, mildly stunned.

"Mrs. Burnside's a grass widow," Colonel Hapgood whispered in her ear. "Her husband went off to the gold rush in forty-nine and never came back." He sighed. "Her son joined the army in the war, against her wishes—he was only seventeen—and got killed. Essie Burnside doesn't have a high opinion of women letting themselves depend on men."

"Gossip, indeed!" Mrs. Bellow, outraged, glared after Mrs. Burnside. "Why I never! Never! I wouldn't stoop to anything so paltry—"

"That's right," Mr. Pepperdine said. "You only tell it when you're absolutely sure it's true."

Mrs. Bellow gave him an indignant look. "There are other boardinghouses," she announced.

"Yes, indeed." Mr. Pepperdine spooned more potatoes onto his plate. "This is your third this year, isn't it?"

Virginia City, Nevada, November 1887

"There have got to be better places to sleep." Tim reached under his bedroll and extracted a rock. Then he got up and pitched the rock through the tent flap. It careened wildly down the slope.

"Goddamnit!" someone below them yelled.

Tim lay down again and stared at the ceiling of the tent, his hands behind his head. Then he poked Sam, who didn't appear to be listening. "Number one, we've taken about enough silver out of this claim to feed us and the stock. Number two, we think there's silver in there, but if I eat beans any longer I'll be too unhealthy to enjoy it when we find it. Number three—" He poked Sam again. "You got me into this, so wake up and listen to me. Number three—if we get a job, we can work this diggings on our own time."

"A job?" Sam stared at him with suspicion.

"In the Ninevah," Tim said. "John Ormond used to know my dad in the army. He offered me a job. I thought I could probably get him to take you on, too."

"Offered you a job?" Sam sat up slowly, propped on his elbows. He obviously ached all over. "Why didn't you tell me?"

"Because I thought you'd want to take it," Tim admitted, "and I wanted to stick with this for a while."

"You could take the job," Sam proposed hopefully, "and I could work the claim here."

"Not on your tintype," Tim said. "All for one, one for all. That's our motto."

Sam considered the angles.

"It's going to snow soon," Tim said, "and it's going to be colder than an igloo in this tent."

"Yes, sir, Mr. Ormond," Sam said. "I've had experience. Experience and education."

"College boy, eh?" John Ormond asked. "What was your field of study?"

"Well, I tried to cover as much ground as I could, sir," Sam replied.

Sitting behind an ornate oak desk, Ormond considered Sam thoughtfully. The office in the Ninevah Mine building was luxurious. "Any engineering experience?"

"No," Sam said regretfully, "not exactly, sir."

"Well, I can give you a job in the drift," Ormond offered. "Since you're a friend of Holt's"—he glanced at Tim—"and because I hate to think of you boys up on that mountain all winter. Check in at the foreman's office at the mine works, and they'll give you a chit for equipment. You haven't got any union notions, have you?"

"No, sir." Sam didn't look as if he had any mining notions, either, but Tim gave him a push toward the door.

"Your alternative's probably shoveling shit in the livery stable," Tim hissed.

Sam glowered at him, but he jammed his hat on his head. "What the hell's a 'drift'?"

"A mine passageway. It follows the vein," he whispered as Sam went through the doorway.

"Now then, young Holt, have a seat," Ormond invited.

Suppressing a grin, Tim sat in the leather armchair opposite the desk. Sam had looked pretty upset, but Tim didn't suppose his own job was going to be any bed of roses, either.

"I can give you a job as a junior engineer, in the drifts," Ormond said, confirming Tim's expectation. But he softened it by producing a bottle of whiskey and a couple of glasses from the cabinet behind him. He poured two shots and handed one to Tim. "I have a great respect for your father, young man. I'm glad to help his son. What are you doing out here, anyway?"

"We had a sort of difference of opinion," Tim admitted, embarrassed. "About my staying at Harvard. To be truthful sir, I wanted to be out doing something, not just studying it."

Ormond smiled. "Well, a little rebellion's a healthy thing in a young man. Shows you've got gumption. You're writing home, I hope?"

"Oh, yes, sir. My dad knows I'm all right."

Ormond grinned. "You telling the whole story?"

Tim looked sheepish, but he grinned back. "Not exactly, sir. I told him we'd found some silver."

"Not a lie, but not exactly the whole picture, eh?" Ormond said. "Well, you do your job in the Ninevah, and in a while you can write him that you got a promotion. I can use a young man with gumption, from the right kind of family. These damn ignorant miners are driving me crazy."

Tim put his glass down on the desk. "I appreciate your trust, sir."

"It's all right. You go see Mr. Stebbins downstairs. He's my chief engineer, and he'll get you started."

The interview with Obadiah Stebbins, a brusque, self-educated older man, proved to be a lengthy one, and Tim emerged from the mine office ready for dinner and as much sleep as he could manage. He was due at the Ninevah Mine across the street at seven in the morning. Since the biggest ore body in the Comstock Lode had been discovered to be beneath the streets of Virginia City itself, the mine-works' adits were in the center of town, squeezed unexpectedly between buildings.

As Tim turned the corner onto Flowery, the one-block street that ran beside the Ninevah mine works between the southern ends of D and C streets, he saw a familiar figure playing with a spaniel puppy on the lawn of Ormond's three-story, mansard-roofed house. It was the girl whose pony cart he had extricated from the traffic snarl that day he had come to town for timber.

Tim stopped, staring in spite of himself, thinking that she was the prettiest girl he had ever seen. When she saw him halt hesitantly on the board sidewalk, she smiled. The fall breeze ruffled her dark hair.

"Hello!" she called. "I remember you. I never thanked you properly."

"I'm Timothy Holt. I'm going to be working for your father." He didn't know what else to say. *God, you're beautiful. Will you marry me?* seemed to be out of the question.

She stood and came over to the wrought-iron fence that bordered the lawn. "I'm Isabella Ormond." She gave him her hand, while the puppy tugged playfully at her bootlaces. "Are you a miner?"

"I'm an engineer," Tim said, snobbishly grateful that he didn't have to admit to being a Cousin Jack with a pick on his shoulder. "A junior engineer," he added, trying for a modicum of truth.

"You're the one!" Isabella said delightedly. "Daddy told me about you. He used to know your father."

Tim found himself suddenly thankful for his father's mere existence. "Yes, I guess he did. It was nice of him to take me on."

Isabella giggled. "He said you poor boys were stuck up on the side of Sun Mountain in a tent, and if you stayed up there all winter, they could haul you down and put you up in the middle of Union Street as ice sculptures."

"I reckon they could." Tim bent to scratch the puppy's nose through the fence. "We're staying at Molinelli's Hotel now." The pup chewed on Tim's finger, and he smiled. "This is a nice little gal."

"Her name's Columbine," Isabella said. "She's my graduation present. She's a purebred springer spaniel."

"Graduation? High school?" It couldn't be college; she looked too young.

"Mmm-hmm." Isabella rolled her eyes. "Miss Alderson's Academy in San Francisco. I wanted to go to school here, but Mama thought I should be 'finished.' "

"And are you?" Tim asked.

She smiled, then pirouetted once around. "I can walk with an encyclopedia on my head, use the proper fork on a lobster, paint in watercolors, play the piano, speak passable French, awful Italian"—she grinned at him slyly—"and know when I've talked too long on the front lawn to a boy to whom I haven't been properly introduced."

"But your father knows my father," Tim protested. "That practically makes us cousins."

"Well, not exactly," Isabella said. "But it helps." She looked as if she knew she ought to go inside but didn't really want to.

Tim tried to think of something to keep her standing there, just for a few more minutes. He had finally met her again—and he even looked respectable this time, in a clean sack coat and his good hat. He had never seen anyone like Isabella. Her small, heart-shaped face held both innocence and mischief, and her soft blue eyes had a faint shade of lavender in them. She looked like a painting, blue wool dress and cape against fading lawn against pale yellow house, with an urn of deep-yellow chrysanthemums in their last bloom on the walk behind her. A modern impressionist painting, all broken light and shards of color.

"Maybe I could take you to church on Sunday," he ventured, trying to think of something she might agree to.

"Maybe you could," Isabella said.

He thought she was flirting with him a little, enjoying the experience of being old enough to be courted and being out of Miss Alderson's clutches. "Where do you go to church?" he asked her.

"The Methodist Church," Isabella said. "Are you a Methodist?"

"Sure," Tim said. He didn't see why he couldn't be.

"I always go with my mother in the morning," she said. "To keep her company. But we have prayer meeting at night. Maybe you'd like to go to prayer meeting."

"I would if it's the only way I can see you," Tim said frankly. He leaned a little closer to her, across the fence. She smelled like lilac water.

Isabella picked up the puppy, which wriggled against her breast and tried to lick her nose. "I'd have to ask Daddy, of course," she said demurely.

"Do," Tim said.

"In fact he's up there watching us now," Isabella murmured, and Tim spun his head around to see John Ormond leaning out his office window across the intersection on D Street. Tim moved back from the fence hastily and raised his hat with a half bow to Isabella. "I think I should be going."

"Probably," she agreed. She let him take a few steps and then called after him, "I'll talk to Daddy. And you can take me sleighing. That's a lot more fun than church."

VII

The hoist rattled downward at a speed that terrified Sam. With three other miners crammed in with him, the cage plummeted through blackness and heat, giving him only brief, eerie glimpses of the first four levels of the shaft—cavernous openings in the earth lit by uncertain candle glow—and then gone again as the cage dropped past them, as if in a descent into hell. At the fifth level, it thudded to a stop, and the cage door swung open. A miner, stripped to the waist and blackened with dirt, stepped forward to meet them, splashing through standing water, and Sam was mildly surprised not to find himself face to face with the devil.

"You the new man?" he asked.

Sam nodded. The level they were in was a man-made cavern, lit by whale-oil lamps. Three tunnels, or drifts, radiated out from it. Narrow track, laid for the ore cars, disappeared into the darkness of the drifts.

"I'm Ross Bent, the station boss on this level. I'm putting you on as mucker on the west drift." He pointed into the blackness of a tunnel. "Just follow the boys. They'll show you what to do."

The other men were already shedding their shirts and disappearing up the drift. Sam followed them at a trot, unbuttoning his own shirt and tying it around his waist as he caught up to them. The tunnel was narrow here, hardly more than the width of the track, and braced with huge, square-set timbers. The air was thick with dust. The light from the other miners' candles cast looming, undulating shadows on the rough-hewn walls. Sam followed them, coughing, until the passage ended at the face of the drift. An empty ore car stood before a mountainous heap of broken rock and the solid wall of the drift face beyond it.

One of the other miners, whose name was Hobbs, rammed the pointed end of his candle holder into the timbering, then turned to Sam. "We got to muck this out and tram it back to the hoist before they finish drilling." He jerked a thumb at the other two men, who were hacking at the face of the drift with picks. "Where the hell's your candle?"

"Here." Sam reached into his shirt pocket and pulled out the holder and one of the three candles he had been given in the hoist room.

"Oh, for Christ's sake." The other mucker looked at him in exasperation. "You light your candle *before* you leave the station. We're fifteen hundred feet underground, and there ain't no windows if the lights go out. You don't ever rely on another man's candle, you got that?"

"Yes. Sorry." Sam lit the candle and stuck it in the timbering as he had seen the other men do.

"You ain't no Cousin Jack," Hobbs growled. "You're as green as grass, aren't you?"

"Yeah," Sam said. "But I catch on fast."

"Well, catch onto this," Hobbs said. He handed Sam a shovel. "That's a one-ton car, and we got to load four of them an hour. You get half an hour's rest and ice every hour."

Sam coughed again. "I can't breathe."

"Powder gas in the air," Hobbs said. "Ventilation's no good down here. Ormond's too mean to put in decent blowers."

A muffled explosion reverberated somewhere in the distance beyond the drift. The noise rumbled in the narrow passage, and a shower of loose pebbles rained down on them from the roof.

"Damn it!" Hobbs muttered.

"That son of a bitch!" one of the other miners yelled.

"They're blasting somewhere," Hobbs told Sam. "They're supposed to wait till the shifts change to do that. They're going to kill somebody, but Ormond doesn't care."

"He's going to care!" the other miner threatened.

"Yeah, you tell him, Yellan." Hobbs sounded sarcastic, yet resigned. He picked up his shovel. "Start mucking," he told Sam.

In half an hour, Sam's hands were blistered raw, and his whole body was drenched with sweat, which ran in rivulets through the dust and grime on his arms and chest. It might be cold somewhere above in the open air, but in the depths of the mine, the heat was like a cauldron's. Out of sheer pigheadedness, he kept up with Hobbs, and Hobbs looked at him with a certain respect as he laid down his shovel beside the second filled car.

"I'll tram this one back alone," Hobbs offered. "You sit down a minute. You can take the next one."

Sam nodded and sank in exhaustion to the floor of the drift. God in heaven, how had he gotten into this? The face of the drift swam before him in the uneven candlelight. Shore, the fourth miner, and Yellan had squared the rock face and were double-jacking it—drilling holes for the dynamite charges that would blast loose another pile of ore. Yellan drove a steel rod into the rock face with an eight-pound sledge while Shore held the rod and turned it between strokes. This was skilled work, more skilled than mucking. If a mucker didn't handle his shovel correctly, he only exhausted himself; a powderman who slipped up might smash his assistant's hands to pulp—or blow them all to hell. As Hobbs came back with the empty ore car, Shore and Yellan traded places, Yellan holding the drill rod while Shore hammered it deeper into the rock.

"Up and at 'em, college boy," Hobbs said with a weary grin, and Sam heaved himself to his feet. Hobbs shook his head. "Your hands are a mess, aren't they? I thought you said you'd been digging a claim up the mountain."

Sam looked at him balefully as he shoveled. "Not this hard."

"I hear your pal got a job with the high-and-mighty engineers," Hobbs continued, grunting as he swung the shovel over the edge of the car.

"Is that easier?" Sam asked. *It must be. Anything would be easier,* he thought.

"Not so much if you're at the bottom of the barrel," Hobbs replied. "Old Stebbins runs his juniors hard. Easier than this, though. The pay's better. Man gets treated like a human being."

"There's a cure for this," Joe Yellan said without turning around. "Back the union, lad, and the union'll back you."

"Balls," Hobbs grumbled. "I pay my dues—and you will too, kid, if you know what's good for you. But the union's got about as much clout these days as—"

He broke off as Yellan jumped back from the rock face with a curse. Sam heard a hissing sound and turned to see a jet of water and steam shoot from the drill hole.

"Clear back!" Yellan warned. "If that blows, you'll get scalded good."

The water spat and steamed as it hit the pile of broken ore. Hobbs moved away from it edgily.

Yellan put the drill rod down, and as he pulled on a pair of heavy leather gloves, he looked at Hobbs. "Go tell Bent they'll have to pump this level soon as we shoot. Maybe before."

"Keep mucking," Hobbs told Sam. "Over here, on the other side of the car. The bosses don't let you stop for water unless you're drowning." He took off down the drift.

Boiled is more like it, Sam thought. He watched the water uneasily. It had slowed from a spurt to a trickle, but it was steady, and the heat of it added to the temperature in the drift. Through steam and candlelight and rock dust, the drift had a stygian aura that surpassed any of his childhood imaginings of hell.

Yellan was turning the drill rod again. Wearing the leather gloves made the work slow and clumsy, and Sam saw that Yellan and Shore were both tensed, alert, and ready to drop the drill and sledge and dive for the other end of the tunnel. Sam tried to remember what Charley Lawrence had said in the letter that Janessa had read to them at dinner: The last of the big pumps had shut down a year ago. The Ninevah and the Consolidated ran small ones as they were needed, but the levels below this one were all flooded.

Tim and I should have paid more attention to that letter, Sam thought, disgruntled. He would have if he had thought he was going to end up down here.

Hobbs came back, and they went on mucking, keeping one eye on the face. Yellan and Shore finished the hole without further surprises. While they started on the next one, water seeped from the first hole, and the drift got hotter.

They stopped twice to cool down in the ice room on the level above them, plunging their arms and faces into tubs of ice lowered by the hoist. They trudged back to the drift carrying lumps of ice that melted before they got to the face.

At midday they stopped to eat lunch, sitting on the floor of the drift, away from the spreading pool. Sam wolfed down a sandwich and a wedge of cheese, washed down with water, now lukewarm, from his canteen.

"Leave a bit for the Tommy-knockers, lad," Shore advised as Sam was about to stuff the last crust in his mouth.

"I don't believe in hobgoblins," Sam muttered. He leaned morosely against the side of the drift, the rock digging into his bare back.

He had heard all the stories about the little folk who lived in a hard-rock mine. The man who didn't give them their due was likely to find his tools missing or his candle blown out by the quick, unexplainable gusts of air that whispered through the drifts. Or worse,

because the Tommy-knockers were firmly and passion-
ately believed to give a death warning, a thin tapping
inside the rock when a cave-in was coming. Some believed they had their origins in the souls of buried
miners who had died while trying to pick their way out
of a rockfall, and if so they would most certainly be
vengeful toward the living who showed them no re-
membrance.

Joe Yellan reached over and pinched a bit off Sam's
bread before he could put it in his mouth.

"I'm hungry, damn it," Sam protested.

Yellan's face was harsh in the half darkness, his
profile illuminated on one side only by yellow candle
glow, like a mask. "You're ignorant, Brentwood, and
you've got no notion how close you work to death down
here. No one plays stupid games with bad luck in a
mine." He took the bit of bread and put it, with a crust
from his own dinner plate, in a crack in the rock.
"Down here you'll respect the mine, and the rock, and
anything that may live in it. And if you don't, I'll have
you thrown off this shift." He stood. "Now get to work."

It took the whole of their ten-hour shift to muck
the rest of the ore from the drift floor and to drill a
half-dozen holes, tamp the charges in them, and fuse
them. Joe Yellan wrapped the powder in screws of oiled
paper to keep them dry—all the drill holes were running a little with water—then loaded them carefully in
each hole, some with more powder, some with less,
according to some arcane knowledge that Sam could
only guess at. The fuses that he cut and poked into the
holes were also of varying lengths. Now he tamped
mud around the fuses to hold them in place.

"Ready to shoot," Yellan said. The other three
gathered well away from him, their candles and lunch
pails in hand. Yellan cut a series of notches in another
length of fuse, lit it, and as sparks spat out from the first
notch, held it to a fuse. He lit the rest as Sam watched,
suppressing the urge to bolt.

"That's it," Yellan said. The fuses spat and burned

with a red glow like a line of malevolent eyes. Yellan cupped his hands to his mouth. "Fire in the hole!"

They set off quickly up the drift to the station. Behind them came the muffled boom of one explosion, then another. Pebbles fell from the ceiling in a little shower of dust.

"Better get that pump working," Yellan told Ross Bent as he passed the station. The floor here was wet with standing water, and water dripped from the ceiling.

"Yeah, yeah," the stationmaster said. "It'll be dry as your granny's parlor by morning."

"If it isn't, happens he'll lose some carpenters when they start timbering," Yellan retorted.

He swung into the lift, and Sam slunk in next to him, then leaned wearily against the wire cage. Yellan looked at him. "Now you're a miner, lad." He didn't sound congratulatory.

It snowed two weeks later, and Tim took Isabella Ormond sleigh riding. Her father seemed to view him as a presentable suitor, more for his family connections, Tim thought, than for his own fine self, which was frequently rather grimy from the mine. That morning he had washed, shivering, scrubbing himself in a tin tub brought up to his room. Molinelli's Hotel was a sort of midpoint between luxury and a flophouse, but if you wanted a bath, you had to ask for it, and you'd better not ask too often.

The rented livery stable nag was feeling frisky, cavorting now in the snow along A Street as it pulled the sleigh. Isabella was bundled in a fur wrap and a fur hat, beneath which her face, pink cheeked, peeped out. Her hands were tucked into a matching muff. Columbine, not exactly to Tim's delight, was in her lap. Tim had a sheepskin coat over his suit, and he wore a wide-brimmed felt hat pulled well down over his eyes. The snow was still coming down.

"Isn't it beautiful?" Isabella enthused. "I love winter."

The mountains were transformed. Snow blanketed

the bare dirt and dusty scrub of the hillside and hid the shambles of abandoned mine adits and the rutted mud in the streets. As they crossed Taylor Street, they saw, far down the hill below them, the red and white spire of the Catholic church, St. Mary's in the Mountains, gleaming against the snow.

"Funny to think of sleighing on top of all that money, isn't it?" Tim mused.

"I suppose so," Isabella said. "I never thought about that. They've been mining right under the city for as long as I can remember."

Tim chuckled. "It's almost cannibalistic, isn't it? Or like the beast that's reputed to swallow its own tail."

"I suppose we do seem strange to outsiders," Isabella allowed.

"Every place is strange to outsiders. This one just seems a little more otherworldly than most." He thought of the blackness of the mine shaft, with the fitfully lit circles of the stations radiating from it, and thought of Dante. " 'All hope abandon, ye who enter here.' "

"Is it that bad down there? Daddy says you've been doing very well."

"Maybe I wasn't talking about the mine," Tim said, looking at her. He took the reins in one hand and put his right hand over hers. He found himself patting Columbine's nose instead. Isabella pretended not to notice, but he thought he heard a faint giggle.

"Tell me about your work, Mr. Holt," she said.

"Can't you call me Tim?"

A child's sled swooped past them, and the livery horse pranced and snorted.

"I'd have to consider whether I have known you long enough," she said. "And whether I wish you to call me Isabella."

"Well, do you?"

"I think so." She scooted over a little bit closer to him.

Tim turned the sleigh onto Sutton and then back along B Street, past the Miners Union Hall, a two-story brick building with a curved façade with the union emblem on it. The lettered streets—A, B, C, and D—ran parallel across the hillside, while the others ran up and down it. They passed the Knights of Pythias hall and the opera house, with its walls plastered with posters. He turned the sleigh cautiously down the slope of Union Street. They crossed the railroad tracks, and Tim urged the horse into a trot as they headed away from town.

"We shouldn't go too far," Isabella said.

"I'm not," Tim responded. "Just up to the hospital and back." St. Mary's Hospital sat on a hill past the outskirts of town. It was just the right distance for courting purposes. "The work is going all right," Tim said, getting back to their previous conversation. "I wish your father spent more time in the mine himself, though. I'm sure he can't know about some of the stuff the foremen are getting away with."

"Such as?" Isabella asked.

"Safety precautions—or the lack of them, really. There ought to be ventilators in there to clear out the powder gas. And they ought to clear the whole mine before they blast."

"I'm sure Daddy does the best he can," Isabella said.

Tim realized she didn't really understand what he was talking about. She had probably never been in her father's mine. "I'm sure he does." He reached over again to take her hand. "I don't suppose that dog could sit on the other side, could she?"

"She might," Isabella said. She tucked Columbine under her right arm and slipped her left hand into Tim's.

"You wanted to see me, sir?" Tim stepped into John Ormond's office two days later, at the end of his shift.

Ormond looked up from his desk. "Sit down, Holt. You look bushed."

Tim smiled. "It's hard work, sir."

"That it is. But I like to see a young man with his

mind on his work. Isabella tells me you're worried about conditions in the mine."

Tim looked uncomfortable. "Well, yes, sir, in some cases." Ormond appeared to be listening seriously, so he went on. "We need blowers down there to clear the powder gas, sir. It's practically unbreathable in places after they blast."

"I see." Ormond looked thoughtful.

"And I worry about the structural integrity of the setup, sir," Tim went on, encouraged. "A lot of rock is being pulled out down there. Square-set timbering's a good system, probably the best, but there's still a risk of cave-in. I do feel we ought to clear all the drifts before we shoot in any one of them. Especially if they're shooting above a working shift."

"Ah, those union men." Ormond ran his hands through his hair. "I can tell they've been at you. We've been using square-set timbering in Virginia City since the sixties and never had a major cave-in caused by anything but the miners' own carelessness." He poured Tim a drink. "These Cousin Jacks are an uneducated lot, and they always blame accidents on everyone but themselves. Bad luck, Tommy-knockers, the mine owners—usually the mine owners, when the men don't like the rate of pay."

"Have you been down there when they're shooting, sir?"

"Hell, yes," Ormond answered. "Not that you need to be, mind you. That's the powderman's job, not the engineer's. No, the problem is, we pay a fair wage, and they're looking for an extravagant one. These men got spoiled by the boom days, when they made more than any other miners in the country. We were getting rich, and we figured they ought to, too." He grinned at Tim. "That was an error. Never feed your dog a steak, my boy. The men have to understand that you can't mine low-grade ore at a profit and pay double wages. This is a business, not a charitable institution."

"I see," Tim murmured.

"I thought you would," Ormond said. "I thought

you ought to understand the situation. Especially if you're going to court my daughter."

Tim flushed. "Yes, sir."

"I'm not against that, mind you." Ormond smiled again. "If I was against it, you wouldn't be taking sleigh rides with her. I have a great respect for your father, and you seem to have a good head on your shoulders. If you play your cards right, you can go a long way out here." He stood. "Well, I'm glad we had this little talk. I hope I've relieved your mind."

Tim stood, too. His drink was untouched. "I think I understand the situation, sir."

"Good. Good. Well, it's the end of the day, but I've still got a stack of papers to go through. The owner's work is never done, eh?" He paused. "Oh, and Holt—"

Tim turned back by the door, by the framed map of the Ninevah Mine that hung on the red-papered wall.

"Don't discuss the mine any more with Isabella, will you? She doesn't really understand business."

The lift rattled to a stop in the hoist room, and Sam staggered out. He was filthy from head to toe, aching and feverish. His lungs hurt when he breathed. Three weeks ago he would have thought he was getting sick. Now he knew that that was just what men felt like after a ten-hour shift in the mine.

An arctic wind blew through the open door of the hoist room, and Sam pulled his shirt on. He limped through the door into the change room, where the other miners were washing in freezing air, using cold water dipped into basins from the tubs in the middle of the room. Walls and floors were wet and gritty, and the only furnishings were waist-high shelves to hold the basins, and hooks for hanging up their clean clothes, if they had any.

Sam pulled off his shirt, washed as quickly as he could, shrugged his shirt back on, and buttoned it up. He would change in his room at the hotel. Any clothes left hanging on the hooks all day were almost as dirty as everything else was ten hours later. Molinelli's wasn't elegant, but it was better than most of the places the miners went home to. He managed that dubious luxury only because of the silver that he and Tim, on their days off, had been able to take out of their own claim. They had christened it the Hopeful, back when they had been naïve.

"You were off over three tons today, Brentwood," Ross Bent said as he passed him, heading for the basins.

"We had to stop while they pumped again," Sam said indignantly.

"Doesn't matter," the stationmaster countered. "Two tons per man an hour, regardless. If you can't muck faster than that, you're out."

"Damn it!" Sam shoved the basin away from him. It bounced against the wall and splashed cold, dirty water over the edge. He pulled his coat off the hook, jammed his arms into it, and stalked out, seething. It was snowing again outside, and he turned his coat collar up and headed for the pay room.

"I've quit." Sam slung his empty lunch pail into the corner of the hotel room and glared at Tim, daring him to make something of it.

Tim was sprawled on the bed, his fingers laced behind his head. He propped himself up on his elbows and stared, brooding, at Sam. "You what? We've got about six cents between us, and you quit?"

"I'll think of something," Sam muttered.

"For instance?"

"I don't know." Sam pulled off his filthy shirt and trousers and took clean ones out of the drawer. "If you don't like it, go home to Daddy."

"I've got a job," Tim pointed out.

"I'll work the Hopeful for a while," Sam decided.

"Oh, very good. In six feet of snow, all by yourself."

"Don't worry, you'll get your share."

"I'm not worried. You aren't going to mine any-thing but ice cubes. Look, I know what it's like down there. I talked to Ormond today about conditions, but he gave me the runaround. I don't blame you for wanting to quit." Tim looked at him sympathetically. Sam had talked him into coming to Virginia City in the first place, but Tim knew that Sam hadn't had to talk very hard. And he couldn't help feeling sorry for anyone who had spent time at the bottom of the Ninevah Mine. Waldo Howard at the *Beacon* had told him there had been a lot more cave-ins than John Ormond was admitting to. "You could go home, too, you know," he said quietly. "Not to Madrona—to Independence. See if you can't work things out with your dad."

Sam, not answering, just looked at him, his face dark, his rakish good looks grim as he appeared to be concentrating on buttoning his shirt. He tucked his shirt in and pulled his braces up. Finally he said, "I'll go back in the Ninevah first." He put his coat on and combed his hair in the mirror.

"Where are you going?" Tim said.

"Out." Sam put his hat on. "I got paid. I'm going to spend it."

VIII

Restless, Sam stood on the sidewalk in front of the hotel, his hands in his pockets. The saloons and most of the stores along C Street were lighted, their windows glowing through flurries of snow. In the boom days, Virginia City had been a twenty-four-hour-a-day town, and even now many of the businesses stayed open in the evening to accommodate the miners coming off their shift. The American Saloon and the bar in the Silver Dollar Hotel were crowded. Sam crossed the street. He had eight dollars' pay in his pocket and a perverse urge to spend it all and worry about it tomorrow. Eight dollars wouldn't last long anyway.

He had one whiskey and then another in the Silver Dollar, but then, still restless, he walked out on the street again. The snow and the lights had a festive look. It would be Christmas soon, and the stores had holly wreaths and cardboard cutouts of St. Nicholas in their windows, but Sam was not touched by the displays. After his mother died, Christmas in his childhood had generally consisted of Sam, his grandmother, and later—after his father remarried—his half sister, Eden, and her nurse sharing a quiet dinner. A practical present, generally new clothes, would have been sent from faraway places to Independence by his father and stepmother. Grandmother Claudia had always tried to make up the difference with new skates and dolls, but Sam had achieved no fondness for the season.

Last week Tim had gotten one Christmas package

from Oregon and another from Janessa in Los Angeles and had sent presents in return. But Sam knew there would be nothing from Independence; the one outraged letter his father had written him had been sufficient to assure him of that.

Across the street, Hooper's Dry Goods was doing a brisk business. Sam strolled over, more to get out of the cold than for any other reason. He didn't want to drink anymore; the first two hadn't made him feel any better. Inside, a miner's wife in a shabby wool cloak, plainly counting pennies in her mind, was looking wistfully at a curly-headed doll, and in the corner a woman in a red velvet cape trimmed with dark fur was trying on a hat in front of a standing mirror on the counter. The hat was dark red with jet beading, a quantity of silver aigrettes, and dark lace ruching. She cocked her head thoughtfully at her reflection and patted red-gold curls into place under the hat. She turned, trying to see the side, and caught Sam's face watching hers in the mirror. He didn't look away when their eyes met in the glass. She smiled a little and turned toward him.

"What do you think?" she asked.

He saw that she was in her thirties, certainly beautiful, but overdressed for Thursday night in Hooper's Dry Goods.

"Wrong color." He came over and stood behind her as she turned toward the mirror again, pensive. "That's not the right red for your hair. That cloak's fine, but this is too purplish." He grinned at her in the mirror. "And it has too many feathers on it."

"I like feathers," she declared. "But the color's no good?"

"Nope." He leaned over and whispered in her ear. "It makes that nice hair look dyed."

"It's not!" she said indignantly.

He smiled at her lazily. "I know."

She looked at the hat again, and after a moment she took it off and put her own back on. It was black velvet, also with too many feathers.

"Let me do that." Sam took the black grosgrain ribbons out of her fingers and tied them under her chin.

She smiled at him, not coquettish but interested. "I'm Annie Malone." She held out one black-gloved hand.

"Sam Brentwood." He held the fingers a moment longer than necessary, and they looked at each other thoughtfully, assessing unspoken signals that might or might not amount to anything.

"How are you at toys, Mr. Brentwood? I have three little boys and a girl to buy for."

"Yours?" Sam inquired.

"No, we never did have any. I'm a widow," she added by way of explanation. "These are my house-keeper's children. What do little boys like, Mr. Brentwood?"

"Drums," Sam said promptly. "Horns. Whistles. Anything that makes noise."

"She won't thank me for that."

"Are you buying for your housekeeper or her boys? Toy soldiers then. Wooden swords. Marbles. A wagon." Odd how easily he could remember the things he had wanted.

They walked to the toys at the other end of the store. She picked up a bisque doll with blond curls and a blue tam o' shanter. "This is for Belle, Emma's daughter," she told him. "I always wanted one, but I never had anything but a cornhusk doll—and was lucky to get that." It seemed that Annie, too, could remember what she had wanted.

They picked out a set of wooden blocks, a box of a dozen brightly painted tin soldiers with cheerfully fierce expressions, and then looked at the sacks of marbles arrayed under a small Christmas tree.

"Which are the best?" Annie asked.

"Aggies," Sam replied. "Glassies are all right, but you have to have an aggie for a shooter." He picked up an agate marble and a smaller glass one and set the glass marble on the floor. He knelt, the aggie between his thumb and finger, to see if he could still do it. His shot sent the little glass sphere hurtling across the floorboards and under the foot of a portly gentleman in a clerical collar, who sat down on the floor suddenly and with some surprise.

Annie pressed her gloved fingers to her mouth as Sam apologized and helped the gentleman to his feet. Sam didn't look particularly repentant, and the affronted cleric appeared to be about to blister him with a condemnation of grown men who played infants' games in stores, until he caught sight of Annie.

"Mrs. Malone." The minister tipped his derby and made a half bow.

"We're awfully sorry, Reverend. We got silly." Annie hustled Sam to the counter, where she paid for her purchases, and they fled outside into the snow.

"Oh, my lord, did you ever?" Annie burst out laughing.

"I thought the old fellow was going to give me the riot act," Sam said. "How'd you tame him so fast?"

"I gave him a new set of pews for the church last month, that's how," Annie explained. "This is a silver town, Mr. Brentwood. Money talks. In Virginia City it even talks to God."

She set the parcels down at her feet. Sam leaned against one of the lathe-turned pillars that supported Hooper's balcony. They looked at each other, suddenly quiet, uncertain where they might be going from here.

"I could carry those for you," Sam suggested.

Annie looked at him, trying to decide what she wanted to do. She knew he was too young; ten years younger than she was, at least. But his dark eyes and reckless-looking face held something beyond what she normally encountered in Virginia City. He knew things— such as when a hat had too many feathers. Annie could tell that his clothes had been good when they were new, of fine cut and quality material. And he knew how to stand just close enough to be suggestive and not insulting, how to hold her fingers just a moment too long, so that no one else noticed. She thought that he probably knew a lot about that.

She picked up half the parcels and handed them to him. "You could take me to dinner, if you wanted to."

Sam accepted the parcels. "I do want to." He gave her a rueful smile and a shrug of his shoulders. "But I haven't any money."

Annie nodded. She put her arm through his, her black-gloved fingertips resting lightly on his coat. "Then I could take you to dinner," she said.

Tim stopped in front of the hoist room, blinking in the jagged sunlight that bounced from the heaped-up snow in the mine yard. It was three days before Christmas, and the dusty evergreens on the windowsill looked pitiful behind the reflected figures of two men with shotguns. They stood one to either side of the door, with Joe Yellan glaring at them from five paces away, a sheaf of printed notices in his hand.

"You've no right to keep me out!" Yellan said furiously. "I'll work my shift, and I won't be searched by company thugs!"

"Don't need to search you, Cousin Jack," one of the men said. "You got in your hand what we want." He started for Yellan. "There ain't gonna be no union agitators in this mine."

Yellan backed away. "Who the hell are you?" he shouted. "You don't belong here."

"Company hired us. We belong, all right. Maybe more'n you."

"This is legitimate union business, and I have a right to put up notices in the change room."

"Naw, you ain't," the man with the shotgun said. "You ain't got a union, neither. What you got is a miners' social club, and if you're smart you'll keep it that way. 'Cause a real union's gonna get blasted to kingdom come if it makes any trouble in this mine. You got that?"

Joe Yellan stood, as stubborn as a bull, feet planted in the snow, glaring at John Ormond's thugs, his breath puffing out from his mouth in little clouds of steam. The man with the shotgun raised his weapon. The sound of the lever being rammed back made a loud clack in the silence.

"You got that, Cousin Jack?" the first man said. "Now give me them notices." He lunged at Joe and grabbed him by the shoulder.

Yellan swung his empty fist and caught the man across the chin. The other thug raised his shotgun, and Tim hurled himself at the weapon and dragged the barrel down.

"Stop it!" Tim shouted. "You can't shoot a man over a piece of paper!"

With the others' attention distracted by Tim, Yellan sprinted out of the yard. The company men advanced on Tim.

"What do you think you're interfering with, sonny?" one of them inquired. "A tea party?"

"I'm not sure," Tim replied evenly. "But I don't think I like its looks." He went into the pump room, a shed beyond the hoist room and the pay room, and found Stebbins poring over a map spread out on his desk.

"What are those two gorillas doing out there?" Tim demanded.

Stebbins sighed. "Keep out of that, Holt. You ain't been here long enough to understand what's going on. If the union's gonna butt heads with John Ormond, you don't want to be in the middle."

"You think I have a choice?"

"Yeah. You can stay out of union shenanigans, or you can get in trouble. Now, how well do you know the Number Three pump?"

"Kissing cousins," Tim answered.

"Good, because it's balking like a mule. They're walking around in about a foot of water down there, and I ain't got time to rip it apart. Get over there and see what you can do."

Beyond Stebbins's desk, in the cavernous shadows

of the shed roof, were the pumps. Stebbins's "Number Three pump" was actually the only pump. The biggest no longer ran. It was the Cornish Pump, with a 125-ton flywheel capable of raising a million gallons of water a day. Number Two, an antique that dated to the sixties, would probably blow up if it was started.

Shutting down the big pumps had been a dominolike process. As the payout of the Comstock Lode had declined, mines went out of production and ceased pumping their own shafts. Because most of the workings beneath Virginia City were connected by the maze of shafts and tunnels, each pump that was shut down placed an additional burden on the others. Inevitably, they, too, were shut down because it simply wasn't profitable to run them. That had ended deep mining. No one went much below the two-thousand-foot level now, and pumping was done as needed with smaller pumps.

Tim inspected Number Three, forgetting the company thugs in his search for the problem. When fired up, the steam engine that drove the pump whistled merrily. Tim continued his inspection, but the engine looked sound.

"Runs like a teakettle till you hook up the pump," Tim reported later to the chief engineer. "There's something jammed in the intake, I'll bet."

"You're probably right," Stebbins muttered, and Tim looked at him suspiciously. To clear the intake he was going to have to go down in the shaft and take it apart. Not a task the chief engineer would have relished.

"Take your overshoes," Stebbins said.

Tim grinned and picked up a pair of waterproof boots from the corner. He pulled them on, then went back to the hoist room, across the slush in the yard.

The company men were still here. They seemed to have been hired for size. They were beefy, no-neck types, in shiny blue serge suits, bowler hats, and hobnailed boots.

Tim pushed past them. "Maybe Ormond will send

you some coffee," he said. He hoped they were getting cold.

As he hung his coat on a hook in the change room, he saw with some amusement that Joe Yellan, by opening a back window and climbing through it, had posted his notices, after all. They advertised a meeting that night in the Miners Union Hall and listed a litany of grievances, primary among them low pay and callous disregard for the miners' safety.

As Tim went down in the hoist, he was troubled by conflicting emotions. The miners worked in abominable conditions—some a necessity of the business of mining itself, but others due solely to stinginess. Still, it did seem to him that to call John Ormond a bloodsucker on a handbill in his own mine was a bit much. Also a consideration was that Tim had fallen head over heels into first love with Isabella Ormond.

When the hoist splashed to a stop, Tim, a candle in hand, got out and waded through standing water, to see the situation at the end of the drift.

"Has Stebbins got that pump up yet?" Ross Bent asked Tim as he passed.

"We're working on it," Tim said. He held the candle up and looked at the drift face. Water was running down it steadily, and the rock looked slick and slimy. Water dripped from the ceiling timbers, too, and one had a deep puddle under it. Tim lifted the candle in the steamy air. The timber was bowed down, warped by the steam, perhaps, or just loosened from its place by water.

"That needs replacing," he said. "Look at this, Bent."

The stationmaster glanced at it. "It's not out enough," he said brusquely. "It'd take half a shift to get it loose."

"Or a single blast," Tim said. "If it doesn't come down the next time you shoot, it'll be a death trap afterward."

"We're getting ready to shoot now," Bent said.

"Soon as the pump's working." He looked exasperated with Tim for having pointed out the risk. "I can't go against orders."

"Well, the pump won't be repaired until you retimber that roof," Tim said. "Get some carpenters down here and get it fixed." He strode back toward the hoist.

"Who the hell do you think you are to give orders?" Bent yelled after him.

"I'm the man with the pump," Tim replied. He knew he was overstepping his authority, but he could almost see the timber buckling. If it came down tomorrow and buried some poor devil alive, it would be cold comfort to be able to say "I told you so."

Tim clanged the cage door closed. "Fix it, unless you want me to leave you up to your nose in water."

After a grisly three hours in the pump shaft, during which he had nightmares about being buried alive himself, Tim found the clog: a piece of grating somehow sucked into the intake, which had drawn a layer of gravel into its mesh until the whole snarl produced an immovable blockage. Tim cleared it by hand, clinging like a monkey to a webbing sling and the side of the shaft.

When he nearly had it, he slipped, slithering down the last few feet of the shaft with frightening speed. The sump was beneath him, full enough of hot water to scald him to death. He grasped at the end of the pump rod and clung, swinging above the water. Slowly he pulled himself up, wrapping his feet around the rod. The steam made his head swim. He inched up the rod another foot and grabbed the webbing, praying it wouldn't break. With another lunge, he was back in the sling.

He waited until his heart quit pounding, then he cleared the rest of the intake. Twenty minutes later he emerged, lacerated and coughing, to the sound of furious voices outside the pump room.

"You've done it now," Stebbins informed him. The chief engineer was sitting at his desk with a woolen shawl around his shoulders—it was icy cold on the surface—trying to ignore the shouting in the yard. "Some of the miners found out you told Bent to retimber that roof and that Bent didn't want to, and now they're having it out with the station bosses and those louts Ormond sent." He caught Tim's arm. "No, don't you go out there. You've made enough ruckus."

"I'm an engineer, damn it. I'm supposed to be concerned with safety." He pulled his boots off. They had done him very little good. He was soaked from head to toe.

"Pay some mind to your own, then," Stebbins advised him. "I've worked in the mines all my life. You won't change things, son. Hard times bring hard economics."

"Not at the price of some man's life!" Tim said indignantly.

"At any price." Stebbins cocked a thin gray eyebrow at Tim. "Ormond's given orders: No one but the superintendent is empowered to order a repair from now on. You haven't endeared yourself in that quarter, lad. He wants to see you."

"I'll see him," Tim muttered.

"Not now, you won't," Stebbins said. "You stay out of the yard."

As he spoke, the voices outside rose to a furious pitch, and a rock smashed through the pump-house window. The reverberating blast of a shotgun followed it, and Stebbins dived for the floor under his desk.

Tim flung the door open. The miners in the yard were running now, scattering as they ran through the streets, their footsteps eerily silent in the snow. One miner lay still, facedown. Tim started to run to him, and a company guard grabbed his arm.

"Leave him be, sonny."

"Take your hands off me!" Tim swung at him and connected with something; he wasn't sure what, because the guard swung his shotgun and cracked Tim across the ribs with it. Tim dropped and staggered up again.

"You made enough trouble," the guard said. He spat in the snow, daring Tim to try again. Tim advanced cautiously. He didn't have a gun, but he didn't think the guard would go so far as to shoot him, although he wasn't sure. If he could wrestle that shotgun away from him . . .

"Ormond's right mad at you," the guard said. "Maybe we'll just get you out of his hair."

"Forget it," the other guard said abruptly. "They got him." He sounded satisfied.

Tim turned to look and saw that two miners had crept back warily and were dragging their fallen comrade away. His body left a bright-red track in the snow.

"Oh, God," Tim whispered.

"Give them something to think about," the guards said. They watched the progress impassively, shotguns cradled now across their arms.

Stebbins came out of the pump house. He took Tim by the arm. "Come in. There's nothing else you can do now." He looked soberly at Tim. "I'll say one thing: You've got nerve."

Tim tossed a pebble up at Isabella Ormond's window. When he caught a brief flash of movement in the lamplight behind it, he moved back into the shadow of the porch.

In a few minutes Isabella, bundled in a dark cloak, came around the back of the house. It was six-thirty and fully dark, except for the pale glow of a half-moon on the snow.

"Daddy would kill me if he knew I was out here," she whispered. "He's furious with you."

Tim led her into the deeper shadows behind a building around the corner. "I know." He had had a blistering interview with John Ormond earlier that evening. In one breath Mr. Ormond had informed him that he was a whippersnapper, a naive fool, and too big for his britches. Tim was to do exactly what Mr. Stebbins told him and not one thing more. Furthermore, Tim was forbidden to call on Isabella for two weeks, during

which time he was to reflect on the error of his ways
and learn which side his bread was buttered on. Tim
had not been able to get a word in edgewise, but he
hadn't been able to think of a word that would not have
gotten him fired. Thank goodness the miner who had
been shot was probably going to live.

"He'll calm down in a day or so," Isabella soothed.
"I'll talk to him when I think it's a good time. I couldn't
bear it if you didn't spend Christmas with us."

"I don't know," Tim said dubiously. "I can't go
back with my hat in my hand and tell him I think he's
right. I don't."

"Then don't," Isabella whispered. She took his hand
and led him across the street, where they could sit in
the portico of the Presbyterian church. She leaned her
head against his shoulder. "Just shake hands and don't
argue with him. That's all he wants."

Her hair, under her cloak's hood, smelled like
lilacs, and the warm, soft feel of her in his arms was
heady and inviting. Tim sat with his conscience chewing at him both because he had not argued with John
Ormond and because now he was here, skulking out of
sight, with Ormond's daughter.

"It will be all right." Isabella turned her face
toward his. She lifted her lips, and Tim pushed his conscience away and kissed her.

And so it came about that on Christmas Day Tim
found himself sitting, in a stiflingly overheated room, at
John Ormond's dinner table, listening to Mrs. Ormond
discuss her work among the poor.

"It's very difficult," she complained over her bowl
of turtle soup. "They can be stubborn and not willing to
be helped, so many of them. If they do manage to come
upon a few dollars, most will only spend it on drink."

"It's a cheap oblivion," Mr. Palmer, a schoolteacher,
said. "It buys forgetfulness. Maybe that's a help." He
was young and balding and had been invited to round
out the table as a dinner partner for Isabella's older
sister, Laney.

"They simply can't learn to save," Mrs. Ormond went on. "That's all it is. No responsibility." She frowned at the notion under her severely crimped fringe of gray curls. She was a stout, square-jawed woman with a look of certainty. A rope of pearls adorned her aqua satin gown. "I'm sure your mother has encountered the same situation in Portland, has she not, Mr. Holt?"

"I expect people are pretty much the same anywhere," Tim murmured. He didn't think Mrs. Ormond would be enlightened by Alexandra's views on the poor, since they corresponded rather more closely to Mr. Palmer's than her own.

As Mrs. Ormond continued to inform him about how the poor ought to conduct their lives, Tim looked around the dining room. It was papered in dark red, which was the fashionable color just now. Large paintings in heavy gilt frames hung on the walls. Most of the paintings were of some sort of game, most of it dead, arranged beside a shooting bag or in a retriever's mouth. Tim found the artwork an admirable appetite suppressant.

On the table was a meal that would have fed the poor for several weeks if it didn't give them indigestion: a ham, a standing rib roast of beef, mashed potatoes drenched in butter, fruit preserved in a gelatinous syrup, green beans that had been boiled and put up in summer, then boiled again in preparation for dinner. On the sideboard stood a mountainous plum pudding, which Mr. Ormond would light as a cap to the evening's festivities. There had been sherry before dinner, and claret with it. Apparently Mrs. Ormond's strictures against strong drink did not extend to her own table.

"Tell me about your family, Mr. Holt," Mrs. Ormond requested, having disposed of the poor.

"I have a younger brother and sister. Mike's still in school, and Sally's going on five. And an older sister. That's Janessa."

"Is she married?" Mrs. Ormond inquired.

"No, ma'am. She's in school in California. She's going to take up medicine."

"Good heavens," Mrs. Ormond said faintly.

"Well, I call that intrepid of her," Mr. Palmer commended.

"Isabella has no such pretentions," Mrs. Ormond informed Tim confidentially. She didn't appear to care how Mr. Palmer would characterize it. "Isabella has bent all her studies to womanly pursuits and to learning how to keep a proper household. She goes with me when I do my visiting among the less fortunate and is always so good with the little ones."

"Mother!" Isabella blushed.

"Come now, my dear," Mr. Ormond said genially to his wife. "You make her sound like a drudge. Isabella has great talent at the piano and at painting. She makes the sun shine around here, don't you, Puss?"

Tim saw that Laney was looking grimly at her plate. Laney, unfortunately, favored her mother and was not thought to have Isabella's prospects. Isabella had confided that her parents would be satisfied if Laney could snare Mr. Palmer.

"Now, let's light the pudding!" Mr. Ormond said after a pair of silent and efficient maids had cleared the table. "A proper Christmas pudding to celebrate the happy season." He beamed at them over it, including Tim in the general good cheer. "Come and help me, my boy. We'll let bygones be bygones," he murmured as Tim held the matches while Mr. Ormond uncorked the brandy bottle. "Everyone's entitled to a mistake or two, as long as they learn from it." He splashed the pudding liberally with brandy, and it blazed up as he applied a match to the liquor in the plate.

After dinner they retired to the parlor, where, as Mr. Ormond said coyly, there were "one or two little surprises to exchange."

Tim, who had agonized over Isabella's present, produced a book of Elizabeth Barrett Browning's poetry, for which she thanked him prettily and gave him in return a silver watch chain with a miniature ingot on it.

"Comstock silver, my boy," Mr. Ormond said. "From the Ninevah Mine."

A Christmas tree, adorned with red glass balls and ornaments of paper lace, dominated the room. The parlor smelled appealingly of pine, but the temperature, like that of the dining room, seemed to Tim to be at least ten degrees above what was needed, and the sensation was not lessened when Mrs. Ormond produced mulled cider to drink. After all the presents had been opened and Isabella had happily displayed a necklace of pearls, similar to her mother's, the gift of her parents, she was urged by her father to the piano stool to play Christmas carols for them.

They gathered around as she propped her sheet music on the piano and sang "God Rest You, Merry Gentlemen" and "Angels We Have Heard On High."

Snow was falling again outside the heavily draped parlor windows as she began "The Wassail Song."

The room seemed to be getting hotter, and Tim mopped his brow with his handkerchief, feeling guilty about being so hot when he knew that some of the miners' shacks were probably pitilessly cold. He forced himself to concentrate on the carol. The last verse seemed to have an ominous air about it:

> Good Master and good Mistress,
> While you're sitting by the fire,
> Pray think of us poor children
> Who've wandered in the mire.

Isabella's youthful soprano rode happily on the music, and as she finished the song, her right hand touched her new pearls briefly with proprietary pride. Tim glanced at Laney and saw that she had picked up the abandoned book of poetry and was reading it.

All in all, it was not an entirely successful party.

"To Christmas." Annie Malone lifted her champagne glass and looked at Sam Brentwood over its rim. The flicker of the fire made her face young and carefree, easing away the fine triangular wrinkles at the corners of her eyes.

"To good company," Sam responded, smiling back. They were sitting on cushions piled on the carpet in front of the fireplace. Its white marble pilasters glowed as rose-gold as Annie's hair. A silver bowl of nuts and figs rested beside the ornate brass kindling basket, and Sam and Annie were sharing a nutcracker and tossing their shells into the fire. Annie's housekeeper, Emma, had departed, laden with the gaily wrapped presents for Belle and the boys, and the gas lamps in the parlor were turned low so as not to compete with the firelight. Sam's Christmas offering, a pair of tortoiseshell combs that had taken nearly his last dime, were tucked into Annie's hair. Her gift to him had been more practical: a new overcoat ordered from the best store in San Francisco.

"I hope it isn't going to bother you," Annie had said as he opened it, "that I have money."

"While I don't?" Sam asked. "You deserve money." He tried on the coat and admired his reflection in a monstrous gilt mirror. The coat had a fur collar and felt heavy, luxurious, as if it would protect him forever from vexation and privation. "Not that I don't want money," he said as he carefully refolded the coat and hung it over the back of the settee. "But I don't resent the fact that you have it. I don't believe in spiteful pride."

"Good," Annie approved. She had arrayed herself for their solitary holiday dinner in black silk taffeta and diamonds. Not too many diamonds, remembering Sam's strictures about feathers.

Sam smoothed the coat with his hand and came to stand by Annie. "Can I say 'thank you'?" he asked huskily.

Annie smiled at him, and he kissed her lingeringly. When his hands began to move caressingly down her back, she gently pushed him away, and they went and sat by the fire. They would make love, she knew, but not just yet.

So now they sat on Annie's paisley Turkish cushions and cracked walnuts. Annie was half lying on the cushions, feet crossed at the ankles, eating a fig.

"Odalisque," Sam said.

"What's that?"

"The sultan's harem girl," he answered. "They spend all their time lounging on cushions."

"I've heard of them," Annie said. "But I never heard them called a whatever it was you said."

"Odalisque." Sam scooted a little closer so that he knelt by the dark pool of her skirt.

"You know more words I never heard of than anybody I ever met," Annie said.

"Here's one for you." Sam pulled her feet into his lap and took her shoes off. "Fetishist."

"What's that?" Annie asked, laughing.

"Someone with a passion for strange objects," Sam said. "Women's feet, for instance."

"Oh, for goodness' sake." Annie pulled her feet back. "I never went to school much past fourth grade, but I bet Miss Woodie wouldn't of taught that one in spelling class."

"Why'd you quit?" Sam asked.

"Ma needed me at home. There wasn't anybody but me to mind the little ones while she worked. Ma took in washing, to help us get by. Pa wasn't any use. All he ever did was drink. He was a railroad man, but he got his leg hurt somehow and couldn't work anymore. I think that's what made him so mean." Annie looked broodingly at the fire. "I don't tell most people all this. But you told me about your folks. Franz and all. Pa used to try to get in bed with me sometimes, too. You got a word for that?"

"My God," Sam said. He put an arm around her. "Yeah, I have a word for it."

"I never would let him. I got a paring knife and put it under my pillow. I told him I'd kill him if he tried it. I lit out when I was sixteen."

"How did you wind up here?" Sam lay down on his elbow behind her, so that her head leaned against his shirt front, his arm over her waist.

"Lots of people were heading this way. Those were the boom days, Sam, when everybody thought the streets were paved with silver, and they were nearly right. I met Joe on the trail. We lived in a tent the first year, and then we struck a vein. It just didn't ever seem to run out. I had champagne for the first time in my life, sitting in that tent, with my feet on a trunk filled with new clothes I'd bought and didn't have any place to hang up. That was before this house was finished. Joe wouldn't go to a hotel. He said we'd go straight from that tent to this house, so we'd always remember the difference."

"Do you miss him?" Sam whispered.

"Sometimes. Not as much as I used to. We weren't married very long. Joe and the vein gave out about the same time."

"How long ago was that?"

"Ten years. But I was careful with the money. I put it in railroads and steel, not silver mines. I saw what happened to Eilley Bowers."

"The Washoe seeress," Sam recalled. "You'd do fine. Big gold earrings and a gypsy scarf." He took her hand and turned it palm upward. "It's already crossed with silver, isn't it?" he murmured.

"I can't see the future," Annie said. "Eilley Bowers couldn't either, poor thing, or she wouldn't have ended up like she did."

"Maybe I'll tell your fortune," he offered. He spread her hand out, then traced the lines in the palm. "You will meet a dark stranger," he said solemnly. His lips brushed the side of her neck.

"Does it say anything about how old he is?" Annie inquired.

"Does that bother you?" Sam asked.

"Well, it ought to," Annie said. She sat up.

"But does it?" He stretched out on the cushions, head propped on one hand, and looked up at her, the firelight giving his face a reckless and unpredictable look.

There was something indefinably untamed about him, Annie thought, not quite civilized, and older than his years. And the physical reaction he produced in her owed nothing to his age but a great deal to that feral charm.

Outside, bells began to peal, faint but joyous, welcoming parishioners to the evening service at St. Mary's. Annie leaned toward Sam. He reached up and pulled the tortoiseshell combs and then the pins from her hair, letting it flow over her shoulders, cascading like water between his fingers. He was not as inexperienced as his age might have suggested. He knew, for instance, how to unhook a set of stays with one hand.

IX

Christmas in Southern California was a different proposition entirely from anything Janessa had encountered in either Oregon or Virginia. In December it was still shirt-sleeve weather in the daytime, although the surrounding hills were bare and brown. They were always brown, Mrs. Burnside said, except in April, when the land turned magically, beautifully green for a month.

Janessa thought longingly of going home for the holiday, but she had decided against it. She needed the time to cram for the exams she would take in January, and she knew she wouldn't study at home; Christmas on the ranch was too much fun. There would be parties, theater expeditions, maybe even skating if the river froze in time. Janessa glared balefully at a cloudless sky, then went into the school's basement, where she was allotted a small cubbyhole cupboard to stash her books, to retrieve Hamilton's text on obstetrics.

A dozen students were in the hallway, also rummaging for notebooks and texts. Janessa opened the door of her cupboard, giving it a good yank because it always stuck. It seemed to her that there was a sudden small, alert silence in the hall behind her, and then the thing tumbled at her feet, bloodless and white, the flayed tendons of its fingers curled as if to grasp her skirts.

Janessa dropped her satchel of books and stumbled backward in a spilt second of terror before she saw the

141

thing for what it was: a severed arm from the pathology laboratory. It reeked of formaldehyde, and there was a wet smear on the floor where it had slid along the tiles.

An outburst of guffaws ringed her, twelve howling men holding their sides, dropping their books in laughter.

Janessa bent and picked up the arm, weighing it in her hands. The skin felt cool to the touch, and slick. She looked at the men and resisted the urge to fling the thing at them.

"Can we lend you a hand, Miss Holt?" someone chortled, creating another burst of stamping and guffaws.

Janessa put the arm on the floor, fetched the Hamilton text from her cupboard, and put it in the satchel with the rest. Then she picked up the arm again and walked down the hall with it, past the laughing men. As she pushed open the door at the end of the hall and went into the pathology laboratory, she could hear the voices behind her: "God, she's a cool one."

"A real cold fish. That's what happens when they try to act like men."

"She's half-Indian, did you know? She's not even white. They aren't like regular people."

"Then how'd she get in here?"

"Her old man's got money. I heard her ma was some Indian squaw he took for a tumble. He's a big man in Oregon."

"That doesn't give him the right to pass off his half-breed brat on us."

Stone faced, Janessa presented the arm to Milton, the ancient pharmacist who ran the lab as part of his multiple duties as building manager, druggist, and embalmer.

The men watched her come out and march up the stairs, her back straight.

"I tell you what," one of them said. "Let's try it on Miss Thoms. I bet she cries."

Janessa arrived five minutes late for class and slid into the seat beside Charley. He sniffed suspiciously. She had scrubbed her hands under the pump, but she knew she smelled of formaldehyde. A faint snicker could be heard behind her. Eliza Thoms gave her a sympathetic look from her usual seat in the corner.

"Miss Holt," Dr. Dunbar said with elaborate sarcasm, "if you are eager to begin your holiday early, please let me know. Otherwise, since this is the last class of the term, I am hopeful that you would strive to be completely with us."

"I'm sorry, sir," Janessa murmured. "I was delayed."

Charley nudged her, under cover of picking his pen off the floor. "What happened?"

"I'll tell you later," Janessa hissed at him. She opened the textbook and tried to concentrate on Dr. Dunbar's lecture. It was difficult: She knew her face was scarlet, and she was still quivering with fury.

Dr. Dunbar's obstetrics lesson was the last lecture of the last day of the term, and most of the students were restive. They fidgeted in their seats, shuffling feet and notebooks, as Dr. Dunbar droned on in much the same manner as the fly that circled his head in ever-narrowing orbits. The students watched with interest to see if it would land on his head.

"Perhaps Mr. Carstairs would describe for us the proper approach to be taken with a difficult lying-in?"

Dr. Dunbar looked at Mr. Carstairs, who jumped and stared at him wildly. A silence settled while Mr. Carstairs tried vainly to pretend that he had not been daydreaming. Janessa raised her hand.

Dr. Dunbar glared at her. "Miss Holt, if I require your opinion, I shall ask for it."

"You haven't asked for it all term," Janessa said.

"Indeed? Very well, since you have volunteered, you may now offer it."

"It is useful to have the mother either kneel or stand, sir, so that she is laboring with the force of gravity and not against it."

"Women are not animals in the barn, Miss Holt. May I ask where you picked up this dubious piece of advice?"

"From my mother." There was an audible snicker

behind her at that. "The technique was also used with good outcome by Dr. Robert Martin in Portland," she added stiffly.

"Yes, I believe I've been told you did a preceptorship with a Dr. Martin." Dr. Dunbar peered at her through his pince-nez. He was a small man, with a dark vandyke beard and beady eyes that seemed to drill through any student he was questioning. "Do you have any other tidbits to offer us contrary to common knowledge and common sense?"

"No, sir. I am here to learn obstetrics from you. I have made certain general observations, however."

"Pray enlighten us."

Janessa gritted her teeth. She knew he was baiting her, but she wasn't going to back down. "I have observed that contrary to the usual practice among the well-to-do, a new mother seems to mend more quickly if she is up and about in a few days rather than keeping to her bed. Among the Indians, the women are generally up the same day, and they have relatively few postpartum difficulties."

"Miss Holt, what a delicate and gently bred white woman may achieve is not to be compared to a savage whose constitution has already been inured to privation. And now if you will permit me, I will explain to you why I have declined to call upon you these past few months—for precisely the reason you have just demonstrated. This is a medical lecture hall, not a medicine show. I will not have an ignorant female spouting Indian mumbo jumbo and antiquated techniques learned from some frontier hack. If you wish to study medicine at this college, I would advise you to concentrate on modern techniques and the opinions of those who know what they're talking about."

"Yes, sir." Janessa managed to get the words out without her voice breaking. *I am twenty-six years old,* she told herself grimly. *I am not going to let this supercilious son of a dog make me cry.*

"Now, if you gentlemen can turn your attention to the matter at hand"—Dr. Dunbar addressed the class, ignoring Miss Thoms as well—"we will try to answer the question that Mr. Carstairs found perplexing."

As Dr. Dunbar expounded on the accepted procedures to be followed in a difficult birth, Charley passed a note sideways to Janessa under the edge of his desk: *Women just have the babies. What do they know about it?*

She smiled and tucked the note into her textbook. She would like to see Dr. Dunbar and his patron saint, Dr. Hamilton, author of the text, lying on their backs in bed, posteriors elevated, trying to push a baby uphill for the convenience of some doctor. Preferably Dr. Dunbar would be surrounded by seven or eight unsympathetic female physicians who would tell him with each labor pain that it wasn't nearly as bad as he thought it was, and in any case it was man's lot in life. *God's will, Dr. Dunbar. We must all accept God's will.*

Janessa's mouth twitched, and she looked sideways at Charley, who was listening to Dr. Dunbar with every indication of pious attention. *Good old Charley,* she thought. She was aware that the other students thought he was something of a stuffed shirt, primarily because he didn't get drunk with them or engage in asinine stunts such as putting the anatomy-lab skeleton, in gown and mortarboard, in a chair at the dean's desk.

Charley was thirty, and he had gotten that kind of thing out of his system years ago at the University of Virginia. He hadn't been above it then, as Janessa recalled, but people had to grow up sometime. She was also aware that Charley could have gone to the University of Virginia for his medical training. She didn't accept his glib explanation that the gap between his undergraduate studies and medical school was a handicap. Most medical schools didn't even require an undergraduate degree for entrance.

Charley wasn't ever going to admit it to her, but she knew he had come to California because the university admitted women, albeit reluctantly. He had known he was her last chance, she thought. Something to cling to while she got her nerve up. He had been right, too.

If it wasn't for Charley, she might have fled by now from the hatred that was sometimes so palpable that she could feel it wrapping around her, like a vapor. Eliza Thoms was finding it tough going, too, and she had only her sex to live down.

As Dr. Dunbar concluded his lecture, his students were already stuffing their pens and books into their satchels, eager to begin their holiday. With Charley beside her, no one made further remarks to Janessa, and she was grateful for his solid presence—not to fight her battles for her, but just to be there, friend and confidant, whom she could cry in front of if she felt like it.

"Don't forget Christmas dinner," she told him as they parted at the corner. Charley wasn't going home, either; it was too far. "Mrs. Burnside says you're invited."

"I'll be there," he said. "What happened to you before old Dunbar's lecture?"

Janessa told him.

"You want me to walk you home?"

"For heaven's sake, no," she said. "They aren't going to pop out at me from behind a bush and say 'Boo!' I'm all right now. I was just angry."

"Good," Charley said. "As long as you stay angry, you'll be too pigheaded to let them win." He set off up the street with a wave of his hand.

Janessa, turning her own way, saw the dean bearing down on her. She waited for him uneasily.

Dr. Francis looked at her speculatively. "Walk a way with me, Miss Holt," he requested.

"Certainly, Doctor."

"I understand you were the victim of an unfortunate incident of hazing."

"Yes." That seemed a little too curt. "You warned me when I applied," she added.

"I did." The dean was a tall man, with dark red hair going gray and a stalking gait like a heron. He modified his steps to match hers. "It is the intention of this university to graduate female physicians. Those of us who made that decision believe that it will benefit both the university and the practice of medicine. But a statement of principle is just that. It cannot alter the convictions of those who disagree with it, and there were many who disagreed. We can change the status quo by admitting women, but it may take another generation to change minds. Are you still prepared to put up with that?"

"Do I have any choice?" Janessa asked. "I mean that seriously. I'm not being flip."

"Not if you're going to stay here," Dr. Francis said. "If women are going to be successful as physicians, they must prove that they can do so with no special concessions. Otherwise, we give credence to the arguments of the opposition. I cannot threaten your fellow students into refraining from putting cadavers into your cupboard, or even from insulting your birth and breeding, because I would not do so for a male student. For that same reason I am not offering to carry your satchel as we walk or patting your hand and calling you 'my dear.' It may not seem fair, but those are the facts. You are fighting the battle for future female students, whether you like it or not."

"I don't, much," Janessa said frankly.

"The vanguard is never a pleasant place to be," the dean sympathized.

"What an unusual gift." Mrs. Bellow regarded the stethoscope in Janessa's lap with an uncertain air. Her expression said plainly that she thought candy might have been more appropriate.

Dinner concluded, Mrs. Burnside's boarders had gathered in her parlor to exchange gifts. These were mostly token gestures, but everyone had given everyone else something. Fifi, adorned for the occasion with a gigantic red bow, was sprawled on the hall floor, eating hers: It was a shinbone, and she wasn't allowed in the parlor until she finished it because she drooled. Mr. Anderson and Mrs. Bellow were of the opinion that dogs and shinbones belonged in the backyard, but they knew better than to express that in Mrs. Burnside's company.

Janessa knew that the stethoscope Charley had given her was nickel plated, and the best that could be bought.

"Your father wrote me that they were sending you the bag," Charley said, admiring it. "This is my contribution to it."

Smiling, Janessa slipped the stethoscope into the new black-leather satchel at her feet. "I'm afraid I wasn't so practical." She handed Charley a wrapped package.

Charley opened the present, and his eyes lit up. It was *Departmental Ditties* by Rudyard Kipling, bound in green calfskin. "Oh, famous! I've read some of his work in magazines."

"My brother Mike adores him," Janessa said. "I thought you might have a touch of the same wandering foot."

Mr. Pepperdine peered over Charley's shoulder. "He's the fellow who writes about India."

"Nasty heathen climate," Mrs. Bellow said. "And dirty heathen people. I should think you'd prefer nice stories about your own kind."

"I'm going to be a doctor, Mrs. B.," Charley said cheerfully. "Under the skin, they're all my own kind."

"That's an interesting supposition," Colonel Hapgood said. "If the skin were removed, Mr. Lawrence, could you tell a man's nationality?"

"I expect you could distinguish race by bone structure," Charley answered. "I doubt you could get much closer than that. One man's guts are pretty much like another's."

"Mr. Lawrence!" Mrs. Bellow exclaimed in an aggrieved tone.

"Certainly not," Mr. Anderson said, affronted.

Miss Gillette listened in fascination.

"You've done it now," Mrs. Burnside said to Charley. "They'll be fighting for a week, trying to prove their innards don't look like a Chinaman's."

"Well, I can't prove it," Charley said. "They haven't let us do torso dissections yet."

"And where do you get these torsos, young man?" Mr. Anderson wagged a finger under Charley's nose. "That's what I want to know."

"Poorhouse deaths mostly," Charley replied. He wondered if the conversation was getting a little out of hand. "Sometimes someone wills his body to the school."

"Ha! Grave robbing," Mr. Anderson said. "Don't try to fool me, young man. I know what those schools are up to! I read the *Police Gazette*."

"Not at all," Charley protested mildly. "Not these days, I assure you." Twenty years ago, religious opinion had been so violently against dissection that there hadn't been any other way to obtain a cadaver. He suspected that robbing graves still happened occasionally, but Janessa was giving him a look that said that if he knew what was good for him, he wouldn't say so.

"And what if nobody dies, eh?" Mr. Anderson was not to be deterred.

"Why, then we wait for a hanging," Janessa said with as innocent a smile as she could muster.

There was a faint moan from Mrs. Bellow, and Mrs. Burnside stepped in. "You two are extremely naughty," she told Janessa and Charley. "Clarice has gone home, so you just go in the kitchen and fix the eggnog until you can behave yourselves."

"Yes, ma'am." They left, trying to look penitent.

"Knowledge, Mr. Anderson," Miss Gillette said behind them, her words passionate, the voice of a believer. "We must have knowledge."

Janessa took the pitcher of eggnog out of Mrs. Burnside's wooden icebox and poured its contents into the punchbowl. "You're hopeless," she told Charley. "How could you?"

"Thirst for knowledge," Charley said. "Just ask Miss Gillette."

"Try to confine yourself to a thirst for eggnog," Janessa said, but his expression was so mischievous that she put an arm around him and kissed his cheek. "Merry Christmas, you devil."

Charley put his hands on her shoulders and returned the kiss, on her lips. Janessa blinked at him in surprise. "Merry Christmas," he said blandly.

Janessa gave the eggnog a stir, thoughtfully. "Do you suppose we ought to put some whiskey in this?" she asked him.

"Oh, I should think so," Charley said.

Janessa got the bottle from the top shelf next to the coal stove, brought it back to the table, and poured a dollop in.

"I'll carry it," Charley offered. He picked up the cut-glass bowl and edged carefully through the swinging door. Janessa followed. In the dining room she paused before the mirror. She had a sprig of holly in her hair. Her reflection looked unexpectedly jaunty to her.

"Excellent," Mrs. Burnside approved. She began ladling eggnog into the cut-glass cups that were arrayed on a tea table. Fifi leaned against her shoulder, breathing heavily, lending a moist odor of dog breath to the scent of cinnamon and pine. Mrs. Burnside put a saucer of eggnog on the floor for her, and another under the table, where Fifi couldn't get at it, for Bill, the marmalade cat.

"I suppose it was too much to hope for," Mrs. Bellow said as Fifi, having finished with the shinbone, polished the bowl with a tongue the size of a washcloth and looked around for more, "that that animal would not be allowed to join us."

"It's Christmas," Janessa defended. She scratched Fifi's ears contentedly and thought that it was a mercy that Mrs. Burnside didn't keep a cow. After four months' acquaintance with her landlady, Janessa was certain that if she did, the cow would undoubtedly be in the parlor, too.

Mrs. Burnside lifted her cup of eggnog in a toast to her boarders. "To good company. To Christmas." She smiled at Miss Gillette. "To knowledge."

*   *   *

When Charley had gone and the other boarders, possibly aided by the doctored eggnog, were asleep, Janessa lay under her quilt, staring at the un-Christmas-like vista of palm trees outside her window. The eggnog didn't seem to have had any effect on her. This was the first Christmas in years that she had spent away from home, and her life felt oddly rearranged by it—or by something.

Finally she got up, put her wrapper on, and slipped downstairs, feeling carefully with her toes in the darkness for the floor below the bottom step. Fifi had a habit of sleeping there and was perfectly invisible in the dark. A thud and an oath from the hall always meant that someone had fallen over her.

She wasn't there now, though, and Janessa padded silently into the kitchen, in search of hot milk. A light beneath the door from the parlor off the dining room caught her eye, and she backtracked, skirting around the dining room table, to investigate.

Only one gas lamp burned in the parlor, turned low. Janessa thought that it must have been forgotten, and she was about to go in and turn it off when she noticed Mrs. Burnside sitting in her chair, with Fifi on her feet. The old lady looked up, and in the dim light Janessa saw the sheen of tears on her wrinkled cheeks.

"Whatever is wrong?" Janessa hurried over and knelt beside her landlady.

"Oh, my dear, I thought you were all asleep." Mrs. Burnside wiped her face with her handkerchief.

"I couldn't sleep," Janessa said. "Are you all right?"

" 'All right' is a relative term. I always get melancholy at Christmas." Janessa saw a half-filled cup of eggnog beside Mrs. Burnside on the table, and the whiskey bottle with it, with a spoon in a red-glass candy dish. "I got the news about Claude at Christmas."

"Your husband?" Janessa whispered.

"No. He was a feckless man, and he's been gone too many years to count. Claude was my son. He was all I ever had, and he was killed the week before Christmas."

"How terrible for you." There wasn't any right thing to say to something like that and no solace to be offered, really.

"It was a long time ago. But sometimes I miss him so." Mrs. Burnside looked at Janessa. "And why can't you sleep, child? You are too young for tragedy, I hope."

Janessa wrapped her arms around her knees, wriggling her toes under the warmth of Fifi's fur. "I don't know. I just don't seem to be able to."

Mrs. Burnside found a clean cup and ladled eggnog into it. She added another dollop of whiskey from the bottle and handed it to Janessa. "You and Mr. Lawrence didn't use quite a heavy enough hand."

Janessa sipped the eggnog. Mrs. Burnside's hand was plenty heavy enough.

"Would it have something to do with Mr. Lawrence?" Mrs. Burnside asked.

"I don't think so." Janessa thought about it. "He kissed me," she said, surprised.

"Heavens, you mean he never had before?"

"No. We're friends. Charley's like a brother."

"Not entirely, it would appear," Mrs. Burnside remarked.

"It's Christmas." Janessa waved the cup as if to explain the oddities of the season.

"You don't appear to have thought this out very well," Mrs. Burnside said. "I had always assumed the two of you were unofficially engaged."

"I never thought about getting married at all," Janessa confessed. Not entirely the truth, but close enough. She had certainly never thought about marrying Charley. "A husband wouldn't want me to practice."

"Men are like that," Mrs. Burnside agreed. She refilled her cup and Janessa's with another addition from the whiskey bottle. "Have some more, dear. At least you'll sleep."

"I don't understand men," Janessa confessed.

"I do," Mrs. Burnside said. "They're a test sent to try us."

Janessa smiled. "That's what one of my professors' wives always said. But I think she meant . . . well—"

"Sex?" Mrs. Burnside asked. "That's both underrated and overrated. "I suppose you know about—?"

"Well, I know how it's done," Janessa replied. "On paper, at any rate." She giggled. It must be the whiskey. "But I never . . . I'm curious, though. I've thought about it, just to see . . ."

Mrs. Burnside chuckled. "Like Miss Gillette, seeking knowledge?"

Janessa hooted. "Exactly."

"Well, I wouldn't," Mrs. Burnside advised. "There are consequences."

"I know," Janessa spluttered. "We've studied those. Oh, lord, if Charley could hear this conversation, he'd never kiss me again!" She laughed harder, and in a moment they were both laughing and rocking gleefully.

Janessa laid her head against Mrs. Burnside's chair, and the old lady put an arm around her. "What men don't know would probably do them a lot of good to hear," she observed.

Janessa awoke the next morning with a splitting headache and a new appreciation of her landlady, who, she guessed, had had a lot more whiskey than Janessa but was her usual chipper if somewhat acerbic self.

Honestly, I must be totally depraved, Janessa thought, gulping down a cooking spoonful of Lydia Pinkham's Vegetable Compound. *And talking about sex with Mrs. Burnside!* Unmarried ladies, no matter what their age, were not supposed to know about sex, much less discuss it in a drunken gab session with their landlady. Of course, one couldn't pursue a passion for medicine from the age of nine and not know things, but that knowledge had heretofore been strictly academic. Even when Janessa had thought she was going to marry Brice Amos, she had envisioned love only as a sort of rosy cloud, filled with walks in the rain, a young man who

tenderly kissed her fingertips, and other such staples of
ladies' magazine romances. She thought about what
Mrs. Burnside had said about Charley and flushed. She
didn't think Charley was the sort to stop at kissing
fingertips, if he got going.

Janessa put the bottle of Lydia Pinkham back on
the shelf. She had her doubts about its efficacy but
knew it to be about twenty-percent alcohol, which might
be what she needed right now. Mrs. Bellow swore by
it, and Janessa had a pretty good idea why: Mrs. Bellow
didn't approve of alcohol, but it probably had never
occurred to her that by dosing herself with Mrs.
Pinkham's compound she was imbibing a good shot of
the demon substance. And thank goodness Mrs. Bellow
hadn't heard that conversation last night. . . .

Finding the notion of breakfast revolting, Janessa
went back to her room and pulled out a textbook,
Diseases of the North American Population. It was difficult to let her mind stray toward dangerous subjects
while examining an illustration of someone's enlarged
liver.

The medical students sat for their exams a week
after the holidays. Janessa had seen Charley only infre-
quently since Christmas because, like the rest of them,
he did little else but study. When she encountered
him, she found her gaze shying away, then sliding back
in reluctant speculation. But he seemed so much his
usual self that she decided finally that Mrs. Burnside
had been wrong; Charley and she strayed no farther
from their old, comfortable familiarity.

The exams were a murderous process, in which
Janessa was relentlessly determined to do well, to spite
Dr. Dunbar and Dr. Osterman, and her fellow students
into the bargain. The dean, catching up to her on the
steps again, gave her the once-over and remarked that
she looked like a fresh corpse. Sleep, he added, was
generally held to improve performance. Janessa just
shook her head, went back to Mrs. Burnside's house,

and shut herself in her room with books and a pot of coffee.

Staggering up from her desk at the end of the last three-hour examination, she thought that she could sleep for a week. Shoving her examination book at Dr. Dunbar, she left without waiting for whatever acid comment he might have it in mind to make.

It was cold outside, as gray as a tin roof, with a biting wind. Janessa stood still on the porch, head thrown back, letting the cold shake her into enough energy to walk. A group of men came out the front door, shouting loudly at each other, asking how they had done, groaning theatrically at the possibility of failure.

They had not so much to prove, Janessa thought. Examinations were a game to them, and a failed exam could be taken over, despite the dire threats of Dr. Dunbar.

They rollicked past her down the steps, and Mr. Felts skidded to a jovial stop and backtracked to her side. "Miss Holt! Freed from the toils of care, eh?"

Janessa looked at him warily. "For the time being, Mr. Felts."

"Then y'ought to celebrate. Get out of that schoolmarm's outfit. It doesn't fool me for a minute." He sidled closer and lowered his voice confidentially. "I bet you've got something pretty to wear. I won't change my mind about female doctors, but we could be friends, if you know what I mean."

She stared at him, revolted, afraid that she knew exactly what he meant. "I think you ought to go catch up with your friends, Mr. Felts." The others had continued on their way, leaving her standing alone with him on the porch.

"Aw, come on now, Miss Holt. Jannie. Can I call you Jannie? You know you aren't bad looking, even for an Indian, and a girl's got to use what she can to her advantage, you know?"

Janessa backed away from him. "Mr. Felts, I hope I am misunderstanding you."

"Oh, I don't think so," he said cheerfully. He seemed impervious to suggestion. "You're not a prissy one. You take anatomy with the men, don't you? And your family's not too hidebound, either, from what I hear about your mother. So how about giving me some of it, and maybe you won't find any more arms in your cupboard."

Janessa, more in exasperation than in fury—Mr. Felts was so stupid and so young—drew her hand back and smacked him solidly across the cheek with her open palm. When maidenly protests did not serve, this was an accepted tactic for conveying to a gentleman that he had misconstrued one's character or wishes—or so said the *Ladies' Home Journal,* which also said that a lady should never find herself where she might be insulted in the first place. However, that august publication conceded that in cases of emergency . . .

It didn't work with Mr. Felts, who was laboring under a deadly misapprehension, probably that she was being coy. He grabbed her left hand and said, "Hey, come on, Jannie. If Lawrence can bring his fancy piece to school with him, you can let the rest of us have some."

Janessa drew her right arm back again, clenched her fist, and punched him in the nose.

Mr. Felts flew backward down the porch steps and sat down abruptly on the paving stones with an anguished howl. Blood ran down his upper lip and, ineffectively stanched by a pale and undecided mustache, dripped onto his white shirtfront. "You broke my nose," he said indistinctly, his voice muffled by pain. "You broke my *nose!*"

Janessa went down and peered at it. "I don't think so," she informed him. "But if you say one more word to me, I will."

She straightened and walked away, noting that as she did so, several interested faces popped out the windows above them.

"Felts is the laughingstock of the campus," Charley informed Janessa when he appeared at Mrs. Burnside's house the next morning after breakfast. "He has a bandage on his nose, and everyone says you punched him."

Janessa dragged Charley into the parlor, out of earshot of the other boarders. "Will you be quiet?" she hissed at him.

"Well, someone should have punched Felts in the snoot," Charley said. "I applaud your initiative."

"And what does Mr. Felts say?" she inquired.

"Felts isn't saying. He's sinking with mortification. But apparently there were witnesses, and they all have plenty to say. One of the campus wags composed a short ditty about it for the banjo and played it outside Felts's room." Charley's eyes were dancing with amusement.

Janessa glared at him. "I just got tired of him. It was unfeminine but effective."

"What did he do? His nose looks like a potato."

How satisfying. Janessa relented and grinned at Charley. "He made unwanted advances." She lowered her eyes and pretended to swoon. She didn't think she would tell Charley what Felts had said about him. Charley would probably damage something worse than Felts's nose if he heard about that. Nor did she want Charley to hear that particular piece of gossip.

But evidently Charley had already heard it. "Am I making your life difficult?" he asked, serious now.

"No," she said flatly. "You are probably the only reason I've stuck it out. Charley, if you abandon me to save my reputation, I will punch *you.*"

"All right, all right. Just asking."

"Good. Now are you going to take me on a picnic or not?" They had planned to celebrate their survival of examinations with an afternoon on the river.

"The basket's in the buggy," Charley said.

Janessa saw a rented gig hitched outside the gate. "I wangled four lemon tarts out of Clarice for dessert," she said.

Charley sighed. "I ought to move in here. I think Mrs. Gonzales makes her piecrust out of adobe." Mrs.

Gonzales was Charley's landlady, and she did her own cooking.

"Absolutely not," Janessa said. "That would be an utter scandal. You'll just have to starve."

They took Fifi with them because she was really a water dog and loved the river and because there seemed to Janessa to be something plainly platonic about picnicking with a 130-pound Newfoundland chaperon for company.

The Los Angeles River flowed past the Vache Frères vineyard east of the college, and unless it had been raining, it wasn't really much of a river at all. It meandered over a rock-strewn bed, and one could wade across it almost anywhere. They spread their picnic on a flat rock that had been smoothed by water over the years, and watched Fifi galumphing in the shallows, pouncing on frogs. The river never froze here. The cycle of life in Southern California seemed never to find an end or a rebirth. It just went on and on. ·

Janessa unlaced her shoes, rolled down her stockings, and put her feet in the water. In a second she snatched them out again, her toes curling.

"Snowmelt," Charley said, chuckling.

"I ought to have known. But the air's not cold."

"This is a strange and insidious place," he said. "Rather like falling down Alice's rabbit hole. When you come out the other end, everything seems to be very slightly askew, or not what it ought to be."

"Just the place for a snark," Janessa murmured.

Fifi came splashing through the shallows and lumbered onto the rock with them. She shook, sending a spray of cold, dog-scented water over them. The sky was brilliant, and the sun glinted off the water. Following heavy rains, the river was capable of becoming a muddy torrent, bearing splintered boards and uprooted trees downstream. Then it would flatten almost instantly into clear, deceptive shallows. Janessa felt that she, like Alice, might suddenly find herself growing to enormous size or forgetting familiar bones and ligaments and reciting instead strange and unintelligible names for things.

The examination results were posted two days later. A bulletin board full of lists, as grimly unarguable as those of the recording angel's, proclaimed each student's standing in each course taken. Somewhere on each list was a red line, consigning those who fell beneath it to the territory of failure. The hall was full of milling students—upperclassmen as well as those of Janessa's year—whooping with joy to find their names clinging to the paper above the line, or groaning with despair.

Janessa wriggled through the crowd unbothered. Even Mr. Felts, whose nose was still adorned with a bandage, was more concerned with his position on the awful lists than he was with her. She found her name, inscribed in fine script on each appropriate list, and her heart began to pound jubilantly. She was first in histology, fifth in anatomy, second in physiology and materia medica, and—oh, blessed revenge—first in obstetrics.

She located Charley's name, found him also to be within a few places of the top in each course, and retreated, allowing herself just a small, malevolent smile at Mr. Carstairs and Mr. Felts, who had flunked physiology.

Dr. Osterman passed her in the hall. "An excellent showing, Miss Holt," he murmured. "Although one trusts you will work a little harder on your anatomy this term."

She looked after his departing back. The old devil. Fifth was quite respectable in a class of twenty students, particularly a class with Charley in it. Charley had taken first honors. He seemed to have an almost encyclopedic memory for the names of minute parts. Janessa grinned, entirely satisfied with that first in obstetrics. Dr. Dunbar must have gritted his teeth while he graded her examination, but he was an honest soul; he wouldn't lower her marks for spite.

* * *

Neither, she discovered as the second term began, would Dr. Dunbar apologize. There was simply a cessation of his remarks concerning "Indian mumbo jumbo" as well as a tendency to invoke her name when he wished to shame the ignorant:

"The symptoms and principal method of treatment of puerperal fever? Quite blank, are we, Mr. Jurgen? Come, come, even Miss Holt has managed to grasp that procedure.

"And for a premature infant that fails to thrive, Mr. Carstairs? No? Dear me. Perhaps Miss Holt will enlighten us."

Goaded, Janessa cornered Dr. Dunbar in the hall. "I wish you would stop holding me up to the rest of the class, sir. It is making me disliked."

Dr. Dunbar's eyes registered eloquent surprise above his pince-nez. "I was under the impression that you were already disliked, Miss Holt."

"Exactly, sir." She looked back at him stubbornly.

"I am aware that you feel that you already have enough to try you, Miss Holt," Dr. Dunbar said. "I assure you that if you succeed in becoming a physician, you will encounter a great deal more."

"I had hoped, sir, not among my colleagues," she retorted.

"Oh, most particularly among your colleagues," Dr. Dunbar informed her. "You may practically count on it. So I shall continue to make use of what weapons I have on hand to stir the laggards into attention. You may think of it as character building."

"I see." Janessa began to turn, teeth gritted.

"Miss Holt."

She turned back.

Dr. Dunbar's eyes glinted with a certain amount of amusement now. "I have noted, however, that no more surprises have been left in your cupboard. It may interest you to know that you are acquiring a certain amount of respect in this college. Possibly aided by a modicum of fear," he added. "Considering the state of Mr. Felts's proboscis. You will have to content yourself with that."

*   *   *

Janessa, sitting at the old school desk in her room, filled her pen and thought. Her dad would want to know how she was doing, but he had enough on his mind right now. It wouldn't do to sound like a school-girl complaining because some bully had dipped her braids in the inkwell.

Thank you all for the wonderful leather bag. With the addition of Charley's stethoscope, I now have a kit to do any doctor proud. I hope you will be proud of me: I took first place in obstetrics and histology, and second in physiology and materia medica. (Fifth in anatomy, alas, but I intend to ask Charley to tutor me.)

The weather has been relentlessly sunny. We are still eating our lunch under the sycamore outside the brewery across the street from the school. The "medical student's lunch" has become an institution: beer from the brewery, a nickel sack of broken crackers from the cracker company, and a slice of cheese from the French grocery up the street. Clarice has offered over and over to pack me something better, but the only place to keep it cold is in the pathology laboratory, and by lunchtime it always smells like formaldehyde.

Last week all of Mrs. Burnside's boarders decided to have a barbecue in the backyard on Clarice's day off, and Mr. Anderson set fire to the steak, which Mr. Pepperdine put out with his hat. I am becoming quite fond of all of them—even Mrs. Bellow, who is a dreadful old gossip and spends all her time talking and knitting endlessly, like Mme. Dufarge, verbally chopping off the heads of miscreants. Miss Gillette is the secretary of the local League for Women's Suffrage, which I intend to join. (Mrs. Burnside says that women should vote because men have let the country go to hell in a hand basket.) Miss Gillette and Mr. Anderson got into a blazing row about it at the barbecue, which was how Mr. Anderson came to set the steak on fire, through not attending to it.

I had a letter and a Christmas package from Tim, and I think—by the various things he didn't say, and the way he didn't say them—that he has met a girl. He was very closemouthed about Sam, too, so I suspect that Sam is up to something, although he is apparently still mining, which surprises me. Shame on me for not being more charitable, since it's so close to Christmas. Goodwill toward one's fellow man seems to wear off awfully quickly, once the decorations come down.

Please give my love to Alexandra, and to Mike and Sally, and Stalking Horse and White Elk, and everyone else. Please tell Dr. Martin that I will write to him as soon as I can. I owe him a great deal (and you, too, for being patient with me) and I know he will be pleased to hear of my marks. I miss you all dreadfully, but everything is wonderful here.

> Love,
> Janessa

X

Portland, January 1888

"No, that isn't the whole story," Alexandra said, handing Toby back the letter. He was silent. "Well, do you think it is?"

"No, I expect not," Toby said. "But her marks are certainly wonderful, and if she doesn't want to tell us about the rest, I don't see why she should have to."

"Do you think I ought to write to Charley Lawrence?" Alexandra asked musingly. She took the letter back again, pondering it.

"I do not," Toby said. "Janessa knew she was going to have an uphill battle. That's why it took her so long to make up her mind. I don't think it will help to cosset her now. And from what she didn't say, I think matters between Janessa and Charley are at a delicate point at the moment."

"And I oughtn't to stick my oar in?" Alexandra chuckled. "You may be right. I wish I knew about Tim, too, though."

"I wish I knew about any of them," Toby said, exasperated. "Mike spends all his time making up lurid adventures and illustrating them with stereopticon slides and Marjorie White's photographs." Marjorie was a family friend and a successful photographer.

"Mike has a very visual sense of a story," Alexandra defended. "Do you know what he said to me? He said, 'If only you could make them move.'"

"He feels confined here," Toby said. "And I feel like a jailer. He told me yesterday that he knew I

163

intended him to inherit the Madrona, and he didn't want it."

"Not want it!" Alexandra looked shocked.

"He said he wanted it to come home to but not to be chained to."

Alexandra pounded her fists on the cushions of the settee in helpless fury. "If only he hadn't gotten sick. I always tried to take such good care of him, and I let him get sick!"

"You didn't." Toby took her hands and held them still. "Dr. Martin told you that you were in no way responsible. And you and Janessa nursed him until you were almost dead yourselves. Alex, we're lucky he lived."

"Then why do I feel responsible?"

"For the same reason I do." He bent his head and laid it against hers. "I don't suppose logic has much to do with it."

Alexandra sighed. "They all have such troubles. I want to shield them, make things come out right for them. Sally's the only one who's truly happy."

"Sally's five years old," Toby said. "The world's her oyster. Maybe if she's lucky, it'll stay that way."

"It usually doesn't," Alexandra said darkly. "Mine didn't." Alexandra had been six when the war began. As a young woman, she had hardly been able to remember a time when the world had been her oyster.

"That's life," Toby said. "It also comes round again. You survived. I survived. Why do you believe our children to be incapable of it?"

"Oh, I think they're capable. I just wish they didn't have to." She smiled up at him and touched his face. "Do I sound stupid?"

"No, you just have the most strongly developed maternal instinct of any woman I ever met. You mother the ranch hands. You even mother Juanita. I saw you putting a mustard plaster on her back and lecturing her about lacing her stays too tight."

"I didn't used to be like that," Alexandra muttered. "Maybe I'm just getting old."

Toby snorted. Alexandra was thirty-three. "If you're

old, where does that leave me? You're just six years older than Janessa. Maybe you could manage to stop mothering her," he suggested.

"Maybe I could."

"Good." Toby picked her up and set her down on his lap. "You can divert yourself by marshaling your equally excellent talents as a hostess. We have to have a party."

"Well, certainly. We have a party every spring."

"This will be different. A party with a lot of people you probably don't want to know."

Alexandra cocked her head up at him. "A political party?"

"Yes." Toby shook his head. "How I let Willis Larken talk me into this. . . . But they all say I've got to do it. It's a kind of ritual courtship."

"I see. And whom are we courting?"

"The state legislature. All the people who are running for the state legislature. All the people who will elect the people running for the state legislature."

"That's quite a mixed bag," Alexandra said.

"You don't know the half of it," Toby said. "We'll probably be lucky if there aren't a couple of fistfights."

Alexandra thought that that was probably an exaggeration, but experience had taught her that Portland took its politics seriously. The party was planned with as much strategy—and as many campaign meetings between Alexandra and her formidable mother-in-law, Eulalia—as Napoleon might have expended on his invasion of Russia.

"Toby simply never thinks about the logistics of things," Eulalia declared, seated amid an ocean of lists and menus.

"Well, he knows we will," Alexandra said. She knew perfectly well that if Toby had planned a party, Eulalia would have replanned it anyway.

"His father was the same way," Eulalia said. "One day, he said to me, 'We ought to invite some folks out here.' And the next day he came back from town with

fourteen people. There was nothing to feed them but
stew and corn bread, but that was all anybody else had
either, so it didn't really matter." Eulalia tilted her
head, looking at some point that seemed to be on the
far side of the wall.

Looking into the past, Alexandra thought.

"Whip was a loner himself," Eulalia continued,
"but he was always worried that I would starve for
company. So every so often he'd provide it." She sat
quite still for a moment, watching something that Alexandra couldn't see. Then she said, "Well! This will be
the biggest affair Portland has seen in years. Lee thinks
that Toby has an excellent chance of winning."

Lee was General Leland Blake, Eulalia's second
husband, and first husband of Cathy Blake, who had
given Eulalia her own land grant as a wedding present.
As a military wife, she had said, she was not likely to
stay in one place long enough to farm it. There had
been more to it than that, Alexandra thought. From
things that Dr. Martin had let drop, Whip Holt and
Cathy Blake had been in love with each other before
they had each married someone else. At any rate, the
Blakes and the Holts had been intertwined for years,
beginning with the wagon train west and those first,
possibly impetuous marriages. Leland and Eulalia's
adopted son, Henry Blake, was married—after a stormy
courtship that also included a previous marriage for
both parties—to Cindy, Eulalia and Whip Holt's daughter and Toby's sister.

For that matter, Alexandra was a distant cousin of
Eulalia's herself. Sam's grandmother Claudia Brentwood
had been Cathy Blake's sister. And Dr. Martin's first
daughter-in-law had been Lee and Cathy's daughter,
Beth. Unable to keep track of so many widows and
widowers, and the marriages and begats, Alexandra had
sat down one day and worked it out on paper. It looked
as impressive as the Hapsburgs, she thought, and Oregon's history was certainly tied up in it.

"I think he's going to win, too," she told Eulalia. "I
hope it's not just wishful thinking."

"Do you want to go to Washington that badly?" Eulalia inquired crisply. She had no patience with political wives, having been married to a general long enough to have encountered a lot of them.

"It might be fun," Alexandra replied. "But I don't think it would break my heart if I didn't. I'm more worried about Toby. Now that he's said he'll do this, I'm afraid he'll feel foolish if he loses. Toby hasn't had much practice at failure."

"And you think failure takes practice?" Eulalia asked.

"I do. Except for the Antelope Horn, Toby has been very successful at everything he has turned his hand to. When we lost that ranch, it nearly killed him." She took a cookie off a plate that was half-buried under a pile of crossed-out menus and bit into it.

"Well, then," Eulalia said, ever practical, "maybe it would do him good to lose."

"I don't want to find out," Alexandra said firmly. "He's just got to win, and that's that."

"Who's got to win?" Sally spied her mother and grandmother in the parlor and trotted in. "Hello, Grandmama, are those cookies? Can I have one? Can I sit in your lap? Who's got to win?" Sally beamed at Eulalia, whom she adored. Even though she would be seventy soon, Eulalia was still a beauty. Her pale skin was softly wrinkled, and although her once-dark hair was completely gray now, her violet eyes had not faded. She had kept her figure, which this afternoon was regal in violet silk. She always smelled of lilac water. Sally climbed up into Eulalia's lap while Eulalia inspected the child's hands and white kid boots to see if they were going to do anything irreparable to the violet silk.

"You're in my lap," Eulalia said, "and you may have a cookie if you don't get crumbs on me." She handed her one. "And your father is the one we want to win."

"Win what?"

"The election," Eulalia said.

"What's an election?"

"It's a vote to see whom we want to lead us," Alexandra said.

"What's a vote?"

"That's when men get to say whom they like best," Eulalia said, "and the person that the most men like wins."

"Wins what?"

"Never mind," they both said together.

"I can read," Sally informed her grandmother.

"Can you, dear? Can you read 'A cat sat on the mat'?"

"That's not interesting," Sally said scornfully. "I like the newspaper."

"Heavens."

"Pond's Extract is the people's remedy," Sally informed her.

"She reads all the advertisements," Alexandra explained. "They have big type."

"Frogs make it," Sally said.

"No, they don't, darling. That's just in the picture."

"Oh." Sally appeared disappointed and looked up at Eulalia. "It was a picture with a big frog pouring something into a pot from a pitcher, and an assistant frog stirring it with a ladle."

"What are you going to do about the children's schooling if you take them to Washington?" Eulalia asked.

"Let them take part of their schooling in Portland and part in Washington, I think. With some lessons in between, if they need it, to make sure they keep up." Alexandra shrugged. "We'll see how it works. They're both bright enough. It might keep them from getting bored, the way Tim did. Mike wants desperately to go places and see things. I don't think I could bear to tell him he couldn't go. Dr. Martin says it won't do him any harm if we don't stay for the hot weather."

"Will it help resign him to being an invalid, do you think," Eulalia asked, "if he gets a taste of other things?"

"I don't know," Alexandra said fretfully. "But I have to do something. He's miserable."

"Poor boy. His grandfather was just the same when his arthritis got so bad. He used to get such a desperate look, like something in a cage. Michael looks like you, but he reminds me of his grandfather Whip more than I can tell you. Something about his eyes." Eulalia blinked.

"He must have been an amazing man," Alexandra said.

"Oh, he was. He was."

Sally patted her grandmother's cheek, feeling some emotion unfamiliar to her in the old lady's voice and in the arms that lay clasped gently around her waist. "Are you sad, Grandmama?"

"No, child." Eulalia smiled at her. "I've loved Lee for years, but I loved Whip before that. A second love never erases your first. They may be equal, but they occupy two different parts of your heart."

Sally looked thoughtful. "Does Daddy still love Tim's mama?"

"I hope so, dear," Alexandra said. Surprisingly, she realized that she really meant that. "And we all love you." She lifted Sally from Eulalia's lap, kissed her, and gave her another cookie. "And now we have a party to plan. You may stay if you will play with your paper dolls on the rug and be very quiet."

Eulalia picked up the discarded menus, brisk now. "I have an idea: This needs to be an Oregon party. Nothing at all imported. Everything we feed our guests has to be grown in Oregon."

"That's it!" Alexandra snatched up a pen and a clean sheet of paper. "Eulalia darling, you're brilliant."

"I'm an old lady," Eulalia said. "I've had time to practice."

The "Oregon Party" went down in the social annals of Portland, and in the process set a fashion for home-grown boosterism in a society that, like most cities, had hitherto considered "imported" to be synonymous with "better."

There were Oregon beef and Oregon mutton, Oregon oysters and trout, and, of course, Oregon salmon.

Walnut pies and strawberry and raspberry tarts, green peas, asparagus, and custards made with Oregon cream. Alexandra had been forced to make-do with California wines, but there were iced kegs of beer made with Oregon hops. As a final stroke of inspiration, she had laid the tables with cloths made from Oregon flax and decorated them with hothouse flowers, Oregon grown, displayed in Oregon cantaloupes carved into bowls. Anything that had not ripened with the unusually early spring was taken down from the pantry shelves, having been preserved the previous fall. The party was held in early May, and the madrona trees obliged by blooming. Smoky-white clouds of blossoms balanced on their branch tips, as white as china against the glossy green leaves. The madronas lit up the garden and created an almost bridallike archway for the carriages coming down the drive.

Everyone who had been invited came, creating the oddest combination of people. There was the requisite contingent of politicians and important men, with their important wives and important daughters; but Alexandra, who had a talent for giving spice to a party, had invited others, some for love and some for a touch of devilment.

Rufus Gooch, Portland's resident inventor, was in attendance—a coup from Alexandra's point of view, since he rarely went anywhere. Her excitement was shared by neither Toby nor Eulalia, since Rufus was reputed to be crazy. He arrived on a bicycle, his long, gray hair and beard flying, in a dull black suit, which he kept for funerals.

Calvin Rogers, the hot-air balloonist who had lived in a cabin on the ranch for many years, looked more presentable. In what Eulalia had to admit to be a stroke of genius, Alexandra persuaded him to inflate his balloon in the field and give safely tethered rides to anyone with a yen to see the countryside from two hundred feet in the air. As General Blake remarked, as he watched Calvin working the bellows under his red and yellow balloon, the Oregon decor was nicely complemented by the Oregon eccentrics.

The general, who was retired, wore his best dress uniform, resplendent with gold braid and a plume in his hat, which he doffed in a dashing fashion to the ladies. He felt a little silly in it at his age, as he remarked to Eulalia while dressing, but he was enough of a realist to know that he was a famous man himself, and a reminder of that would do no harm to his stepson's campaign.

Michael, who loved anything flamboyant, followed him everywhere, when not being recruited to carry trays of sherry and lemonade about, and pestered him for as many tales of military exploits as General Blake had the patience to tell.

"Why didn't you wear your sword?" Michael wanted to know.

"It gets in the way at parties," the general assured him gravely. Lee Blake scanned the crowd milling in the garden with amusement. "The ladies take up too much room, you see," he confided to Michael. "With a sword on, you're apt to get permanently stuck in someone's bustle."

Michael considered that notion with a gleam in his green eyes. "Why do they wear all that stuff?"

"Women's fashion is a mystery," Grandpa Lee told him. "Which means I have no idea. When I was a boy, women wore skimpy little things, more like a shimmy than a dress really, not more than two or three yards of material in the whole thing. Then they just gradually got wider and wider, until there was no telling what was underneath. Look at Mrs. Larken." They contemplated the lady in question, in a stout gown of gray bombazine, with a mountainous bustle of red and gray striped wool. "She could keep her pug dog well hidden in that bustle. I wouldn't be surprised if she did."

"Mama says that during the war, the Confederate women smuggled morphine inside their hoopskirts," Michael said.

"Yes, they did, poor things. One could hardly blame

them. Our blockade had made drugs almost impossible to get, and their hospitals had no morphine. I once had to search a woman who was suspected of smuggling. I can confess to you now that when I found she had only drugs and no messages, I let her go. Gave her back the drugs. I've always been glad I did that."

Michael looked perplexed. "But weren't they the enemy?"

"Yes, and no," Lee said. "They were our country-men. That was what the Union was fighting for, to keep us all one country. Your grandmother Eulalia was from South Carolina. When your father and grandfather went to war, they were fighting against men she had known, danced with at parties, grown up with. It was a terrible time for all of us. We mustn't ever let it happen again."

"Could it?"

"I don't believe so. I think we've been tried in that fire. But that's partly the reason your father is running for the Senate: to make sure that the East and the West remember that we're one country now. This continent is so big, you see, and we are all so different. We need to be reminded sometimes that there's nothing wrong with difference. Your dad wants to see that Oregon remembers it, too. The factory owners and the unions must understand that we're all one state and settle their differences without trying to knock each other over the head."

"What about the foreigners?" Mike asked. "The Chinese?"

"If they're here, they're not foreigners," Lee an-swered. "They're Americans. We were all foreigners to start with, except for the Indians. Foreigners built this country."

"Then why does everybody want to keep them out now?"

Leland squeezed the boy's bony shoulder. "Folks have a mighty short memory, Michael."

"I believe you have my soapbox, General." Toby came up to them, smiling, and held out his hand to Lee. "I hope you don't mind if I quote you."

"By all means," Lee said. "Feel free." He surveyed the garden admiringly. "This is quite a party. At least half the population of Portland is here, I should think."

"And a fair contingent from Salem," Toby said, "most of whom are staying with us. It's a full house."

Michael saw his mother with her eyes on him and went guiltily back to the house to get another tray of lemonade. The garden was full of ladies admiring Alexandra's flowers, and he drifted among them with the tray, making polite responses when they said how much he had grown and asked about his health.

The Misses Langley, who were twins and in their sixties and never got anything right, wore gray taffeta dresses, not identical, but conveying that impression. They were under the misconception that Toby was running for governor.

"Not governor?" Miss Dora Langley asked, disappointed, when Michael gently corrected them.

"I was certain our nephew George said governor," Miss Cora Langley put in. "Not governor? You're certain, dear?"

"Yes, ma'am. My dad's running for the Senate."

"What a pity. I think he would have made a very handsome governor."

"Why, Cora dear, I believe the Senate is quite important, too."

"We must ask George."

"What do you think about the Chinese labor question?" Michael asked them, fishing. The Misses Langley fascinated him. They reminded him of the comics who came on in the middle of serious plays to remind the audience that it was only a story, after all, and keep them from taking it too seriously. Michael wondered if real life had provided the Misses Langley for the same purpose.

"The Chinese? Well, dear, I do feel they ought to be watched. They all look just alike, you know. You can't tell one from the other, so shifty. And of course they all smoke opium, which is very injurious to the lungs."

"George feels they ought to be repatriated," Dora said, "although I don't see the point in doing it twice. If they've been patriated once, that ought to be enough."

"That's the trouble with foreigners, dear. They just aren't satisfied."

Michael circulated further with the tray, filing the Misses Langley away in one corner of his brain until he wanted them again. He could call them up at will—not just their words but their expressions, mannerisms, the squirrellike cock to their heads when they were explaining something. They were part of a vast population that inhabited his brain, including his teachers and the minister and various members of his own family. When he wanted to make up a story, he could bring them out, dress them in costumes of his choosing, and assign them parts to which they seemed suited. When he read a book, Mike always translated its characters into the three-dimensional humans that he knew. It never seemed real to him until he had done that. His family had played Shakespeare in his mind—Grandpa Lee as King Lear, Sam as a young Macbeth—as well as the adventures of his own devising, set against the backdrop of Marjorie White's photographs.

Michael set down the tray in the kitchen, where Abby was taking a pan of chocolate lace cookies out of the oven.

"Watch it, Mike, honey, you'll burn your fingers," Abby warned.

"I'm careful," Michael said. He scooped up a cookie on a spatula and flipped it over on the breadboard until it was cool. Nothing was worse than burning your mouth with chocolate.

"This is a wingding of a party," Abby said. "You want to do me a favor, honey? Take some port and a tray of good glasses into your daddy's study. He's got all the men in there where they can be private." Abby put the decanter on a tray. "Smoking big cigars and smelling up the place, I'll bet. It'll take Amy a week to air it."

He took the tray and slipped through the back of the house to Toby's study, dodging the crowd of people in the front parlor and hall. In the study he set the tray on the big library table that his father used to spread maps out on. Toby and Willis Larken and six others were gathered around it under pungent blue clouds of cigar smoke. Michael recognized Ephraim Bender, Donald McCallum, and Noell Simpson, who had been out to the house steadily in twos and threes since his dad had decided to run.

The other three men he didn't know, but he knew they weren't businessmen. He tried to put his finger on how he knew. One looked to be in his fifties, the other two were younger, in their twenties. They wore heavy, round-toed work shoes that had been polished, and they looked less sleek than the others.

"Thanks, Son," Toby said. "This is my son Mike. Mike, this is Mr. Bruder and Mr. Lansky." He nodded at the two younger men. "And Mr. Boyle." He indicated the older man. "I believe you know everyone else."

"Yes, sir." Mike looked longingly at the leather armchair in the corner, wondering if his father would let him stay and listen.

"Sorry, Mike, this is private talk."

"Political talk?" Michael asked wistfully.

"Secret machinations and sharp bargaining," Toby said with a grin.

Michael grinned back. "All right."

"Tell your mother we'll make an appearance as soon as possible," Toby said.

"Cora and Dora Langley think you're running for governor," Michael said from the door.

"Well, they can't vote," Toby said. "Thank God."

When Michael had closed the door, Toby poured himself a glass of port and passed the tray down the table.

Lansky poured his and drank some as if he didn't care much what was in it. "Now listen to me, Mr. Holt. You will not get the support of the union men if you won't make some concessions."

Donald McCallum bristled. "We're making a concession by asking you here at all, Lansky."

Lansky half rose. He was a muscular young man in a cheap suit. "Then maybe we'll just leave and go talk to the strike committee!"

"Sit down, Sasha." Bruder pushed him into his seat again. "We don't want it to come to a strike. That's why we're here."

"You're a hothead, Lansky," the older man, Boyle, said. "This isn't a contract meeting." He turned to Toby. "But you haven't given us any reason to back you, Mr. Holt, and that's the truth. You've just as good as said you're not going to support an anti-Chinese act."

"I have," Toby confirmed. "And I won't. On the other hand, I *will* support any legislation that prevents employers from hiring cheap labor at a starvation wage that undercuts the unions."

"Toby, we can't afford what these men are asking," Willis Larken said.

"That's between you and them," Toby said. "But I'll tell you what you can't afford, Willis—you can't afford to hire Chinese and starve them to death, not and have any conscience to go on with."

"Let me worry about my conscience," Willis grumbled.

"We'd all better worry about it," Toby said. "Now you listen to me, all of you, and when I'm through if you don't like what I have to say, you'd better go support the Republicans. Because, thanks to you, the Democrats are stuck with me now."

He glanced at Noell Simpson, Portland's congressman—a Democrat and a party man—but Simpson didn't say anything; he just sat turning his wineglass in his fingers, apparently admiring the color of the port.

Then Toby looked at Boyle and Bruder and Sasha Lansky. "You were happy enough to have the Chinese

build the railroad. And there weren't any complaints
about them forty years ago, when every white man in
the state was trying to get rich quick in California. If it
comes to that, you're happy enough to have them now,
to do the work no white men want. It's when the
Chinese start doing the same work as the white men
that you want to throw them out. As for you, Willis,
and you, McCallum, I've heard you sound mighty pious
about the poor Chinaman, but what you really want is
cheap labor. Not one of you gives a damn about these
people we brought over here. Well, now that they're
here, we're responsible for them. Their children who
are born here are United States citizens. That means
they have a right to the same things we have, and that
includes a job, at a decent wage. If you union men shut
them out of the union, you cheapen everything you're
supposed to stand for."

Boyle banged his glass down on the table. "You
want us to take coolies into the union?"

"I heard my stepfather explaining to my son today
that this country was built by foreigners," Toby said. "I
couldn't fault that. Shall we discriminate against foreigners now? Then which foreigners should it be? How
about the Irish, Boyle? Or the Scots? Or the Ger-
mans?" His glance rested on McCallum and Bruder.
"How about Russians?"

Lansky gave him a dark look, but he seemed
uncomfortable.

"We're all in this country together, gentlemen,"
Toby said. "You had better get used to it."

They sat around the table, glaring at him.

Finally Boyle said, "Well, it's a rare politician in
my experience who's willing to piss off both sides in an
argument. Maybe you're as honest as they say you are."

"Of course he's honest!" Ephraim Bender said.
Bender was the land developer. What he wanted was
peace and harmony and an enlightened and progressive
Portland portrayed in Eastern newspapers.

Donald McCallum, the railroad chairman, looked

less enthralled. "Honest doesn't necessarily preclude stupid," he muttered.

"Neither does dishonest," Sasha Lansky said, glaring at McCallum.

"We said we'd back you, and we will," Willis Larken said with a grin. "You warned us."

"You'll support the unions?" Boyle asked.

"I'll support the unions."

"All right, then." Boyle stood and looked at Bruder and Lansky. "We ain't got a prayer of getting an anti-Chinese candidate in past these." He jerked a thumb at Larken and McCallum. "We'd better make our pact with the devil this election and take half a loaf."

The discussion that had taken place in Toby's study was repeated, in various incarnations, throughout the rest of Oregon as the campaign progressed.

Willis Larken put Toby's opinions before the chairman of the National Bank at the Friday afternoon backroom poker game, from which Toby, due to the pressures of campaigning, was absent.

"Damn it, Larken, I don't want to talk politics."

"Then talk money," Willis said.

"I talk money all day. I want to play poker."

"We will," Willis said. "As soon as you cough up a campaign contribution."

"Holt hasn't got any coolie labor," the chairman said. "And there isn't a ranch hand's union. What does Holt want, anyway?"

"A halo, probably," Willis said. "That man has more conscience than anybody I ever met. But he can help pull Oregon together, and I can stand his conscience while he does that."

"Oh, for— all right, I like Holt, but he's too honest, that's what I think, and I think we're going to be sorry, but all right. Now will you deal, damn it?"

Harry Boyle, Will Bruder, and Sasha Lansky took a similar message to the union halls.

"Let a coolie in the union?" Stubbs, a fellow laborer in the Union Pacific switchyards, looked at Lansky as if he had sprouted horns. "I'll go and beg on the street corner before I'll let some squint-eyed Chinaman in. We're trying to get rid of the little bastards!"

"I didn't say we had to let them in," Lansky snapped. "I said Holt won't support repatriating them, but he will support a union wage for everyone. Who's going to hire a Chinaman if they can get us for the same price?"

"Well, I don't know, but that's the same as saying they're as good as me." Stubbs took another drink.

"I came here when I got tired of hearing I wasn't as good as somebody else. Peasants in Kuznetsk aren't encouraged to have unions," Lansky said.

"You ain't a Chinaman," the other man growled. "You're just a dumb, stupid Russian."

Lansky snorted. "Then, since you are so much smarter than me, you go vote Republican. They're going to put up Barrowby—I read it in the paper today—and you know what a friend of the union he is."

"I'll take Barrowby before I take a Chinaman."

"I'm not asking you to let him marry your sister, you ass!" Lansky threw his hands in the air. "Mother of God, haven't you got any sense?"

"I've got sense enough to know when I'm being insulted." The level of whiskey in Stubbs's bottle was pretty low, whereas the level in his bloodstream was fairly high. "You leave my sister out of this."

"Nobody said anything about your sister."

"You did."

"I only said you didn't have to—"

Stubbs's fist shot out and connected, not very effectively, with Lansky's chin. Lansky grabbed him by the wrist, socked him back, and in a minute the union hall was full of wrestling, swearing men.

"What's it all about?" a latecomer asked as he sidestepped a flying shot glass.

"Lansky told Stubbs that Toby Holt says he has to let his sister marry a Chinaman," another man explained. "At least I think that was what it was. Doesn't make much sense to me, but politics always gets folks emotional." Another missile, this time a shoe, flew overhead, and he flattened himself under an overturned table.

The Misses Langley discussed it with their nephew George over Sunday dinner.

"I've always thought Josiah Barrowby was underbred," Cora said. "His jaw, you know. Like a bulldog's. His bottom teeth stick out."

"That doesn't affect his politics, Aunt Cora," George Langley said. "Barrowby may not see the need for repatriation, but he'll keep these coolies in their place."

Dora sighed. "I cannot feel that he's quite honest. I've been shortchanged twice in his store. I was sure of it."

George resisted the temptation to put his head in his hands. Dora was always sure she had been shortchanged, because when she had five dollars on Monday she never could understand why she didn't still have five dollars on Thursday, since she never remembered having spent it.

"That doesn't affect his politics, either," George said, but they both gave him shocked looks, identical round stares, their eyes wide, from opposite ends of the table. George found these Sunday dinners something of a trial. "Of course we want our man to be honest," he muttered. "I just meant, well, we want him to be practical." He found that he hadn't really considered that aspect of a race before, since self-serving was the generally accepted if unspoken definition of a politician. He had to admit that he thought Toby Holt was honest, and he might want an honest man if his own back was ever to the wall someday. The only question was, did he want an honest man now?

"Well, I don't like that jaw," Cora reiterated. "I wouldn't want to be represented in Washington by it. What if they thought we all looked that way? I think you'd better vote for Mr. Holt, dear."

"Oh, yes," Dora said. "But he's not running for governor, did you know? Such a pity. He would look so *lovely* in a parade."

XI

"White Elk!" Toby spotted his assistant foreman coming down the steps of the foreman's cottage, which White Elk shared with Stalking Horse, his foster father. Toby waved his arm at him, and White Elk turned his steps toward Toby. His normally jaunty face was somber. Toby frowned. If White Elk was worried, Toby knew why. "How is he?"

"He is old," White Elk replied. He hooked his thumbs in his belt loops and stared at his boots.

"No better?" Toby asked. Old Stalking Horse had developed a persistent cough a month earlier and seemed unable to shake it off. Toby had known the Indian since he was a baby. He had helped Toby break his first horse.

White Elk didn't answer, and Toby slung an arm around his shoulders. They were all old, Toby thought, the generation he had depended upon for so much: Stalking Horse, Lee Blake, Robert Martin. . . . The doctor was too old to practice at all now and had sent a pleasant young man about Alexandra's age to examine Stalking Horse. But he had had little to say except that a body ran down eventually.

"I'm going into town," Toby said. "To Chinatown."

White Elk blinked in surprise.

Toby grinned at him. "I've got all these blasted politicians yakking at me about what sort of stand I ought to take concerning the Chinese, and it occurred to me while I was shooting my mouth off that I've never asked the Chinese what they want. I don't even know any of the Chinese here. I find that people often have very odd notions about what other people need. It's occurred to me that mine might be wrong."

"I will go with you," White Elk offered.

"You're certainly welcome. But why?"

"I don't know any Chinese, either. They seem to me very wonderful and strange. Like the carnival. Or a play in the theater."

Toby chuckled. "And you want to see the elephant? Well, come along, then." It might do White Elk good to have some diversion and to see that the diversity of man, although wonderful, was inclined by its very nature to breed prejudice. White Elk had grown up among white people on the Madrona, but he had not met with universal acceptance in Portland. Perhaps because he had not been brought up in a tribe, among the Indians' own prejudices, White Elk had found that hard to understand and sometimes harder to bear.

They saddled their horses and made the ride into Portland at a brisk clip. It was a blazing June day, not hot but brilliantly lit with sunlight, the air thick with the scent of flowers. The usual aroma of sawdust and fish overcame the flowers as the men neared the center of town, and then, through that familiar smell, White Elk caught the faint, exotic odor of incense in the air, alien and beckoning.

Their first stop was Mr. Li's drugstore. The front windows of the shop were hung with dried turtles and bunches of herbs. White Elk recognized some of the herbs, but others he had never seen. Small red boxes with black calligraphy on them were stacked in a pyramid beneath the herbs.

Inside, the shelves were filled with boxes made of paper and rice straw and lacquer, with Chinese labels on them, and the room was dusty with the driftings of Mr. Li's herbs and powders. Mrs. Li came out from behind the counter as Toby and White Elk walked in. She had black hair in a knot on her head, and a canvas apron over baggy, black-cotton trousers and tunic. On her feet she wore heelless, heavy-soled slippers with round, embroidered toes.

"Mr. Holt." She bowed to Toby and cast an alarmed glance at White Elk's Shoshone face. Toby was surprised that she knew who he was. "You come this way. I will bring you to my husband." She ducked behind a curtain, and they followed her. *Mr. Li and White Elk will probably stare at each other,* Toby thought, suppressing a grin.

Mr. Li's back room, which served as his drugstore office and mixing area, was pungent with the odors of his trade. The smell was sharper than the incense they had sniffed in the street, but not unpleasant. White Elk looked curiously at the baskets of plants and ginger root, and the strings of onions and seed pods that dangled from the ceiling. On a long table was a big mortar and pestle, and beside it on a lacquer tray, little heaps of who knew what, ready to be ground into medicine.

When they came in, ducking their heads past the low door and the hanging pods, Mr. Li was counting something on an abacus, then making entries in a ledger filled with neat columns of Chinese characters. Looking up, he stopped and bowed gravely to them both. He was small, only a little taller than his wife, and wore a tunic and trousers similar to hers. His hair was braided into a long queue behind, and on his head he wore a round, black cotton cap. He had a thin beard with a little gray in it, of the sort that announced him to be a man of substance.

Toby and White Elk bowed back.

"Mr. Li," Toby began, "it is good of you to see me. This is White Elk, who is the assistant foreman of my ranch."

"Please, you are welcome," Mr. Li said. He drew forward two carved armchairs with tasseled cushions. He gave White Elk a look that a scientist might accord an aborigine, very nearly the look that White Elk was giving him, and Toby almost laughed.

"You will pardon me for my ignorance," Mr. Li

said, touching the tips of his fingers together, "but I do not understand why it is that you wish to speak with me."

"You are a leader among the Chinese," Toby said. "Probably the most successful man of your race in Portland, and with much influence. If I am to represent Oregon fairly—"

"If you win," Mr. Li said gently.

"If I win," Toby agreed, feeling that maybe he had been pompous. "What I mean is, I can't hope to represent the Chinese without knowing them, without knowing what they need from me."

"We do not vote, Mr. Holt," Mr. Li remarked. "It is not encouraged."

"Well, I represent you anyway," Toby said. "And maybe that needs working on."

"Mr. Holt, you do not know us well, although we have been under your nose all your life. You have had business dealings with us—you have even been to our country, I am told—and still you do not know us."

"I suppose I don't," Toby said, frustrated. "Will you tell me?"

"I suspect that it may be like trying to tell a fox what it is like to be a hare," Mr. Li said with a smile, "but I will try."

He clapped his hands and waited silently until a curtain on another side of the room was pushed back and a girl came through it. She was young, in her late teens, dressed in a dark-blue tunic and trousers much like Mrs. Li's but embroidered at the neck and cuffs. She bowed to her father, but her eyes slid sideways with interest toward the newcomers.

"My daughter, Mai," Mr. Li said. He spoke to her in Chinese, and she hurried out. "We will have tea," he explained to Toby. He settled back in his chair, hands folded in his lap, waiting again.

Perhaps, Toby thought, talk would come with the tea.

When Mai returned, she carried a lacquer tray with a blue and white teapot and small white cups. She set it on the table and poured tea into the cups. It was pale, almost the color of wheat, with a faint greenish tinge. She handed them each a cup, and when he sipped it, Toby found it surprisingly strong and very hot. Mai looked at Toby and White Elk again curiously, moving just her dark eyes, her head still demurely downcast. She looked as if she wanted to stay, but Mr. Li made a shooing motion with one hand, and she went back through the curtain. Toby saw her pause for a moment on the other side, looking back, before the curtain dropped into place.

They drank the tea, and Mr. Li made no further remarks until it was finished. The cup felt impossibly small in Toby's hand, as if he were drinking out of a thimble.

Mr. Li set his empty cup on the tray. "I have lived in this city for twenty years, Mr. Holt. I worked on the railroad. The second year I was here, I sent to China for my wife. We were not married then. My parents arranged it all. We did not meet until she arrived here. That is the way it is done, you understand."

"I do, and I don't," Toby said. "What if you had not liked each other?"

Mr. Li smiled. "That is irrelevant. My parents would not have selected an ill-tempered woman, or a lazy one. My wife's parents would not have selected a young man with no prospects. Respect is important. Liking comes with time."

"What were your prospects, working on the railroad?" Toby asked. He had seen the railroad camps and had worked on the railroad himself, surveying.

"On the railroad I earned enough to send money home to my parents," Mr. Li said. "In America my prospects were much greater than they were in China. The land of my birth has a rigid society. What one is born, that is what one stays. I was born a peasant, like my ancestors. There are no guarantees here for us, Mr. Holt. Only opportunities. I am a businessman now. Mai was born here and is old enough to marry. I can ask much greater things of the matchmakers than my father could expect for me." He smiled. "Also for her younger brothers. I have made inquiries in China for wives for them already. They are twelve and thirteen, and these things take time."

The fact that further Chinese immigration was now illegal might account for some of the time, Toby thought. "And Mai?" he asked.

"Ah, I see that you do not understand us, Mr. Holt. If you are to understand how we live among you, you must first see how we live among ourselves."

"I'm trying." Toby wondered what White Elk was making of it. White Elk sat perfectly still, just turning the little porcelain cup in his fingers.

"For Mai, I must find a husband here. A suitable man in China, one with the position that I can now require for my daughter, would expect things I cannot give him. Birth. An ancestry of the merchant class. Little feet." He raised his eyebrows questioningly at Toby.

"I'm familiar with the custom," Toby said grimly.

"Americans do not approve," Mr. Li said. He dismissed Americans. "It is an ancient custom in China, but foot binding is not for peasants. A woman with bound feet cannot do work. That is the point, of course. But a Chinese husband of the proper class would require little feet." Mr. Li smiled. "I am modern. For my sons' wives I require only beauty and health and a modest dowry."

"I see," Toby said.

"In some ways, we are very American here," Mr. Li continued. "In others, not at all. And I must be frank, Mr. Holt: We do not trust Americans."

"We must trust each other if we are to live together," Toby said.

"Americans," said Mr. Li, "insult our women in the streets. They hold demonstrations demanding that we be shipped back to China. They cheat us in their stores. They catch our young men in alleys and cut off their queues for amusement. When we work for Americans, we are paid half what other men are paid, then are threatened for 'stealing jobs.' You make it very difficult for us to trust you, Mr. Holt."

"And yet you stay," Toby said.

"We are here," Mr. Li said. "We have very little to go back to, and we struggled very hard to leave. China is an ancient country, a civilization thousands of years older than yours. We find it amusing that you consider us to be barbarians. And yet, as you say, we stay. China is very beautiful. But for so many of us, it has nothing but the beauty and great poverty to offer. Perhaps I could go back. I still dream of China in my sleep, and I am rich. Wealth is portable. But most of us here could not, particularly if they are uprooted by force. Perhaps I stay for them. Or perhaps just because it is easier. My sons do not want to go. They have never seen China, and longings for it do not trouble their sleep."

Toby wondered what it would be like to leave home forever to live on the other side of the world. His mother had left the South, and now Oregon was home to her. Certainly it was home to her children. He thought of living in the East and felt suddenly that his collar was too tight—the same reaction that Tim had always claimed he had. But the East, his East, was still his own country. Mr. Li's position seemed very complicated by comparison.

"What do you want," Toby asked him, "that I can try to offer? Schools? The vote?"

"We want to be left alone," Mr. Li answered. "To be Chinese, but to live here. Not in fear of our own overlords or of your race." Mr. Li stood. "Come. If you want insight into my race, I will show you."

They followed him through the curtain into the shop. Mrs. Li was behind the counter again, making up a parcel for a small boy who wore a conical straw hat that was tied under his chin with a red cord. Mr. Li pushed open the front door in a cheerful jangle of brass bells, and they went out onto the sidewalk. Mr. Li's store was near the corner of Second Avenue and Pine Street, and he led the way across Pine to a blank-walled building halfway down the block, whose walls had been plastered with notices of all shapes and sizes, written in Chinese on flame-colored paper.

"This is our means of communication," Mr. Li explained. "And if you read it, you will know what we are. It is most revealing." He pointed with a finger to a new notice, its paper still crisp. "Pu Wen advertises that he is opening a school for boys of good character and studious bent. So you see, Mr. Holt, we do not need your schools."

He pointed to another notice, this one weathered and fraying at the edge. "Here Lo Shan advertises for a husband for his niece in China. He says that she is strong, hardworking, and of an exceptionally even temper. He does not mention that she is walleyed, but everyone knows it, which is why his notice has been here so long. And here"— another fraying notice—"the matchmaker seeks a wife for a middle-aged client of good means. Again, no name is mentioned, but everyone knows it is Su T'si, who has one leg shorter than the other and a wicked temper. Here I advertise the receipt of a shipment of ginseng. And this is news from China. Here is only a date, in the middle of next month."

"What is the date?" Toby asked. He noticed that White Elk had drifted off and was walking along the sidewalk, looking about him with curiosity. The bulletin board was less interesting to White Elk than the inhabitants. Toby, on the other hand, found it eye-opening.

"Ah, the date." Mr. Li clasped his hands behind his back and stared off in another direction. "An arrival time, so to speak."

"Of an illegal ship, full of illegal immigrants?" Toby inquired. "Somebody's illegal bride?"

"Possibly," Mr. Li conceded. "Your government's Chinese Exclusion Act directly negates the Treaty of 1880 between our countries. There are too many of us in China, Mr. Holt. More than China can feed, and we will come somehow."

"I see," he said. "I doubt that that act can be

rescinded. It comes down to the matter of wages again. When your people will work for almost nothing, they are a threat to the white workers."

"And if they do not work for nothing, they are not hired. Our young men are between a flood and a fire, Mr. Holt. And so will you be if you try to untangle this coil. Life is most difficult."

"I could have told you that without bothering to open my front door this morning," Toby said dryly.

Mr. Li chuckled. "Let us continue our tour." He strolled along the sidewalk, Toby following him, to view other posters and notices. "Here is news of this country: An Industrial Reform Party has been formed in Washington, D.C. We are interested in industrial reform, in case we should find ourselves on the list of things to be reformed. Similarly the labor parties, and the Equal Rights Party. You have so many factions here. These parties never win elections, I have noticed, but they bump things along. They are signposts, and we read them carefully. Is your President Cleveland going to beat this Mr. Harrison?"

"I hope so," Toby replied.

"Now here," Mr. Li said, "we have matters closer to home: a Chinese man killed in Salem. A Chinese woman abducted and raped in Seattle and left naked on the street. Only a small sentence in your newspapers, but of more interest to us here." He tapped two new sheets of paper, filled with careful calligraphy. "Here is a plea to form vigilante committees of our own, and here, an offer to teach anyone interested the use of firearms. That is not in our nature, but you see that we, too, struggle with change and fear. . . ."

White Elk ambled down Pine Street, wondering how he could contrive to talk to Mai. He had no idea why she intrigued him so and felt an intense reluctance to ask himself, probably because he knew this wasn't a good idea. He turned down the alley that ran behind Second Avenue anyway, prowling past the back stoops, where fish and octopi lay drying on mats and an occasional quilted bed cover hung airing on the railings. Second-story balconies jutted over the street. On them, old women sewing and old men gossiping bit their words abruptly into silence as White Elk passed.

Then he saw her, shelling peas into a colander on what must be the back steps of the drugstore. She had a straw hat over her hair now, to shade her eyes, and she looked up at him suddenly from under it. White Elk tried to think what he could say and wondered if she even spoke English. She hadn't spoken at all in her father's office. He took off his hat and held it in one hand. She just looked at him, so he bowed awkwardly, and she giggled.

"My name is White Elk."

"I am Li Mai." She did speak English. She was the smallest woman he had ever seen, with pale gold skin and black oval eyes. The eyes studied him. "You don't look like an American."

"I'm as American as they come," White Elk said with a grin. "I'm Shoshone."

She cocked her head at him mischievously. "I thought Indians wore feathers."

White Elk sat on the stoop by her feet. They might have looked big to a Chinese aristocrat, but they weren't much longer than his hand. "And I thought Chinese girls wore chopsticks in their hair."

Mai pretended to be shocked. "Would you eat with something you kept in your hair? Chinese girls wear hair ornaments in their hair—when they are doing something nicer than shelling peas." Her English was like her father's, educated in its speech patterns, but more mellifluous than Americans', overlaid with the tonal patterns of her native tongue. It made White Elk, who knew himself to be besotted already, think of birds. She went on shelling peas, deftly stripping them from their pods into the colander in her lap. She dropped the pods into a basket at her feet, and her jade earrings swayed with each small movement.

"I never saw an Indian before," she informed him. White Elk took a handful of pods and began to help her. "Now that you've seen one, how do they strike you? On the whole?"

"Very fierce," Mai said. "Like a bandit. Aren't you supposed to be with your Mr. Holt?"

"Probably," White Elk admitted. He ate one of the peas and dropped the rest into her colander. He could feel a row of interested eyes boring into his back from the balconies. "All the old parties upstairs are watching us," he said. "Am I going to get you into trouble?"

"Probably," Mai said. But she put another handful of pea pods into his lap with a little smile.

White Elk sat down in the chair beside Stalking Horse's bed. "Grandfather, I have done something very stupid."

"It will not be the first time," Stalking Horse said with the trace of a smile. His face had aged even more in the weeks that had passed since Toby's and White Elk's introduction to Chinatown, and his dark eyes were so sunken that they seemed to be hooded by his brows. He looked at White Elk affectionately. "But if you have not lost one of Alexandra's prize horses or shot anyone, you will doubtless survive it." He chuckled at White Elk's guilty expression. "Tell me what it is, and I will decide whether or not to get out of this bed and beat you."

"Yes, Grandfather." The day had long since passed when Stalking Horse, even with his health, could have beaten White Elk, who was as tough and wiry as a panther; but they maintained the respectful fiction that he could. White Elk put his hat on the braided rug by his boots and scratched his head, perplexed by his own folly. "I have fallen in love with the daughter of Mr. Li."

Stalking Horse closed his eyes. "You are right," he said finally. "That is stupid." He sounded almost admiring, as if to have thought of anything that idiotic must have taken enormous mental effort.

"I am sorry, Grandfather." White Elk looked at his boots.

"Hand me my medicine."

White Elk took the cup of camomile tea from the little table beside the bed and held it while his foster father drank.

"That tea is dreadful," Stalking Horse complained. "The young doctor says that it will help my digestion, but I think I would prefer not to eat." He took a deep, careful breath. A kettle of water steamed on a brazier beside the bed, and Stalking Horse looked at White Elk through the clouds, which were supposed to ease his lungs. "And is this child in love with you?"

"Yes."

"Of course. Otherwise you would not have a problem, only a broken heart, which is more easily mended. Do you want to marry her?"

"We haven't gotten that far," White Elk said. "But yes."

"And how does Mr. Li take to that?"

"Mr. Li won't even let me court her."

"But you have been seeing her anyway." Stalking Horse sighed. White Elk could hear the breath rattle in the old Cherokee's chest. "Even as a child, to tell you that you couldn't have something was to make you desire it earnestly. This is my fault."

White Elk looked at him indignantly. He might be stupid, but he wanted to reserve that stupidity to his own initiative, not Stalking Horse's prompting.

"I brought you up away from your own kind," Stalking Horse continued. "Prejudice is not reserved to any one race. We are all prejudiced against those who are different, and we all believe that our own way is the true way. Mr. Li may even be right: It is always better for like to mate with like, if only because to do otherwise angers so many people. I gave you Indian knowledge, taught you Indian hunting skills, told you your heritage. I never thought to provide you with Indian girls."

"You couldn't have ordered me a wife from a matchmaker," White Elk said, "like Mr. Li is trying to do with Mai. I wouldn't have stood for it."

Stalking Horse snorted. "I should have introduced you to some suitable women. When you were younger and—malleable. It is easier for a young man to fall in love than you think."

White Elk grinned. "That isn't love."

"It's an excellent start," Stalking Horse said with asperity. He reached out and took White Elk's hand. The old man's hands were pale from being indoors, blue veined and frail, but his grip was still strong. "Before you court this woman further, remember Janessa, who has spent her life trying to be two kinds of people at once. I know that neither you nor Mai has had an easy time among white people, but at least you are each all one race, a race that you know. It's the way of creation, like to like." His eyes fluttered closed wearily. "Go against it, and you may break your heart past mending."

XII

The pace of life on the Madrona quickened throughout the summer. As fall and the elections approached, Toby's campaign was in full swing, and Alexandra watched a parade of politicians and party men come and go, usually taking Toby away with them to make a speech or kiss a baby. Tim wrote, in a tone that Alexandra thought far too brisk and brittle to be truthful, that things were going swimmingly, and he expected to be rich any minute as he and Sam were still working the Hopeful, in pursuit of the same elusive vein of silver that had evaded them all year.

Janessa came home for a flying visit, played with Michael and Sally, talked somberly and unhappily to White Elk and the doctor about Stalking Horse's health, and then took the train back to Los Angeles, where she had persuaded Dr. Dunbar, of all people, to let her spend the summer assisting him at the hospital.

Michael proved to have grown four inches and required new knickers and shoes. And Sally's reading ability improved to the point that Alexandra put unsuitable material on the top shelf of Toby's study and hid the stepladder. Juanita asked if Sally couldn't go to school. Alexandra decided that she could and talked the school principal into it. The school board was well acquainted with the precocious Holt children.

White Elk took over the foreman's responsibilities almost completely for Stalking Horse and in his free time vanished on errands unknown. If either Toby or

Alexandra had thought to wonder where he was, the answer would have made them distinctly uneasy.

"I am supposed to be taking this pot of soup to Mrs. Soon," Mai said with a conspiratorial smile. "It is very fortunate that Mrs. Soon lives so far away."

White Elk pulled Mai into his arms under the shadow of a dilapidated warehouse. It was an abandoned building on the far edge of Chinatown, which they had adopted as their spot to court away from disapproving eyes. Not an easy task, since neither of them could think of anyone who wouldn't disapprove. He took the handle of the lidded lacquer pot out of Mai's hand and set it on the ground. "I thought you weren't coming."

"I had to think of an excuse," she replied. "And then I had to wait for the soup. And now I feel bad because Mrs. Soon is ill, and I am using her for my own wicked ends."

"Not wicked," White Elk said firmly, but he knew that was only his own opinion. Mr. Li would have called it something much worse. He led Mai farther into the shadow of the building, and they sat on the steps of the old loading dock.

"Very wicked," Mai said mournfully. "My father is trying to find me a husband. I am bad and undutiful to go on seeing you, but I do it anyway."

White Elk felt a cold knot in the middle of his chest. "You won't let him marry you off to someone?"

Mai shook her head. "No. I have told him I will not marry anyone I do not like. I can just go on not liking them. But it is very hard." She sighed and stared at the embroidered tips of her shoes.

"Then marry me," White Elk said. "And we'll tell them after we've done it." He didn't think she would. They had been through this before.

"You don't understand. You are not Chinese. I owe my father duty. The family is very important to us—more important than anything. It is all we have. If we dishonor the family, then we have done the worst we can do."

"I understand honor," White Elk said. It was dishonorable to go on seeing each other on the sly, too, but he didn't want to rile up her conscience any more than it already was. "I even halfway understand about your family. But you've got to feel like you owe yourself something. If your father didn't want you to get notions like that, he shouldn't have brought you up in America."

"That is what he says." Mai gave White Elk a reluctant smile. "That is irony. But I still cannot run away with you."

"Only as far as the end of Chinatown," White Elk said. He'd have to settle for that, for now. Maybe with time. . . . He pulled her into his arms again, impatient, feeling as if there wasn't time. He loved her now.

Mai kissed him, snuggling into his arms as if trying to make this stolen meeting last, make it compensate them both somehow for her refusal and for her divided loyalties.

We can't go on like this, White Elk thought. Either he would go crazy, or her father would find out—or both. But he couldn't think of what to do. The Chinese community was like a closed door, behind which was something beautiful and baffling. Even Mai struck him that way sometimes. White Elk looked down at her delicate oval face and those beautiful, mysterious, slanting eyes. Maybe Stalking Horse was right about like mating with like, but it was too late for that. White Elk didn't want an Indian girl; he wanted Mai.

Scenarios passed through his mind in which they ran away to live alone on the Antelope Horn in the Dakotas; in which he pleaded his case with such eloquence and persuasiveness that Mr. Li changed his mind; in which Mr. Li had a heart attack and fell down dead—White Elk was a little ashamed of that one; but none of them seemed very likely to come to pass.

In the meantime, Mrs. Soon's soup sat in its pot at their feet and got very cold indeed.

* * *

At the beginning of September, Alexandra, in the last throes of getting Mike and Sally ready for school, with a stack of clean pinafores in one hand and a scarf tied around her head, opened the door to find an irate Mr. Li on the front porch.

His round black hat fairly quivered with rage as he informed her that he must see Mr. Holt. At once.

Good heavens, Alexandra thought, silently blessing the fact that Toby was at home, as she had no idea what she would have done with Mr. Li otherwise. She escorted him to the study, where Toby greeted him with a startled look.

Mr. Li came to the point with un-Oriental directness. Alexandra had barely closed the door when she heard the sinister phrases "my daughter" and "uneducated barbarian" and "absolutely forbid it" through the oak door.

Sally and Mike appeared at Alexandra's side with the unerring instinct with which children are drawn to crises they aren't supposed to know about.

"What does the Chinaman want, Mama?"

"Golly, he looked mad!"

"I haven't the faintest idea, darlings," Alexandra said, shooing them away before Mr. Li could raise his voice again and enlighten them.

In the study Toby was having little success in placating his guest, although Mr. Li managed to get enough of a grip on his temper to stop shouting.

"Now wait a minute," Toby said. "White Elk is not a barbarian, and he certainly isn't uneducated. He went to school with my children, and he was generally at the top of his class."

"He is not Chinese," Mr. Li said.

"No," Toby conceded, since that was inarguable.

"His race live in tents. Nomads. Like Mongols." Mr. Li sniffed. "They do not even have an alphabet."

"White Elk is hardly an illiterate nomad off the plains," Toby said. "And there have been many great leaders among the Shoshone."

"And would you want your daughter to marry him?" Mr. Li demanded.

"I wouldn't object," Toby said. "My daughter is half Indian."

"Ah," Mr. Li said sympathetically. "Of course. That would make it very difficult for her to find a suitable husband. I am very fortunate not to have that difficulty in my family."

"That wasn't what I— Oh, never mind. I'll do what I can, Mr. Li." Toby knew he wasn't going to get anywhere. Mr. Li expected his daughter to respect her ancestors and follow her family's traditions, which was pretty much what Toby expected of his own daughters. Unfortunately, those traditions were worlds apart, and Toby was aware that his views on race relations were held by his own people to be somewhat eccentric, even on the frontier. "I'll do what I can," he repeated helplessly, wondering what on earth was going to occur.

"Where's White Elk?" Toby asked Alexandra as they stood side by side on the porch, watching Mr. Li's departing back.

"In the barn?" Alexandra guessed.

"Right." Toby set off in that direction. As long as he wasn't in Chinatown . . .

He found White Elk in the barn, giving Trout a bucket of oats. Trout had improved out of all knowing since Tim had ridden him, and White Elk had broken him to be a useful mount, if occasionally somewhat too exciting for the unprepared.

"That horse doesn't need oats," Toby said. "He needs to be knocked between the ears with a two-by-four."

White Elk laughed. "He has better manners than he used to." Trout rolled an eye at Toby and snorted.

"He's demented," Toby insisted. "And he bites. I think you ride him to show off."

"Maybe," White Elk conceded. "I'll give him to Tim when he comes home. I just want to keep Trout mannerly till then. It would be a pity to waste Tim's work. That was a good ride."

"It was," Toby admitted. He leaned against a stall door, out of Trout's reach. "I had a visitor just now," he remarked. "Mr. Li."

White Elk stopped with the empty bucket swinging from his hand. "Did he, er, happen to mention me?"

"Forcibly," Toby said. "You know darn well he did."

White Elk upended the oat bucket and sat on it. He took off his hat and pushed the hair back from his face. Toby didn't think he looked very tractable.

"Mr. Li was pretty steamed," Toby said.

"Yeah, I bet," White Elk said. "Look, if it's any help, I didn't do this on purpose."

"Didn't do what? Seduce the daughter of a respectable Chinaman or somehow forget to mention it to me?" Toby, having known White Elk since he was about eight, felt he could speak to him much as he would have to Tim.

"Fall in love," White Elk replied. "I didn't mean to fall in love with her. I was just curious, but it got out of hand."

"So it seems."

"And I didn't seduce anybody. I want to marry Mai. I don't know what Mr. Li would do if he thought I'd—"

"I didn't mean it literally," Toby interrupted. "I figured you had more brains than that. The question is, what are you going to do now?"

"I don't know," White Elk confessed. "He's forbidden me to see her."

"Which hasn't stopped you," Toby said dryly.

"Well, no. I don't suppose you could talk him into it?"

"I tried. I spoke glowingly of your character, ambition, education, and general purity of soul. He was unimpressed."

"Oh, boy."

"You're not planning to run away with her, I trust? The Madrona isn't nearly far enough."

"No," White Elk said gloomily. "She won't do that."

"Well, I'll think on it," Toby said. He saw Alexandra coming toward them across the yard. "Maybe Alex can think of something. She's good at . . ." As she neared them, he saw the expression on her face, and his voice fell into an uneasy silence. There were tears on her cheeks.

White Elk stood. Alexandra put her hands on his.

"Is it Grandfather?" White Elk knew by looking at her face that it was.

"He's gone," she whispered. "Just now." Tears streamed down her cheeks. "He was asleep. It was very peaceful."

White Elk's fingers clenched hers for a moment. "I'll go to him," he murmured. He walked away across the yard, head bowed.

"White Elk—" Alexandra said.

"Let him go, honey," Toby said. "He needs to mourn."

"We all do," Alexandra said sadly.

White Elk sat with his chin in his hands, on the edge of the white iron bedstead in his room in the foreman's cottage. In the next room, he could hear Juanita and Alexandra laying out the body for burial, and outside, the sound of the undertaker's carriage bringing the casket. Telegrams had been sent to Janessa and Tim, and to Cindy and Henry Blake in Washington, and to all the others who had loved the old man over the years. They would all come back for the funeral, and White Elk knew he must do his private mourning before then.

Stalking Horse had been his foster father since White Elk was around eight, when he had been found, half-starved and completely distrustful of the world— and white men in particular—by a troop of cavalry after his mother and the last of his people had been drowned in a flood. For a few years Stalking Horse had shared the upbringing of White Elk with an Englishwoman named Pamela Drake Randall, and then the old Cherokee had taken over sole responsibility. Stalking Horse had taught him to hunt and fish, to ride a horse, and most important, to live satisfactorily with a foot in two worlds. He also taught him to follow after him as foreman, as any son would assume his father's vocation.

It had been an accepted idea for years that when Stalking Horse was gone, White Elk would be foreman of the Madrona. An hour before, when the women had come to take care of the body and had gently shooed White Elk from the bedside, Toby Holt had brought up the subject again:

"It's yours," he had said. "You know he would have wanted that. But you'll have to give it all you've got for a while."

White Elk realized that. He would have to take hold, now, today. The ranch hands were good men by and large, but there had inevitably been a certain amount of grousing, particularly among the newer ones, about taking orders from an Indian—never very loudly, and never where Toby Holt could hear it, but White Elk was well aware of it. Stalking Horse had been a venerable and intimidating figure, able to enforce his orders with a long, hard look. White Elk was younger; he would have to pay more attention. If he didn't, he would have problems he might not be able to undo.

Mr. Li couldn't have discovered a better way, White Elk thought forlornly. If Mr. Li could have mentally willed any action that would have prevented White Elk from courting Mai, he could not have devised anything more effective than the death of Stalking Horse.

Miserable, White Elk stared at his boots, listening to the women on the other side of the wall. Alexandra was softly singing "Rock of Ages" as she worked. The old, familiar hymn sounded both comforting and lonely to White Elk. He had lost his foster father and for all intents and purposes had lost Mai too. He would not be able to see her now for a long time. Would it be too long? Long enough for her to forget him?

The mourners gathered in the rain around Stalking Horse's newly dug grave in the family cemetery. The undertakers had erected a canopy by the grave for the Reverend Mr. Wilson and the Holt family, but beyond it the ranch hands stood, hats in hand, heads bowed to the drizzle. Other souls rested in the ground beneath the solitary grove of pines that marked the cemetery; Clarissa, Tim's mother; Mary White Owl, Janessa's mother; and there was a stone for Whip Holt. Whip had been killed in a landslide, his body never recovered, but a rough granite cross remembered him. Stalking Horse's stone was shiny among the others. It had no birth date; Stalking Horse had not known it. But it gave his name, the date of his death, and the simple words "Old Friend" beneath it.

"I heard a voice from Heaven, saying unto me, from henceforth blessed are the dead who die in the Lord: even so saith the Spirit; for they rest from their labors."

Janessa, in black, stood between White Elk and Charley Lawrence, who had come with her. Tim and Sam had come home, too, Sam looking slightly rebellious, as if Tim had cajoled or threatened him into coming. Eulalia and Lee Blake were there, of course, and Dr. Robert Martin, nearly as frail as Stalking Horse had been, in a wicker wheelchair with his wife, Tonie, beside him. Toby's sister, Cindy, and her husband, Henry Blake, had come from Washington, where Henry was attached to the army's general staff. The Blake children had been left in Washington with the servants to care for them. The funeral had been postponed to wait for them.

". . . We humbly beseech thee, O Father, to raise us from the death of sin unto the life of righteousness; that, when we depart this life, we may rest in Him; and that, at the general Resurrection in the last day, we may be found acceptable in Thy sight. . . ."

And how on earth did you know when you were acceptable, Alexandra thought, human nature being what it was? How could you ever know? She supposed you simply had to trust. That must be it.

Alexandra stood beside Toby, with Michael and Sally under her wing. Michael had tears running down his cheeks, and Sally, who had never met death before, had her thumb uncharacteristically in her mouth. She stared with large, bewildered eyes at the flower-covered coffin. Alexandra smoothed Sally's hair, tied back from her face with a little black ribbon, and looked at White Elk. He was immobile, expressionless; he might have been a figure carved from redwood; and Alexandra knew him well enough to recognize that as a sign of deepest mourning. It would do him good to have Janessa and Tim home, she thought. A bond had always existed among the three of them, and Janessa and Tim had both lost a parent. How hard it always was, she thought, thinking of her own parents, both long deceased. She drew Mike and Sally a little closer to her.

The mourners began to sing as the undertaker's men lowered the coffin into the wet ground. The mortician's black horses snorted and shook their heads, their black plumes sodden with the rain.

"Mama!" Sally's voice was a bereft cry of incomprehension, and Alexandra lifted her into her arms.

Afterward, they gathered around the fire in the parlor, ate the inordinate amount of food that was set out, and told stories, remembering happy times, wrapping the gentle, reminiscent laughter around themselves as if for warmth.

Charley stood a little to one side, watching Janessa among the family he was meeting for the first time. They were an oddly assorted lot, he thought, possibly eccentric by anyone's standards. But he began to see something of the pride and stubbornness, the kindness and goodness of heart, and the almost visual flicker of pure energy that ran through all of them and that had shaped Janessa.

He was beginning to have a sense of the regularity with which this family took into itself those not born of it by blood but rather by some kinship of the spirit: Stalking Horse and White Elk, for instance; or General Lee Blake and his son, Henry, who was so like him in apparent singleness of purpose that Charley was startled to learn that Henry had been adopted in his teens. Janessa, too, had come into the family as a stranger at nearly ten, even though Toby was her father. The Holts and their connections seemed to attract those who should be theirs through some sort of homing instinct.

It was those who had been born to the household who seemed to possess a rebellious streak. Charley watched Toby Holt and his son Tim with some amusement. They looked like the same person, at different ages, preparing to argue with himself.

"You look older," Toby observed.

"I am older," Tim said.

"I had a letter from the dean," Toby remarked. "He asked after you."

"You may give him my regards," Tim said solemnly.

"I did," Toby said. "I told him you were engaged in the mining business currently and couldn't see your way clear to returning. I hope that was stuffy enough for you. Don't be a standoffish ass."

Tim chuckled and abandoned the carefully blank-faced expression he had maintained since his arrival. "I'm not. I'm just not going back."

"Well, that being settled, how is the mining business? Can I retire and live off your generosity yet?"

"Not just yet, so quit needling me. Dad, I swear there's silver in the Hopeful, and I'm making a good salary in the Ninevah in the meantime."

No, you aren't, Toby thought. *Not if you're working for John Ormond.* "How is Mr. Ormond?" he asked.

"He sends his regards," Tim said. "He talks about you a lot. What was he like, in the army?"

"He was a stiff-necked brass polisher," Toby responded. "Most cheese-paring man I ever met, too. He changed any?"

Tim gave a snort of laughter in spite of himself. "Not noticeably. He's got a very pretty daughter, though."

"I wondered what the attraction was," Toby said. "Look, Tim, think some more about Harvard. Now, don't get defensive; I just said think about it. You don't want to work for John Ormond for the rest of your life."

"I don't intend to," Tim said.

"If you marry his daughter—and without any other job prospects—you may have to," Toby said.

When Tim nodded gloomily, Toby realized that he *was* thinking about marrying the girl. "Don't leap into anything," he suggested gently. He knew better than to say much more. Tim was testing his wings, and Toby knew he was on tricky ground. Any criticism of Miss Ormond was likely to produce the opposite of the desired result. Toby couldn't say he really wanted John Ormond in the family. Toby hadn't liked Ormond in the army, and he was willing to bet he wouldn't like him now. He noticed Sam Brentwood, moodily nursing a glass of whiskey by the fireplace. "How did you get Sam here?" Toby inquired, by way of changing the subject.

"Dragged him," Tim said.

"I don't know that last respects mean much, if you don't want to pay them," Toby pointed out.

"I don't care whether he wants to pay them or not," Tim said. "I'm paying my respects, and making Sam show up was part of it. Dad, I'll miss Stalking Horse something awful, and I wanted him to have a good send-off. Even if he knows Sam didn't want to come, he'll know I cared enough to bring him."

"Yeah, I reckon he will." Toby slung an arm around Tim's shoulders. "We'll all miss him, Son. I think you did right." They slipped away out of the crowd together, to watch the rain from the front porch, in the fresh air. *He's going to be all right,* Toby thought, meaning Tim. *He's going to do okay. You can't kick*

*them into line, I guess. You just have to do your best
and then turn them loose.*

Michael sidled up to Sam. Sam looked surly and as
if he wished to be elsewhere, but Michael was drawn
by the irresistible lure of the exotic. Sam had been in a
silver camp, where fortunes had been dug, prospectors
had gone from rags to riches and sometimes back again,
and men had shot each other in midnight duels on the
streets of a twenty-four-hour-a-day town. Michael saw
Virginia City as a panorama in his mind's eye, with all
of these events taking place simultaneously against a
backdrop of snowcapped mountains, with ore trains
winding their way laboriously down the zigzag grades.

"Hey, Mike," Sam said, as the boy came up beside
him. Sam looked around the parlor and shook his head
at the men in tailcoats and silk hats and the women—
and even children—in sooty black. "Like a bunch of
crows. Don't you expect them to caw any minute?"

Michael laughed. He knew he shouldn't, but Sam's
description was so apt. Most of the women even had
feathers in their bonnets, and their bustles stuck out
behind. "The ladies are really more like black chickens," he whispered. "But the men have the right kind
of tails to their coats."

"I believe you're right," Sam agreed solemnly. He
inspected the group through an imaginary lorgnette. "I
wonder what Stalking Horse would have made of it."

"He would have known we loved him," Michael
said, feeling ashamed of himself for laughing, but really
it hadn't been at Stalking Horse, only at how all the
people looked. "When I was so sick, when I was little,
Stalking Horse came to see me every day, and he
always brought me something. A frog or a little boat
he'd carved, or a pretty rock. I have a whole rock
collection that he brought me that year, one piece at a
time. I'm glad you came, Sam."

"How are you feeling these days? You make up any
more stories?"

"Oh, lots," Michael said. "But I don't know enough.

I wish you'd tell me about the silver mines. And I feel fine," he added rebelliously.

"Sure you do. You can't help it if your mother coddles you too much. No wonder you're always pulling at the leash. No one wrapped me in cotton wool when I was sick." He looked regretful as he thought about that for a moment. "The silver mines aren't all that interesting. And they're hotter than the devil's cookstove. But Virginia City gets right lively. Did Tim tell you about the time Hal Goode put the snake in Weedpatch Johnson's long johns, and they shot it, out on the porch of Roseanna Dawn's fancy house?"

"No!" Mike looked at Sam hopefully.

"Well," Sam said, "Hal Goode and Weedpatch had been on the outs for some time, due to an argument over a silver claim. Their feud kept escalating, and in January Hal dug up a rattlesnake out of its den where it was hibernating and took it over to Roseanna Dawn's, where he'd heard Weedpatch had a special girl. The rattler was as cold as a poker in that weather and about as lively, and Hal sneaked up the stairs and hooked Weedpatch's drawers out of the girl's room with a stick through a crack in the door, stuffed the snake in them, and pushed them back. Well, Roseanna keeps her house pretty warm, her clientele being inclined to take off their clothes, and the rattler warmed up quicker than Hal had intended. Hal wasn't quite out the front door when there was an almighty row, with the girl screaming and climbing the bedpost like a monkey and Weedpatch tearing down the stairs, wearing only a six-shooter. He knew who'd done it, see, and—"

"Samuel Brentwood!" Eulalia Blake appeared at his side and snatched Michael bodily away from him. "What do you mean telling an innocent child a story that any decent Christian man would be ashamed to bring up in mixed company! And in a house of mourning!"

"Grandmama—" Michael wanted to know what happened when Weedpatch caught up to Hal Goode. And what had become of the rattlesnake?

"Michael, you go to bed!" Eulalia gave him a push

toward the door. She whipped around and glared at
Sam. "With no concern for his state of health! And after
you connived to drag his brother off to that heathen
outpost!" Eulalia was furious. "You are an irresponsible
troublemaker, and it is a pure wonder to me that any
son of Andrew Brentwood's could behave in this fashion!"

"Yes, ma'am," Sam said. "It's a pure wonder to
him, too. There's just no accounting for wickedness, is
there?" He stalked out, picking up his hat and jamming
it on his head, before she could answer him.

"Mama, you'll bust a stay." Toby had come in from
the porch as Eulalia was letting Sam have it, and he put
an arm around her waist. "Simmer down."

"I am just outdone with him," Eulalia said, seething. "He's hopeless! How could any son of Andy's have
grown up this way?"

"Ask Andy," Toby replied grimly. "If you can get
his attention."

Sam, knowing that he would be persona non grata
in the parlor now, found a wicker chair in an unlighted
corner of the porch and sat in it, propping his feet on
the porch railing. He lit a cigar and stared out at the
rain and the night. You'd think he had taken the kid
into a whorehouse, he thought, irked. He liked Mike,
and he thought it would be a shame if all the old
biddies in the house turned him into a mama's precious
pet. Sam wouldn't have minded having Mike for a little
brother. He sure beat the hell out of Lydia's precious
Franz, whom he had never even seen. Sam gritted his
teeth. He had told Tim he didn't want to come, so Tim
could just blame himself when his grandmother took
out after him about Sam's telling the rattlesnake story
to Mike. Sam shot a venomous look over his shoulder at
the gathering displayed in the lighted parlor window.
He still didn't see what was wrong with that story.
Hell, Annie had thought it was funny. She had laughed
and laughed. Sam was surprised to discover how much
he missed her.

*   *   *

White Elk managed to accept the condolences of the Holts and their kin, of the neighboring farmers, and the Madrona ranch hands without letting his eyes spill over. He hadn't cried since he was ten, but staying under control was harder than he would have thought. He felt orphaned more irrevocably than when his mother had died in his childhood. As soon as it seemed decent, he slipped away from the house and went home to the achingly empty cottage. He looked into Stalking Horse's room. Eventually he would have to sort his belongings. There were things, White Elk knew, that the old man had wanted to go to Tim and Janessa and to Toby, Alexandra, and the little children. He hadn't bothered to write a will; a scribbled list was in his desk. Stalking Horse had known that White Elk would follow it.

Tomorrow, White Elk thought. He didn't think he could stand it tonight. He paced restlessly, looking for something, or nothing—for a ghost, maybe, to keep him company. Having gotten away from people to mourn in solitude, he was now lonely. He had only lit one lamp, and the cottage was either black with shadow or yellow-gray in the circle of the lamp. He looked out the darkened window of the front room. Across the yard, the bunkhouse spilled light onto the mock orange shrubs beneath its windows. Someone had gotten a guitar out and was singing "Swing Low, Sweet Chariot." Bill Eddings, probably. His low, mournful baritone drifted across the yard as the others joined in. White Elk went to the window and opened it, the better to hear:

"Swing low, sweet chariot . . ."

"You reckon he's in heaven, Bill?" someone interrupted. "Do Injuns go to heaven?"

"He was a Christian," Bill answered, "so I reckon."

"Myself, I never thought the old man was more'n half a Christian. He was raised up with all them Injun spirits. A leopard don't change his spots."

"Well, he was buried a Christian, so I guess maybe they'll give him his choice," Bill said, then continued his singing.

"I looked over Jordan, and what did I see . . . "

"Injun heaven might be a sight better," Coot Simmons speculated. "Hunting and fishing for eternity. I never did much fancy a harp and halo."

"You all don't know anything about it," another man said. "It ain't like renting a room at a hotel."

"Well, you don't know, either," Coot said. "You ain't been, an' you ain't likely to go."

"A band of angels comin' after me . . ."

"For Gawd's sake, Bill, play somethin' that ain't a dirge."

White Elk closed the window and ran a hand through his hair. They were mourning after their own fashion, and he wasn't angry, but he had no desire to join them. None of them had ever really understood Stalking Horse, he thought; they never understood what it was like to have a foot in two eras as well as two worlds. Stalking Horse had been born in another age, when the West was unsettled and the Indians were still free in it, lords of their own land. White Elk went into his bedroom and pulled off his boots. Everything was different now. It had been different before Stalking Horse had died—the old man had seen the world change—but now the difference had a finality, something like the closing of a door.

In the morning White Elk found the world not so much changed as he might have hoped. Ranch hands who sat up all night conducting a wake with a guitar and a bottle still had hangovers, and the new foreman's skin was still a different color from theirs.

At seven o'clock, when there was still no one to be seen in the barns, White Elk banged the bunkhouse door open and began pulling them out of bed.

"Awww." Coot Simmons opened one eye. "Don't you people ever sleep? We figured to take a day off, out of respect." He had been nursing a toothache with creosote and clove oil, topped off with liberal internal applications of whiskey. Now his jaw was so sore that he couldn't even chew eggs, and he looked as if he had the mumps.

"Yeah, respect," Bill Eddings mumbled sleepily. He pulled the down pillow over his bald head like a hat.

"My grandfather was up at five every day of his life," White Elk said. "So if you want to respect him, you can do the same." He looked around the room. "And this place is a pigsty. Mrs. Holt would raise hell if she saw it." The double bunks around the wall were a shambles of crumpled blankets and bare ticking. The floor was a sea of old newspapers, wood shavings from someone's whittling, and piles of what were possibly clothes—if they weren't rags. It was hard to tell.

Coot sat up, yawned carefully around his toothache, and scratched under the armpits of his red undershirt. "We ain't had much time to sweep up." He glared at White Elk. "The old man never cared, neither."

"He was too sick to smell, then," White Elk said. "When you finish up tonight, we're going to take a mop and bucket to this place."

"Aw, ain't Injuns just the cleanest folks," Howie Janks muttered from under his pillow.

White Elk pulled the blanket off and hauled Howie up. "Folks don't pass out when they get upwind of us, either," he commented. "Now you listen to me. I've got a job to do, and I aim to do it, and I'm not going to take any guff from you boys. Now get up and get to work. We've got hay to bale and a load of horses to ship by the end of the week. If you've got time on your hands after that, a fence in the south pasture needs mending."

They got up and dressed and filed unhappily out to the back door of the Madrona kitchen, where they ate breakfast at a long trestle table in a room next to the pantry. Abby Givens presented them with cold bacon and leathery eggs for their sins, and everyone but Coot ate it, grumbling. Coot had tied a rag around his jaw and knotted it on top of his head; it looked like he was wearing rabbit ears. It made speech difficult and eating impossible. After breakfast, the men trudged out to work.

By noon, White Elk knew that he wasn't going to see Mai for weeks. Stalking Horse's illness, Toby's campaign, and White Elk's preoccupation with Mai had combined to leave the Madrona hands on a loose rein for several months. They were good men, at heart, White Elk knew, or Toby wouldn't have hired them. But they were also inclined to idleness when unsupervised; otherwise, they would have been homesteading their own spreads instead of baling hay for someone else.

"Most men need to be ridden," Stalking Horse had been known to say. "Just like the horses. They do not think in the long term. If you leave them idle, they will be idle, like a horse. It is the exceptional man who can ride himself, set his own goals, and achieve them, day after day. You are one of those, which is why you will be the boss after me. But always understand that it is not a fault in other men that they cannot do this; it is just human nature."

White Elk discovered that in the last month human nature had resulted in more than a pigsty in the bunkhouse. The morning's baling, when he went to check it, proved to be hopelessly sloppy and the hay had to be rebaled. The loose fence in the south pasture had become a downed fence, and four horses were missing—probably getting sick on apples on the Givens place up the road, where Abby and Amy's brothers farmed.

White Elk sent Howie Janks for the horses, baled three bales of hay himself to prove that he knew what he was doing, then hitched the mules to the ranch buckboard.

He pointed at Coot. "Get in."

"Huh-uh. Ain't going." A twinge shot through his tooth into his jaw, and he made an anguished motion with his hand three inches away from it, afraid to touch it. "Ow, damn!" He could still swear.

White Elk advanced on him. "Get in the wagon, or I'll sit on you and pull the tooth myself." He took a pair of baling pliers out of his back pocket and wiggled them at Coot, who paled and got in the wagon, accompanied by unsympathetic hoots from his friends.

The dentist used much the same procedure, but at least he had chloroform. Driving the wagon back through Portland, White Elk looked wistfully down Pine Street toward Chinatown, but he didn't turn. Too many responsibilities were on his shoulders, including knocking twenty surly cowboys back into shape. Mai haunted his dreams at night, but reality sat beside him, chewing on a wad of blood-soaked rag and glowering at him over it.

XIII

Virginia City, September 1888

Tim and Sam jerked out of a doze as the Virginia & Truckee Line steamed into the Virginia City depot at twilight. The platform lights were on, and an unusual number of people seemed to be awaiting the train. Tim poked Sam.

"Looks like a reception committee. You do anything I don't know about before we left?"

"Not that I can remember," Sam said cheerfully.

"I wonder who they're waiting for." Tim recognized Joe Yellan among the crowd of miners.

"Big union yahoo," Sam guessed. "That was the scuttlebutt."

"How do you know that?"

"Oh, I get around." He stretched lazily. "If the union's going to make it safe for us common types, I may take up mining again." His eyes roved over the crowd and lit on Annie, waiting in her buggy at the end of the platform. He smiled. "Right after I rest up a little."

Sam picked up his carpetbag, and Tim followed him down the steps. A furious yapping greeted them, and Tim saw Isabella, with Columbine lunging hysterically at the end of her lead. Tim pushed his way through the miners, nodding at the ones he knew.

"Welcome home!" Isabella tucked her arm through Tim's and beamed up at him. "We all missed you. Mother's expecting you for dinner tonight."

"I'm pretty tired," Tim said dubiously. He whispered in her ear, "I missed you, too. I'd sure like to see you without the entourage."

"That wouldn't look nice," Isabella said primly.

Tim gestured toward the crowd behind them. "What's all the commotion?"

"Oh, Daddy's so annoyed." Isabella clucked her tongue sympathetically. "Those troublemakers in the mine have brought in a union organizer. They're even threatening a strike. Daddy's just worried to death. He says the union's going to be lucky if their man doesn't get himself ridden out of town on a rail." She squeezed Tim's arm. "Now don't you ask him anything about it. Mother's just gotten him calmed down."

"The question won't cross my lips," Tim promised. He thought it had better not. He probably wouldn't be able to keep his own mouth shut if Mr. Ormond got started on the union. "I'll tell you what: dinner and then a walk. Just us two. All right?"

"Well . . ."

Columbine, in an excess of enthusiasm, ran around them in circles until she ran out of leash. Tim, finding that he and Isabella were tied together at the knees, took advantage of it and declined to help her unsnarl them until she gave in.

"All right. But you'll have to look absolutely pious at dinner, or Mother will make Laney go with us."

Poor Laney, Tim thought. How trying for her. He hoped she was going to marry the schoolteacher. If she didn't, she would spend her life as an old-maid aunt and unpaid babysitter. Isabella was too young and too pretty to have any understanding of the trial of being plain. But Tim, with his inborn sympathy for the underdog, thought that when he married Isabella—and he did plan on marrying her—he would see that they did something for Laney. He hefted his carpetbag. "I'll walk you home, and then go and change. And I promise to look as pious as a parson so that your mother won't ever suspect that what I really want is to get you into a dark corner outside and kiss you."

Isabella giggled. "Without Laney," she said demurely.

"What are you going to do now?" Annie asked. "If there's any silver in that Hopeful mine, I'll eat my hat." She leaned back on the settee and propped her toes on an ottoman. Sam was lying with his head in her lap, and she trailed her fingers through his dark hair.

"I might get a job in the Ninevah again," Sam answered.

"You'll just quit again," Annie said. "Besides, how do you know they'll take you on?"

"Oh, I had an offer." He reached an arm out for a peach from a bowl on the tea table and took a bite. "Before Tim dragged me up to Portland."

"You didn't tell me," Annie said suspiciously.

"Well, I don't tell you everything."

"You might make peace with your pa, too," Annie said. She knew he ought to, and she knew she was hoping that he wouldn't. If he made peace with his folks, he might leave for Independence.

"When hell freezes over." Sam ate the rest of the peach and tossed the pit back in the bowl. "We could join the circus. You could be the daring bareback rider, and I could tame the tigers. We could be the toast of two continents."

"Annie Laurie Malone and Professor Samuel Brentwood," Annie said, going along with it. "It would look swell on a poster." She liked when he made up scenarios of what they might do together. It was always something silly and improbable, of course, not something they might really do. She didn't think he'd go back in that mine, either.

She knew she ought to quit lending him money. It probably wasn't good for him. She was a cradle robber; there was no point in trying to put a nice name on it. It was just that with Sam lying in her lap, sweetly amorous and saying how he had missed her, it was getting harder to think about that, harder to throw him out.

*   *   *

Sam did go back to work in the Ninevah, much to Annie's surprise, but he came straight to see her after his shift. He had taken to leaving a change of clothes at her house, too, to put on after he had washed off the mine grime in Annie's palatial, marble-floored bathroom. Annie knew that she oughtn't to let him do that, either, but when he described to her in plaintive tones the oversize mixing bowl that Molinelli's Hotel provided for a bathtub, she gave in.

Annie's house was huge, ornate, and up-to-the-minute in all respects. Water for the tub was piped in from the boiler in the kitchen, not carried in cans, and it flowed away again through a drain in the bottom, which was worked with a lever. The bathroom walls were paneled halfway up with polished, brown-marble slabs. Above the marble were pastoral scenes, executed by an itinerant artist, of shepherdesses dressed in fanciful romantic costumes. The floor was covered with hooked rugs, and the room was lit by a gas chandelier with tulip-shaped glass and warmed by a fat-bellied porcelain stove.

Annie knew that Sam liked her house and loved luxury. He would slide into the steaming water, prop his toes against the foot of the enameled tub, and soak, as happily as a crocodile, until he felt clean again. He hated to be dirty. Annie thought maybe he hated that more than anything else about the mine.

The fifth night after he had gone back to work in the Ninevah, Sam limped in late, grimy and wretched looking as always, but with a certain secretive jauntiness. It wasn't anything she could put her finger on, and he wasn't forthcoming about it, but after he had bathed, he drained the water out of the tub and refilled it. Annie was going over accounts at the little secretary in her bedroom when he came in behind her, wrapped in a Turkish towel and leaving wet footprints on the carpet. He put wet arms around her shoulders, and Annie pushed the ledger away from the drips.

"I have something for you," Sam said.

"You're wet."

"I have a present for you. Come on." He pulled her out of the chair.

"You're wet," Annie said again. "You'll spoil my dress."

Sam chuckled and turned her around and started to unlace it.

"You're no present," she informed him.

Sam twitched the dress down over her shoulders and unhooked her bustle. "You have a filthy mind. This is a real present."

"Then why do I have to undress for it?" Annie asked, giggling, but she let him lead her into the bedroom in her shimmy.

"Because it's to take a bath with." Sam produced a gold-foil box and handed it to her.

Annie blinked. It was bath oil, an expensive French scent—more expensive than Sam could afford. "How did you pay for this?" she demanded.

"None of your business. It wasn't with your money. I'm not that much of a cad." The smile had abruptly disappeared from his face.

Annie sighed. "I didn't mean that," she said penitently.

"Then quit checking up on me. You're not my mother."

The towel slipped from his hips, and Annie eyed his muscular young body pensively. "I'm almost old enough to be." She sounded sad

"Horseshit." Sam smiled, suddenly jaunty again, pulled her into his arms, then kissed her neck. He took the bottle from her and, after pouring some of the oil into the water, began untying her chemise.

His emotions seemed to fluctuate like quicksilver tonight, Annie thought, and there was a bright flush of excitement in his cheeks. He looked reckless, as if he were doing something dangerous and was driven by the pleasure of the danger. Annie thought the recklessness and the mood were not her doing; she was only being swept into them. But she let him pull off her clothes and drag her, laughing, into the tub with him.

Sam pulled her into his arms on top of him in the scented water. The water sloshed over the side of the tub onto the marble floor. Laughing and floundering, Annie gave in to the silliness of the moment and the desire that Sam always evoked in her, but as they kissed she thought, *He's up to something.*

Tim climbed out of the lift cage on the third level of the Ninevah, and the little group of miners fell silent and watched him uneasily. Tim set off up the drift and heard their low voices pick up again behind him. He knew it wasn't animosity, just caution. The first thing the union organizer would have told them was to quit broadcasting their intentions publicly. What the mine bosses knew about, the mine bosses could put a stop to. As an engineer—and a known suitor of John Ormond's daughter—Tim was on the other side of the fence, wherever his sympathies might lie.

Tim looked at the newly timbered ceiling at the end of the drift and shook his head. It was just barely good enough. The mine superintendent had given the word that "good enough" would suffice; time and money were not to be wasted. Tim silently wished the struggling union good luck. They would be meeting somewhere in secret, he knew, with the organizer to tell them the next step if they really wanted to fight. Tim didn't know where or when—it wouldn't be in the Miners Union Hall—and he didn't want to know. That way if anyone asked him, he wouldn't have to lie. He had been careful to ask Sam no questions—not that he saw much of Sam. Tim grinned. Sam had rolled in around midnight the night before and fallen asleep in his half of the bed almost before he had pulled off his boots. If Annie Malone didn't throw him out occasionally, Sam wouldn't come back to the hotel at all.

Holding his lantern close, Tim studied the face of

the drift, looking at the way the ore lay. The miners seemed to be right on the vein, but he thought it was beginning to dip a little. If they had to follow it down, they would spend a lot of time timbering. This drift had a lot of clay. The Comstock Lode was a notoriously unstable geological formation, laced with thick sheets of clay, which swelled when exposed to the air, exerting a tremendous pressure on the timbers. Even when there was enough timbering, a crew constantly had to haul away the encroaching clay. When there wasn't enough timbering—or it wasn't adequately braced, the clay could bust the whole thing right out of the rock.

Tim ran his lantern over the drift walls. They glittered with a fairylike beauty that was lost on the men who mined them. Hard-rock miners were too concerned with staying alive to appreciate the charm of what appeared, in places, to be diamond-studded walls. Quartz crystals mingled with the ore and reflected the lantern glow and candlelight in brilliant splendor. Tim's lantern caught the further glow of two red eyes above a heap of ore: a rat, looking for leavings from the lunch pails. The mine rats were quite tame, for rats, and they followed the crews from drift to drift. The food that was left for the Tommy-knockers generally ended up in a rat's belly. In Tim's opinion, the Tommy-knockers, whose tiny tapping sounds were held to indicate rich ore or warn of a cave-in, were probably rats.

"You're out of luck," Tim apologized to the rodent, his voice sounding loud and cavernous in the drift. "I don't have anything."

The rat scuttled away. Tim followed it. It was nearly the end of the shift. The crew would be back from their cooling-off break in the ice room after a few more minutes, to fire the charges that were set up in the face in the seven-point pattern that would blast the rock in upon itself, then lift it out with the final charge onto the tunnel's floor. The procedure would advance the drift about three feet. Tim thought he would take another look at it in the morning and see what Stebbins thought.

Voices came faintly around a bend in the drift:

"Well, I say we ain't gonna get anywhere till we find out how the hell they knew. Not two minutes into a meeting before we find one of Ormond's hired guns outside the door. Now you tell me how he knew where to look."

"I know damned well how he knew where to look," Joe Yellan growled. "I just don't know who told them. Billy Pitts told me the company would put a spy in if they could."

"Shhh!" They saw Tim's lantern and broke off as they came around the bend.

"You boys ready to shoot?" Tim pretended not to have heard the talk. Billy Pitts was the union organizer. Tim knew Yellan didn't think Tim was a spy, but they wouldn't talk around him anyway.

"Pretty near," Yellan answered. "But it wants more timbering."

"Yeah, I know." Tim was sympathetic. He knew he wouldn't get anywhere with Ormond if he tried to insist on it. "Fire it and get out." He headed on up the drift.

Behind him, he heard Joe Yellan's voice: "Fire in the hole!" Almost simultaneously, a faint rumbling sounded from somewhere else in the mine and then a slow, faint creak of timbers. Tim stiffened. He thought, for no reason that he could grasp at first, of the rat. He saw it in his mind, outlined by lantern light, scuttling down the drift. Then he heard Stebbins's voice, still in his head: "The mine rats know. If they start scramming, you scram, too."

He yelled, "Get out!" and ran as Yellan and his crew came pounding behind him. It was too late. The charges behind them blew, and Tim heard the sound of breaking timber and a roaring all around him. He stopped, afraid to move, as a violent blast of air blew out his lantern. A man careened into him in the darkness.

It was pitch dark, terrifyingly dark. Tim didn't need light to know they were sealed inside the earth.

That first blast of air had come from ahead of them up the drift, before they felt the wind from Yellan's charges. Miraculously they were unhurt, but they were trapped.

Someone made a faint moan, and Yellan's voice said, "Mother of God," very quietly. There was the quick flare of a match, and Yellan relit his candle. The air was thick with dust and gas as they pushed their way up the drift, coughing. Thirty feet ahead, the drift stopped. Where the tunnel had been was now a mountain of rubble and broken timber, with water dripping steadily down it from the broken roof. Tim looked at the miners' faces in the flickering light and saw fear on every one of them. They looked desperately at the wall of rock.

"What do we do?" he quietly asked Yellan.

"We wait, lad," Yellan answered. "For them to dig us out."

"It'll take days," Shore said.

"If the rest doesn't come down." Hobbs looked at the sagging roof of their narrow cavern.

Tim realized that this was Sam's old crew. It was only because Sam had quit in a fury and been replaced before he had hired on again that he wasn't buried here with them. Sam was safe, with another crew on a different level—if they weren't buried, too. Tim had no idea how much of the badly timbered mine had come down with the double blast.

Penrose, Sam's replacement, sat on the ore-car tracks and put his head in his hands. He was a little man—as small as a Tommy-knocker, the others teased him—with a Cornish accent thicker than Yellan's. His empty lunch pail clattered against the tracks, and he kicked at it in helpless fury.

"Bide still!" Yellan hissed. He cocked his head, listening, but he could hear nothing.

"At least two hundred feet," Hobbs estimated somberly, nodding at the blocked tunnel. A single blast on the drift face would take out only three feet of ore. To dig and blast through two hundred feet, timbering as they went, could take two weeks.

Water was beginning to trickle down the walls now, and the air steamed like hell made real. The water was scalding to the touch.

"Get up off the floor," Yellan ordered. "The water'll burn you bad."

It was already beginning to pool on the floor. The drift sloped slightly downward toward the station, and ordinarily the water ran down it into the sump, where it was pumped to the surface. The sump was like a cauldron. A man had fallen into it the previous year, only hip deep, but he had died of the burns. Tim looked at the water puddling around his boots.

"How deep will it get?" Tim asked.

Yellan shrugged, his face grim. "How long is a string? But we'd better find something to sit on."

"It'll come up," Penrose whispered. He was standing now. "We'll be cooked alive. Damned bosses'll leave us to cook!"

"Happen they might," Yellan agreed. "But that's our own mates t'other side of the fall. They won't leave us."

"Is there any other way to get at us?" Tim asked. "Besides through the drift?" He wasn't sure how anyone's nerves, including his own, could stand the waiting. Did men go mad in a cave-in? he wondered. Were the rescued dragged to the surface screaming, insane?

"There's the old west drift," Hobbs said. "It fell in, and they timbered it up. Yonder." He took Yellan's candle and walked ten feet back down the tunnel. Dimly, Tim could see the boarded-up face of an old cave-in behind new timbering. "Doesn't go nowhere. The vein didn't pan out. That's why we kept on south."

Tim tried to orient himself in his mind, picturing the maps on the pump-house wall. Slowly he began to get his bearings. "It goes toward the Sutro Tunnel, doesn't it?" he asked Yellan. The Sutro Tunnel was the main drainage and ventilation shaft for the vast, interconnected workings beneath the city.

Yellan nodded. "Toward it, not to it."

"How far?" Tim asked.

"Within ten feet at the end," Yellan replied. "But look here, lad, it might as well be from here to the moon. Drift's caved in at this end and unstable as hell. That's why they stopped it. Another cave-in could have dropped the Sutro Tunnel with it. They won't try from that end—get themselves killed, like as not."

"We could try it, though," Tim proposed. "From this end. Couldn't we?"

Yellan gave him an appraising look, as if trying to decide something. "We couldn't dig it all. We'd have to blast." He held his candle to the roof. The timbering bulged at the bottom, and a fissure ran through the stone. "One more blast could bury us permanent. Best that we sit tight out of the water and wait." He looked at the others and bent his head toward Tim casually. "We'll try it if the water gets too deep," he said in a low voice.

"And will it?" Tim whispered back.

In the candle's flame, Yellan's face loomed at him oddly, like an apparition. "Happen it may."

Twelve hours later they lay in darkness and silence atop the rubble of ore in front of the drift face. A single candle flickered from its spike in the timbering. They only had two each left, besides Tim's lantern, and they would light the next from the guttering stub of this one. It was so hot that they were drenched with sweat, and Tim, like the miners, had shed his shirt and undershirt. His sodden pants rubbed and chafed at his skin. There was no food, not even a crust in a lunch pail. They drank the hot standing water that pooled on the floor and then promptly sweated it out again.

Far-off in the depths of the mountain, they could hear the distant concussions of heavy blasting—the rescue party working toward them. Tim peered at the water again and pulled out his watch and looked at it. The tunnel would fill with water in four days at this rate, and it would be a week, minimum, before the rescue party could make a breakthrough.

Tim took a mental inv. ntory of their tools: a pick, a shovel, whatever powder was left in Yellan's powder case, and the sledge and drills, which would all be dull. A drill needed to be resharpened and tempered by the blacksmith after cutting about six inches of hole, and Yellan and the crew had been coming off their shift. They had no timber to set in the tunnel as they dug it out.

Tim leaned his head on his arm, watching the single candle flicker almost imperceptibly. A faint draft of air was coming from somewhere, through some fissure in the rock. At least they had that. He felt sick to his stomach with the heat and the sense of desolation that enveloped him like a shroud. He hadn't wanted to die, he thought, but he was going to, buried in the earth with everything he cared about far away on the surface.

He closed his eyes and slept, then woke, groggy and sick, to look at the scalding water again. It was higher. He sat up and saw that Yellan had lit another candle from the flickering remnant of the old one. Tim shook his head, trying to clear it from the heaviness of the heat. He still didn't want to die, but he thought he would rather go from being crushed quickly by rock than scalded to death. He poked Yellan.

"If we don't try now," Tim said, "there won't be much point in it."

Yellan got up, staggering a little, and righted himself. "Better to try than to lie despairing." He looked at Tim. "How old are you, lad?"

"Twenty-two." Tim managed a shaky grin. "And I'd like to get older."

"Happen you won't," Yellan said. "But we'll give it a shot." He shook the other three awake. "We're going to clear the west drift," he told them. "If nought else, it might take some water off."

They struggled to their feet and followed him blindly, as unprotesting as sleepwalkers, to the boarded-up face of the old cave-in. Hobbs looked willing to try anything; Shore and Penrose looked like zombies, their bodies willing to work but their minds shut off, turned to some inner landscape to block out terror.

"When we've cleared a few feet," Tim said, "we can yank timbers out of the end of the drift to use here. Maybe ten feet worth. That's all we can chance coming down."

The end of the drift didn't go anywhere anyway, but they couldn't risk taking too much of the open corridor with it. They were in a tunnel that was perhaps a hundred feet long, with the old west drift midway along it. Maybe they would find salvageable timber in there, Tim thought.

Water fell from the ceiling to splash at their feet.

"Right," Hobbs said, looking down at it. "Let's get to it."

They began the most agonizing work that Tim had ever known. They upended an empty ore car that had been knocked off its tracks in the explosion, then straightened its axle, which had been bent by the blast, with the sledge. That done, they loaded the tools into it and dragged it, bumping along the track, to the old drift. Yellan carried his powder case and coil of fuse with infinite care from place to place, hacking out a dry ledge to set them on. He reckoned he had enough powder in the case for one good shot. If it got wet, they were as good as dead.

With the pick they pried open the boarded-up mouth of the old drift and began to clear it. There was room for only two of them to work, and a third to muck the rubble into the ore car.

"No one works more than fifteen minutes," Yellan decided, his watch in hand. "Fifteen minutes on, and fifteen off."

Even at that pace, they were light-headed with exhaustion in an hour. When the ore car was full, it was dragged to the face of the working drift and dumped, then dragged back, leaving half the width of the drift to haul the cannibalized timbers through when they would need them. They slogged through hot mud that clung to their feet and worked by candlelight, one candle to light the old drift, and one lit only when they needed to move the ore car. They were hoarding Tim's lantern against a need for it deeper in the old drift.

After a while, they stopped counting hours, keeping tabs only on the fifteen-minute marks on their watches. Yellan cut a catch basin in the rock wall with the pick, to save clean water. The hot water made them retch òn empty stomachs, but Tim made them drink it anyway, stubbornly quoting from vague memory of a lecture that Janessa had once given him on dehydration.

They worked for two days. They cleared thirty feet of rubble from the old drift and shored up the tunnel with salvaged timber shaped with a miraculous treasure: a rusted carpenter's ax found in the debris. When salvaged wood would not do, they pulled down the timbers bit by bit from the end of their own drift until they were afraid to go near it any longer, for fear of its collapsing. Once Tim found in the rubble a chunk of gold-bearing pyrite, shining in the candle flame with an ironic glitter; as useless in their trap as any other form of money.

The old drift sloped downward and drew the water from the main tunnel until it slopped around their ankles as they worked. Their skin began to blister and loosen from the muscle tissue until they could feel it crawl over their bones when they touched it. They were haggard, emaciated wraiths, half-parboiled and, Tim thought, all a little crazy. Shore began to sing "The Wreck of the Arethusa" and "Whiskey Johnny," and at first they all joined in, but in the middle of each song he would trail off and begin again, a fragment of a different song, and the rest would stumble to a stop, perplexed. After the third try, as if he could not help it, Shore sang the same lines over and over:

"Oh, I drove three mules for George McVane,
And I drove them three mules on a chain,

Nigh one Jude, and the middle one Jane,
And the one on the stick she didn't have no
name."

They worked, then rested, slumped on piles of
rubble above the water, and worked again. Shore kept
singing the same four lines, a repeated, bewildered
litany in a thin, thready voice, until Penrose flung his
shovel down and screamed at Shore to stop.

". . . drove them three miles on a chain—"

"Stop it, damn yer eyes!" Penrose lunged at him,
grabbing him by the shoulders.

". . . the one on the stick she didn't have no
name—"

"Shut up!" Penrose shrieked. They fell, wrestling
in the mud and rubble, until Yellan pulled Penrose
away and Tim yanked at Shore, shaking him, trying to
get past those unseeing eyes. "Stop it!" he hissed. "Sing
something else or stop it!"

"No name," Shore whispered. He sat down abruptly
on the rock, swaying from side to side.

"Leave him," Yellan said. "He'll do no more, poor
man."

After twelve more hours, in which they lost all
sense of time while the fear of cave-in never left them,
they had cleared the old drift to its ending. As they had
advanced down the drift, they lifted Shore and took
him with them; he never spoke or tried to stand.

The makeshift timbering creaked, and the original
drift behind them was a mountain of rubble from its
face to the opening of the tunnel. To hold the water
back, they had, in desperation, dammed the mouth of
the drift; but water was seeping through anyway. In the
original drift behind them, it lapped waist high. To go
back would be to die.

Yellan looked at the fissured and unsteady rock
face before them.

"No more timber," Tim reported. He staggered,

almost too weary to stand. His hands and feet were raw and bleeding. His skin had blistered from the water and the rock, which was hot to the touch. His lungs felt as if they were burned.

Yellan hacked at the rock with the pick. "We'll dig all we can, and then we'll have to use powder. You might say a prayer, lad."

"I have been," Tim said grimly. "All the ones I know."

They felt a faint, distant shudder in the earth. Hobbs and Penrose looked up from their rest. Shore didn't move. The rock quivered again.

"Rescue party," Hobbs said. "Too far off."

"They should have come this way," Penrose said. "The cowardly bastards."

"Would you, if we be out there, and they in here?" Yellan asked, looking at the rock overhead. It made a faint creaking sound, like a moan.

"They've got more to lose," Tim said.

"And we've got damn all," Penrose snapped bitterly.

"Then just dig," Tim whispered. It would be so easy not to dig, just to lie down—if it weren't for the water. They were pursued by the water, terrified and driven by it.

Wordlessly, they began to hack at the rock in turns, breaking it with the pick, prying pieces loose with the ends of the drill bits. Shore never moved, even when they shifted him to drag the ore car past. It snagged and lurched on the ancient, broken rails. Shore's eyes followed it. They glittered wildly in the candle glow.

"Tommy-knockers told me," he said suddenly. "Little Tommy-knockers said die, and I came down to die." His grimy, haggard face looked as ancient and demonic as a harpy's in a cave.

Tim hacked at another piece of rock. How many more feet to the tunnel? Ten had been Yellan's guess. So close! So close if the earth didn't fall in upon them first. A rhyme from his childhood came into Tim's head,

from whatever unconscious depths his mind had begun
to lapse into:

> How many miles to Babylon?
> Threescore miles and ten.
> Can I get there by candlelight?
> Yes, and back again.

He remembered his mother bouncing him on her
knee and reciting it. He wondered how long it would
be until he was as mad as Shore.

XIV

The pick struck the rock face and snapped. The tip, long since dulled almost to the point of uselessness, broke off and clattered away into the darkness. Tim pried a last piece of stone out with the broken end and stepped back in disgust. The sweat streamed from his filthy body and dripped from the torn shirt-sleeve he had tied around his forehead.

"That's it, Joe." Tim dropped the pick in the rubble at Yellan's feet. "We shoot it, or we sit here and rot."

Yellan got up from his rest, and Hobbs and Penrose stopped shoveling. Yellan looked at the three of them. Shore was as useless as the broken pick; Tim was the youngest and strongest. "Have you ever double-jacked a drill, lad?" Yellan asked him.

Tim shook his head.

"There's a trick to it. Think you can learn?"

"Have to."

Yellan nodded. He took the carefully hoarded lantern and lit it. They blinked and squinted as the drift burst into what seemed at first to be piercing light. Yellan held the lantern up, running his hands over the rock face, prodding it with his fingers, studying how the rock lay, trying to get inside it with his mind. There was enough powder for one shot. If it failed, they were goners. If it didn't fail, it still might bury them.

When he had chosen his spot, Yellan took up the starter drill, a foot-long octagonal rod with a chisel tip.

It was dull. They all were, but nothing else was available. A dull drill could still punch a hole, given enough muscle behind it. And enough time.

Tim held the drill where Yellan told him to, near the center of the face and angled downward. The steel chewed into the raw palms of his hands.

"Give it a quarter turn between strokes," Yellan instructed, "so it don't stick in the hole." He swung the sledge.

It was mindless work, requiring concentration on the steel and a rhythm of the back and hands but no real thought. After a while Tim discovered he became lost in the pattern and the rhythm, and his mind went blank. It was, in its way, an anesthetic.

It took two hours to make the first hole, thirty inches deep and cut with drills. With every six inches, they stopped to scoop out the rock dust with a long-handled, miner's copper spoon and to change drills. Each drill was longer and thinner than the last, beginning with the starter drill—the bull steel—which was an inch and a quarter across the tip. The last was three feet long with a three-quarter-inch tip.

The next two holes formed the base of a triangle and were angled up and in, to meet the first hole at the apex of a pyramid, within the rock. "Up" holes were harder to cut than "down" holes and seemed to Tim to take forever. When he looked down, he saw blood dripping from his hands on the rock.

"Hobbs!" Yellan said. "You take a turn."

Tim slunk off with relief to lie on the rock pile. He tore the other sleeve off his shirt and fashioned it into bandages, which he wound around his hands. Only in his lack of calluses was he the weakest of the three. Hobbs and Penrose were in desperately bad shape, and Tim knew he would have to go back to the drill. He looked at Joe Yellan and thought that the man would kill himself if he kept this pace. Yellan was double-jacking with Hobbs, swinging the sledge while Hobbs turned the drill. Ordinarily double-jack men took turns at the sledge, but Hobbs was too weak to trade off. He would slip with it and kill Yellan.

Tim got up, tightening the bandages on his hands with his teeth. "Give me the sledge. I'll take a time with that."

"I want my fingers, thank you," Yellan said.

"I drove spikes for the railroad one summer when I was sixteen," Tim said. "I can hammer a drill." He grinned at Yellan. "If you don't trust me, put Penrose on the drill. We can't afford to lose you."

"So we can't," Yellan agreed. "We've not another powderman." He pointed at Penrose solemnly. "Up with you."

Penrose got up mournfully, like a sheep being led to slaughter.

"If you want to say prayers," Yellan said, "we'll wait."

Penrose, eyes closed, shook his head, and Yellan made a long-drawn-out rasping sound, which the others finally recognized as laughter. "Open your eyes, you daft fool," Yellan said. "If you die from concussion, it'll be the roof falling in."

Tim and Penrose drilled the edger hole at the right of the pattern with no mishaps; then Tim and Yellan worked on the left-hand edger. The last was the lifter at the bottom. By this time all the drills were so blunt, it was like trying to hammer plain rod through the rock, and two of the drills had bent. Yellan, Penrose, Tim, and Hobbs traded off on the sledge and the drills every two minutes. They were so far past the point of exhaustion that their muscles twitched and quivered, and the men found it hard to stand or hold their hands still. Finally, the seven-point pattern was drilled. It had taken them fourteen hours. The lantern was nearly burned out.

Yellan took his powder case and fuse carefully from the ledge where he had put them. Except for Shore, who had long since ceased to know where they were, the men watched Yellan in tense silence as he made up the powder-filled paper cartridges and fitted them with carefully cut lengths of fuse. With elaborate care he tamped them into the drill holes and packed them in with mud, leaving the rattails—the fuse ends—hanging out. He moved with what seemed to Tim half his normal speed, as if the motion of the world were slowly grinding to a halt. Still slowly, in an almost dreamlike pace, he cut a length of spitter fuse from the coil and notched it—seven notches, one for each charge. Maybe he moved slowly because he was loath to light the fuses, Tim thought; the charge would either free or kill them. Or maybe it only seemed slow to Tim, prolonged by his own terror.

"Get Shore," Yellan said, and the world's speed seemed to snap back to normal.

Hobbs and Penrose took Shore, unprotesting, under his arms and lifted him. They half dragged him to the end of their drift, to the mound of rubble that was heaped against the rising water. With Tim's help they overturned the ore cart and put Shore beneath it. Hobbs and Penrose crawled in under its overhanging side, and Tim went back to Yellan.

"Get out of here," Yellan growled.

"Not till you go. If you drop the spitter or pass out and break your leg, you're going to need me."

Yellan gave Tim a long, appraising look.

"All right, then." He lit the end of the spitter, and it sparked from the first notch. He touched it to the center fuse, then lit the others in turn. He nodded at Tim. "Go!"

"Fire in the hole!" They set off down the drift as quickly as they could. Hobbs and Penrose reached out from the shelter of the ore cart and pulled them under.

They crouched, waiting. "Our Father, who art in Heaven . . ." Penrose murmured.

They heard the roar of the blast, the three center charges first, followed by the outer ones. A wall of air buffeted them, and the dimming lantern went out, leaving them in blackness. Penrose moaned as rock began to pepper the sides of the ore car. They choked on billowing dust and powder gas. And then there was silence, and one last rattling pebble.

"Are we alive?" Penrose whispered.

"You're talking, ain't you?" Hobbs asked shakily.

A timber creaked overhead, and they scrambled suddenly, frantically, from the ore car, blundering in the darkness.

"Bide still!" Yellan hissed. He took the last candle out of his pocket, and it flared into a tiny flame. "Now move quiet, you dumb fools."

Bringing Shore with them, they inched down the drift. The roof sagged and creaked ominously. A mountain of rock was in front of the drift face, and the face was still standing. *No good*, Tim thought dully. *Oh, God, it wasn't any good.*

Then he jerked his chin up, sniffing like a hound. From somewhere came the unmistakable, blessed smell of fresh air.

They flung themselves at the drift face, searching for it, hacking at the rock with drill steels, pulling at it with their bare and bleeding hands. A piece of rock fell away suddenly, and Tim put his hand into open air. With the broken pick, they opened a two-foot gap and slithered through it like demented monkeys, shrieking and splashing in the shallow water of the Sutro Tunnel.

Shore stood docilely, waiting to be led. Protecting their little candle, they set off down the gentle slope of the tunnel. At first the light at the tunnel's mouth was a faint glow washing into the blackness. Next it became a flame, and then a searing white pain that caused them to cover their eyes. At the tunnel's mouth, they staggered blinded into the daylight and dropped in the dirt. Dimly, as he fell into unconsciousness, Tim heard shouting in the distance.

He woke in a hospital bed, with bandages on his head, chest, and hands, like a mummy. The room was square and white, the bed an oblong of white with white iron foot rails. A white-aproned nurse looked at him as he opened his eyes, and then she went out into the hall to call to someone.

He woke again to find a doctor by the bed, with Sam and Isabella. Joe Yellan was in the bed beside his, sleeping, and beyond him Tim could see the small huddled figure of Penrose.

"Where are the others?" he rasped.

"Just rest," the doctor said.

"Goddammit, where are the others?" Tim tried to sit up.

"Tell him!" Sam snapped.

"Shore's on the third floor, with a nurse," the doctor said. "He can't be left alone."

"Where's Hobbs?"

The doctor looked at Sam, and at Joe Yellan, whose eyes were open now, watching them. "Mr. Hobbs didn't make it," he said wearily.

"He was alive!" Tim insisted.

"His heart stopped," the doctor said.

Isabella sat on the bed and took Tim's bandaged hands. "He was dead when the rescue crew got to you," she explained.

"We heard the blast when you broke through into the Sutro Tunnel," Sam said. "We figured out what had happened and got there about when you did. We thought you were all dead for a minute, pal. You've been out for three days."

"You're a hero," Isabella said softly. "Daddy's taking care of the hospital bills for all of you."

Tim closed his eyes, thinking of Hobbs and of the short-cut timbering that had been set in the drift on John Ormond's orders. "Tell him thanks," he responded quietly. Isabella didn't know, didn't understand.

A week later, Tim stood outside the Ninevah hoisting works, looking grimly at the stark landscape of smokestacks and wooden trestles, the heaps of waste rock shadowed by smoke and steam. He looked older now, thinner, his bones accentuated by the gaunt lines of healing scars. The creases around his mouth and eyes were harsh, and very little trace of youth was left in his face. He watched the miners filing into the change room to go down into the earth for a ten-hour shift and two dollars' pay. He watched until the last man had gone inside, then he turned and walked across the street to the mine offices.

Tim pushed open John Ormond's office door without knocking. Ormond was at his desk. "You canned Joe Yellan," Tim said.

Ormond put his pen down. "Due to his own carelessness, Joe Yellan spent a week in the hospital, where, incidentally, I paid his bill."

"Joe Yellan spent more than four days in the pits of hell," Tim said. "I know because I was with him. And if it hadn't been for Joe Yellan, we'd be there yet."

Ormond spread his hands. "A terrible experience for you. Terrible. Mining is a dangerous business, Holt, with risks we all accept. I've been in some dicey situations myself. But this is precisely why we don't encourage our aboveground staff to be down in the drift when the miners are shooting." He smiled avuncularly. "We couldn't have afforded to lose you, son. And Isabella would have had a few words to say to me about it." His expression hardened again. "But a powderman's responsible for his powder. I can't risk another cave-in because Yellan can't set a charge properly. We lost a week's work in that drift."

Tim stood glaring at him, his own face hard, scarred hands hanging at his sides. "Hobbs is dead, and Shore's never going to be right in his mind again because of faulty timbering. You canned Joe Yellan for union activity."

"The damn unions are a cancer," Ormond retorted. "They'll gut this country and strangle the economy, out of greed."

Tim looked out the window. He could see the mine yard from it, as ugly as sin. It made a hell of a tombstone for the men who died below it, he thought. "Greed seems to be a pretty universal human impulse," he said. "I guess a man's got to consult his own conscience about how he's willing to make a living."

"Precisely," Ormond agreed.

Tim didn't know whether or not Ormond was deliberately misunderstanding him.

"You think it over, son. I think you'll come to the same conclusions I have. Those union men don't think about the good of the country. They don't think about anything but their own demands. Pick your friends from your own class, Holt—that's what I believe in."

"Me, too," Tim said. He looked at Ormond with disgust. "We just aren't using the same criteria."

He walked out, down the stairs, and past the smoky desolation of the hoisting works and waste-rock dump. If there was beauty in silver, it was hard bought and only apparent in the final product. And even that, in the right circumstances, was as illusory as the fairy light of the quartz crystals underground. Virginia City was built on that illusion, on the capacity to see only the fine houses, not the gaping wounds hacked out of the earth between them or the raw ugliness of the mine leavings.

He walked through the commercial district and past the opera house to the Miners Union Hall. No serious meetings would be held here now, but the miners still came to play cards and conduct such other social activities as they had no reason to conceal. As he entered, though, eyes turned to him silently, and all movement ceased. Company men were not welcome in the union hall.

Tim saw Penrose in the corner, nervously shuffling and reshuffling a deck of cards, alone. Tim went over to him, while the eyes followed. "Where's Joe Yellan?" Tim asked.

Penrose looked up at him darkly. Tim could still see bandages above his shirt collar. "Ask John Ormond," Penrose said bitterly.

"I just came from there," Tim replied. "I want to talk to Joe. Or to Billy Pitts."

"Has Ormond sent you?" Penrose asked.

"Ormond wouldn't send me anywhere, except maybe to the devil," Tim answered.

"Then what do you want with them?"

Penrose looked nervous, Tim thought, and embarrassed. They had been in danger together, and it made a bond between them; but now, aboveground, Tim was still a company man and maybe an enemy. "I want to join the union," he answered.

"Engineers don't join the union," someone said behind him. "Engineers are management."

"Well, I want to work for the union."

"Look, Holt," Penrose said. "You're a good man, as I've got cause to know. But you're management and courting Ormond's daughter."

"And I might be a spy?" Tim said. "Isabella Ormond doesn't know enough about what goes on in her father's mine to spill a secret if I told her. And I won't—not because I can't trust her, but because I won't involve her in a fight that has nothing to do with her. Isabella is completely innocent of her father's actions, and if I can manage it, she's going to stay that way. I won't have her name dragged into it." He turned to look at the men behind him. "You got that?"

"Beneath that argumentative and long-winded breast beats the pure heart of a lover," a voice said, and Tim turned to find Sam behind him, grinning. "You boys can trust Tim," Sam said. "He's about the most honest man I know." He pulled up a chair to the table, across from Penrose. "And you might as well trust him, because he's also the most pigheaded, and if he wants to find Joe and Billy, he will."

"And you vouch for him, Brentwood?"

"Yeah," Sam said. "I vouch for him. He's my cousin." He grinned at Tim. "Sort of."

"All right, then."

They were meeting in a cabin among the rows of miners' shacks along the gulley below F Street. A kerosene lantern hanging from a beam provided the only light. Joe Yellan was sitting beside Billy Pitts, the union organizer, at the rough plank table, and the one-room shack was crowded with twenty other men, Sam among them. On the stoop a union guard with a shotgun across his knees kept a watch for the uninvited.

"Ormond isn't going to like this." Billy Pitts looked

at Tim appraisingly. Pitts was young and earnest looking, with gold-rimmed glasses on the end of his nose,
but he had a reputation as a union tough and an accomplished brawler. The Ninevah was the third mine he
had organized.

"I can't help that," Tim said stubbornly.

"Well, we can use you," Pitts allowed, "especially
if you'll spread the word to the men we can't get at so
easy. With Joe out, we need a voice in the mine. But
you better keep your head down. Ormond'll fire anybody he thinks is organizing. And I'm taking your word
about the girl."

"We've been through that," Tim said.

"I vote him in," Joe Yellan said.

Pitts looked around him at the other miners. They
nodded. "All right, Holt, sit down. Now let's get to
business."

Pitts regarded the miners. "There are two things
you're going to have to swallow, all of you, if you're
going to follow through with this and not just end up
knuckling under. If you knuckle under once you start,
you're dead."

The miners nodded again. They were willing now.
Since the cave-in, they were mad enough and scared
enough to take the risk.

Pitts removed his glasses. "First, you have to strike,
and that means every man in the mine walks out and
stays out. If you walk, the Consolidated Mine may
walk, and then you'll really have some clout. But you'll
need a strike fund and some backing."

"We got that," Yellan said.

"All right. Second, you'll have to keep the scabs
out. The company'll hire anyone who isn't scared to
cross you, and if that doesn't work, they'll bring them
in from outside. And they'll bring hired guns with
them, men like the couple of thugs Ormond's got already. Every man in this union's got to have a gun and
know how to use it."

"I don't like that," Tim objected. "Nobody scabs
unless he's desperate to make a living, just the same as

us. If we start killing other miners, we've lost our soul, and we're no better than Ormond."

A miner spoke up. "That's right. I ain't no murderer. I got a wife and kids."

"And how long are they going to have you if we go on like we are?" another asked.

"We got to defend ourselves."

"Not with murder!"

"Quiet!" Billy Pitts slammed his hand down on the table. "Nobody shoots a scab unless the scab shoots first. But when the time comes, you'd better be prepared to shoot back at company guns because they're sure as hell going to shoot at you. And if you aren't prepared to risk that, you might as well just go back to Ormond with your tail between your legs and take whatever crusts he's got a mind to throw you." He looked at Tim. "You got that, Holt?"

"Yeah," Tim said. "If it's only in defense, I do."

Pitts looked at the others, at the miners who had been the most vocal. "And you get hold of what Holt's talking about, because he's right, up to a point. If you start a war, you'll lose all sympathy in this town, and right now, since the cave-in, you got some sympathy."

"Till they forget," Yellan muttered. "They forget quick."

"Then we'll act quick," Pitts said.

"Sam, what the hell are you doing getting mixed up in the union?" Tim demanded later that evening when they were walking back to Molinelli's, through the half-empty streets.

"I got a living to make," Sam said. "Like everybody else."

Tim thought he looked evasive, but that was Sam's usual expression anyway. Evasion came naturally to him. He wondered uneasily if Sam had more conscience than he had thought, or less. "Well, thank you for speaking up for me."

"I'm not sure I did you a favor," Sam said.

*   *   *

By the end of the week, they had gotten agreement to strike from more than ninety percent of the Ninevah miners, and quiet contributions to the strike fund from a number of Virginia City residents who didn't want to buck the powers of the town but who were privately appalled by the cave-in and by John Ormond's subsequent firing of Joe Yellan. Billy Pitts ruthlessly removed the now almost catatonic Shore from the hospital and displayed him on the streets of Virginia City for an afternoon. Tim didn't like the tactic, but it brought in two thousand dollars in contributions.

The strike was set for the first of October—a new month and a new start, Billy Pitts had explained. Most of the lower level of management—the engineers and the blacksmiths and station bosses, prodded by Tim—had agreed to strike with them, including, to Tim's surprise, old Stebbins. The Consolidated miners were waiting to see how the Ninevah men fared before joining the walk-out.

The union leaders held a hasty conference as they gathered in the mine yard before the first shift on October first. Billy Pitts and Joe Yellan were lying low, since their presence would be a dead giveaway.

"You sure you know what you're doing?" Penrose whispered to Tim.

Tim nodded. The weather was turning cool, and he was wearing a leather jacket over his shirt. A pistol was hidden under it, if he needed to defend himself. He hoped he wouldn't. "On my signal. Three blasts on the quitting whistle, and you turn and walk off, without a fuss if you can help it. Anyone inside will walk out with you."

Penrose shook his head. "No, I meant do you know what it'll cost you? Ormond'll fire you sure, and then what about the lass?"

"He'll try to fire all of us," Tim replied, "but he can't if we stick together. Isabella will know I had to take a stand, whatever her father thinks."

"Happen you're putting too much faith in love," Penrose muttered.

"Happen I'm not," Tim said. Isabella loved him, and in his mind he already counted her as his girl, not John Ormond's. "Women have more conscience than men, if you ask me."

"They got a convenient conscience," Penrose said. "Same as any of us. You'll see."

The miners were gathering for their shift, nervously swinging lunch pails that they weren't going to use—for lunch, anyway. Tim knew that pistols were stashed in some of them. Sam grinned at him and gave him a thumbs-up sign.

"Get ready." Tim clapped a hand on Penrose's shoulder and headed for the pump room.

Inside, Stebbins was at his desk, and the hoist engine was clattering and whistling with a full head of steam.

"Maybe you better think twice," Stebbins suggested as Tim put his hand on the lever that operated the whistle.

"I thought you were with us," Tim said.

"I am," Stebbins claimed. "But look." He pointed out the window at the mine offices across the street.

Tim saw half a dozen big men in heavy blue suits and bowler hats coming out the open door. They all carried shotguns. Tim had never seen any of them before. Hired guns. Other men moved in a group behind them; men in work clothes, who peered nervously past the company guards. Scabs. "Damn it!" Tim said, infuriated. It was too late to turn back now. If they didn't walk out today, the miners would lose momentum, lose heart, lose the war. His hand jerked on the lever, and the quitting whistle shrieked. Tim blasted the whistle twice more and sprinted for the door. He looked over his shoulder at Stebbins. "You coming?"

Stebbins got up. "Reckon I am. The more fool I."

The Ninevah miners were already confronting the scab crew and the company guards in the yard. Joe Yellan and Billy Pitts had appeared from wherever they had been hiding, to stand at their head.

"This mine is shut down," Billy Pitts declared.

With his sleek hair and his gold-rimmed glasses, he still looked more like an accountant than a union tough, but a shotgun was under his arm to match those of the company guards.

John Ormond waded through the crowd, a furious little bull of a man. "Nobody shuts my mine down, you damned thieving blackguards!" He looked at Joe Yellan. "You don't work here anymore. Take your rabble-rouser and get out before I shoot you." Ormond's eyes traveled over the others. "The rest of you men are docked half a day's pay for holding up work. And if you don't get down there in five minutes, you're all fired." When he saw Tim, his eyes narrowed. "Except for you, Holt. You're fired now, you ungrateful, insubordinate son of a bitch. And if you ever so much as speak to my daughter again, I'll ship you back to Oregon in a box!"

Ormond was so mad, he was almost hopping. He hadn't said anything Tim hadn't expected, but that wasn't what worried Tim. What worried him was the crowd of uncertain-looking men behind the guards. How the hell had Ormond learned about the strike in time to get a crew of scabs together? How had he known to hire enough guards to get the scabs down into his mine?

Joe Yellan and Billy Pitts were no doubt wondering the same thing, but the answers could come later. Right now a war was brewing in the Ninevah mine yard. If the replacement crew got down in the mine, the union had lost its best chance.

Yellan looked the new men over and cocked his shotgun. The scabs backed off a step. More guns were sliding out of lunch pails and jackets among the striking Ninevah miners.

"We don't want bloodshed," Yellan warned. "Just how bad do you boys want to work?"

The new men didn't answer. They were unarmed; apparently Ormond had neglected to mention that his job offer might be over someone's dead body.

"And what's the company paying you, eh?" Billy Pitts shouted. "Do you know that ten years ago a Virginia City miner made four dollars a day for an eight-hour shift? What's the company giving you for a ten-hour day, eh? And do you know how many men this mine has killed in the last year alone?"

"If you want to be a miner, sign a union card!" someone else yelled.

"We got to eat, too!" one of the new men called out.

"Eating ain't the only factor in staying healthy!" a Ninevah man shouted back. He brandished his pistol, and the other Ninevah men took a step forward. "Now git!"

"Get these rabble-rousers off my land," Ormond ordered. He nodded at the company guards, then turned and walked swiftly away through the crowd as the thugs leveled their shotguns.

Nothing like having the courage of your convictions, Tim thought, watching Ormond's retreating back. A shotgun blast exploded in the dirt at his feet. "Take cover!" he shouted.

Tim heard another shotgun blast and saw a miner go down in the dirt. A crack of rifle fire answered from the top of the waste-rock dump, where Pitts had stationed a few men out of sight, in case it came to this. The union men in the yard scrambled for positions behind and beside the hoisting works and the pump shed as the company guards took note of the rifles on the waste-rock dump and backed off a step. They had no cover.

It's a standoff, Tim thought, crouched behind an ore car beside Pitts and Joe Yellan. He raised his head cautiously. The wounded miner was writhing in the dust, trying to sit up, and blood was pouring from his thigh.

"I'm going to get that man before he bleeds to death," Tim told Pitts. "Cover me, but for God's sake hold your fire if you can." They were in the center of town; it would be too easy to kill an innocent bystander unlucky enough to be crossing the street at the wrong time. Public opinion would turn swiftly against the side that did that.

Tim inched out, hands spread to show he wasn't armed, and knelt down by the miner. He tied his bandanna around the man's leg.

A guard chuckled. "If it ain't the Red Cross."

The scabs had scrambled to safety back across the street, but the heavyset guards hadn't moved. Another of them spat, then shouted, "You can shoot us and get strung up for murder, or you can get the hell out of here before we shoot you. You're trespassing on company land. We got Sheriff Tomes behind us."

"Then where is he?" Tim yelled back. He knew Carl Tomes didn't want to take sides; he had said as much when Tim and Joe Yellan had talked to him the previous night. His job was to keep the peace, he had said, which meant arresting any fool who killed someone. He would have told John Ormond the same thing. Sheriff Tomes was in his office down the street, probably watching out the window. He wouldn't run the strikers off the mine-works land unless they opened fire first. Tim and Joe had gotten him to promise that much.

"He'll be here," the guard responded. "When we get a dispersal order from the judge."

"Then I reckon you better get it," Yellan called, allowing himself a small smile as he settled more comfortably behind the ore car. The strikers knew that the judge was on a hunting trip, pursuing bighorn sheep around Tonopah. That was one reason the union had picked today to walk out.

The guard glowered at him. Tim suspected they had already tried that. The guard motioned to his men. "We'll be back," he warned. "If there's any damage to company property, you'll be charged with it."

"Better round up your scabs first!" a Ninevah man shouted. "Looks to me like they're headed clean out of the country!"

The guards swore and set off after the frightened new men, while the Ninevah men hooted at their backs.

Tim motioned to a couple of miners to get the wounded man out of the way, then he yanked the hoist-room door open. A few senior-management men were clustered inside, wondering what to do. Tim jerked his thumb in the direction of the guards. "Any man who's not willing to honor the strike, get out and go with them."

As Tim, wondering *Now what?* himself, walked back to Yellan, a miner named Fenno came skidding and slithering down the side of the waste-rock dump behind them.

"They got a spy!" Fenno sputtered, panting. "That's how they got wind! Ross Bent just came and told me."

"Ross Bent's a station boss," Tim said, "and he wouldn't join our strike."

"No, Bent's union," Billy Pitts corrected. "They got a spy, we got a spy." Behind him, Yellan was talking in a low voice to Fenno. Pitts shrugged at Tim's angry look. "You don't know everything."

Yellan, his face hard, turned to Tim as Fenno scrambled back up the rock pile. "We were right about that, seemingly," he told Tim. He spat and picked up his gun as he looked at Pitts. "It's Brentwood."

XV

Ross Bent had instructed Fenno to report his findings quietly, and Fenno had done so. But that duty discharged, Fenno felt free, in his indignation, to tell the world. In less than a minute, the mine yard was full of furious, shouting miners, howling for Sam Brentwood's blood.

Sam, suspecting what might be coming, tried to slip away through the crowd, only to be collared by Penrose. Sam was a lot bigger than Penrose, but Penrose had outrage on his side. By the time Sam had extricated himself, his escape route was blocked by Pitts and Yellan. The mob was behind him. The company guards across the street looked back dubiously, possibly deciding if they ought to rescue their man. They apparently determined that he wasn't worth it, for they stayed put.

"We got a problem," Pitts told Sam grimly.

"Grab him!" someone yelled.

"Find a rope!"

"Get a bucket of tar!"

"That's too much trouble." A burly miner meaningfully slapped an ax handle across his palm.

Hands reached out to grab Sam, and he fought them off, kicking and thrashing.

"Stop it!" Tim pushed his way to the center of the scene. He wanted to wring Sam's neck and knew that he was going to have his work cut out for him to prevent the mob from doing something worse. "You can't act without proof!"

"Reckon Ross Bent's word is good enough," Pitts said.

"How do you know he's not Ormond's man?" Tim demanded. This elicited howls of protest from the miners, most of whom had known Ross Bent for years.

"All right! All right!" Tim held up his hands. "Maybe you're right." He knew they were right. "But if you turn on your own, even for this, you've lost everything you stand for. Pitts, you know that." Tim slipped his hand inside his jacket, feeling for his gun, in case they didn't know that—or didn't care.

The miners had a cruel grip on Sam, having pinned his arms behind his back.

"Pitts, call them off," Tim demanded.

Pitts looked at Tim through his gold-rimmed glasses. His eyes were icy.

"Call them off!" Tim repeated. He pointed the gun at the organizer. Tim knew he couldn't shoot Pitts, but he was banking on the hope that Pitts wouldn't let an internecine war get started. "If there's a lynching, there won't be a union," Tim insisted. He flicked his eyes at Yellan. "You know that, Joe."

Yellan shifted his feet. He looked at Sam with loathing and at Tim with bewilderment. "I been in a bad place with you, Holt, and I counted you honest. And why do you want now to save a back-stabbing liar's hide?"

"Because his family and mine go back a lot of years," Tim admitted with disgust. "And because I don't want his corpse on your soul, or mine." The angry miners might start with a beating, but Tim knew that if they started at all, Sam would end up dead.

Yellan looked at Pitts. "Maybe I owe Holt a life."

Pitts grimaced, but he was well aware that Tim's revolver was pointing at his vest buttons. "All right, you're square now," he said curtly to Joe Yellan. "Although it strikes me you've overpaid." He gestured to the miners. "Let him loose."

They flung Sam away from them, angry but not angry enough to counter their respect for Joe Yellan.

"Get out," Yellan growled at Sam. "Out of the union, out of the mine. Get out of my sight."

Tim stuck the gun back in his jacket, grabbed Sam, and solidly punched him in the jaw.

Sam staggered and stood staring at him, his hand on his jaw. "What was that for?" he asked thickly.

"You damned Judas," Tim said. "Why did you take Ormond's money?"

"I needed it."

"You son of a bitch, I'm going to beat your brains out." Tim lunged at him again. Sam dodged and swung back, connecting, and Tim went sprawling in the dirt. Tim picked himself up, and the two men swung at each other, while the miners formed an interested circle around them. Sam was a street fighter, quick and nasty, but Tim outweighed him, and he was mad. His fist connected with Sam's jaw again, but Sam hooked his boot behind Tim's ankle, and then they were rolling in the dirt, while Tim punched Sam in the face again and Sam tried to wrap his hands around Tim's throat. Tim straddled him, his chest heaving and murder glittering in his eyes.

"Hell, he might as well have let us do it," one of the miners said as Tim repeatedly bashed Sam's head against the ground.

Another shook his head sagely. "Pounding relatives ain't a thing you leave to strangers."

Sam kneed Tim in the groin, and Tim lost his grip on Sam's collar. Sam rolled out from under him and managed to get to his feet. His fist caught Tim in the stomach, and Tim doubled over. As Sam launched another jab, Tim dodged the blow and caught Sam in the ribs with a punch that sent him spinning. Sam's hair was caked with dirt, and his nose was bleeding. Both men were gasping for breath. Tim, spitting blood, came after him.

They grappled and fell in the dirt again, with Tim astride Sam. Tim hit him twice more in the face. When Sam didn't move, Tim stopped, head hung low, gasping for air. When he had gotten his breath back, he stood, grasped Sam's shirtfront, and hauled him to his feet.

"Get out of my way," he growled at the miners. They eyed him with respect, and the circle parted, leaving a path down which Tim propelled Sam. At the end of the mine-works yard, he pointed Sam at John Ormond's office building and the disinterested company guards. Tim put a foot on Sam's backside and sent him staggering across the street toward them.

"And get your stuff out of my hotel room!" Tim shouted after him. "I don't want to see your lying face again!"

He turned and stalked up the street without looking back at Joe Yellan and the miners in the Nineveh yard. Because he was a relative newcomer, an outsider whose past was linked with Sam Brentwood's, a man who had courted Ormond's daughter and had worked for that man as a management-level employee, he knew without asking that their banishment of Sam went for him, too. And worst of all, in spite of his beating of the company spy, he had deprived the miners of the pleasure of extracting their own revenge.

Annie Malone's maid opened the door and gave a little shriek at the apparition on the porch. Sam's shirt was in shreds, his face almost unrecognizable beneath dirt and blood. His left eye was nearly swollen shut. He staggered past her across the marble hall into the parlor and fell on the green velvet settee. He coughed, spat out a piece of tooth, and rolled over on his stomach, his head and arm hanging off the edge.

"Go tell Annie," he said thickly.

Tim pulled off his clothes and limped to the tin washtub, which had been filled by an irritable hotel maid who had given him to understand that she was a busy woman with other work to do, and right-thinking people didn't bathe in the middle of the morning. Tim lowered himself into the water, wincing as it crept into the cuts and scrapes. He felt as if a horse had rolled over him, and he took a vindictive consolation in the fact that Sam probably felt worse. He hoped Sam felt like hell, he thought venomously, picking up the sponge and gritting his teeth as he dabbed it across his face.

When he had sponged away the mud, blood, and bits of gravel, he sat looking sourly at the muck floating in the water and let the heat soak into his aching muscles. Finally he got out, dried off with the minuscule towel provided by the maid, and packed Sam's things into his carpetbag. He set the bag in the hallway outside the door.

The hotel manager passed by with a clipboard in his hand. "Checking out?"

"Mr. Brentwood is," Tim answered. He retreated into the room and lay on the bed, wondering how long he could afford to stay here. He had ten dollars, and Sam had effectively forfeited for him any claim that Tim might have on the miners' strike fund. He had had a pretty short career as a union activist.

I could wire Dad, he thought. *Eat crow and go back to Harvard. Dad might send me some money even if I don't go back. So much for independence.*

No, he was damned if he would ask his father for help. He'd go back to their mountain camp at the Hopeful.

He slept for twenty-four hours, said farewell to civilization with a dinner at the International Hotel, and spent the rest of his money on coffee, flour, sugar, cornmeal, and cans of beans and tomatoes. He eyed them with loathing, got the mule and his horse out of the livery stable paddock where they had been loafing, and headed up the switchback of Geiger Grade toward the Hopeful.

As he had expected, Sam was nowhere to be seen. The Hopeful didn't look as if it had been worked in months, and spiderwebs hung in the narrow tunnel beyond the adit. Cursing Sam, Tim swatted with his hat at the monstrous spiders that inhabited them.

*　　*　　*

"You're lucky they didn't string you up on the spot," Annie Malone said knowingly. She looked across the breakfast table at Sam, who cradled his head in his hands.

"You already said that," he muttered. "My head aches like it's going to divide down the middle."

"Telling you twice doesn't make it less true," Annie said. "I saw it done once." She cut a bite of fried egg. "Fellow was a claim jumper," she volunteered. She took another bite of egg and a sip of coffee. "They had a trial first, sort of. The judge sat on a packing box and said, 'Is there anybody here who thinks this varmint ain't guilty?' Nobody said he did, so the judge said, 'I sentence you to death by hanging.' But they'd already thrown a rope over a pine tree. Whole thing took about three minutes."

Sam looked up. "That's a hell of a story to tell at breakfast." His lip was still swollen, and his left eye was ringed with a greenish-black bruise.

"If talk about hanging makes you sick, you'd better steer clear of those union boys," Annie advised. "They might do it yet if they catch you alone." She put her fork down in exasperation. "Sam, what has gotten into you? I gave that strike fund five hundred dollars because I know what it's like trying to dig a living out of a mountain, and you go sneaking around for John Ormond. That's a dirty and dishonorable way of dealing."

"So's living off a woman," Sam muttered. "That was mentioned once or twice by the boys. All in good fun, of course." But he looked like it had bitten some.

Annie snorted. "I've got a thick skin, and so do you. But John Ormond's a measly old miser, and his wife snubs me on the street. I'm ashamed of what you did for him."

Sam hung his head. "I'm sorry, Annie."

No, you aren't, Annie thought. *You're just sorry you got caught.* "Well, what's done is done," she said. "You'd better lie low here for a while."

Tim sat down on the empty bucket he had been

using to haul rock out of the Hopeful and looked with
aggravation at the corner where his drift ended against
solid rock. Protruding from it was a crystalline chunk of
quartz with a black streak of silver ore through it.
Maybe it was another false start, a pocket that would
end nearly as soon as he started to dig it. Maybe it
wasn't, though. It was bigger than any he and Sam had
found before, tantalizing with promise. Tim looked with
disgust at his pick and then at his hands, which were
bleeding again. They looked lumpy and misshapen. The
scars from the cave-in were still healing, and Sam's
teeth hadn't done them any good, either. And now he
didn't have Sam to help dig. Tim knew where Sam was.
He could go over to Annie Malone's, where Sam was
probably lolling around and letting Annie put beefsteak
on his eye, and forgive him, then make him come back
and help with the Hopeful. But Tim didn't much want
to. If he saw Sam again, he would probably put him in
the hospital.

Tim studied the silver ore. He could shoot it,
putting to good use what he had learned in the abandoned drift from Joe Yellan—if he could drill the holes
alone. It was done all the time on small claims, but it
was even harder than double-jacking. He sighed and
stood up. He'd give it a try. Anything was better than
sitting out here keeping company with a mule.

After a while he fell into the rhythm of the drill, as
he had before: a quarter turn of the drill steel with the
left hand, strike with the right with a four-pound sledge,
turn, strike, turn, strike. It was back-breaking work.
Turn, strike, turn, strike. He let his mind wander,
consoling himself with thoughts of getting rich, of spir-
iting Isabella out of her father's house, of honeymoon-
ing with her in Paris. They would send her father a
telegram from aboard ship and dance under the stars on
deck. In their stateroom, the best to be had, he would
take the pins from her hair, while the liner steamed
toward France. He would slip the dress from her shoulders, hold her to him—

The sledge hit the drill off-center and smacked into

his thumb. Tim dropped it, cursing, and stuck his thumb in his mouth. After that he avoided such physical daydreams and just thought about money.

It took him a little over two days to drill seven holes around the silver ore. He tamped the charges in gingerly, added the rattail fuses, lit them, and ran.

"Fire in the hole!" he warned the mule as he stood back from the adit and waited. The mule shook its ears and snorted. They heard the overlapping blasts of the explosion, and the mule snorted again as the ground shook. Dust and smoke billowed from the adit.

"What do you think?" Tim asked the mule. "Think we're rich? I'll buy you a straw hat." He waited until the dust and powder gas cleared a little, then stepped cautiously inside with a lantern.

Quartz crystals thickly veined with silver glittered at him from the rubble on the drift floor. He looked at the newly exposed face. The vein went on into the mountain. Unfortunately, the direction it took was down.

Tim groaned. He felt like a kid looking at a ripe peach tree whose fruit was just out of his reach. He'd have to sink a shaft. But he couldn't sink one by himself: Comstock formations were too unstable just to start digging, and square-set timbering wasn't a job he could do alone. And this one, because of the angle of the vein and the wide bands of clay that he could see around the ore, looked particularly tricky. Tim sighed and began to pick through the ore, dropping the best chunks into the ore bucket. He needed some experienced help, and given his current standing with the miners' union, that wasn't going to come cheaply.

Help proved, in fact, to be a thing he couldn't buy at all. When he poked his nose in the door of the Miners Union Hall, he found a pistol barrel poking back at him.

"Hey, hold on," Tim said.

"Get out of here," Ross Bent ordered. The pistol barrel didn't waver.

"Look, dammit, just let me talk to Joe Yellan."

"Yellan ain't here. But he and Pitts left orders. You're out, Holt."

"I don't want in," Tim said irritably. "I want to hire some men. Union wages. I've got a vein in the Hopeful I can't work alone."

Bent laughed heartily. "Well, you're in a right fix, aren't you? Hear that, boys? The spy's got himself some silver he can't get at."

A chorus of satisfied guffaws came from the men behind him in the union hall.

"I'm not a spy, and you know it, Bent," Tim said.

"You're Brentwood's cousin," Bent said. "You came to town together, worked a claim together. I don't figure we need to know much else."

"Well, if you weren't a knothead, you'd know I didn't have anything to do with it."

"You saved his neck for him."

"I wasn't about to let you lynch him just to prove I didn't like him," Tim retorted.

"Too bad. He wasn't worth it. Fact is, Holt, now you're tarred with the same brush, and we ain't gonna work for you. The union's got to take a stand against spying, or some other weak soul will try the same trick when he gets hungry enough." Bent grinned maliciously. "You might try to hire those new men Ormond's trying to replace us with."

"Those men don't know their ass from a flat rock," Tim growled. "I need an experienced powderman and a carpenter."

"Well, you won't find them here." Bent prodded him with the gun barrel. "Now get out."

Tim backed off and stood in frustrated fury on the sidewalk as the door banged shut in front of him. The only other miners with the experience he needed were working in the Consolidated Mine. He might possibly hire a couple of them away, but he doubted it. The Consolidated was about ready to strike, too, and the union sympathizers among them would follow Billy Pitts's orders. The others would be busy trying to keep a struck mine going and wouldn't have any truck with him, either, because of the hand he had taken in the Ninevah strike. The Consolidated owners wouldn't let him get near the mine, anyway. Like John Ormond, they probably wanted to shoot him on sight. He felt like a pariah.

He slouched moodily down the street, going nowhere in particular, and nearly bumped into Waldo Howard outside the *Virginia City Beacon* office.

"You look like a lost soul," Waldo observed.

"I feel like one," Tim confessed. "I want to punch somebody." He gave Waldo a succinct description of his visit to the union hall.

"You got yourself in a pickle," Waldo agreed. "Come on, I'll buy you a drink. You look like you need to let off steam."

"You sure you're not embarrassed to be seen with me?" Tim snarled.

"I'm neutral," Waldo said. "I report the facts, but I don't take sides. Can't afford to."

"Well, both sides are mad at me."

"That's about as impartial as you can get," Waldo observed. He took Tim into the Silver Dollar, parked him at the bar, and made sympathetic noises while Tim recounted his plight. Waldo had reported on the Ninevah strike from the beginning and printed periodic updates on its progress—carefully phrased so as not to annoy either faction—but it was cramping his style. Waldo liked a story with pepper.

The mine was still shut down, but John Ormond hadn't budged an inch. Waldo wanted to print his opinions and was of a mind that an edition that didn't net its editor several threats of horsewhipping wasn't a good newspaper. Unfortunately, he was so far in the hole financially, he couldn't afford to offend any advertisers and was forced to look elsewhere for ways to liven up the facts. Sam Brentwood's near lynching, followed by his fistfight with Tim Holt, had been a boon.

"I don't suppose you're thinking about taking on Billy Pitts," Waldo asked, hopeful.

"I'd like to," Tim admitted, "but it wouldn't do any good. I'm not going to get beaten up for your sake, Waldo, just because the news is slow."

"That's a shame," Waldo said. "If you ask me, Pitts needs it. He's near as bad as Ormond."

"He gets results," Tim pointed out.

"Yep, but I don't like his methods. Men like Pitts haven't got any sense of perspective. Can't see any shades of gray at all, just black and white."

"Most people can't see gray," Tim remarked. "At least that's what my dad says."

"Your dad's a man of sense and perception," Waldo said. "If there's one thing I've learned in the newspaper business, it's that there are anywhere from two to ten sides to everything, and people will balk at the damnedest stuff. They'll accept a politician's taking bribes and chasing women but throw him out because they find out he's a card player. In the army they'll take orders from a commander who's an obvious coward and unfit for his post, and then mutiny because there are beans for supper again. Newspapermen are just as bad. We write editorials trumpeting the justice and virtue and all-over purity of one side or the other. We feel wishy-washy if we admit they might both be right."

"Well, I don't think John Ormond's right at all," Tim said.

" 'Course he isn't," Waldo agreed. "But Billy Pitts is a little bit wrong. One doesn't prevent the other. If I weren't so broke, I'd take on both those bastards."

"What's stopping you?" Tim asked. He knew—Waldo's lament was not an unfamiliar one—but he didn't have anywhere to go and was killing time until dark. He was planning to toss a pebble at Isabella's window then, when there was less chance of being shot. Waldo was good for quite a while if you got him going, because he both loved the newspaper business and hated it. He was a terrible businessman and slightly lazy, but he burned with a reporter's fiery passion whenever a good story came along. In between, he got bored with the everyday news, which was why his paper was always a losing proposition: Waldo didn't have the patience to spend time on the obituaries and the civic clubs, which were what people really wanted to read about. Now that this last fling with journalism had run aground, Waldo was trying to sell the *Beacon;* but Tim would bet that Waldo would have another newspaper within two years. He listened with half an ear as Waldo warmed to his subject.

". . . had to lay off my printer's devil, and the paper mill won't send me another shipment until I pay this bill that's sort of been hanging around for a couple of months."

"Is that the same bill you were moaning about last time we talked?" Tim inquired. "If so, I don't blame them."

"Well, maybe more than a couple of months," Waldo conceded.

"You've got no head for business," Tim said. "That's your problem. The publisher can't spend all his time chasing fires. How do you plan on putting out a paper without paper?"

"Well, I got the Readyprint," Waldo answered. "The news service hasn't cut me off yet, and the advertising sheets are free."

Readyprint carried advertising, mainly for patent medicines, on one side, with the other blank for the local paper's use. For some small, struggling publications, it was their sole source of newsprint. Readyprint news was also available by subscription and carried national and world events. It saved small papers typesetting time. Both arrived weekly by train, and the *Beacon* would come out the following day. The *Beacon* had never quite been able to make a dent in the *Territorial Enterprise*, which had been a Virginia City institution since the boom days, but Waldo had given it a good try because he figured someone ought to—the *Enterprise* had been bought out ten or fifteen years earlier by a bunch of mine owners, and it hadn't spoken for the common man since.

"I'll go down fighting," Waldo vowed. He signaled to the bartender for another drink. "Go down fighting, that's what. What are you going to do?"

"I'm going to go see my girl," Tim replied. "Soon as it gets dark."

Waldo chuckled. "I wouldn't be in my twenties again for anything. How's Miss Ormond holding up?"

"I haven't seen her since the strike. I haven't had a chance."

"Oh." Waldo looked as if he might be about to say something else, but he didn't.

"That's why I have to see her tonight," Tim continued. "Poor kid's probably worried to death about me."

"Probably," Waldo said. "You think her old man'll ever give you his blessing, after what you did?"

"Give me his curse, more likely."

"So what are your plans, then?"

"I'm going to elope," Tim said.

"Oh," Waldo said.

"As soon as I get the money together. That's why I need to work the Hopeful."

"Of course," Waldo said. "Does Miss Ormond know about this yet?"

"Not that I hit silver. I'll tell her tonight. I expect that'll relieve her mind some."

"I expect," Waldo agreed. "Looks like it's getting dark out there. Maybe you ought to go relieve her mind while you're still sober. I might be here when you get back if you want to tell me about it."

Tim strolled down C Street, whistling "The Foggy, Foggy Dew" under his breath. It was a tune that always reminded him of Isabella.

"All night long I held her in my arms,
Just to keep her from the foggy, foggy dew. . . ."

He turned down Flowery, thinking how appropriate that name was for a street that held his true love's residence. At Isabella's gate he paused cautiously to see if Columbine was in the yard. Columbine was useless as a watchdog, being nearly brainless, but the slavering hysteria with which she greeted anyone she liked would be bound to draw the attention of the entire household and possibly of the neighbors for miles around.

There was no sign of the dog, so Tim eased along the side of the yard and climbed over the low iron fence under Isabella's window. He tossed a pebble at the glass. Nothing happened. A light shone in the room, and Tim knew Isabella ought to be in there changing for dinner. He tossed another pebble. He saw a quick movement, and Isabella appeared at the window. She put her hand to her mouth and stared at Tim.

Tim motioned to her to come down. She shook her head. *She must not understand,* he thought. "Come down," he called softly. "I have good news."

Isabella put her finger to her lips in an urgent gesture. She backed away from the window and in a few moments slipped into the yard from the back of the house.

"You can't stay here. Daddy will have a fit."

"Not if he doesn't see me," Tim said. He put his arm around her. "Boy, I've missed you."

Isabella leaned her head against his chest. "Tim, how could you? How could you go against Daddy like that? He says I mustn't ever see you again."

"I've got to follow my conscience, honey," Tim explained gently. "That's important. And if you knew what really went on in that mine, you'd agree with me. But it's going to be all right—honey, I hit silver in the Hopeful!"

Isabella didn't say anything.

"And as soon as I get enough of it dug, you and I are going to elope. What do you think of that? We'll have a Paris honeymoon, just like a couple of nabobs, and I'll build you the prettiest house you've ever seen."

"Run away?" Isabella looked at him, astonished. "Tim, I couldn't."

"You love me, don't you?"

"Well, yes, but . . ."

"And I love you, Isabella, so that's all that matters."

"No, it isn't." She wrung her hands in anguish. "I can't. I just can't. Daddy would never speak to me again for the rest of my life."

"Well, that wouldn't be much of a loss," Tim said, "but I bet he would, too."

"You don't understand. He's my father. How can I run away from him? How can I run away from Mother and Laney? From home?"

"You're scared, aren't you?" Tim asked.

"No, I— All right, I'm scared! This is my home. I've never been out on my own. I don't know how."

"And you don't trust me to take care of you?"

"Yes, I do. But I can't just leave them." Isabella looked up at him, tears running down her cheeks. The streetlight illuminated them plainly and painfully for her unhappy lover. "They would hate me if I ran away. I couldn't bear it."

"You aren't ever going to see me again, are you?" Tim's voice had gone flat now, a monotone, expressionless.

Isabella shook her head. "I can't," she whispered. "I can't go against Daddy. I can't make all that trouble."

"All that trouble." Tim shook his head, marveling. "And isn't that just about the worst thing you can do," he said sarcastically. "Get everybody all stirred up just because you love somebody."

"Tim, don't. You just don't understand." Isabella looked up at him, her eyes red.

"No, I don't, do I?" Tim turned on his heels. He vaulted the iron fence with a quick careless leap and was gone, striding down the sidewalk, hands in his pockets, singing.

"And the only, only thing that I ever did wrong,
Was to woo a fair young maid.
I woo'd her in the wintertime
And in the summer too;
And the only, only thing that I did that was wrong,
Was to keep her from the foggy, foggy dew."

*   *   *

Waldo was still standing at the bar in the Silver Dollar. Tim stood next to him without comment.

Waldo cocked his head at Tim. "That was quick."

"Yeah."

"I was afraid something like that might happen. You want to get a bottle?"

"I don't feel much like getting drunk," Tim said.

"That's all right. I'll get drunk. Never say Waldo Howard won't mourn another man's sorrow." He put two dollars on the bar and took the bottle of whiskey to a table, motioning to Tim to follow. Waldo uncorked the bottle and poured a shot. "What happened?"

"It was too much trouble," Tim said.

"What was?"

"Eloping with me. What she said was it would make too much trouble, but she really meant that it just was too much trouble. I wasn't worth the grief she'd have to go through."

"She's young, you know," Waldo consoled.

"So am I," Tim countered. "I just didn't think I was so green, to be taken in like that. I thought I could tell when someone was lying to my face. Maybe I can't. I didn't know when Sam was lying, either."

"Sam's slick," Waldo said. "He ought to be selling snake oil. You aren't green, kid; you just ran up against a master. You're green about love, though—she wasn't lying; she did love you."

"Not enough." Tim stared gloomily at the floor of the bar. It was spread with sawdust, and he watched a cockroach scuttle through it to a hole under the table.

"For the prices they charge, this place is none too clean," Waldo muttered. "Look, kid, maybe she didn't love you enough, but there are degrees of love. You have to figure that into the equation. Gals who never said boo to a goose on their own don't generally up and defy their daddies. If you want the independent type, you ought to be courting Annie Malone."

"Oh, God," Tim moaned. "Do you know what Sam's father and stepmother would do if they found out about that? For two cents, I'd tell them," he added vindictively.

"You let Sam cook his own goose," Waldo said. "If you want something to do, you can come back to the office with me and help me set up the Readyprint. It just came in, and there isn't anything like reading the nation's news to convince you that you haven't got a corner on misery. Be glad you're not in Los Angeles like your sis. They've got a scarlet fever epidemic breaking out there. All we have is a plague of stupidity."

XVI

Los Angeles, October 1888

"Dr. Goulard's Indian Elixir and Celebrated Prepared Prescription are absolutely guaranteed to provide
instant, lasting relief for bilious cholic, green sickness,
nervous derangements, and all diseases arising from the
indiscretions of early youth. In addition, my prescription has proven to be an infallible specific for the red
menace, the dreaded scarlet fever now sweeping your
fair city. One bottle provides certain cure—"

"Charley, how can they?" Janessa glared with outrage at the medicine-show wagon parked near the commercial district on Aliso Street. Dr. Goulard, in a top
hat and tailcoat, stood on the folding platform that let
down from the back of the wagon. His assistants, a
small boy and a middle-aged Indian in fringed buck-
skins and a headdress of scarlet and white feathers, held
up the product as the doctor extolled its virtues.

"To claim it will cure scarlet fever," Janessa said
indignantly, "when so many people are dying of it."

"Well, it won't cure syphilis, either," Charley said,
"which is what he means by the 'indiscretions of early
youth.' It might cure nervous derangement. It's probably about fifty percent alcohol."

"Nature's remedy," Dr. Goulard boasted, as the
crowd of prospective buyers gathered around him. "Guaranteed to be entirely vegetable. Safe for man, woman,
or child. Prepared from the famous cure of the Hualapai
Indians. This child was brought up on it. Step forward,
boy, and show these folks what a fine lad you are. And

Chief Tall Walker here is ninety-seven years old this month. Taken a dose of elixir every day of his life. Isn't that right, Chief?"

"That right," the chief said. "Ugh." He grunted and flexed his arm.

"And how's your health?"

The chief picked up a stout board from the floor of the platform and broke it across his knee. "Health good."

The crowd murmured, visibly impressed. Dr. Goulard's wagon was painted with bright Indian designs and bore a sign on its roof offering his elixir and pre-scription at a dollar a bottle. "The Invalid's Hope and Friend. Thousands of Satisfied Customers." The crowd pressed around the wagon. Small children jumped up and down trying to see the Indian.

"What about you, madam?" Dr. Goulard held out his hand with a flourish, a bottle of elixir balanced on his palm, before a tired-faced woman in a sunbonnet. "My elixir makes dull care begone, gives you vim and vigor to start the day! And you, madam." He pointed at a woman holding a small girl by the hand. The girl was staring at the chief, who stared back at her impassively. "Protect your family from the dreaded scourge! The fearful threat of scarlet fever, which causes strong men to shrink as if at some fanged and dreaded beast, which ravages whole cities, may be made to pass your loved ones by, as docilely as the plague of the Lord passed over the Israelites, if you have fortified them with my prepared prescription, savior of thousands. How will you face yourself if you deny them this infallible shield?"

"I'll take a bottle!" A slim young man in a dusty suit pushed his way through the crowd from the back. "For my sister Mae. She's always been puny. I been worried sick about her getting scarlet fever."

"You may restore her strength as well with a bottle of Indian Elixir," Dr. Goulard suggested.

"Yeah, I better have some of that, too." The young man pulled two crumpled bills from his pants pocket.

"This is too much!" Janessa glared at Dr. Goulard as he handed the young man the bottles.

"He's a shill," Charley said. "A plant, to buy the first bottle. He works for Goulard."

"Well, these other people don't," Janessa said. "Playing on their fears like that, telling them it will be their fault if their children die—he ought to be horse-whipped." She started forward.

"Little lady." Dr. Goulard beamed at her. "My Indian Elixir will keep the roses in those cheeks."

"You and your Indian Elixir ought to be run out of town," Janessa said indignantly. She turned to face the crowd of hopeful buyers. "This stuff won't cure anything," she told them. "Scarlet fever is infectious, or contagious, or both. You can't prevent it with a bottle of hogwash, which is just about all that's in here."

"Now see here, madam—" Dr. Goulard bent down from the platform and pulled at her arm.

Charley folded his arms across his chest and waited. Janessa was going to start a riot, but she had truth on her side, and Charley wasn't about to stop her.

Janessa pulled away from Dr. Goulard's hand. "You people listen to me. The only way to prevent scarlet fever is to stay away from crowds like this one and to boil or burn everything that's been touched by a scarlet-fever patient. Don't put your trust in anyone who tells you he can cure it with stomach bitters or 'prepared prescriptions' or any other chicanery."

"He's a doctor, ain't he?" the woman with the little girl asked. "He ought to know."

"If this man has a medical degree, he stole it," Janessa replied. "He's no more a doctor than you are."

"And what do you know?" a man challenged.

"I'm a medical student. I'm not a doctor yet, but I know a quack when I see one."

"Get this woman out of here," Dr. Goulard murmured to the chief.

The chief looked as if he weren't sure how he was to manage that, but he climbed down off the wagon and gave it a game try. "You come on with me, ma'am.

You're disruptin' the doctor's show." He seemed to have lost his Indian accent and acquired a distinct Midwestern twang.

"You're a disgrace to your tribe," Janessa said. "Whatever it is. My mother was a real medicine woman, and she'd have died laughing if she saw that getup. You two ought to be ashamed of yourselves, taking these people's money and making a child help you. And a block from the medical school, too. Dr. Francis would have you run out of town if he saw you."

Dr. Goulard looked a little unsettled by that news, but he held his hand up to the crowd. "Pay no attention to this woman, folks. The poor thing is obviously disordered from studying matters unsuitable for a female." He bent down. "I said, get her out of here!" he hissed to the chief.

The chief tried to take Janessa's arm, but she shook him away.

"You people are being taken in by an unprincipled con artist," she told the crowd. "And he's not any better." She pointed at the shill. "That man works for Goulard—he hasn't got any sister."

"That is a base calumny!" The shill stuffed the bottles in his coat pocket and pressed his hand to his heart. "If you could but see my poor sister Mae—the most pitiable creature. I am certain that this elixir will restore her to strength."

"Poor girl," someone said sympathetically.

"Have any of you ever seen this man before?" Janessa demanded.

"Well, I ain't," someone else said. "How about it, buddy—you work for the doctor?"

"I am new to your fair city," the shill said defensively.

"There now," a woman said. "And with a sick sister, poor man."

"Indeed, madam. If she were well, the poor creature would be here with me to give the lie to this accusation."

"If she existed at all, you mean," Janessa said. "Forty bottles of that elixir wouldn't cure a wart."

"Goddammit, Chief," Goulard said, "get rid of her!"

"With scarlet fever in the city, you people shouldn't even be out in a crowd," Janessa persisted. "How do you know these men aren't coming down with it themselves?"

The crowd stirred uneasily.

"I got children at home," a woman muttered, backing away.

"I don't care, I want some of that elixir!" a man said.

"Where you think they been before this? Maybe they brought the fever with them!" someone else said.

"You can't catch scarlet fever out of the air. You get it from dirty living."

"They don't look any too clean to me."

The chief took note of the shifting mood of the crowd. "You want her got rid of, you do it, boss," he muttered to Dr. Goulard.

"Madam, I shall have you arrested for interfering with a man's livelihood." Dr. Goulard bent down to shake his fist at Janessa as the crowd began to rumble.

When a tomato splattered against Dr. Goulard's top hat, Charley got ready to intervene if things got too physical. Heaven knew where the tomato had come from, Charley thought. Crowds always seemed to be able to produce tomatoes when they needed them.

"Save the elixir!" Dr. Goulard shouted.

The small boy on the platform watched with fascination as a tomato struck the brown-glass pyramid of bottles. The pyramid buckled in on itself and toppled with a satisfactory crash. The chief ignored the crashing bottles and sprinted for the driver's seat of the wagon.

A barrage of tomatoes splattered the wagon, and a half-dozen citizens who wanted their tonic anyway surged forward, snatching bottles off the platform. Dr. Goulard snatched them back.

"Get inside, you damn fool!" the chief shouted, trying to untie the reins.

A tomato hit a man who was trying to get a bottle off the platform, and he turned and punched the man who had thrown it. The shill was seen scuttling into the back of the wagon. He reached out and dragged the little boy in with him. The crowd had run out of tomatoes and were searching through market baskets for whatever else was handy. Potatoes began to hum through the air.

Charley decided it was time to get Janessa out of there. He waded through the brawl that had broken out.

"My good people, wait!" The doctor stood on the jolting platform and raised his arms. A potato hit him solidly on the forehead, and he fell backward.

"Come on, you ninny." Charley grabbed Janessa by the hand. "The police'll be here in a minute." She hung back, but he pulled her along. "They're fighting with each other now. They aren't going to listen to a lecture on health."

"I didn't mean for this to happen." Janessa gasped as he dragged her, at a half run, past the commercial district and the Vache Frères vineyards.

"Of course you didn't." At what Charley considered a prudent distance they stopped, puffing, and looked back. A full-scale riot was going on around Dr. Goulard's wagon, which was too hemmed in by irate citizens to move. "Here, sit down." A bench for cable-car patrons had been erected at the corner of the vineyard. Charley pushed her down onto it. "You're a dangerous woman."

"To use a child like that!" Janessa fumed. "That little boy."

"He's probably old Goulard's son," Charley said. "Ten years from now he'll have his own show. Grandpa Goulard's Toxic Elixir. With the same old Indian."

"Hmmph!" Janessa glowered at the melee down the road. Charley was right. The police had arrived. "Indians have enough to hamper them in their lives, without making a laughingstock of themselves."

"Indians have to make a living like the rest of us. And not all of them have the advantage of being Toby Holt's daughter," Charley said gently.

Janessa looked as if she was going to retort, but she didn't. "I suppose you're right. Maybe I'm not grateful enough for the luck of the draw."

"None of us is," Charley said. He put his arm around her, not seeming to notice that he'd done it, and she leaned her head against his shoulder. "I could have ended up as a sharecropper's kid when the war was over. My mother married again, after my dad was killed. Married a Yankee. Not a rich man, but a good one. He did all he could for us, saved me from a hell of a lot. I never thought at the time that I'd be grateful for that, but I am. I used to hate him. Now I guess I'll figure out eventually how to thank him."

Janessa smiled. "I never thanked you properly, did I? For coming home to Madrona with me. You always seem to be there when I need shoring up."

"You make yourself sound like a dam about to break," Charley said. "There's nothing wrong with you, Janessa. Except maybe for a conviction that you can save the world."

"Well, can't I?" She gave him a crooked smile. "Someone ought to be able to. Oh, Charley, those people are so ignorant, looking for some sure cure, some miracle elixir to solve their problems."

Charley shook his head. He tightened his arm around her. "There's no cure for stupidity, honey."

Down the street, the police were thoroughly outnumbered by Dr. Goulard's critics and his supporters, who had banded together to repel outside interference.

Somehow the story of Janessa's routing of Dr. Goulard spread throughout the medical college, and she found herself a minor heroine when she appeared the next day in the dissection laboratory.

Dr. Osterman raised his scalpel at her in salute and said, "Ah, Miss Holt, fresh from your triumph over the forces of ignorance." His white hair stuck out wildly, and clenched between his teeth was a cigar that dribbled ash on his black-oilcloth apron. Leaning toward her over a pallid and much-used cadaver, he looked almost maniacal.

Janessa wasn't sure whether he was teasing her or not but decided to pretend that he wasn't. "Thank you, sir," she murmured. "When last seen, the enemy were in full flight."

"I saw it from the window," Mr. Jurgen said. "I damn near fell out. Best show you ever saw. They even threw tomatoes."

Eliza Thoms gave her an admiring look, and even Mr. Felts looked impressed. "I say, Miss Holt," he said tentatively, "what made you do it?"

"I got mad," Janessa answered. "All those people crowded together out there, probably spreading the epidemic, and that two-faced quack telling them that his potions would prevent it."

"Well, they got their comeuppance," Mr. Jurgen said. "When they finally shook loose from the police, they drove right past here in that damn silly wagon, and we pelted them with a few odds and ends dipped in formaldehyde."

Janessa stifled a laugh. "Oh, I wish I'd been watching. I trust it wasn't anything essential from Alphonse here." She pointed at the cadaver.

"No, old Alphonse is too much the worse for wear already," Mr. Jurgen said. "Just some nonessential bits of pig intestine that no one was using, and a sheep brain."

"Naturally, I do not in any way condone your behavior," Dr. Osterman said, but Janessa could see his lip twitching. "I do, however, share in your indignation. In a time of epidemic, the voracious will always prey upon the weak, and I fear we are in for it."

"How bad is the epidemic, sir?" Charley asked.

"Getting worse," Osterman replied. "It may burn itself out if it can be confined, but I doubt it. The dean does not yet feel that the college is in any danger, so in the meantime we will eat, drink, and be merry. You are invited to a sherry party tomorrow evening in honor of Dr. Dunbar's nephew, who is visiting from Washington."

They brightened at that. "I never thought of old Dunbar as having a family. Always assumed he'd sprung full grown from his own top hat."

"Fancy his having a nephew."

"And liking the fellow enough to waste sherry on him."

"Well, I call it sporting of him."

"Now if you feel that you can return your attention to the thoracic cavity . . ." Dr. Osterman continued.

There was a general bustle as the men hung up their coats and tied aprons over their vest fronts. Janessa and Eliza Thoms, who wore white shirtwaists and dark vests very similar to the men's, did likewise. Mr. Jurgen, who was smoking a cigar, retained it, clenched between his teeth in the manner of Dr. Osterman.

The dissection laboratory was illuminated by a skylight and a large gas chandelier. The floor was covered with sawdust, and boxes of sawdust sat beneath the table to serve as disposal bins for anything that couldn't be fitted back into Alphonse. The cadaver, stored in a formaldehyde bath when not in use, was bloodless now, gray and desiccated. Three students had vomited during their first introduction to Alphonse, but they were used to him now and treated him with jocular friendliness, which helped to suppress the conscious knowledge that this was a fellow human being, who had once been as alive as they.

"Today we will continue our consideration of the heart-lung system," Dr. Osterman said. "Not forgetting, however, our examination in the musculature of the extremities tomorrow. Those of you who feel on shaky ground in that area may ask my permission to spend further time with Alphonse tonight."

"Yes, sir. Please, sir," Mr. Felts and Mr. Carstairs said together.

"What appalling lack of confidence," Dr. Osterman said. "Very well. Now, as to the thoracic cavity—do I have a volunteer to prepare Alphonse for us?" Opening the cadaver and pinning back the muscles and inner organs to expose whatever was to be studied was a privilege. Osterman would turn down any volunteer he didn't think competent, but there was a rivalry among the best to be allowed to do the job.

Mr. Jurgen presented a scalpel to Janessa with a low bow. "Miss Holt, will you do the honors for us today?"

Osterman nodded. "An excellent choice. By all means, Miss Holt."

"I hope you won't have a swelled head now that you've been elected queen," Charley whispered to Janessa as they hung up their aprons on hooks on the dissecting-room wall.

"I promise to remain the same, simple, unspoiled girl I always was," she said solemnly. Her eyes danced. "Oh, Charley, I have never been so pleased. To have one of them volunteer me. They've all hated me for so long. I feel as if the ice is finally beginning to break."

"You've earned it," Charley told her. "You're a tough kid. I've always said you were."

"But what am I going to do about that exam tomorrow?" she asked, her face suddenly falling. "I wanted to spend some time on Alphonse's feet, but Felts and Carstairs got ahead of me. I know they want the feet, too, because Felts was moaning about the mess they're in."

"Why don't you let me tutor you?" Charley suggested. "I'm a whiz at the feet. It's all memorization."

"It's easier when I look at it," she said. "Drawings just don't stick in my mind."

"Never fear." Charley's eyes gleamed. "I know just the thing. You meet me here at five."

"No one's here then," Janessa protested. "That's Milton's supper time."

"Precisely," Charley said.

When Janessa came back at five, Charley was waiting for her at the laboratory door. It was closed, and the lab was dark, as she had expected. Milton took his supper at five, and no amount of pleading by the students could persuade him to postpone it by so much as a minute.

Charley produced a brass key and proceeded to unlock the door.

"Where did you get that?"

"Swiped it from Milton," Charley said. "I'll leave it on the floor, and he'll think he dropped it." He pulled open the long drawer in which Alphonse resided. He extended the cadaver's feet and studied them, picking the one that seemed the least hacked up. "Give me a saw."

Janessa stared at him and then ran for the saw. She watched in delight while Charley sliced back the mottled flesh in classic amputation technique and sawed neatly through the bone. "Thirty seconds," Charley said.

"Liston couldn't have done better," Janessa remarked dryly. Liston was an English surgeon who, before the common use of ether, had made a reputation for himself for the speed with which he could remove a leg before the struggling patient could pull free of the assistants holding him down. Some surgeons still operated that way, even with ether. It was flashy, and they liked it. Although the story was told of Liston that he had once amputated a leg at such speed that he had also inadvertently removed his assistant's thumb and index finger and the patient's right testicle.

Charley pushed Alphonse's drawer back in and found some oilcloth in which to wrap up the foot.

"Thank heavens," Janessa said. "I thought you were going to tell me to put it in my purse."

"Anyone coming?" Charley asked.

She cautiously poked her head out the door. "No."

"Come on, then." They hurried out of the lab and up the stairs. Janessa carried the foot under one arm, like a package from the butcher shop, with her shawl draped over it. They nodded grandly to Mr. Felts and Mr. Carstairs, who were lounging on the front veranda, and swept down the stairs to the street.

"Have dinner with me," Charley suggested. "And

then we'll take Alphonse's piggies home, and I'll instruct you in them."

"Well . . ." Janessa hesitated. "Somewhere outside, maybe."

"By all means," Charley agreed. Alphonse's "piggies" smelled strongly of formaldehyde.

They rode the cable car for six blocks—their fellow passengers sniffed and edged away from them slightly—then alighted at a Mexican restaurant near Alameda Street. It had tables set on a flagstone terrace, under a grape arbor. They settled themselves at once, with the foot in Janessa's lap.

"Would señorita wish me to take her shawl and parcel?" the waiter inquired.

"Oh, no! No, thank you, I believe I'll just keep them with me."

When he came back with a glass of lemonade for Janessa and a pottery mug of beer for Charley, she thought he sniffed rather loudly, but he made no further comment.

They ate beans and enchiladas in the pleasant shade of the arbor. "It's awfully hot," Janessa whispered. "Do you think the foot will be all right?"

Charley inhaled, then grimaced. "Maybe it's a little high," he admitted.

She giggled. "Imagine what Felts is going to say when he finds one foot's gone."

"He and Carstairs can draw straws for the other one."

A stout gentleman with an Airedale on a leash was staring at them from the next table. The terrier was straining at the leash, nose quivering.

Charley touched Janessa's hand. "I think we'd better go."

They paid for dinner and fled down Alameda Street, giggling like a pair of guilty children. On Mrs. Burnside's porch, they hesitated. The landlady stuck her head out the front door.

"You missed dinner. Good evening, Mr. Lawrence."

"Good evening, Mrs. Burnside." Charley took his hat off. "I persuaded Miss Holt to dine with me."

Mrs. Burnside sniffed. It seemed to be everyone's immediate reaction. "What is in that parcel?"

There was no point in trying to get around Mrs. Burnside. "It's a foot," Janessa answered. "And I simply have to study it," she added before Mrs. Burnside could say anything. Fifi stuck her head around Mrs. Burnside's skirts and barked at the parcel.

"In the parlor." Mrs. Burnside pointed at the hallway. "Get off the porch with that thing before the neighbors call the authorities. Where in heaven's name did you get a foot?"

"Charley stole it for me," Janessa said, moving inside, with Charley following.

"Gallant of him," Mrs. Burnside conceded. She threw open the parlor doors. "Miss Holt and Mr. Lawrence require this room to conduct the study of an anatomical specimen," she advised those gathered within. "I would suggest that those of you who are faint of heart take your after-dinner coffee on the veranda."

"What sort of anatomical specimen?" Mrs. Bellow demanded.

"Just a foot," Charley said.

"It's sort of old," Janessa added.

Mrs. Bellow fled. No doubt she would have expressed her outrage had she not felt quite so sick to her stomach at the moment. The others followed with more decorum, although Mr. Anderson appeared ready to notify the authorities.

"Grave robbing! I said so!" he declared.

"My good man," Charley said, "if I were going to rob a grave, I should take the whole corpse."

Janessa kicked him.

"This is a specimen from the laboratory at the college," Charley assured Mr. Anderson.

When they were alone and the door firmly shut against Fifi, who seemed as enthralled with their specimen as the Airedale had been, Janessa unwrapped it. They spread the oilcloth out on the hearth and knelt beside it. Charley took a scalpel and a pair of forceps from his pocket.

"Very well, Miss Holt. The muscular layers and their functions, if you please, one by one."

They spent the rest of the evening on it, until the other boarders came in from the porch and went to bed. Mrs. Bellow and Mr. Anderson did not cross the threshold, but Colonel Hapgood opened the door and waved to them genially, and Miss Gillette pressed Janessa's hands.

"Miss Holt, I do admire you so much." She looked at their topic of study with a curious eye. "Fascinating," she murmured.

"Miss Gillette is a poet," Mr. Pepperdine said, also coming in to bid them good night. "All learning is wondrous to her."

"Mr. Pepperdine, you are making fun of me," Miss Gillette said, but she didn't sound annoyed.

Charley picked up the foot. He investigated the contents of Mrs. Burnside's sewing box and helped himself to a spool of thread. He put his hat on. "Till the morrow."

"What about that?" Janessa pointed at the parcel.

"I'll keep custody of it for the evening," Charley said. "There are no dogs at my house."

When Janessa arrived for dissection lab the next morning, Charley was already among the group of students standing outside the door waiting for Milton to let them in.

"It was gone!" Mr. Felts was saying indignantly. "Mr. Carstairs saw it! Of all the low, sneaking—"

"What is your difficulty, Mr. Felts?" Dr. Osterman inquired. Milton came down the hall behind him to unlock the door.

"Someone took one of Alphonse's feet!" Mr. Felts yelped. "And after we reserved them!"

"Right or left?" Charley inquired. Janessa thought he looked particularly pious, not at all like a man with a foot under his frock coat.

"Left. What does it matter?" Felts sputtered.

Milton unlocked the door, and they surged in to view the theft. Mr. Felts pulled Alphonse's drawer open triumphantly. "Look!"

There was a guffaw, quickly suppressed, from Dr. Osterman, and a howl of laughter from his students. The foot had reappeared, neatly sewn on in cross-stitch with red embroidery thread.

In honor of Dr. Dunbar's sherry party, Janessa got out one of her best dresses. She had worn proper blue serge suits and white shirtwaists for so long in her effort to prove herself a serious medical student, she was beginning to feel like a nun. This dress was of fine teal-blue wool with a moderate neckline draped in ivory lace. Her teal kid shoes had satin bows across the instep. She wore a choker of pearls, pearl drops in her ears, and a straw Empire hat with a teal ribbon.

Mrs. Burnside looked her over with approval. "Just right," she pronounced, and waited with interest as the doorbell rang, to see what Mr. Lawrence thought of it.

"You'll knock 'em dead," was Charley's remark.

"Who? Dr. Dunbar?" Janessa laughed. Dr. Dunbar's attitude had changed some—enough to work her to death all summer—but not that much. In Dr. Dunbar's opinion, you could be feminine, or you could be a physician. You could not be both. It appeared to be the only way he could cope with the idea of Janessa at all.

"Well, you knock me dead." Charley gave her his arm. He looked dashing himself, in a Prince Albert coat and top hat. He had rented a gig, which he had tied outside, and he handed her into it carefully.

Dr. Dunbar lived a mile from the medical college, in an old adobe house shaded by live-oak trees. The carriage drive was lined with buggies and saddle horses hitched to the post-and-rail fence that followed the drive. The front walkway was lit with luminarias, little candles set in sacks of oiled paper weighted with sand. There was no lawn, the climate of Southern California not being conducive to one, but the front yard held a

rock garden planted with pampas grass and lilies of the
Nile. In the pleasant cool of the evening, the guests
were gathered on a stone terrace under the live oaks,
and a maid in a white cap and apron was circulating
with trays of crystal sherry glasses. The dean and a
number of doctors from the hospital as well as the
medical school were present.

"He must think highly of this nephew," Charley
murmured, dazzled by this display.

"Steve Jurgen told me he's a hotshot physician
from Washington," Janessa whispered. "Very upper crust.
No one below congressmen need apply for an appoint-
ment."

"Sour grapes," Charley said, grinning. "That's what
Jurgen wants to be. Well, let's go meet old Dunbar's
pride and joy. Even if he is a dope, we can still have
some sherry."

They saw Carstairs and Jurgen on the terrace and
joined them. Mr. Carstairs had his wife with him, a
small woman with a frizz of blond hair. She eyed Janessa
suspiciously as they were introduced, her nose twitching like a rabbit's.

Heavens, Janessa thought. *What a pariah I am.*
She knew that female medical students were popularly
supposed by male students' wives to be man-hunting
femmes fatales. She wondered how on earth she could
possibly explain to Mrs. Carstairs that she wouldn't
want Mr. Carstairs, even if he was being given away
with a pound of tea.

"Have you heard?" Mr. Jurgen was saying. "There's
been another outbreak of scarlet fever, and this one's
spreading like fire. It'll be citywide—you watch."

Charley shook his head. "And here we are, like
damn fools—pardon me, ma'am—doing what we tell
everyone else not to: standing around in a crowd, baaing
like a bunch of sheep."

"Surely there is no danger in these circles," Mrs.
Carstairs said.

"Scarlet fever's no respecter of persons," Jurgen
said. "Not even Dr. Dunbar's dear boy. Although I

must say he certainly looks impervious to most troubles
likely to befall the common man."

"You're jealous," Charley said. "Where is this
paragon?"

"Over there with Dunbar. Just inside the door."

They peered through the crowd around the french
doors leading from the terrace into the house. In the
doorway they could just see the top of Dr. Dunbar's
head and looming over him a tall blond man with
immaculate curls and the leonine air of a man who
knows himself to be handsome. Janessa found herself
looking into the eyes of Brice Amos, the man who had
jilted her in college.

XVII

"Ow!" Charley laid his hand across Janessa's, and she realized that she had been digging her fingernails into his other arm. She unclenched her fingers carefully.

Charley looked at her face and then back at Dr. Dunbar's nephew. "Is that who I think it is?" he whispered.

"It is." Janessa straightened her shoulders. "I think I'd like a glass of sherry."

"Certainly." Charley hailed the maid in the starched cap. "Anyone else? Jurgen? Carstairs? Mrs. Carstairs?"

"Maybe just a little," Mrs. Carstairs said. "Goodness, he's a handsome man, isn't he, Miss Holt?"

Charley gave Janessa her sherry and tucked her other arm through his, as if he weren't sure what she might be going to say. Her face had a dangerous look.

"Exceedingly handsome," Janessa said. "Traffic has been known to stop for him."

"Oh, are you acquainted with him?"

"Only briefly," Janessa replied. "Quite briefly, in fact."

"We knew Dr. Amos in our undergraduate days," Charley said. "In Virginia. I had no idea he was related to Dr. Dunbar."

"His sister's son, I believe," Mr. Jurgen said.

"Aren't you going to go say hello to him?" Mrs. Carstairs asked. "Do bring him over to chat."

"In a moment," Janessa said.

Charley guided her through the crowd toward Brice

282

before she could protest. "Might as well get it over with," Charley said. "Do the polite thing and then relax, I mean. Dunbar will be in a snit if we don't pay our respects."

"I don't want to talk to him!" Janessa protested.

"If it comes to that, he probably doesn't want to talk to you," Charley said. "No one likes someone who reminds him of the time he was a cad. But you've got to do it. You'll be darting around corners the whole time he's here if you don't, and Dunbar will think you've lost your mind."

He made no mention of the fact that it might be painful for her, but just the sight of Brice's face brought back with such clarity that scene on the bridge that Janessa flinched as if it were a raw spot on her skin. She stared at Brice Amos with a mixture of anger and humiliation and the last shreds of an emotion that she had always assumed to be love.

And then they were in the doorway, and Charley was shaking hands with him genially. "Charley Lawrence. We met briefly while you were at Hollins. My sister Nan was a student there. You remember Miss Holt? Extraordinary meeting you out here."

Brice's eyes touched Janessa's and leapt away, but he held out his hand. "Certainly. How pleasant to see you once more. I wasn't aware that you were acquainted with my uncle."

"I'm one of his students," Janessa replied evenly.

"Of course. You always did have a crazy idea to be a doctor, didn't you? Well, well, so you're actually going to do it."

"I am giving it every effort," she said from between clenched teeth.

Dr. Dunbar turned from his conversation with the chief of the Los Angeles County Hospital to beckon Brice into their talk, and Charley and Janessa made an escape for which Brice Amos was no doubt as grateful as they.

"There," Charley said, satisfied. "It's like smallpox vaccination: Now you're immune."

"My smallpox vaccination made a nasty red boil," Janessa grumbled. "And I have a scar."

Charley led her over to a massive Spanish oak bench under a live-oak tree. He brushed the prickly leaves, which the trees shed year-round, from the seat, and sat them both down on it. "Janessa, are you still in love with that son of a bitch?"

"I beg your pardon." She gave him the frosty glare appropriate for a gentleman who has used bad language.

"Don't get fine haired with me," Charley said. "Are you in love with him?"

"Of course not," she said. "He's two-faced, egotistical, pleased with himself, mercenary—"

"And handsome," Charley interrupted. "Let us not forget his fine blond curls. You didn't answer my question."

Janessa's lips quivered. "I don't know. No, of course not. It's just that . . ."

"That he gave you the brush-off while you thought you were in love with him," Charley said. "That tends to freeze progress in its tracks. I've always thought you would have dumped him if he'd given you enough time."

"Why?"

"Because he's two-faced, egotistical, pleased with himself, and mercenary," Charley said, "and I can't stand his curls. Wishful thinking."

Janessa laughed. "Have I ever told you that you're a comfort to me?"

"Oh, I'm good at that," Charley muttered.

The next day they both found they had more important matters to trouble them. Brice Amos presented a guest lecture in his uncle's class, through which Janessa sat stone faced. Following that, as the polite applause died away, the dean came into the hall and took the podium.

Dr. Francis looked at them solemnly. "There are times in every doctor's career when he must weigh the good of his patients against his own welfare—sometimes against his own life. That is a choice that is coming a little earlier to you than to most. But before I continue, I want to emphasize that it is a choice for you because you are not doctors yet. No one will be stigmatized at this college because of his decision." His eyes rested on Janessa and Eliza Thoms. "Or hers."

The students shifted in their seats, knowing what was coming. Rumors had been circulating all morning.

"We now have a full-fledged epidemic in this city, and not enough doctors to go around. Classes will be canceled at this college for the duration of the epidemic because the professors are too badly needed to spend even a few hours of their time teaching. And you are also needed, those of you who are willing.

"We need doctors to take shifts at the clinics and the hospital, and doctors to go to the homes of the sick. For those of you who doubt your capabilities, let me say that I would not ask this if I did not have confidence in you. A paper will be posted outside the door. Please sign it as you leave if you are willing to volunteer, and return at five o'clock. Thank you."

Conversation and speculation erupted as Dr. Francis left the room.

"Are you signing up?"

"Hell, yes! Where are you going to get clinical experience like that?"

"You don't think they're going to send us out alone, do you? I mean, what if somebody's really sick?"

"Then they'll really be in trouble, if they get you, won't they?"

"Aren't you worried about catching it?"

"Of course I am. But I might as well find out now if I've got the guts for this before I spend any more on tuition." That was Mr. Jurgen, pushing his way through the crowd to the sign-up sheet. "Hello, Miss Holt. You're signing up, aren't you?"

"I am," she answered gravely.

She noted that Mr. Jurgen had Mr. Felts by the scruff of the neck. "Felts here doesn't think he's up to it."

"Tut, tut, Mr. Felts," Janessa said. "Where is your dedication? Your marriage to the Hippocratic ideal? Your nerve?" She put a pen in his hand.

"I didn't mean that," Felts protested indignantly. "I just don't feel I've had enough training. Probably just get in the way."

"Never fear, Felts," Jurgen said, guiding his hand. "A use can be found for us all."

When they returned to the college in the evening for their assignments and a crash course in clinical training, four-fifths of the students were there. Brice Amos was sitting on the veranda, smoking a cigar. Mr. Jurgen, coming up the steps with Janessa and Charley, detoured from the crowd to shake his hand.

"I think it's splendid of you to join us, sir. It's an example of service we won't forget."

"Dear boy, I'm only waiting for my uncle," Brice said.

"You're not volunteering?" Jurgen looked taken aback.

Brice tapped the ash off his cigar. "I can't stay for the duration," he explained genially. "I have to be back in Washington next week, so I mustn't get ill. A lot of important people depend on me. I couldn't risk that."

"Of course not," Jurgen said. "Well, it's been nice meeting you." He rejoined Janessa and Charley. "And I thought I'd misjudged the man," he muttered indignantly.

"And you hadn't?" Charley asked.

"Dear boy, he couldn't possibly find time for our little epidemic! He has important patients in Washington."

Janessa looked over her shoulder at Brice as they passed through the front doors. She pulled at Jurgen's sleeve. "Did he really say that?" she demanded.

"That is nearly a direct quote."

Janessa stopped, letting the others bump around her. Charley looked back at her, worried, but when she didn't move, he moved on with Jurgen. Janessa hardly noticed that she was creating a bottleneck in the doorway, as students and professors jostled past her. She stared at Brice Amos as if he had suddenly turned green. It should have been a relief to discover that what she had wanted for so long—and couldn't have—was no good anyway. But it wasn't. She felt sick in the pit of her stomach at the agony she had suffered for this man, at the self-delusion she had practiced to justify that agony.

Brice, having noticed her staring at him, looked uneasy. He beckoned. "Er, Miss Holt—"

Janessa jerked herself into motion and walked over to him.

"Er, Miss Holt, I do trust—" He peered at her nervously. "That is, I hope that you won't, er, see fit to make our acquaintance general knowledge. I mean, it wouldn't be good for you, and—"

"You are a weasel," she said distinctly.

"Now, Miss Holt—Janessa—you don't want to make a scene. No use digging up the past, eh?"

Janessa stared at him. The reason for his worry was beginning to sink in. "You think I'm going to go around telling everyone you jilted me!"

"Well, not exactly—but I didn't jilt you. We had no firm understanding. At any rate, you do look upset, and I hope—"

"Don't give it another thought," she said. "I'd be more embarrassed than you are if anyone ever found out I was that stupid. And you're even a poorer excuse for a doctor!"

She marched across the veranda and through the front door, fuming. In the lecture hall, Charley and Steve Jurgen had saved her a place, and they looked at her curiously as she slid into it.

"You pin his ears back?" Charley whispered.

"Never," she muttered under her breath, "never fall in love with someone because he's good-looking."

"Stupid reason," Charley agreed.

Janessa glared at him. "Men do it all the time."

"Women are supposed to be smarter," Charley pointed out.

Jurgen raised his eyebrows at this exchange, but he didn't say anything. He looked as if a certain amount of light was beginning to dawn on him.

As the last student scrambled into his seat, Dr. Francis walked in and looked them over. "First, let me say how very proud of you I am. That is probably the last thanks anyone will have time to give you until this is over, so make it last."

There was a small chuckle from the students.

"First-year students will be assigned to assist the staff at the hospital. Second-year students will see patients at the clinic. Third-year students will be sent to patients' homes. None of you will be able to go home again—unless you live alone—once you have begun treating patients. I have had beds set up on the second floor for the male students, and on the third floor for the female students. Two of my staff nurses will also sleep on the third floor with the women.

"You will practice scrupulous disinfecting procedures. You are to bathe with carbolic soap, and all clothing worn while seeing patients will be boiled before it is worn again."

Dr. Francis gave them a wintry smile. "And *you* will boil it." There was a faint groan at that. "We have no one else. The only prevention that we know of for this disease consists of quarantine and antiseptic measures. You will wash all food thoroughly before eating it and boil milk before cooking with it. Don't drink fresh milk. A small kitchen is on this floor, and we will use it to prepare our meals. I devoutly hope that some of you know how to cook."

Eliza Thoms glared at Mr. Carstairs, who was looking at the women students expectantly.

"I'll learn if you'll teach me," Steve Jurgen whispered to Janessa.

"She can't boil water," Charley whispered back, then winked at Janessa.

"You will monitor yourselves for signs of fever and take your temperature every day. Anyone with any sign of fever, inflammation of the throat, or nausea is to report to the clinic immediately. You are not to dose yourselves. I will now turn the floor over to Dr. Dunbar, who will refresh your memory on the further symptoms and management of this terrible disease."

As if they weren't burned into her memory, Janessa thought. They had all gone home and read and reread them after Dr. Francis's announcement that afternoon.

Dr. Dunbar reviewed them anyway. In truth, very little could be done for scarlet fever other than to isolate the patient and allow the disease to run its course. A liquid diet was advised when the patient could eat at all, and ice might help to bring down the fever, which could rise as high as 105 degrees with terrifying suddenness. Those who survived the fever itself might suffer permanent kidney damage or deafness.

"You're taking a terrible risk," Mrs. Burnside said when Janessa returned home to pack after the lecture.

"I have to," Janessa said. "If I were already a doctor, there would be no question." She didn't mention Brice Amos. She handed Mrs. Burnside three sheets of notes from Dr. Dunbar's lecture. "Here. Watch for these symptoms and take these precautions. Tell all your boarders to take their temperatures every day and not to go out if they can help it. Don't go to church. You can do your praying at home."

"Such a dreadful plague," Mrs. Burnside said, studying the notes. "And the young and the old always seem to be the ones to catch it. My little sister died of it, years ago."

"They're the weakest, that's why. Rest as much as you can. And take good care of Colonel Hapgood."

"You wait a minute," Mrs. Burnside said. She went upstairs while Janessa stood alone in the hallway, with Fifi leaning against her companionably. Even now, the other boarders wouldn't go near Janessa. She didn't blame them.

Mrs. Burnside came back down with a bundle of old dresses over her arm. "You take these," she urged. "I won't have you boiling your good clothes."

*   *   *

If Janessa had expected to see her first patient in the morning, she was mistaken. The waiting room on the first-floor clinic at the college was full when she got there, and she worked through the night. In the morning, after four hours' exhausted sleep, she drove with Charley and Steve Jurgen to the Sisters of Charity Infirmary to put in a stint there. Those who could afford it went to the hospital or stayed at home and let a doctor come to them; the clinics were for the poor. And because the poor were also the uneducated and lived in crowded conditions, their numbers here were legion. Janessa saw old men, terrified mothers and their children, and housemaids who had been thrown out by their employers as soon as they got sick.

While they stared at her uncomprehending, she explained how the disease was spread by microbes, which couldn't be seen; told them how to boil clothes, bedding, and kitchen utensils; and knew, despairingly, that most of them wouldn't follow her instructions.

At six o'clock she returned to the college and boiled what she had been wearing. The students had set up a big pot over a fire in the field behind the college building and were stirring it in the falling dusk like witches around a cauldron.

"Double, double, toil and trouble," Charley said, dropping a shirt and trousers in, and then with elaborate care, a pair of long johns. "Fire burn and cauldron bubble."

"Eye of newt, and toe of frog," Janessa said, and then, laughing, the rest took up the chant, circling around the pot, stirring it with broomsticks.

"Wool of bat, and tongue of dog,
Adder's fork, and blindworm's sting,
Lizard's leg, and howlet's wing . . ."

Macbeth seemed an appropriate enough work to quote, under the circumstances; and after the horrors of the day, the macabre laughter provided release.

"For a charm of powerful trouble . . .
Fire burn, and cauldron bubble!"

Dr. Francis and Dr. Dunbar watched them from the porch.

"Let us hope the charm provides sufficient trouble for the streptococci bacillus," Dr. Francis said.

"At any rate it is making doctors of them," Dr. Dunbar remarked. Although he was thinking harshly of his nephew, he didn't mention it as he watched the students with approval. Miss Holt wore an old dress that looked as if it belonged to someone else: its excess girth belted tightly around her waist with a sash, its skirt scandalously too short, exhibiting high button shoes and several inches of black stocking. The shoes were not improved by having been washed with carbolic soap. The men wore flannel shirts and blue-denim jeans. No one wanted to boil a wool suit. They looked less like doctors than the participants in a drunken farmhands' revel.

"They have learned the first great lesson," Dr. Dunbar said with satisfaction. "The lesson that is only learned by doing."

Dr. Francis raised an eyebrow in question.

"That dignity and personal safety are not important to the service of medicine."

The little boy was burning hot to the touch. The older girl who held him on her lap stared at Janessa with dark, frightened eyes.

"He has it," Janessa confirmed. "Are there any more at home?"

"Three," the girl said.

"You must keep them away from him. Where's your mother?"

"She sick, too," the girl answered.

"And your father?"

"He go. Go to pick lettuce in Salinas, not come back. He send a little money sometimes."

Janessa looked at the girl frantically. The little boy

and the mother should be in the hospital, but the hospitals were full. She beckoned to a nun who had been taking another child's temperature. "This one needs to stay," Janessa told the woman. "And probably his mother, too. Isn't there some place?"

"We already have beds in the halls," the nun said.

The little boy watched them dully, too sick to care.

The girl started to cry. "I can't keep the others away. We only got one room." She was thin, with hollows around her eyes. Her black hair was lifeless. She would catch it, too, if she tried to nurse them both.

Janessa looked pleadingly at the nun. "Something. Anything."

"Mother of God," the nun whispered. "I'll try. They'll have to share a bed."

Janessa picked up the little boy. "I'm going to send a wagon for your mother," she told the girl. "And then you must boil all the bedding and everything else she's touched. You'll have to burn the mattress. And wash the floor and walls with a weak solution of chloride of mercury. I'll give you that," she added, seeing the girl's desperate expression.

"Is he going to die?" the girl asked. "Is Mama?"

"We'll do the best we can for them," Janessa said, knowing she was dodging that question. She passed the little boy to the nun and reached into the pocket of her faded dress. "What's your name?" she asked the girl.

"Lupe."

"Lupe, I want you to buy food with this." Janessa pressed five dollars in the girl's hand. "And a new mattress." She knew they would have only one. They couldn't sleep on the floor; she couldn't bear it. "Now you go wait out front for the wagon."

"*Gracias,*" Lupe whispered. She trudged to the door, with a backward glance at her little brother.

Charley saw them from across the room. When Lupe had gone outside, he came over and touched Janessa on the shoulder. "You can't do that for all of them," he said softly. "You'll break your heart."

"I know," she said. "Just . . . some of them. I have to. It helps me get through."

"But how do you choose?" Charley asked.

Janessa shook her head, tears running down her face. "I don't know."

Janessa put her face down on her arms, practically in her plate. Steve Jurgen put a sandwich on the plate, and she raised her head and looked at it suspiciously.

"What's in that?"

"Cheese," he said.

"Did you boil it?" she asked wearily.

He laughed. "It's not local cheese. Finest imported goods. All the dairy farmers are mad at us because we've been telling everyone not to drink their milk. The French Grocery's doing a land-office business in imported cheese."

"For the ones who can afford it," Janessa said, thinking of Lupe. She took a bite anyway.

Charley sat down beside her at the trestle table that had been moved into the lecture hall and began wolfing sandwiches. "The nuns have set up a soup kitchen, and the dean strong-armed the mayor into appropriating funds to bring in milk that we know isn't contaminated."

"We ought to be able to test the milk," Janessa declared. "Get a sample from every cow. Klein identified the streptococcus scarlatina three years ago."

"Every cow? It would take years. And we don't even know it's in the milk."

"We don't know it's not," she said stubbornly. "That's what caused the Marylebone epidemic. If we don't know the source, how can we stop it?"

"I don't know," Charley conceded. Exhausted, he rubbed his temples with his fingers. "It's like trying to sweep back the ocean with a broom. Maybe you're right."

The thought stayed in her mind when she went back to the infirmary the next day and sat for a long time beside the bed containing Lupe's mother and little brother—longer than she should have spared from the other patients. The mother was delirious, clutching the child to her, weeping and thrashing in the throes of the fever, her lips parched, her body covered with the rash that gave the disease its name. Janessa pried the little boy from her and held him in her lap while she spooned ice chips into the mother's mouth and wiped her face with a cold cloth.

Epidemic. It was a fearful word, a tide that swept from God knew where and God knew why to engulf everything in its path. Only those who had had the disease before and survived were immune. The others who stayed well were just lucky.

The students and professors gave all that they had to the battle. They went sleepless and homeless for two months, staggering from clinic to hospital to infirmary, ordering the burning of treasured possessions with the ruthlessness of despots, repeating an endless litany of carbolic soap and boiling water to bewildered patients who had no belief in organisms they could not see.

All that could be done was contain the disease. They could neither stop it nor cure it. They could only hold it back a little. Dr. Francis came down with it.

Lupe's mother died. Her little brother lived. Why one and not the other? Janessa had no idea. She tried to think of an answer for Lupe, who was fourteen and suddenly the "mother" of four children, but she couldn't. She found Lupe a job at the brewery instead. It was the best she could do. And she paid for the mother's coffin.

At the end of that day, she found Charley on the back steps of the infirmary with his head in his hands. He looked up as she sat down next to him, and she saw that he was crying. He wiped his eyes on the back of his hand, not even bothering to be embarrassed.

"What is it?"

"All of them," Charley said. "I lost another patient. We thought she was going to make it. The fever was gone, and she was shedding the old skin, but then her kidneys failed."

"Ohh." Janessa laid her head against his shoulder. They sat there a long time, leaning on each other, not speaking, and then they got up and walked slowly back to the college.

Jurgen, Felts, and Carstairs were sitting on the porch with Eliza Thoms, exhausted but too weary to go to bed. They waved Janessa and Charley into their circle. A bond existed among them all now.

"They think the dean's going to make it," Jurgen said.

Janessa gave a little sigh of relief.

"But he's going to be deaf," Eliza said.

Janessa listened to the chirp of crickets in the dusk as tears rolled down her cheeks. No one had anything to say about female hysteria tonight.

"We wanted clinical experience," Jurgen observed after a moment. "I guess we got it."

"We're thinking about this the wrong way," Janessa said, trying to hold the thought that had been nudging at the back of her mind. "We're counting the ones who died. We should be counting the ones we saved."

"Did we save them?" Charley questioned. "Or did they just not die?"

"Not the ones who got sick," Janessa said. "I don't know about those. I mean the ones who never caught it. The ones we kept from catching it, by preaching antisepsis at them until they had to listen."

"Salvation in a bar of soap," Charley intoned.

"Maybe. Salvation in a test tube is more what I'm thinking. If Klein hadn't found the streptococcus scarlatina, we wouldn't know that carbolic soap would do any good. Think of all the other diseases that are still a mystery. How can you stop an epidemic if you don't have a clue what causes it?"

"Microbe hunters," Jurgen said.

"Bacteriology is the new field," Janessa commented. "I always thought I wanted to be a general practitioner, but to tell you the truth, I think we have plenty of those." The image of Brice Amos rose in her mind. "I've been thinking about the Marine Hospital Service."

"That's not just bacteriology," Jurgen said. "That's epidemic fighting—nasty work. Don't tell me you've acquired a taste for it."

"I just want to know." Janessa pounded her fists in frustration on her knees, covered by Mrs. Burnside's old dress. It had been boiled so many times it looked like a dishrag, the pattern only a series of blotches. "I want to know what causes these things, and then I want to stop them."

"Not a bad life's work," Jurgen said.

"Too rich for my blood." Carstairs yawned. "I'm a family man with responsibilities about to arrive."

"You don't say!" They turned, diverted, to congratulate Carstairs. Then the others stood up, stretched, and went inside to bed, leaving Janessa and Charley on the veranda.

"The Marine Hospital is civil service," he remarked idly. "How willing are you to work with the government breathing down your neck?"

"I'll work however I have to. I want to do something!"

"Make a name for yourself?"

"What's wrong with that," Janessa asked irritably, "if you make it by doing some good?"

"Not a thing. I just wanted to be sure there was more to this sudden passion than a desire not to be another Brice Amos."

"That enters into it," she admitted grimly. "Charley, I am so ashamed of ever having given that man the time of day."

"Love's embers quite blown out?"

"Quite."

"Well, that's a relief."

It was nearly pitch dark on the veranda. Suddenly they didn't seem to be talking about scarlet fever. Janessa leaned forward, trying to read the expression on his face. It was elusive, melting into shadow. "Charley? . . ."

"It's an odd thing about friendship," he said. "I always used to think of you as a buddy. Sort of an extra sister. When you showed up here for school, it all went haywire. I wouldn't want you thinking I talked you into coming here under false pretenses."

"You talked me into coming here because you thought I ought to be a doctor," Janessa said. "I'm assuming you still do."

"Well, of course I do. I wasn't aware that 'doctor' translated as 'nun.'"

Janessa became acutely aware of the smallness of the space between them and the enveloping darkness. "Lots of people don't think a woman ought to try to do two things at once," she said. What an odd courtship they were having—if that was what it was. She was pretty sure it was. Most people hurled themselves into each other's arms first and then decided later if it had been a good idea.

"I don't recommend making love and performing surgery simultaneously," Charley said quietly. "Other than that, I don't get your point."

She gave a shaky laugh. "That's because you aren't normal. Brice would get my point."

"Will you leave Brice out of this?" Charley yelled.

"Shhh!" Janessa looked around, expecting to hear windows thrown open. The men's and women's dormitory rooms were directly above them.

"Sorry. Oh, hell. I was going to wait till we graduated," Charley said grimly, "but if you're cured of Brice, you may go and fall for some other man, so I might as well have my say now. I love you. I think we ought to get married. I've been thinking about the Marine Hospital, too, if that's any help."

Janessa started to laugh; she thought she probably sounded demented. "Most men would have offered a ring instead," she said, when she got her breath back.

"I thought maybe the Marine Hospital was more important to you."

"It is. You wouldn't do it just for my sake, though?"

"No."

They sat, looking at each other in the darkness, knowing there was one more bridge to cross, unsure how to get over it. *If I let myself go with him, I may not stop*, she thought. Odd how that had suddenly become clear.

Charley reached out to put his hands on her arms. His face was intent and certain in the faint moonlight. His eyes had a glitter that she recognized, even though she had never seen it in them before. He bent his face to hers, and her heart hammered under the shabby dress. Once she gave way to him, he awakened sensations in her that Brice Amos had never touched. His hands roved down her back, and she found herself curled in his lap, kissing him, feeling physical desire jolt through her like a rocket. *My God.* She sat back, shaken.

"Well?" Charley looked at her seriously. The fingers of one hand were still resting lightly on the front of her dress, just cupping her breast.

"I will marry you," she said jerkily. "I think I had better."

"And?" His fingers moved just a little, exploring, gently insistent.

"I love you." She gasped.

He pulled his hand away reluctantly. "I think I'd better stop."

"I expect you had," she agreed. "For the time being." Now that they had gone over the bridge, whatever else was going to happen was inevitable and thus would keep. She rested her head against his chest and listened to the thudding of his heart.

They sat for a long time, smiling out at the moonwashed road, until Janessa finally made herself get up and go inside, upstairs to the dormitory room she shared with Eliza Thoms and two nurses.

XVIII

Portland, November 1888

"Well, Holt, I think we can safely say you're in."
Noell Simpson, the Democratic congressman from Portland, raised his glass at Toby in their unofficial campaign headquarters in the Esmond Hotel—unofficial because the November election had not been for the United States Senate but for the Oregon State Legislature. But the popular vote had returned a narrow Democratic majority to the legislature, and this made Toby's election by the legislators in March a foregone conclusion. Nationally, the electoral vote had given the presidency to the Republican Benjamin Harrison, but it, too, had been close. Cleveland had actually received the larger popular vote, and a good deal of ill feeling over that was already making itself felt.

"Tricky times," Toby said. "Maybe we're counting our chickens a mite early."

"Not a bit," Simpson disagreed. "We got a solid majority in the legislature, and not a Democrat in there will cross the party lines if he knows what's good for him—particularly not since a lot of Democratic popular vote came from men who want you in the Senate."

Willis Larken chuckled. "Probably more than they cared about putting Democrats in the legislature."

"More than you cared, certainly," Simpson said, a touch acidly. Like most businessmen, Larken voted his pocketbook. Its interests had just happened to coincide with the Democrats' this time.

"Gentlemen," Ephraim Bender reproved. "This is

a victory celebration. When does your wife arrive, Holt? I want to give her my best regards. I can't think of a better senator's lady to represent Oregon in Washington."

"She'll be glad to know she has your confidence," Toby said, amused. Alexandra didn't like Ephraim Bender much. She thought some of his land-development projects were ruining the countryside. Bender liked Alexandra, though. He thought she projected just the right image to impress easterners with Portland's culture and sophistication. He had been afraid he might get Mrs. Barrowby. The wife of Toby's Republican opponent was reputed to smoke a corncob pipe and wear hobnailed boots.

"White Elk's driving Alexandra into town," Toby said. The Democrats had planned a dazzling victory ball at the Esmond Hotel. Alexandra, refusing to admit any possibility of defeat, had ordered a gown from her dressmaker that was carefully calculated to make every other woman in Portland faint with envy. Ephraim Bender was going to love it.

As Toby spoke, Alexandra swept into the Esmond's parlor, followed by White Elk, who carried a carpetbag, and a hotel porter with a small trunk on his shoulder. She stood on tiptoes to kiss Toby, then beamed at the other men.

"Delighted to see you, my dear," Willis Larken greeted her. "My wife is upstairs dressing."

"I'll join her in a moment." Alexandra turned back to Toby. "Dear, it may not be anything to worry about, but I didn't like the look of things out there."

"What do you mean?"

"Lot of folks gathered in the streets," White Elk said. "Placards and such."

"What kind of placards?"

"I didn't get close enough to read them," White Elk answered. "I didn't think you'd like it much if I got Mrs. Holt in a riot."

"I wouldn't," Toby replied, moving toward the door. "But I want to know what's going on."

"You can't leave," Larken objected. "There'll be a

ballroom full of people wanting to shake your hand in half an hour."

"I'm going outside," White Elk said. "Put your dancing suit on, and I'll give you a report when I see what's up." He handed Alexandra's carpetbag to Toby, then went out the door.

Bender clapped Toby on the back. "I'm sure it's nothing to get worked up about. Folks like to blow off a little steam after an election."

Toby allowed them to propel him up the stairs, but he felt uneasy. Most men didn't have any brains when they got in a crowd, and if they had a placard to wave, it just made them loonier.

White Elk still hadn't returned by the time they were dressed and descending the Esmond's main staircase into the lobby. The double doors to the ballroom were thrown open, and the strains of "The Blue Danube Waltz" floated through them. Alexandra's gown was a deep emerald velvet embroidered with sprays of white wisteria blossoms. She wore a choker of pearls, and a cluster of silk wisteria blossoms in her auburn hair. As far as Toby was concerned, she was the best-looking woman in the ballroom.

He swept her into his arms as they went through the door. As soon as Willis Larken and Ephraim Bender caught up with him, he would have to make the required polite rounds, shaking hands with all his supporters and dancing with their wives. Toby figured this might be his only chance to dance with his own wife.

The dancers swayed and spun to the music, satins and jewelry catching the light from the enormous crystal chandelier that floated above their heads. The pale green walls were adorned with pier mirrors in heavy gilt frames that doubled and redoubled the whirling dancers endlessly, so that they spun at the center of a lamplit universe.

Alexandra smiled up at Toby contentedly. "I hope you know how happy I am. You deserve this victory. And now that Janessa is going to marry that dear man we liked so much, I can't help but feel that things are on the upswing again."

"Oh, I planned it this way," Toby assured her solemnly. "Planned it all."

Alexandra chuckled, and they swayed to the music.

As they spun around again, Toby spotted White Elk standing in the double doors that opened to the lobby. His face was streaked with mud, and he looked worried. Toby guided Alexandra toward the doors.

"It's not getting better," White Elk said when they were close enough to speak quietly.

"What's going on?" Toby asked.

"They're staging a demonstration," White Elk replied.

"Who're 'they'?"

"I don't know. Two demonstrations, really. The bunch with the placards are yelling 'Chinese go home!' and another bunch are arguing with them about how they got the right to hire coolie labor. A third group was mad about Cleveland's losing, but they kind of got shouted down. But they're all grousing about the coolies getting uppity and wanting a white man's wages now that you've given them the idea they're as good as anybody. None of them seem to like you much."

Alexandra, her expression concerned, looked at White Elk's face. "What happened to you?"

"I asked them what was going on, and they asked who the hell I was. When I said I was your foreman, one of them punched me."

"Oh, no!"

"He didn't really have his heart in it," White Elk said. "They're mad at the boss, but not that mad—they figure he's been led astray. It's the Chinese they're really after."

"I'm going out there," Toby declared. "Where are the police?"

"They were coming as I was going," White Elk answered. "But they'll have their hands full."

Toby looked at Alexandra. "You go pacify Noell

Simpson and Willis Larken. Tell them I'll be back as soon as I can."

Alexandra watched her husband's disappearing back. Most men would have left the mob to the police, but she knew there was no point in suggesting that to Toby.

Ephraim Bender appeared at her elbow. "My dear Mrs. Holt, you look ravishing." He dropped his voice. "Is there a difficulty?"

She was too worried to mince words with Ephraim Bender. "A bunch of anti-Chinese hotheads are out there trying to incite a riot, and Toby's in the middle of it."

"This is dreadful." Bender peered out the window and then drew the draperies. "We mustn't let a panic start," he said earnestly. "We have Eastern visitors tonight."

"Heaven forfend." Alexandra glared at him, irritated because his sole concern was to prevent bad publicity. Then she became further irritated because she realized he was right to draw the draperies: If the victory ball degenerated into a horde of stampeding guests, someone would get hurt. She drew the draperies at the other windows and went to look for Noell Simpson.

"They were headed into Chinatown," White Elk said as he and Toby hurried down the lamplit street, in the wake of a helmeted and uniformed policeman. They could hear the rumbling of an unruly crowd ahead of them and see the ominous flare of torchlight. In the distance, a fire wagon crossed the road at a full gallop. Toby and White Elk broke into a run.

On the edge of Chinatown, a mob churned, shouting at each other. More men came to join them, dark figures slipping around corners, drawn by the promise of violence and a focus for their frustrations. A handful of policemen were trying to push them back and herd them together, but the mob had become an amorphous entity, feeding on its own anger. Men with no jobs, men whose wives nagged them because they did not bring home enough money, even, ironically, men who had suffered from prejudice themselves—any man who felt abused by society could be swallowed by the mob, become a part of it, strengthened by its numbers, and find one single, easy cause to blame for all his ills.

"The goddamned coolies think they're as good as white men!"

"White men built this town!"

"We going to hand it over to a bunch of slant-eyed, murdering heathens?"

"Idol worshippers!" An itinerant preacher in a frayed frock coat clung to a lamppost. "The golden calf shall not prevail!"

"Stinking opium eaters ain't going to take our jobs!"

A policeman waded into the crowd and tried to collar the agitator. "I know you, McCarthy. You haven't worked a lick in your life." But the officer was too late. They surged around him, placards waving.

"Heathen devil worshippers!" the preacher shrieked from his lamppost.

The policeman tried again. "Now you folks get out of here. And put those torches out before you set fire to something."

"Might be a good idea!" someone yelled.

"A cleansing fire shall restore righteousness!"

Shoving his way through the edge of the crowd, Toby looked at the preacher with disgust. "He's got to go," he muttered to White Elk.

"Right," the foreman agreed. "You can reason with them later." They stepped back and began to circle around the milling men. Toby knew he stood out like a circus ringmaster in his evening clothes, but fortunately no one was paying much attention to anyone else; they were all too busy getting themselves worked up.

Toby and White Elk got behind the lamppost and hauled the preacher down. "Sin and wickedness!" he shrieked as he fell.

Toby and White Elk picked the preacher up and dragged him around the corner as the other rabble-rousers continued to shout. He twisted furiously in their grasp. "Vengeance is the Lord's!" They hauled him, screaming, down an alley and into the shadow of a back stoop. White Elk sat on the man while Toby took out his handkerchief and gagged him with it. They tied his hands behind him with White Elk's belt.

"No one can hear you anyway, Reverend," Toby said. "They're making too much noise themselves, so you might as well save your breath."

White Elk buckled the end of the belt into the ring in a cellar door. His expression ominous, he bent his face close to the preacher's. "You make any more trouble, I'll come back here and give you sin and wickedness like you wouldn't believe."

Then he and Toby ran back down the alley. The mob was moving now, and a harassed police captain was shouting orders to his men. He recognized Toby in the lamplight. "I thought that was you, Mr. Holt. What did you do with him?"

"Tied him to a coal cellar. You can turn him loose when things tone down."

"They aren't going to," the captain grumbled. "I can hold them for a while, but there isn't any way to disperse them short of shooting them, and I can't do that till they do something besides yell."

"By the time they start to do something else, it'll be too late to stop them. You've got the fire engines out?"

"Hell, yes. They haven't set fire to anything yet, but they will. It's going to be like eighty-six all over again. We couldn't stop that, either. It would take the militia."

Toby snorted. "The governor ran on an anti-Chinese platform. He doesn't like my politics any more than I like his. Anyway, it would take too long to get the militia here. Where are the fire engines?"

The captain pointed. Beyond the crowd, Toby could see the red-and-brass engines, their horses waiting patiently amid the chaos.

"Turn the hoses on them," Toby suggested. "At

least it'll put those blasted torches out, and it may slow them down some."

"Hey! Billings!" The captain called to one of his men.

"Come on," Toby said to White Elk. "Maybe we can get ahead of them." Chinatown was only three blocks wide and no more than seven or eight blocks long. Once the mob got in there, there would be hell to pay. If he and White Elk could slow the mob first and defuse the irrational fury, they might have a chance. Toby could see the fire crews unreeling their hose and beginning to work the pumps. There was nothing like being drenched on a cold night to make a man thoughtful.

They dived down an alley on the edge of Chinatown. All the windows they saw were firmly shuttered. The white citizens who weren't out prowling with the mob were keeping to themselves, unwilling to protest. A small boy leaned out a window, and his mother snatched him back in and slammed the shutters closed.

Toby and White Elk dodged onto Pine Street by the Chinese bulletin board, ahead of the mob. White Elk looked over his shoulder, down Second Avenue. The Lis' drugstore was closed for the night, but lights were glowing in the windows on the second floor.

"Go on," Toby said. "Get them away from here for a while, if they'll go. I don't know what's going to happen."

White Elk, torn between his responsibilities, ran down Second Avenue. At the door of the drugstore, he looked back over his shoulder again, this time at Toby, who, White Elk knew, could get killed, facing up to that mob alone. But so could Mai and her family. He pounded on the door.

No one answered. White Elk pounded harder, insistently. He rang the bell. Finally a window opened above him. Mr. Li shouted down at him, "Go away!"

"No!" White Elk called up. "You've got to get out of here! There's going to be trouble!"

"We do not require your assistance."

White Elk caught a glimpse of Mai's face before her father pushed her back again. "You need all the assistance you can get!"

"We will not run away."

"What about your family?"

"My family is not your concern." The window slammed shut.

White Elk stared up at the window. If he broke the door down, Mr. Li would probably shoot him. Maybe he'd shoot anybody else who tried it. "Then lock your doors!" he shouted, and ran back up the street.

The fire hoses had taken the enthusiasm out of a good number of the rioters, but at least fifty men were spilling down Pine Street, overturning shop stalls and shattering windows. Two of them broke open a door and leapt in irrational fury on the Chinese who confronted them. The Chinese, cornered, were fighting back.

A placard carrier sprawled in the street, his leg bent sideways. "The damn coolies busted my leg!" he howled.

Three others grabbed a Chinese and began to beat him. Farther off, down another alley, White Elk could hear a woman screaming. He looked frantically for Toby and saw him trying to prevent a man from setting fire to an awning.

As White Elk watched, Toby, who could fight dirty when he needed to, kicked the man in the groin and, while he was doubled over, stuck the torch, which had somehow escaped the fire hoses, in a horse trough. The man grabbed Toby around the ankles. Toby lifted him by the collar and hit him in the jaw. Then, before anyone else could jump him, he climbed up on a grocer's wagon and fired a shot over the mob's heads.

White Elk almost laughed. He'd bet Toby Holt was going to be the only senator in Washington who carried a pistol in his tailcoat.

"Now you idiots shut up and listen to me!" Toby shouted. There was another crash of breaking glass, and he fired again, carefully this time, very close to the boots of the man who had done it.

"I said, shut up!"

"That's Toby Holt!" someone shouted.

"Damned coolie lover!"

"The police have sent for reinforcements," Toby yelled. "They've already arrested most of you morons, and if there's any more damage here, I'll identify every one of you in court."

"Yeah, you and who else?"

White Elk scrambled up on the wagon beside Toby.

"Me and about twenty of my ranch hands who have just been deputized and issued shotguns," Toby bluffed.

That gave them pause, but White Elk wondered how long they were going to swallow that story once they had thought about it.

"If you think I'm joking, look behind you," Toby shouted.

Down the street, the police, having dispersed the wet and fainthearted, were advancing purposefully on the rest. Toby's threat had taken some of the steam out of these, and now they wavered.

White Elk jumped off the wagon and tried to look as fierce as he could. He hauled a brawler off his Chinese victim and knocked him flat, and the Chinese scrambled, limping, for the darkness.

"You're a disgrace to Portland!" Toby yelled. He looked a little wild himself, and those who were not actively brawling and breaking windows eyed him uneasily. His hair hung in his face, his evening clothes were muddy, and his coat was split down the back. "You know me. Have I ever lied? You know damn well I back union labor. And I tell you now, you can't solve your problems this way."

A woman who had a little girl by the hand ran screaming from a shop as glass shattered around her. White Elk tripped the man who ran after them. He grabbed the woman and child and boosted them into the wagon, where they cowered in the corner, the woman's arms wound tightly around the child and her head bent protectively over the girl.

"Aren't you all brave?" Toby said scathingly. "Women and little kids."

"Then get them out of our town!" A man advanced on the wagon and began to rock it. "Come on, boys!"

Toby drew back the hammer of his pistol. "I'll shoot the next man who lays a hand on one of these people."

The police arrived and brought the fire engines with them. The crowd, cursing and shouting, was driven back by a blast of ice-cold water.

"You'll be all right," Toby told the woman. "Just don't get out of the wagon." He jumped down and waded into the fray.

The mob, scattered under the sustained impact of the fire hoses, didn't regroup this time; divided from a single, malevolent entity into its separate components, the individual agitators found themselves suddenly not so brave.

In twenty minutes Pine Street was a shambles but deserted, save for the police captain, two of his men, the fire-engine crew reeling in their hoses, and Toby Holt and White Elk. And the victims. Two of the younger Chinese men who had not run but fought back were badly beaten. The woman from the wagon was bathing the forehead of one, while her daughter stood beside her, sobbing.

"You stopped them just long enough, Mr. Holt," the police captain said. "I don't think they would have listened to anyone but you for more than two seconds."

"That's about how long they listened to me," Toby said.

"You want to make a statement, Mr. Holt?" A reporter from the *Portland Oregonian* appeared at his elbow.

"Yeah, I'll make a statement," Toby growled. "Mob violence has no place in a civilized city, and I'm ashamed of this town. And the Boosters Committee can put that in their pipe and smoke it. If they're worried about what the rest of the world thinks of Portland, they'd better work on teaching people to get along with each other instead of jawing about how many square feet of new construction's gone up the last year. Tonight I didn't see anything to recommend us to outsiders."

The reporter dutifully scribbled that on his pad. In the silence Toby lifted his head, listening.

The sound of weeping drifted from the alley that ran behind the Lis' drugstore on Second Avenue. White Elk heard it, too. He ran for the alley in a panic, with Toby following and the reporter behind Toby.

A man dodged out of the alley, and Toby ran after him. Finding himself alone, with no mob to hide him, the man fled in panic, but Toby caught up to him halfway down the block. Toby grabbed him by the shoulder and spun him around. The man's pants were unbuttoned, and his face was raked with scratches that looked black in the dim light. In a rising fury, Toby swung at him. The man went sprawling and came up again with the pale gleam of a knife in his hand. He lunged at Toby.

Toby dodged, feeling the blade slice through what was left of his tailcoat. He shrugged the coat off, and while the knife was still entangled in the cloth, he caught the man a good solid left to the jaw. With his right hand, he twisted the man's wrist until it broke. The man howled. "Leave me alone! She was just a damn Chinee!"

"I ought to kill you," Toby snarled. He twisted the man's good hand behind his back and shook the knife out of his coat. He held it to the man's throat while a policeman came down the deserted street after them.

"I didn't do nothin'," the man whined.

Toby shoved him at the policeman. "Get him where I can't see him," Toby said, just barely under control. "Or I'll kill him." He ran back toward the alley.

A woman was crouched in the dirt by an over-turned dustbin, some distance from the Lis' back steps. White Elk was kneeling beside her. It had taken him a moment to be sure it wasn't Mai. Her face was a mass of cuts and dirt, and her black smock hung in ribbons. Her black-cotton trousers had been pulled completely off, and she clutched them to her, trying to hide herself from the men gathered in concern around her. Her long black hair had come out of its pins and fell in a tangle.

"Get some light here!" Toby shouted, and another policeman came up with a lantern.

The woman sobbed and turned her face away, trying to retreat from the light. The reporter stood behind the others, staring.

"It's all right," White Elk said gently. He tried it again in the awkward Chinese that Mai had taught him, but the woman huddled into a ball and just shook her head.

"Go get Mai," Toby suggested.

White Elk ran up the back steps of the drugstore and pounded on the door. A brief, fierce argument erupted, and then he came back, with Mai's mother. Mrs. Li knelt and spoke to the woman in Chinese, and the woman buried her head in Mrs. Li's shoulder. In a moment Mr. Li came out with a blanket, and they wrapped it around her. Mr. Li picked her up and carried her into his house, his wife following. After a long while, he came out again, quivering with fury.

"She has been raped," Mr. Li grated. "By three men."

"She needs a doctor," Toby said.

"I have sent for one," Mr. Li said. "One of our own. She is a respectable woman, the wife of Mr. Wu, the grocer. She will not let one of your kind touch her." He spoke tersely, from between clenched teeth. "She was returning from a visit to her daughter. She is afraid for me to send for her husband. Wives are considered to be property, and now she is—damaged. She is afraid Mr. Wu will send her away. He may; he is very old-fashioned."

"Surely he wouldn't," Toby said, but they all knew that plenty of white men felt the same way. "We'll get the others. I promise you, we'll find the men who did this."

"It will do no good," Mr. Li said. "It would shame her to face these men, to identify them. And Wu would not permit it."

Toby looked at the reporter. "You're not to use her name."

"No," the reporter agreed, his face stricken. "I've seen a lot, but there're times when I'm ashamed to be human."

"There must be some way we can help," Toby said.

"You can leave us alone," Mr. Li said angrily. "Your kind have done enough."

"Mr. Li." White Elk ventured a step forward. "Please may I speak with Mai? Just for a moment."

"You go to the devil," Mr. Li hissed.

Outrage in Chinatown
Appalling Crime Following Election Night

Portland has prided itself as an enlightened city, but last night that pride was thrown to the winds as a criminal mob perpetrated a savage attack on an innocent woman. . . .

The *Oregonian*, the voice of the white citizens of Portland, had generally held no high opinion of, and little sympathy for, the Chinese. The newspaper's editorials usually took the stand that the Chinese were a detriment to the city or referred to them in patronizing terms. But the reporter who had been with Toby and White Elk the night before had had a bellyful. In a two-column story, he castigated the people of Portland for wickedness beyond that of any heathen, for allowing a climate of hatred to develop that could produce such crimes, and then turning a blind eye to the results.

"There's going to be no end of a stink over this," Toby said, reading the paper at the breakfast table.

"Maybe it will embarrass certain people enough to do more than apply bandages to the problem," Alexandra said tartly. She was plainly thinking of Ephraim Bender and his gospel of Oregon as the new paradise. She looked at Toby over her coffee cup. He had a black eye, and the leading citizens of Portland would take a long time to recover from the sight of Toby returning to the Esmond Hotel with his tailcoat in ribbons and mud in his hair. They had no idea what kind of man they had elected, Alexandra thought, and they had forgotten what his father, Whip, had been like.

"I've got to see her." White Elk paced across the breakfast room like a penned wolf, paying no attention to either of them. "I've got to make him let me see her."

"The Chinese lady?" Michael asked. He looked up from his muffin, interested.

Alexandra made a shushing noise at him. Very little escaped Michael, but he hadn't learned yet when he ought to pretend that it had.

"I'm going to be a Chinese lady," Sally said. "Butterflies in my hair." She took a late-blooming chrysanthemum from the vase on the breakfast table and stuck it behind her ear.

"Where's Juanita?" Alexandra asked. "White Elk, dear, will you stop that pacing? You're making my head spin." She looked at him with affectionate pity. She had always considered him one of her children, like Tim. "I don't think they'll speak to any of us right now," she said gently.

White Elk pivoted in midstride and redirected his steps toward the door. "They're going to speak to me," he said. "They've got to."

"He'll probably sit on their step until they do," Alexandra guessed, looking after him. "Poor boy."

The Lis' drugstore had a board nailed across the door. The windows were empty of everything but a sprig of some dried plant laying forlornly on the sill. When White Elk pulled the bell, no one answered. He pounded frantically on the door and listened to the echo whisper through the silence inside.

Panicked, he ran across the street and pounded on the door of Mr. Wu's grocery. No one answered him there, either. White Elk pressed his face against the glass and then pounded again, harder. Finally the door jerked open, and Mr. Wu glared at him. He looked as if he would like to spit on him.

"Where are the Lis?"

"They go," Mr. Wu said.

"Where?"

"Back to China. On the packet this morning." He looked at White Elk with hatred. "We go, too. Next ship." He slammed the door in White Elk's face.

China. White Elk lurched back from the door, as if the old man had punched him in the gut. He tried to draw his breath, but his lungs felt frozen. *China. Oh, God, Mai!*

He turned and ran down the street toward the wharf, desperately dodging through midmorning traffic, his heart pounding, his breath coming in gasps.

"It's sailed," the harbormaster told him.

"When?"

"Twenty minutes ago. You want to catch it, you'll have to swim."

"Was there a Chinese family on it?"

The harbormaster looked at him sourly. "I don't keep track of them people. If there was, it's a good thing. They ought to all go back."

White Elk took him by the throat and shook him. "It was a little ship. You'd have seen who was on it. Tell me!"

"Yeah, they were on it," the harbormaster rasped furiously. "Stinking Chinese! Now get your hands off me." He looked at White Elk venomously. "We ought to run your kind out, too."

White Elk pushed him away, his temper receding into misery. "Sorry," he muttered, then turned and walked blindly down the wharf, going nowhere.

"Stinking Indian!" the harbormaster shouted after him.

The wharf was crowded, jammed with arriving and departing passengers and crates of vegetables and fish in ice. Coal-black smoke from the steamers' stacks hung in the air, and the hoot of tugboats, the creak and thump of windlasses being unloaded, and the shouts of the longshoremen made an impenetrable din. White Elk dodged past a slat-sided cart full of mooing calves and sat on a stone with an empty mooring ring in its face. Gulls whirled above his head, swooping down for the garbage that floated below the wharf. He watched the black water lap at its sides.

He couldn't blame Mr. Li. The old man had had enough of hatred. Opportunity and freedom had finally not been enough to compensate for terror and hatred. White Elk tried to think what he could have said to change the old man's mind, had he been in time. He couldn't think of a single thing. He stared inconsolably at the water. They could never come back now, even if they changed their minds. As a sop to anti-Chinese feeling, Congress had passed a law barring Chinese who left the country from returning.

Gone. A gull squawked and scooped a piece of lettuce from the boards beside him. White Elk watched it flap away across the distant water. Far out down the river, he thought he could see the tip of a sail, as white and fading as the sea gull's wing.

In the press of strangers on the wharf, someone brushed against his shoulder, and he shrugged the touch away angrily. He felt it again, insistently, and looked up. It was Mai.

He could hardly speak for wondering if the face he saw was a vision born of his own despair. "They said you were on the boat." He clutched her hands, as if trying to make the vision solid, to will her into reality.

She looked down at him, solemn and frightened, and he realized with a lurch what she had done. A bundle was clutched in her hand, a small one, tied up in a peony-flowered scarf.

"I was born here," Mai explained. "I have never seen China."

"You ran away."

"I said I was ill, and I slipped off at the last moment." She was coatless, and she shivered a little in the wind. "I have done something very wicked, my dear."

White Elk stood up, wrapping his jacket around them both. "No. No, you haven't."

"I have," Mai insisted. "You are not Chinese. You can't know. But I have done it anyway. This is my place."

"Even after what happened last night?"

"It is still my country. I will have to take my chances with it."

White Elk turned her face up to his. "And with me?"

Dark, almond eyes looked at him solemnly. "And with you."

White Elk held her to him. He would take her to Alexandra, he thought. After what Mai had done sank in, she would need someone besides himself, some other family around her to ease her pain for the ones she had left. He smiled, looking past her black hair at the river. But Mai was tough. Just like him. They would make it.

XIX

Virginia City, November 1888

Tim stuffed his father's letter into the carpetbag that, with his bedroll, a lantern, and an apple crate, constituted the main furnishings of his tent outside the adit of the Hopeful. So White Elk was getting married to a Chinese girl. Tim shook his head and grinned. And Janessa was going to marry Charley Lawrence. Love in bloom. He was happy for all of them, but his own life looked pretty bleak just now in comparison, especially since it was beginning to snow.

I need a dog, he thought. Another warm body to sleep with. You couldn't successfully sleep with a mule. He knew because he had tried it one night in desperation. Even more than feeling cold, he was lonesome. Sam was over across the valley, lolling around in Annie Malone's bed, no doubt. Tim hadn't seen him since their fight. He hadn't tried because he couldn't think of anything that he much wanted to say to Sam; but, perversely, he missed him anyway. Tim had spent most of his time hacking ore from the Hopeful, but it wasn't a one-man job, and he wasn't making much progress.

He could always sell the claim, he knew, and go home with some money in his pocket. His father hadn't said anything more about Harvard, which seemed to Tim a million miles and years away. He could probably stay and work the Madrona. As what, he wasn't sure. White Elk was foreman. He couldn't take that from him. The wind whistled around the tent flap. Tim thought he could at least go into town and take a room at the hotel again. He could afford to now. But the strike at the Ninevah was still going on—it seemed to be the main topic on everyone's mind—and Tim was considered an outcast by both sides. And he might run into Isabella. In the face of everyone else's nuptial bliss, he didn't think he could stand that. Tim pulled another blanket around him and opened the tent flap, morosely considering the view—the black adit of the Hopeful and the back end of the mule.

"You got any ideas?" he inquired of the mule's rear end.

The mule stamped its feet and snorted.

"Yeah, I'm cold, too. We're all cold."

When he caught himself figuring that he would probably freeze up here—they'd find his body and all be sorry—he got up, threw off the blankets, and picked up his saddle and a lead rope. This had gone on long enough, he thought. If he stayed up here any longer, he'd be talking to things that weren't here, and if he didn't freeze, the stock would.

He saddled the horse and hooked the lead line to the mule's halter. Farther down the mountain, some other cold soul was singing to keep warm.

"I drove three mules for George McVane. . . ."

Tim doubled over suddenly and threw up on the snow-covered ground. When he stopped retching, he pulled himself into the saddle. Shore's face seemed to loom at him out of the flakes of snow. He wondered how long it would be before that song didn't make him sick. Dreams of the black depths of the drift no longer troubled his sleep, but he couldn't hear that song without gagging.

He kicked the horse down the hill, looking for some warm, lighted place.

It was mostly by chance that he ended up in the Silver Dollar. Any place would have done, but he saw Waldo Howard through the window. It was a good thing that Waldo wasn't married: Tim never saw him anywhere but in the *Beacon* office or a saloon. A little blond barmaid in a purple satin dress was pouring

Waldo a drink and looking over his shoulder at his poker hand. The purple dress was cut low at the neck, and high at the hem to reveal a pair of shapely, black-stockinged ankles. The blond hair was probably dyed.

The saloon girls made good money, but none of the respectable women in town would speak to them. In turn, the saloon girls held themselves aloof from the prostitutes in their cribs on Union. There were, it seemed, gradations in morality. The saloon girls were moral by their own standards, but if you went around in a short, purple dress with black lace and poured drinks in the Silver Dollar, you couldn't expect girls like Isabella Ormond to make friends with you.

That was just fine with Tim. He felt worldly and cynical. The last woman he wanted to associate with was one who reminded him of Isabella. Tim pushed open the swinging double doors and went in.

Waldo was playing poker with two men Tim didn't know and Ham Sigmundson, who owned the livery stable where Tim had left his horse and the mule. Waldo waved him over to join them.

"Sit in. These bastards are fleecing me hand over fist." Waldo tossed his cards on the table in elaborate disgust. "I'm out. But I want to see your openers, you thieving Swede."

Ham held up a pair of queens and grinning, raked in the pot. A bottle stood in the middle of the table, and the saloon girl brought Tim a shot glass as he pulled up a chair.

"This is Millie," Waldo said. "She's here to bring me bad luck, aren't you, doll?" He put an arm around her waist.

"I ain't responsible for your cards," Millie protested. "The trouble with you is you don't never look before you leap."

"You in?" The dealer shuffled the deck and looked at Tim.

"Sure."

"This is Tim Holt," Waldo said. "He's got a little mine up on the grade. Tim, meet Eddie Tucker and

Moose Pearum. Eddie's a stationmaster over at th
Virginia & Truckee. Moose hauls freight when he isn
too drunk. You know Ham, the Swedish cyclone." Wald
glared at the money Ham was stacking up in front
him.

"I'm Norse," Ham corrected. He didn't sound in
sulted. He had a round, genial face and smelled vague
of horse.

"Same thing."

"It ain't, either. For a newspaperman, you're plai
ignorant."

"I don't bother with what I don't need to know
Waldo was picking up the cards as they were dealt an
looking at them, hopeful.

"You call me a Swede again, and you'll need it.
Ham picked up his hand as Eddie Tucker dealt the la
card around the table. "I plan on getting you, Wald
You're a doomed man."

"Y'all want to shut up and play?" Moose aske
"Two dollars."

"Call."

"Up a dollar."

"Not me." Waldo tossed his cards back. "Damn.
He pulled Millie onto his lap. "If they don't get bette
next hand, I'm going to make you go sit on Ham."

Tim considered the prospects of four high spade
"Call."

"I'm in."

"Yeah. Me, too."

"I'm in."

Eddie Tucker put his hand down and picked u
the deck. He looked at Moose.

"Three."

Eddie dealt them. Tim took another drink. Th
whiskey felt warm and comforting. Warmer than Isabell
he thought sourly. To his satisfaction, he drew anothe
spade and took the pot from Moose's jacks and Ham
three sevens. Eddie tossed in a straight that hadn
panned out. Someone refilled his glass.

Tim chuckled at Waldo's disgruntled expression. "You weren't even in."

"Waldo's got troubles," Eddy said. "His press is busted."

"Hell of a problem for a newspaperman." Waldo looked at the new hand that Moose had dealt. "Three dollars. I can't afford to get it fixed, either."

"You won't ever, if you keep betting like that," Millie said.

Waldo glared at her. The cards went around again, and Millie proved to be right. Eddie Tucker won with aces and tens.

"Three dollars on a pair of eights," Millie muttered. "Honest to God."

Tim drank more whiskey and didn't object when Millie came to sit on his lap instead. He won another hand, then lost a couple. Someone sent for a new bottle. The Silver Dollar was warm, and the yellow glow of lamplight made it look friendlier than it did by daylight. Millie was friendly, too, and Moose Pearum's Southern drawl reminded Tim of Alexandra's. The companionship of men and the forthright company of saloon girls who spared themselves Mrs. Ormond's airs and graces seemed infinitely preferable to sitting up straight in a starched collar in Isabella's parlor. Isabella could go to hell, he thought. He emptied his glass, and Millie filled it again.

After a while she went to sit with Moose, and then with Eddie Tucker. Millie was impartial. Her business was to keep all the customers happy and to sell whiskey. Tim bought the next bottle. He played some more. Poker was a fine game, he thought. The cards rearranged themselves according to the luck of the draw, a lot like life. But unlike life, at the end of the hand, all uncertainties were cleared up, and a new hand was a fresh start. After another glass of whiskey, he decided there was deep philosophy in that. Isabella, for instance, would be a better woman if she learned to play poker. When he was drunk enough, he favored them with a chorus of "The Foggy, Foggy Dew" between hands.

Waldo got in deeper, and Eddie started winning. They played some more. Moose told Tim how he had ridden with Jeb Stuart during the war, when he was just a boy.

Maybe I'll join the cavalry, Tim thought. That was an honest profession. No women in it. He looked at his cards and found that he had to squint to focus. The light must be getting bad, he thought. He had another drink to see if that would help, and it did.

A painful sound clanged inside his head, of someone hammering on an iron triangle. Tim put his hands over his ears, but it didn't go away. There was a horrible taste in his mouth, like he'd been eating a rat.

He moaned and tried to turn over, but he couldn't quite. He opened his eyes and found he was sprawled on top of a bed, facedown. He pushed up with his arms and managed to roll over. Where was he? Light streamed through a cracked window shade. Tim focused his eyes with an effort, and the dusty outlines of a hotel room coalesced into a kind of queasy solidity. When he moved the room seemed to move. What hotel? He had no recollection. Someone had pulled his boots off, but otherwise he was completely dressed.

He lay spread-eagled on the bed for a few more minutes, then heaved himself off it and shuffled to the window. He squinted past the shade, blinking. The sun glared at him above the ridge of Sun Mountain. Not very far above. It must be three in the afternoon. The taste in his mouth was getting worse the more awake he got, and he had a ravening thirst. He found water in the pitcher on the dresser and drank half of it out of the pitcher. Then he lay back down.

Where the blazes was he? He could look out the window again and see, but it didn't seem worth the trouble. He tried to remember going to bed but couldn't. He couldn't recall the end of the poker game, either. The last thing he remembered was singing "The Foggy.

Foggy Dew" in the Silver Dollar. And "Oh! Susannah."
Moose Pearum had said they used to sing that in the
cavalry. Tim had a vague recollection of singing it while
going up the stairs.

I'm going to swear off whiskey, Tim decided. He
was lucky no one had robbed him, in the condition he'd
been in. Then it occurred to him that maybe someone
had. He sat up suddenly and pitched forward onto the
bed as his head began to pound. He raised himself
cautiously and felt in his back pocket for his wallet. It
was still there. Waldo or Moose must have walked him
home, he thought gratefully. Wherever home was. He
still didn't know.

He shook out the wallet to see what he still had. A
two-dollar bill fell out, and a couple of pieces of paper.
He found a ten-dollar gold piece and a few cents' change
in his front pocket. It didn't look like he'd lost more
than about twenty dollars. He still had a hundred in the
bank, if he hadn't been drunk enough to sign chits on
it. He didn't think he had. He unfolded the pieces of
paper to see what they were.

One was a receipt. From Eddie Tucker. For the
deed to the Hopeful Mine.

Ohhh. Tim leaned forward again until his head hit
the quilt. Vaguely he remembered saying, "It's no good
to me. I can't work it anyway," before he had tossed the
deed on the table and drawn to an inside straight. Tim
slowly buckled until he was lying out flat again, with his
nose in the quilt. Maybe he would just stay here until
someone came to look for him. It didn't seem worth the
effort to move. He didn't feel well enough to think
about what he was going to do next. In fact, if he
moved, he knew he would throw up.

He remembered the other piece of paper, and he
felt around for it behind him on the bed, still with his
face in the quilt. *I'll straighten out*, he thought in a sort
of halfhearted prayer. *Just don't let me have bet that
hundred dollars in the bank*.

He found the other piece of paper and lifted his
head enough to unfold it and look at it. It was a deed,

this one made out to him, but it wasn't for the Hopeful. It was signed by Waldo Howard, and it conferred on Timothy Holt full ownership of the *Virginia City Beacon*, with all its assets—and liabilities. Tim groaned and let his head drop down again, with his face in the deed.

Annie Malone sat up in bed and pulled her wrapper around her. It was too cold to get up until Emma started the boiler and came in to put more coal on the bedroom fire. Before she became rich, Annie had spent a lot of her life being cold. She wasn't ever going to do it again. She fluffed up the lace-trimmed pillows and propped them up against the tall mahogany headboard. Sam was asleep beside her, arms clenched around his own pillow. Annie sat looking at him and thinking.

Sam had been living with her ever since the trouble at the Ninevah. After the first night Annie had said the hell with it and let him move into her bedroom. There wasn't any point in being prissy about it. Emma knew what was going on anyway. So did everybody else in town. In fact, she was a Virginia City scandal.

After a tap at the door, Emma came in to poke up the fire. She shoveled some more coal on the grate and flicked an eye at Sam, as if to say, He still here? But she didn't comment. Finished with the fire, Emma left to start breakfast.

Annie looked again at Sam. He had been here over a month, and Annie knew that couldn't go on. Virginia City was a lot more free and easy than the East, but not that free and easy. A certain amount of license was allowed for unconventional arrangements, but you were supposed to make them conventional eventually. Reverend Phelps had said as much to her at church, which Annie attended minus Sam—she wasn't that brazen.

"You should consider what the Lord has in mind for you," the minister had cautioned, and Annie knew that that new set of church pews she had donated wasn't going to last her much longer.

I'll either have to throw Sam out or marry him, she thought. Marrying him didn't seem like such a bad idea, first thing in the morning and remembering the night before. She'd miss Sam if she threw him out.

Annie thought about Sam's age and hers and sub-tracted them for the hundredth time. She still couldn't make the difference come to less than eleven. But she wasn't in love with Sam, not the way people thought about love, and he wasn't in love with her, so maybe that would be all right. Sam could take her all the places she had always wanted to go, and he would know how to act when they got there. He could teach her how to act right, teach her all the things that he'd just grown up knowing and she hadn't. If she married him, she could meet people who ignored her now, and they wouldn't laugh behind her back anymore. She could stand it if he fooled around on her—she knew that he would—and he could probably stand it if she kept the reins on the money. She would see he had anything he wanted.

She poked Sam in the shoulder, and he turned over sleepily.

"Wake up," Annie said. "We've got to talk."

The wedding of Annie Malone and Sam Brentwood provided Virginia City with a spectacle that would go down in city legend. It was, as Waldo Howard put it, grander than a night at the opera. Annie Malone had a carriage with six white horses, a twelve-piece orchestra to play at the reception, and every citizen of both sexes to see the show. The women were willing to disapprove but not willing to miss it.

Tim sat on the groom's side in the packed drawing room of the International Hotel, next to Waldo. Tim had decided he couldn't blame Waldo for losing the *Beacon* in a poker game, even if Waldo had lost it to him. At least Tim had a place to sleep at night that he didn't have to pay for. He looked around and saw Joe Yellan and Billy Pitts on the bride's side, so he guessed that Sam had been forgiven for Annie's sake. The Ormonds were here, too, on the bride's side, at an elaborate distance from the union miners. Tim gave

them no more than a glance. He was building up a
callus where Isabella was concerned, but he didn't think
it was quite thick enough yet to look at her for very
long at somebody else's wedding.

The groom's side was mostly full of people who
couldn't fit on the bride's. Annie had invited old friends
and new, anybody she could think of—miners and nabobs. There was an interested hush as Sam and his best
man came in through the far door. Sam hadn't asked
Tim, which didn't surprise him. Sam had a chipped
front tooth to remember Tim by. Instead, he had dra-
gooned Eddie Tucker, who had been delighted to buy
Sam's half of the Hopeful, too, and was planning to quit
the Virginia & Truckee and get rich.

Tim craned his neck around the hat of the woman
in front of him to look at Sam. Tim thought he looked as
if he knew just what he was doing. Sam's dark face was
cheerful, almost cocky, as he grinned at Tim over the
heads of the wedding guests. Annie was just what Sam
had been wanting, Tim thought—a get-rich-quick
scheme, with bedroom privileges.

The pianist struck up the strains of the Wedding
March from *Lohengrin*, and Annie's bridesmaids, six of
them, glided down the aisle past the rows of gilt chairs.
Annie had simply picked her attendants from among
women she liked—anyone who occurred to her—and
they were certainly a mixed bag. Tim recognized the
minister's wife; Annie's housekeeper, Emma; the daughter of the president of the California Bank; Mrs. Hooper
from the dry-goods store; the young president of the
Virginia City Civic Improvement League; and a black-
haired woman who ran a boardinghouse in Tonopah and
who had known Annie way back when. Their outfits
were provided by Annie: They all wore identical dresses
of marine-blue lutestring, striped with white, and hats
to match, and carried bouquets of hothouse roses shipped
from San Francisco. Emma's daughter, Belle, was the
flower girl, in a blue-tulle dress with a white sash, and
one of Emma's boys carried the ring on a satin pillow.

Tim grinned. Raised with Alexandra's dictum that

understatement was best, Tim thought the attendants looked like the chorus for *H.M.S. Pinafore*, and he would bet the Ormonds did, too. Well, the hell with the Ormonds. Annie was entitled to whatever she wanted; she was going to get stuck with Sam.

The last bridesmaid marched past in stately splendor, and Annie came down the aisle on the minister's arm. The Reverend Mr. Phelps looked pleased to be shepherding her along the path of righteousness, although he plainly felt a more restrained ceremony would have been suitable for a woman's second marriage to a man she had been living with for two months.

Annie's gown was white satin, with the neckline filled with Brussels lace. The front was draped in lace from head to toe and trimmed with wide, flat bows and chains of orange blossoms. She wore white kid gloves and white satin slippers. The train, also bedecked with orange blossoms, trailed a good six feet behind her, under a more-than-floor-length veil of white tulle. And anybody who wanted to say anything about that was welcome to, judging by Annie's expression. The first time she had been married had been in a calico dress in a sod church. This time she was going to have the whole nine yards.

"Dearly beloved, we are gathered here together . . ."

Mr. Phelps had taken his place in front of the couple, while the bridemaids gathered to one side and Emma grabbed the ring bearer to make him stop bouncing the ring on the pillow. Fortunately, it was tied on with ribbon.

". . . if any man can show just cause why they may not lawfully be joined together, let him now speak, or else hereafter forever hold his peace."

Tim snorted, and Waldo Howard chuckled quietly. "There's no provision for objecting on the grounds of stupidity," Waldo whispered.

"Samuel Fulton Brentwood, wilt thou have this woman to be thy wedded wife, to live together after God's ordinance in the holy estate of matrimony? Wilt thou love her, comfort her, honor, and keep her in sickness and in health; and, forsaking all others, keep thee only unto her, so long as ye both shall live?"

Sam coughed. Was he having second thoughts? Tim could not tell.

"I will," he vowed.

"Annie Laurie Malone, wilt thou have this man . . ."

Annie hesitated, too, and Mr. Phelps looked at her sternly. In his memory, no woman had yet jilted her husband at the altar, and he forced himself not to hope that Annie was going to do it. Surely it was better to be married to Sam Brentwood than to burn in hell. Surely it was.

Annie said, "I will," and Mr. Phelps went on rather hastily.

The prayers concluded and the ring firmly on Annie's finger, he joined their hands and faced the wedding guests.

"Those whom God hath joined together, let no man put asunder." A fly on his coat collar might have also heard him mutter, "God help me, I hope I've done the right thing." Aloud, he said, "You may kiss the bride."

The reception was held in the hotel ballroom, decked for the occasion with white satin streamers. An endless parade of waiters circulated with endless trays of champagne, and the buffet table was laden with oysters, ham, tea sandwiches, and bonbons. The multi-tiered cake, in the center of the table, was frosted in white icing and decorated with holly leaves and berries made of green and red sugar.

Annie and Sam held the silver-tined cake cutter above it, motionless, while the photographer burrowed under the black cloth behind his camera, his outstretched hand brandishing a tray of flash powder. After a pop and a small explosion of light, Emma's boys yelled with glee and chased each other around the tripod. The cake cutter came down on the cake, and Annie lifted the slice onto a plate.

"You're supposed to feed it to him!" someone shouted.

Annie waggled gloved fingers in the air. "Not in my new gloves." She put a fork on the plate and handed it to Sam. Enough jokes were circulating about their ages, without her feeding him.

Sam grinned and picked up the cake in his own fingers. He held it out to Annie. "Bite. It's tradition."

Annie took a bite. Sam ate the other half and gave the bridesmaids a rakish smile. "You ladies want to do the honors? I'm going to dance with my wife."

The orchestra had begun to play, and he held out his arms to Annie. They circled the room, Annie's veil and train looped over one arm. Tim, who had been to a lot of weddings and knew his duty, asked one of the bridesmaids, the boardinghouse keeper from Tonopah, to dance.

"I'm not much of a hand at it."

"That makes two of us," Tim said gallantly. "We'll stumble together." He had taken dancing classes at Alexandra's insistence, and with the ease of the practiced dancer he matched his steps to hers so that after a while she relaxed and quit trying to watch her feet. He thought she was about the same age as Annie, but the years showed more plainly in her face, and her dark hair had threads of gray.

"I'm Tim Holt," he said, since they hadn't been introduced.

"I'm Vina Perkins. You're Sam's cousin, aren't you?"

"I am." She was probably the only person in the room who wouldn't think that was an untactful question. Being from Tonopah, she hadn't read the account in the Virginia City newspapers of his falling-out with Sam.

"Well, what do you think? Will he make her happy?"

"God knows," Tim replied. He watched them dancing. Sam's arm was tight around Annie's waist, and his expression was triumphant. "I think they're happy now."

"I've known Annie a long time. Back when she didn't have a penny to bless herself with. He marry her for her money?"

"God knows," Tim said again. He looked at Annie's

glowing face and red-gold hair, framed in a cloud of roses and white tulle. "She's a mighty pretty woman."

"She always was," Vina said. "She always liked a good-looking man, too." Sam and Annie danced past them, and Vina eyed Sam's dark, reckless face wistfully. "A good-looking man with a touch of the devil. I got to admit, I do, too. Well, I can't blame her. I'd marry him myself if he happened to ask."

Tim chuckled. "Are you a married lady?"

"Yeah," Vina said, "but my man isn't a match for that one."

The dance ended, and Mrs. Perkins was claimed immediately by another partner. The male population of Virginia City outnumbered the female by about three to one. Tim went to pay his respects to the bridal couple now, while any ill feeling on both sides was diluted by bonhommie and champagne.

"Congratulations. I'm happy for you."

"Thank you." Sam put out his hand. "And relieved that I won't be a public embarrassment to you any longer."

"That, too," Tim admitted.

"Have no fear. We're taking my bad reputation to the Continent for a honeymoon."

Annie flashed them a smile and disappeared into the crowd of dancers on the arm of John Ormond, who accorded Tim only a brief, vitriolic glance.

"We're leaving tonight," Sam said. "With ten trunks. We'll sail from New York."

"Stopping in Independence on the way?" Tim inquired.

Sam looked uncomfortable. "I tried to talk her out of it, but she's bound and determined."

"Might as well get it over with," Tim said. He knew Andrew Brentwood well enough to know if not exactly what Andrew was going to say, at least what tone of voice he was going to say it in.

"I got her to tone her clothes down some," Sam said. He brightened. "Maybe I shouldn't have. Maybe we could make Lydia have a heart attack and die." He was smiling, but a certain amount of genuine venom was in his voice.

Tim hesitated. "Look," he said finally, "I don't believe in running down folks' families, but Annie's worth about twelve Lydias. Don't you let them make her think she's not. You married her, and you look after her, even if it means telling your father and Lydia to jump in the lake."

"The Tim Holt acid test of true love," Sam said.

"That's right." They both knew it was the test that Isabella Ormond hadn't passed.

"You watch me," Sam said. "It'll be a pure pleasure."

"Not in a way that'll embarrass Annie," Tim said, noting the gleam in his friend's eye. "Use some tact."

"Use some yourself," Sam suggested. "Quit talking to me like I was your kid brother."

"A little sensitive about our age, are we?"

"Yeah," Sam said, "but it'll pass. Quit trying to pick a fight with me at my wedding reception, will you?"

"I'm not," Tim protested, although he thought maybe he had been. He felt restless and not particularly good tempered. As well he might. His hundred dollars was just about used up.

"And what are you going to be doing now?" Sam inquired.

"God knows," Tim said. That seemed to be all he could think of to say to anything. He hoped God did know. He sure didn't.

"Have some champagne," Sam suggested. "It'll help to blur the edges."

He went off to dance with a bridesmaid. They all wanted to dance with Sam, Tim thought. They disapproved of him, but they all wanted to dance with him.

Tim took a glass of champagne off a tray and circulated moodily. He saw Eddie Tucker across the room and sidled through the crowd toward him, wondering if Eddie was feeling like a rich mine owner yet.

"I hear you're going to be a nabob," Tim said. "Silver doorknobs and French wine."

Eddie looked a little nervous. "No hard feelings, I hope?"

"Not at all. Like I said, I couldn't work it myself."

Eddie chuckled. "That was what Waldo said about the *Beacon*."

Tim groaned. "I don't quite remember that part."

"You were drunk," Eddie admitted. "We didn't pour it into you, though."

"Naw, I poured it into myself. Doesn't matter. I might have done it sober." He snagged another glass of champagne off a tray and handed it to Eddie, then clapped an arm around his shoulder. "Tell you what, though: A man in your position needs an image. Civic responsibility and all that."

"Yeah?" Eddie said, interested.

"Sure," Tim said. "Waldo lost that newspaper to the wrong man. What the *Beacon* needs is a publisher who's up-and-coming. Make yourself a force in Virginia City. Now I'm prepared to give you a good deal, just because I've got no hard feelings. . . ."

Suddenly, Eddie's expression grew wary.

XX

Tim glumly surveyed his fellow wedding guests. Eddie hadn't bit. Ham Sigmundson, too, had failed to see himself as a newspaper tycoon, and Moose Pearum and several other people had been similarly lacking in vision. Tim hadn't even bothered with Waldo Howard. Waldo was going to San Francisco to work for the *Chronicle*, where he didn't have to worry about paying for the paper.

Maybe he should have waited for them to get drunker, Tim thought. The reception was in full swing. Annie had gone upstairs to change into her going-away costume, assisted by Vina Perkins and Emma. Emma was going to live in the house while Annie and Sam were gone. Tim wondered how long they would stay in Virginia City after they came back from Europe. Not long, he'd bet. Annie and Sam both itched for bigger things. Virginia City was a frontier town, even under a veneer of silver.

A murmur passed through the milling guests, and they began to crowd out into the lobby of the hotel. Tim followed them. Annie was coming downstairs. She had on a traveling costume almost the color of her hair, and a little brown hat with a pink flower on it. She held her bouquet up, and Tim watched, amused, while the unmarried bridesmaids tried to pretend they weren't interested. Some of the married ones looked as if they'd like to catch it. Sam went up the stairs and took Annie's hand. He whispered something in her ear. Annie put her foot up on a step, and Sam pulled her garter off.

"You bachelors step up," Sam called, waving the garter.

They crowded around him raucously.

"Perfectly vulgar," Mrs. Ormond said.

Sam flung the garter, and Tim gave Mrs. Ormond a wicked smile as he shot his hand up and caught it. "I wouldn't worry, ma'am," he informed Mrs. Ormond, who was trying to pretend not to notice him. "I'm counting on this to give me better judgment." He stuck the garter in his pocket.

The other men crowded up, slapping Tim on the back and laughing, suggesting that Annie's garter might bring him a wife as rich and pretty as the bride.

"I'll settle for the pure of heart," Tim declared. He noticed Isabella's frosty face beside her mother's. He thought that maybe he was a little drunk, and he'd better tone it down. He moved away to cheer as Annie tossed the bouquet. It sailed over the heads of the laughing bachelors and into the arms of little Belle, the flower girl.

"There you go, Holt," Moose Pearum said. "You're gonna have to wait awhile for her, though."

Tim chuckled and ruffled Belle's hair. "You can do better than me."

Annie and Sam descended the stairs in a shower of rice and ribald advice and made their getaway in a waiting carriage. Eddie Tucker and a few other thoughtful souls had tied a black-crepe wreath, an apron, and a pair of handcuffs to the back of it.

After the carriage had rattled down the street toward the depot, Tim wandered back into the ballroom. The reception would go on till the champagne ran out, although the respectable element, which was to say those who had their wives with them, were taking their departure before things got too rowdy.

"You look like a man at loose ends," Moose commented as Tim, hands in pockets, surveyed the dancing couples. The orchestra was playing a polka now.

"Yep," Tim said. He thought Moose looked pretty drunk, and another idea occurred to him. "We might get up a game," he suggested.

*   *   *

"Holt, I ain't that drunk," Moose said, "and I ain't going to be."

Tim put the deed to the *Beacon* back in his pocket. The damned thing was an albatross. He couldn't even lose it at poker.

"In that case, gentlemen, I'll take my leave of you." Tim stood. "Fine thing when a man can't even put up clear title to his own business to get a little stake."

"Clear title?" Moose snorted. "That paper's got bills three years outstanding. And a press that don't work. You might as well cut your losses and use that deed to light your cigar."

Tim gave him an annoyed look and strolled off across the Silver Dollar's sawdust floor to see who else might have a game going.

"You're a pariah, Holt," Moose called after him. "They'll fold their cards when they see you coming. You couldn't get anyone in this town to steal that paper." Tim didn't answer, and Moose called after him again, "I could maybe get you a job hauling freight, if you want."

Tim thought of the mule teams that lurched their way up the hills to the small settlements where the railroad didn't go. He hesitated, and then Shore's song came unbidden into his mind. He shook his head. "No, thanks."

Portland, December 1888

Alexandra took stock of her Christmas dinner table with a satisfaction that was mildly tinged with the exasperation she knew Toby felt, too. Only Tim was missing. She kept hoping he might suddenly burst through the door in a flurry of snow, his arms full of packages. But there hadn't been any snow—there usually wasn't at Christmas—and there was no Tim, either. Alexandra hoped he wasn't freezing to death in some tent. She had sent him a package with a new sheepskin coat and a

bottle of brandy, among other things, but he ought t
be here, completing the charmed circle of the family
This was the second Christmas he had missed.

But Janessa was here, with a sapphire ring on he
finger and Charley Lawrence at her side. It was won
derful how Charley fit into the family as if he ha
always belonged to it, Alexandra thought. You coul
tell he had little brothers and a sister. He had playe
Ride a Cock Horse with Sally on his knee and told Mik
all about Janessa's routing Dr. Goulard's Medicine Sho
and—not, thank heaven, at this dinner table—how the
had stolen a cadaver's foot and eaten dinner with it i
Janessa's lap.

"She got a hundred percent on the exam, too,
Charley had said, and Toby had given Janessa th
proudest look. It was Alexandra's opinion that Charle
had done wonders for Janessa. She laughed all the tim
now, and her face was softer. That tight look of alway
waiting to defend herself against something had gone
Even her brown hair had more luster and seemed t
spring unbidden from its pins. What a difference lov
made. Love and having put your life on the right track
Alexandra supposed.

White Elk and Mai had joined them for Christma
dinner, too. They had been married two weeks earlie
White Elk looked solid and confident, and the ranc
hands were scuttling to do his bidding the way they ha
done for Stalking Horse. They had made a pet of Mai
Any anti-Chinese sentiments they might have harbore
had vanished with her arrival; and when they heard th
story of how she had left her family to stay in Americ
with only a bundle tied up in a scarf, they had delve
into clothes chests and cupboards to bring her presents
Coot Simmons had brought her a deerhide jacket fringe
in elegant frontier fashion and a pair of deerhide boots
Bald Bill Eddings had given her an ivory comb that h
said he was only keeping for sentiment's sake, anyway
Howie Janks had brought her a bouquet of dried flow
ers and carried them to the door of the big house th
morning after she arrived. "Gawd, you're pretty," h
had announced, shoving them at her.

Mai seemed to have taken it in stride, barring the one night she had sobbed her eyes out in Alexandra's arms. But that was to be expected; Alexandra wouldn't have thought much of her if she hadn't. It was a shame that there was a price on everything worth having, but that was the way it was. Alexandra had no patience with people who waltzed from one thing to another without regrets.

Mai sat at the Christmas table between White Elk and Sally. Sally had been trying to learn to use chopsticks and had thrown a temper tantrum because Alexandra refused to let her continue this adventure at Christmas dinner. The temper having blown itself out, Sally was smiling happily at Mai.

"I wish my eyes would do that," Sally said, and Mai giggled.

"Everyone has the eyes they're born with," Mai said solemnly. "But I'll tell you a secret, little butterfly. I wish I had your hair."

Sally considered Mai, who looked as Caucasian as she was ever going to look, which wasn't very, in one of Alexandra's second-best dresses, shortened and taken in. "You'd look silly," Sally said.

Mai lifted one of Sally's rose-blond curls. "And you'd look silly with my eyes. All the pieces of a person are supposed to match."

"Oh. Then I want some Chinese clothes," Sally announced. "I want to wear trousers."

Mai sighed. "So do I. But I am trying to learn to be American."

Janessa chuckled. "An awful fate. How on earth did women's clothes get so complicated? Look at the pictures in the history books. At the turn of the century they were wearing stuff with less to it than my nightgown."

Eulalia and Lee Blake were at the table, too, Lee assisting Toby in the carving of the turkey. "I have a picture of my mother in a dress like that," Eulalia said. "Painted before I was born. She told me that women who were a little bit fast used to dampen those thin skirts to make them cling and show their shape."

His eyes gleaming, Toby gave Alexandra a look. "Hear that, Alex? I call that a fine idea."

"Of course my mother never did it," Eulalia informed him.

"Sure," Toby said. "Nobody's parents ever misbehaved. At least, not that their kids know about." He caught the interested expressions on Mike's and Sally's faces. "You two aren't listening to any of this, you hear?"

"Mama puts rouge on her lips," Sally informed the company in general.

"Sarah Holt!" Eulalia gave her a reproving look, but she couldn't hide the twitch in her lips. "That is personal and privileged information."

Alexandra put her face in her hands. "Disgraced!" she said, laughing.

"She uses face powder, too," Michael said, with a wicked grin.

"I do not!" Alexandra defended indignantly. "Just a little, to take the shine off my nose."

"My mother always recommended a dampened red ribbon to give color to a lady's lips," Charley said solemnly. "It leaves no evidence behind."

Alexandra responded to Mai's baffled expression. "No lady of breeding would ever be caught painting her face. We just help it out a little."

"I bet Sam's wife paints her face," Mike offered.

"Let us hope not," Toby said. "Old Andy's going to be steamed enough."

"She's older than Sam," Michael informed Mai and White Elk. "As old as Mama."

"That does not exactly constitute one foot in the grave," Alexandra informed him.

"Good thing, too," White Elk remarked. "She'd better have her strength if she's married Sam."

Charley whispered in Janessa's ear. "If I hadn't loved you, I'd have proposed anyway, just to get your family."

"You just be glad you didn't get Sam," Janessa whispered. "That Annie must be crazy."

"Oh, I don't know," Charley said thoughtfully. "I saw Sam. Like you said, men marry for looks all the time."

"Like you said, women are supposed to be smarter." Janessa grinned wickedly. "So I picked you."

"Smart gal," Charley said, unruffled. "That way you know rich widows won't be pursuing me."

Later, happy and full of turkey, they stood together in the shadow of the Christmas tree to watch Toby light the candles. It was an immense red fir, and its scent filled the room. Charley put his arm around Janessa's waist, and she leaned against his shoulder.

"I feel content," she said. "There's just no other word." She smiled up at the china angel who soared from the tip of the tree. "I feel as if I could fly."

"Me, too," Charley agreed. "I don't know how I'm going to wait a year and a half."

"I don't, either," Janessa confessed. Just standing next to him made her catch her breath. "Maybe I should go out with a *dueña*, to keep me from doing something foolish."

"Maybe you should," Charley said. "I feel pretty foolish."

"Stand back and prepare for the grand illumination," Toby announced. He carried a lighted taper in his hand and a step stool to reach the candles at the top of the tree. Alexandra stood behind him with a bucket of water. She was taking no chances.

They gathered around the tree, and Abby and Amy Givens came in from the kitchen to join them. Toby got up on the stool and held the taper to the highest candles, working his way down. They flowered into light, their flames reflected in the glass balls that hung among the popcorn strings.

Sally watched ecstatically, on tiptoe, and Charley lifted her up onto his shoulders, so she could see the angel with her face bathed in ethereal light.

"Isn't she pretty?" Sally whispered, in awe. She reached out a hand as if the angel might alight on it.

"Yes, she is." Alexandra smiled mistily at her daugh-

ter, her baby, and then at her son and husband. The
evening only lacked Tim. "There's nothing like being
home for Christmas, is there?"

Toby awakened slowly, struggling up through the
drifts of sleep and wondering what darned idiot would
come calling at eight in the morning on the day after
Christmas.

The bell jangled again on the floor below, and he
gave up waiting for Amy to get it.

Alexandra opened her eyes and sat up.

"I'll get it," Toby grunted. He pulled a pair of
pants on over his long johns.

A boy about Michael's age, in knickers and a cap,
stood at the door. He handed Toby a telegram. Toby
snatched it open. Telegrams were for momentous ti-
dings or bad ones. But it wasn't from Tim, as he had
half feared. When he saw the signature, Toby grinned.
He held the telegram away from him and squinted. He
was beginning to have the unpleasant suspicion that he
might need glasses. The block capitals leapt out at him
clearly enough—powered possibly by Andy Brentwood's
wrath.

TOBY HOLT, MADRONA RANCH, PORTLAND, OREGON
SAM MARRIED STOP LEFT HIM IN YOUR CHARGE NOW
SEE WHAT COMES OF IT STOP WOMAN COMPLETELY
UNSUITABLE STOP LYDIA DISTRAUGHT STOP DEMAND
TO KNOW WHAT YOU ARE GOING TO DO ABOUT IT STOP
ANDREW BRENTWOOD, INDEPENDENCE, MISSOURI

"You want to send an answer?" the boy asked.

"I do," Toby said. "You wait while I get some
paper."

"No, sir, Mr. Holt. The boss said if you want to
answer, you got to come into town. Said he ain't got
time to send me out here five or six times while you
fight with this fellow by wire." He noted Toby's wrath-
ful expression. "We was closed yesterday," he said,
placating him. "We're right busy today."

Toby relented. "All right. You get on back. But you tell him I'm coming. Wants to know what I'm going to do about it," he muttered as the boy pedaled away on his bicycle. "I'll tell him."

The telegrapher looked up as Toby stomped in. "Thought you might be here," he said.

"Here." Toby scribbled on the message pad and handed it to him.

ANDREW BRENTWOOD, INDEPENDENCE, MISSOURI
SEE THEY GOT THERE STOP SEASON OF GOODWILL
STOP SUGGEST YOU TRY SOME STOP BAD TEMPER
ON TOP OF BIG DINNER BAD FOR YOUR LIVER STOP
TOBY HOLT, PORTLAND, OREGON

"You two ever write letters?" the telegrapher inquired.

"Naw, you can really put your back into a telegram," Toby said.

Andrew Brentwood put his back into his:

TOBY HOLT, PORTLAND, OREGON
HOLD YOU AND YOUR SON RESPONSIBLE LETTING THIS
HAPPEN STOP SHOULD HAVE GONE VIRGINIA CITY AS
ASKED KEPT SAM OUT OF BAD COMPANY STOP TIM
OBVIOUSLY DANGEROUS STOP SAM HAS BROKEN TOOTH
STOP NOW DISASTROUS MARRIAGE STOP

"Did Tim break Sam's tooth?" the telegrapher wanted to know.

"I hope so," Toby said. He reached for the pad again.

ANDREW BRENTWOOD, INDEPENDENCE, MISSOURI
SAM BAD COMPANY ALL BY HIMSELF STOP IF YOU HAVE
LICK OF SENSE WILL MAKE THIS WOMAN WELCOME
STOP OTHERWISE GOING TO LOSE SON STOP GOD
KNOWS YOU HAVE BEEN TRYING STOP

"Maybe you ought to just go to Missouri and straighten him out," the telegrapher suggested. "Be a sight cheaper."

"I'd like to," Toby said. "But I've got other fish to fry." Andy wouldn't take kindly to being straightened out, either. He wondered what Annie Laurie Malone was like. Pretty, Tim had written, and a two-fisted kind of woman. Toby figured she could probably stand up to Andy. Still, he felt a certain amount of relief that she hadn't married Tim.

"I was happy I got mine married off at all," the telegrapher commented as he clicked his key. "Figured I'd have the lot of them underfoot the rest of my life, squabbling with each other and sassing their ma. This Brentwood fellow don't know that the Lord's smiled on him."

No more than a minute of silence elapsed before the key began to tap again. "You got one more shot at him and that's it," the telegrapher said when he had transcribed the message. "I got a stack of them here waitin' to send." He gave Toby the slip of paper. "You give him hell, though."

TOBY HOLT, PORTLAND, OREGON
DON'T NEED YOUR ADVICE STOP YOU ARE PIOUS ASS STOP TIM STILL VIRGINIA CITY ISN'T HE STOP LYDIA IN BED HERE WITH SICK HEADACHE STOP SAM AND WIFE BROUGHT TEN TRUNKS AND PARROT STOP GAVE PARROT TO EDEN STOP LYDIA ALLERGIC TO BIRDS STOP ONLY PEACEFUL PLACE IS TELEGRAPH OFFICE STOP   GOING TO PUNCH YOUR FACE WHEN I SEE YOU STOP WHAT THE HECK AM I GOING TO DO STOP

Toby sat down on a rickety wooden chair that nearly gave way when he threw himself onto it. When he managed to stop laughing, he wrote out his final thoughts for Andy Brentwood.

ANDREW BRENTWOOD, INDEPENDENCE, MISSOURI
TELL LYDIA BRACE UP STOP MERRY CHRISTMAS STOP

When Toby got home, he found breakfast over and his mother and stepfather bundled under lap robes on the porch, watching Sally and Mike try out a Christmas present: a goat cart, painted red, with two silky-haired billy goats to pull it. One goat was trying to eat his harness, while the second was attempting to turn around far enough in his to butt the first.

"Sit down, Son," Lee Blake said. "This is better than the theater."

Mike got the two goats straightened out and ran to jump into the driver's seat before they could become entangled again. Sally sat beside him giggling, her little hands encased in a warm fur muff. The goats trotted off and then veered abruptly to the right when one of them saw a good patch of grass.

"They seem to be perpetually hungry," Lee observed. "They ate one of your mother's gloves."

"I'd ask you what possessed you to give them a goat cart," Toby said, "but I know." He bent down and kissed his mother on the forehead.

"I had one when I was a girl," Eulalia said. "Back home in South Carolina. It was such fun."

"She's reliving her childhood," Lee said.

"One is entitled to at my time of life," Eulalia replied. "This has been the loveliest Christmas I can remember. If I don't have another one, this one will hold me."

"You'll have plenty more," Toby assured her. He was aware that lately he refused even to consider the fact that his mother was getting old. "Are you warm enough? Do you want another blanket?"

"I'm quite comfortable, dear. Oh, look, the children have gotten them going." The goat cart disappeared around the corner of the house. Eulalia cocked her head up at Toby. "Alexandra tells me you had a wire from Andy Brentwood. How are they?"

"In hysterics," Toby answered.

"I wouldn't doubt it." Eulalia sniffed. "That boy is a walking disaster. Born to be hanged, my father would have said. I don't give that marriage very long."

"Well, you can write Andy and tell him so," Toby said. "It'll pep him up. Where's Alex?"

"In the pantry. I offered to help, but she wouldn't let me."

"You helped last night," Toby said. "You rest. Keep an eye on the goats."

"We'll cheer them on," Lee said. The goat cart flew around the side of the house and across the lawn, with Mike and Sally whooping and cheering. "They wanted to get the pony cart out and race, but we nipped that idea in the bud."

"Prudent of you. Don't let Mike get too excited."

"Michael's fine," Eulalia said firmly. "Janessa and Charley listened to his heart and said so." Eulalia had taken immediately to Charley Lawrence, to his good-humored smile and Southern gallantry.

"Well, it's still not normal, and it worries Alex, so slow him down some if you can."

"The goats are doing all the work," Lee pointed out.

"It's an outlet, dear," Eulalia told her son. "It will keep Michael from trying something else that might be dangerous. If you wrap him in cotton wool, he'll rebel. He's just like your father."

"Well, all right. I'll bow to your judgment."

"That's why people have grandmothers, dear," Eulalia said comfortably. "For perspective."

Toby grinned and went in the house in search of Alexandra. He found her, as predicted, in the pantry, seeing what they might have for lunch. Splashing and laughter from the kitchen informed him that Janessa and Charley were washing dishes. Abby and Amy had gone up the road to their father's farm to wish him a belated Merry Christmas and "straighten him out," as Amy had said. Since Horace Givens's wife had died, his farmhouse was generally less tidy than his pigsty. Since Abby and Amy's idea of a good time was to get a new broom and sweep clean, they celebrated holidays by digging their father out of the mire.

Alexandra was considering the merits of half a ham, a wheel of cheese, and a loaf of crusty bread.

"Country lunch," Toby said. "Perfect."

"It doesn't seem very elegant," Alexandra said dubiously.

"I don't think my digestion will stand any more elegance. We all ate like starving hogs last night. And I've got indigestion from conversing with Andrew Brentwood."

Alexandra looked up from the ham. "What did he have to say?"

Toby gave her the handful of crumpled message slips he had dug from his pocket. Alexandra read them one after the other and shook her head at him.

"Toby Holt, you ought to be ashamed of yourself. 'Brace up,' indeed."

Toby laughed. "Old Andy'll calm down when the newlyweds leave and he gets Lydia out of bed. That woman's a cross to bear."

"He loves her," Alexandra said, automatically defending the underdog.

"Lydia's had a tough row to hoe," Toby conceded, "but it doesn't justify her dedicating her life to being a nuisance." He grinned. "Lord, I wish I could have been there when they drove up! Mr. and Mrs. Samuel Brentwood, with ten trunks and a parrot, and the missus in an unsuitable hat."

"How do you know it was unsuitable?"

"Bound to be. Anything flashy is unsuitable in Independence, and from what Tim says, flashy is Annie's style."

"You wouldn't think it was so funny if it were Tim," Alexandra informed him.

"Nope," Toby said unrepentently. "But it's not Tim. And better yet, Tim's not going to marry that girl of John Ormond's, and if you knew Ormond, you'd count that a major blessing."

"You've changed your tune since Tim went to Nevada," Alexandra observed.

"I guess I have at that," Toby agreed. "But it sounds to me as if Tim's been through the mill and come out in one piece, so I guess I'm proud of him."

He found unexpectedly that he was proud of him—for saying to hell with Harvard, for bucking the mine bosses, for saving Sam's carcass from the irate union men, for all of it. Tim seemed to have an unconventional approach to life and a compulsion to take the hard way, but that might not be so bad. That was the attitude that had hauled wagon trains over the Rockies to Oregon. Portland was built on that attitude. "Tim's got a level head on his shoulders. You don't have to worry about him."

"I wish he were home," Alexandra said.

"He'll be home as soon as his pride'll let him," Toby replied. "I give him six months of mining, just to prove his point. Then he'll be home."

It did not occur to him that Tim might not have told them quite everything that had been going on or that an unconventional approach to life and a level head might be opposing forces that could produce results to surprise even their owner.

Virginia City, 31 December 1888

Tim Holt turned up the coal oil lamp in the *Virginia City Beacon* office. The gas had been turned off long ago because Waldo hadn't paid the bill, and even then it hadn't been much of an office. The *Beacon* was on D Street between Union and Sutton, flanked by a saloon and a laundry. A whorehouse was across the street, and behind him Tim could hear the clatter and rumble of the Virginia & Truckee freight yards and the crash of cars being coupled in the night. Having no place else to live, Tim was now sleeping on a camp bed in the office, behind the partition that divided the front desk from the composing room, but the noise of the freight yard was not conducive to rest.

Tim stood at the front window, with his nose nearly pressed against the dingy lettering that said VIRG NIA CITY BE CON. Across the snow-covered street the denizens of Roseanna Dawn's whorehouse were getting ready to celebrate the New Year after their own fashion. Roseanna's windows were brightly lit, and she had put red bows and pine boughs on the front porch. A steady stream of miners and mule drivers lurched down the street between the saloon and Roseanna's place. Inside, Tim could see Roseanna's girls, in trailing woolen wrappers, drinking whiskey around the Christmas tree. A miner staggered up to the door, pounded on it, and nearly fell through, amid a peal of laughter. Farther down the street the girls who operated out of their own cribs—narrow little houses in a row—stood on their porches, their breath making clouds in the air, to drum up customers.

Across town, the rich and respectable would be celebrating at the Washoe Club and the International Hotel with oysters and roast beef and an orchestra to play "Auld Lang Syne" at midnight. Tim knew, because last year he had gone to the Washoe Club with John Ormond and his family. Tim thought of Isabella, and then of inviting one of Roseanna's girls over to drink champagne with him. He had one hoarded bottle, bought on a whim. But it didn't seem a good omen for the new year to spend tonight with someone who had to be paid.

What the hell. He got the bottle out of the composing room, which was as cold as an icebox, and opened it. He poured some into an empty jar and drank it.

"Happy New Year," he told the broken press.

The press, an ancient Washington, stood silent and grimy in the center of the composing-room floor. It looked to Tim like nothing so much as a fire screen with a small coffin stuck through its middle. The twin rails supported the bed, extending like a stuck-out tongue and being held up in the front by a crossbar and a single leg. It didn't look all that complicated, but he had to admit that Waldo had about as much mechanical ability as an elk.

What the hell, he thought again, and went over, champagne in hand, and began to poke at it. He hadn't bothered until now, since there wasn't anything to print a paper on if the press was working, and Tim was no newspaperman. But he had to do something. You couldn't spend New Year's Eve feeling sorry for yourself. That was probably an omen for the coming year, too, like being hungry on New Year's Day. If you did that, Abby Givens had always warned him, you'd be hungry for the rest of the year.

He put the champagne down, slid the bed out onto the supports, and lifted the tympan. The form still held the locked-up type from Waldo's last edition. Tim squinted, trying to read the mirror-image letters. "Union Struggle with Ninevah Mine" it read. So what else was new? Tim found the ink brayer and ink and rolled the brayer over the type. He tore a scrap of newsprint from the tail end of the roll and laid it on the type. He put the tympan back down and ran the bed into the press under the platen. There was a bar to press the platen down, so he leaned on that and then lifted the platen again. He pulled the newsprint off the form and discovered that it was an indecipherable mess.

Tim wadded it up and threw it away, then glared at the press. It occurred to him that a Washington flatbed press wasn't an awful lot different from the one that Gutenberg had invented in the fifteenth century. "The human race has had four hundred years to get smarter than you," he informed it.

He got the coal oil lamp and balanced it on a shelf beside the type rack to give himself more light, then peered at the springs and levers above the platen. Something was moving that should be stationary, making the platen twist when it came down on the form. Tim got a screwdriver and started taking the toggle levers apart. When he had a handful of pieces, he sat down to figure out how they worked.

Ten minutes later, he was drinking champagne out of his jar again, stomping around the composing room, and cursing Waldo Howard, who didn't have the brains to make a blue jay fly crooked. The toggle levers were broken, so that the platen came down skewed and waltzed all over the form. Any idiot could have figured that out. Tim pulled his hair with both hands so that it stood up straight as if he had been electrocuted.

"I'm going to kill you, Waldo!" he shouted into the gloom of the front office. If Waldo had had any brains, the press would have been working. And if the press had been working, Waldo would never have lost it at poker—maybe. Tim had to admit that Waldo had been fighting a losing battle. Maybe the press had just been the last straw, something that would let Waldo jettison the *Beacon* with no regrets.

Tim had never been able to resist machinery. He drank some more champagne and started fixing the toggle levers. Maybe Waldo would buy it back. No, he wouldn't. Waldo didn't have any money. Waldo had lost the *Beacon* to Tim, who had then lost his mine to Eddie Tucker. And Waldo had a new job with the *Chronicle* in San Francisco. Come to think of it, Waldo had left last week, so Tim couldn't kill him.

Tim glared at the press. It looked back at him inscrutably, a deformed fire screen capable of making its views known to the world. Tim inked the form again and put another ragged scrap of paper in it. This time the impression was perfect. "Union Struggle with Ninevah Mine." The story under the head was carefully objective. Waldo had been pretty desperate for advertising when he wrote it.

I could tell them something about the Ninevah, Tim thought vengefully. His eyes strayed toward the type rack. One week's worth of Readyprint was bundled in the corner. It was weeks out of date, but he could always ink the printed side black. And the advertising pages were still good. Dr. Scott's Electric Corsets, and Dr. Michaelson's Celebrated Infallible Fit Powders didn't go out of date. Tim started pulling the type out of the form.

It took him longer than he would have thought to put it back into the font in the right slots, but he got it done as the last New Year's revelers straggled down the street toward home or passed out on the porches of the girls' cribs and were hauled back in bodily so they wouldn't freeze. Snow was falling outside, making a magical, misty landscape glowing under the full moon.

It was 1889, Tim thought, the last year of the decade, the beginning of the run toward the twentieth century, when anything might happen. What would the world be like in eleven years? It occurred to him that a man with a newspaper might have something to do with how things shaped up by 1900. Might be able to give the world the benefit of the insights that Tim, under the influence of New Year's Eve and a lot of champagne, could suddenly see so clearly. *Nobody's always right.* That was a great thought, he decided, and pulled out a sheet of paper and a pencil.

Having committed this message to paper, he somehow ended up on the camp bed between the editor's desk and the type rack.

In the morning he had a hangover equaled only by the one he had had the morning after he won the *Beacon* in a poker game. But the editorial, read and reread over a cup of coffee, still looked good to him. He might not be able to spell when he was drunk, he decided, but he possessed a talent hitherto unsuspected: He could write.

He wondered what would happen if he actually tried to run this newspaper. It would be tight at first, but if he made it lively enough, folks would buy it. People liked newspapers that were unpredictable, "newspapers with pepper," as Waldo once said. And the *Territorial Enterprise*, the only real competition, hadn't had any pepper since the mine owners, bankers, and politicians had bought it. If people read the *Beacon*, then the advertisers would advertise, whether they liked the editor or not. Virginia City was a town that knew which side its bread was buttered on.

Tim did some figuring in his head and some more figuring on paper. It might take six months, but there was at least that much left to run on the lease, and he could continue to live in the office and not pay rent. He had the Readyprint to start out with. The paper mill might be placated with a promissory note from an ambitious new editor. They would know they wouldn't get paid at all if someone didn't get the *Beacon* going—

unless they wanted to go to San Francisco and try to shake it out of Waldo. He could ask his dad for a loan, Tim decided. With a business to put it into, he wouldn't be hat in hand.

I'm going to do it! Even with a hangover, he felt more excited than he had in months. A new year, a new enterprise, a new start. Tim jumped up and surveyed the type font, type stick in hand. He had watched Waldo spike type often enough to know how to do it. You just had to remember to work backward, right to left. His new editorial was suddenly burning a hole in his hand. He had something to say to a lot of people, and, by God, he was going to say it! Laboriously, he began picking letters out of the font:

A Call for Common Sense

In any dispute among men of reason, there is always one ditch to jump: that of blind prejudice. No man seems naturally endowed with the ability to see that his foe may occasionally speak truth or that he himself may occasionally be a darned fool.

The striking Ninevah miners, whom this newspaper perceives to have right on their side, have yet employed some tactics as deplorable as those of the Ninevah management. Broken heads and mob violence and the beating up of scabs have no place in the negotiations of honest men. And in our opinion they will always go a fair way to sinking a just cause.

Compound this with the out-and-out greed of a management that would cheerfully sell its own grandmother for ten cents, and tragedy is lurking around the corner.

The Miners' Union needs to police its own, but for the good of our community, a serious move must come from Mr. Ormond, who, in our opinion, has hitherto worn blinders made out of money. It rests with the right-thinking citizens of Virginia City to think of the safety and well-being of the

men who go down in a subterranean shaft to mine
the rock that has built this town, and to put pressure on Mr. Ormond for the good of us all.

Tim grinned. That ought to start something. He
filled in the corners with such town news as he could
think of and an ad in a neatly bordered box offering the
services of the *Beacon* press for job printing. Under the
masthead he put the date and *Timothy Holt, Editor and
Publisher*. Then, as a precaution, he loaded his pistol
and put it on the front desk. Assuredly, that editorial
was going to start something. But that was why Waldo
had always claimed that a man ran a newspaper: in
order to start something.

Tim got a sheet of Readyprint and laid the blank
side on the form. Old Waldo might not know it, but he
had just given Tim purpose in his life. And a fair chance
of getting shot, of course, but Tim wasn't going to
worry about that. He had something to do that he
wanted to do, and the prospect of getting shot had
never stopped a Holt.

Tim began to whistle as he worked.

The saga of the Holts, America's "first frontier family," continues with

THE HOLTS:
AN AMERICAN DYNASTY

Book 2

OKLAHOMA SOONERS

by Dana Fuller Ross
author of the 25 million copy
WAGONS WEST series

Turn the page for an exciting preview of
OKLAHOMA SOONERS . . .

Nineteen-year-old Cathy Martin, encouraged by Lucy Woods's success on New York's legitimate stage, runs away from finishing school to seek her own fortune as an actress. Her great-aunt Claudia Brentwood comes to Manhattan to set up housekeeping at the luxurious Waldorf Astoria Hotel, to chaperon Cathy and her thirteen-year-old cousin, Eden Brentwood. They are joined there by Eden's half brother, Sam, and his wife, Annie, newly returned from their two year honeymoon trip to Europe.

Friday evening marked Cathy's theatrical debut. Her family could not learn of her performance until after she was a success, an actress. She lied as nonchalantly as she could manage that she was meeting Lucy Woods at the Lyceum Theater, so they needn't worry about her. Somewhat to her surprise, no one made any objection at all. But Cathy didn't think that Aunt Claudia had really been paying attention. And certainly Sam and

Annie hadn't. They just glared at each other all through dinner, and Eden looked frightened by their martial tension.

As soon as dinner was over, Cathy decided to go while the going was good. She put on her wrap and picked up her bag with her sewing kit concealed inside it. She had a needle and a package of pins, which, attached to the tapes she had already sewn inside her dress, would raise the hem to her knees, in accordance with the music-hall producer's specifications. She had bought a pair of black net tights to wear under it and a black plume for her hair, and she felt very giddy and devilish.

If anyone had been paying attention to Cathy, they would have known she was up to something. But Annie had been waiting for two days for a chance to let Sam have it for his infidelities, and Sam, well aware of her mood, had been conspicuously absent from the Waldorf, pursuing his own concerns and returning only when he was sure Annie was asleep. It was Claudia who had bidden him come to dinner tonight. Claudia was the one he wouldn't cross.

When Cathy had gone, Claudia rose from the table and took Eden off with her to put the girls' hair in curl papers. Tomorrow was Eden's fourteenth birthday, and it was Claudia's wish that whatever Sam and Annie had to settle might be settled now, so as not to cast a pall on Eden's lavish party.

As the door closed behind them, Sam got up too.

"I want to talk to you," Annie said with a suggestion of gritted teeth.

"Going to call me on the carpet?" Sam inquired, grinning at her with saturnine sarcasm. He was furious that there was no way to avoid the confrontation. "Mother dear?" he added.

"I'm not your mother!" Annie snapped. "Even though you've been acting as if you were five."

"Been keeping tabs?" Sam looked rebellious. "Why don't you hire a Pinkerton man?"

"The only thing I need a detective for is to find your conscience; it's that small. Do you think I didn't see you, acting like a tomcat with that chorus girl right under my nose? I was just plain mortified."

"And I'm not, I suppose? Coming to you hat in hand every time I want a nickel to spend?" Sam made an obsequious begging gesture.

"You get an allowance. A fat one. And I don't ask how you spend it."

"Shall I confirm your worst suspicions? I spend it on opium. Whiskey and sin. Harlots. I go out and prowl the Bowery every night. I'm just sinking in iniquity."

"Oh, stop it," Annie said. "I know that you bought my Christmas present with it. But why do you have to act like this?"

"Maybe because I'm choking to death on your diamond-studded leash," Sam snapped.

"Well, you didn't mind the diamonds when you married me," Annie snapped back. "And you knew I was going to keep control of my money. Don't be childish." She looked at his restive, angry face. "Aw, Sam, you know you aren't reliable. I'd be crazy to give you a free rein. You've never managed a business. You don't know how to do it."

"I could learn," Sam suggested. "You ever think of that?"

"Yeah, I've thought of it, and it plain gives me nightmares. You'd put money in every get-rich-quick scheme that comes down the pike, draining off my capital.

Before we even left Virginia City you were after me to put money in that gold mine, and I knew it was salted."

"I knew it too," Sam said, irritated. "But I could have turned around and sold it for a big profit."

"Then you're just flat dishonest." Annie put her napkin down and looked at him, trying to see some steadiness in him and not finding any. "They'd have outsmarted you," she said gently. "I knew those boys from way back."

"Yeah, you always know it all. Maybe sometimes I just want to talk to someone who doesn't know so much."

Annie raised her eyebrows. "Like Sukie, that little chorus girl at the party? A good choice: That tart didn't look as if she had enough brains to give her someplace to put a hat."

"She isn't a tart," Sam said defensively.

"As pure as the driven snow," Annie said acidly. " 'Oh, Mr. Brentwood, you're such a *card*!' "

"Oh, Annie, she doesn't mean anything to me." Sam walked around the table, put his hands on her shoulders, and ran his fingers cajolingly along the back of her neck.

"I expected you'd step out on me some, Sam," Annie said stiffly, "because I've got no illusions about you. But I expected you to behave decently, and I didn't expect you to humiliate me. You've gone too far."

"Oh, now, Annie." He let his hands trail around to the front of her neck and run lightly over one breast under the tight silk bodice. "You know you do something to me that no one else can. You always have."

Annie pushed his hand away. "Stop it. You won't get around me like that. You haven't been home in two nights."

"Maybe I was afraid to," Sam said. He tried to put his hand back.

Annie slapped at it and twisted her chair away. "You aren't coming into my bed out of someone else's. I know you're probably out of money and are afraid of making me so mad that you'll be broke the next quarter. Well, you stay home and sober a couple of nights. Then we'll talk about an advance on your allowance."

Sam backed off, his eyes blazing, his mood turning defiant again, as quick and unstable as a gas jet. "The hell with you." He turned on his heel and stalked into the parlor.

"Where are you going?" Annie was behind him in the doorway.

Sam snatched his hat off the coat rack by the front door. "Out!"

The Elysian Music Hall, where Cathy was scheduled to perform, looked menacing by gaslight. The customers crowding through the front doors were noisy and seemed half-drunk already, even the women. And the alley by the stage door was very dark. Cathy made her way into the murky light of the backstage passageway, grateful to be inside. Eddie Gamble, who had intervened with the producer to get Cathy the job, was waiting for her by a dressing-room door.

"In here," he said, preceding her into the room without ceremony.

She looked at him with surprise.

"You're late. And your dress is too long."

"It won't take me but a minute to shorten it," Cathy said. There was something different about Eddie: His brown eyes had a glitter that was less friendly and more demanding. She handed him the sheet music. She couldn't raise her hem until he left. "Please give this to the orchestra for me."

Eddie's hand rested on her wrist, caressing it. "You're on in fifteen minutes. They always put new acts on early," he smiled. "We'll have plenty of time to celebrate afterward."

"Oh, I'll have to go right home," Cathy said.

Eddie bent closer to her. "You aren't going to run out on me tonight," he said distinctly. "Girls who get jobs are supposed to be grateful for them. I'm expecting a whole lot of gratitude."

Cathy stared at him. His smile had grown wolflike and hungry. The knowledge that she had made a mistake hit her like a punch in the stomach. She looked around the dingy room, but there was no way out except past Eddie.

He laughed, and his hand moved up her arm. "Now get that skirt hiked up. This isn't a revival meeting."

Cathy pushed at him. "All right. All right. Just go away."

"I'll wait outside the door," Eddie said. She felt his hand caress her buttocks. "I guess I can wait that long."

When the door closed behind him, she looked frantically for a lock, but there wasn't one. Mechanically, she began pulling up the tapes inside her skirt and pinning them. She put on the black net stockings and slipped her shoes back on. She looked into the cracked mirror and, shaking with horror, pinned the black plumes into her hair. There was no way out now except onto the stage. Somehow she would have to get away from him after the performance.

Cathy looked at the closed door, scared to death of Eddie. *Oh, why did I do it?*

The door opened without a knock, and Swanson, the producer, glared around it at her. "Get out there. You're on next." He inspected the green dress and the sad, silly black plumes. "That damn dress is still too long."

"I can't—it won't—"

"Move!" Swanson pulled her out the door and shoved her at Eddie. He didn't have the sheet music anymore; he must have given it to the orchestra. They led her down the passage, past other dressing rooms filled with performers in various stages of undress. A canvas drop thumped down beside them, and Swanson pushed Cathy out onto the stage in front of it. The orchestra was playing the first bars of her selection, "None Can Love Like an Irishman." The curtain came up.

"Ladies and gentlemen, for your particular enjoyment, Miss Catherine Salton, the New York Nightingale!"

The air in the music hall was dim and smoky. The audience, impatiently waiting to be entertained, was a sea of pale faces in the gloom, drinking beer at smeared tables. The orchestra leader looked at her testily. She nodded at him, her teeth chattering.

"The turban'd Turk, who scorns the world—" she sang mechanically, knowing her voice was flat.

The audience began to shift in their seats.

"The gay monsieur—" Cathy lost the beat, struggled frantically to catch it, and stumbled over the next line. She glanced into the wings and saw Eddie watching her, with a grim-faced Swanson. Terrified, she looked out into the audience again. When she saw their angry expressions and heard their booing, she lost the beat again.

She tried to go on singing, but the words wouldn't come. She couldn't remember the next verse. Some of the audience were pounding with their beer bottles on the table tops, and half of the rest were standing up, shouting at her.

"Ask any . . . any girl you happen to meet—"

A piece of a half-eaten sausage bun smacked against the front of her dress and a beer bottle landed at her feet.

Cathy put her hand to her face and fled, sobbing, stumbling past the canvas drop. One of the tapes holding her hem came loose and straggled around her ankles, nearly tripping her. Behind her she could hear the audience roaring and the clatter of more bottles on the stage.

"Get the curtain down!" Swanson shouted.

The orchestra wound up the song with a crescendo, and the curtain hurtled down. "Get Mirella out there!" The producer was livid. Another canvas unfurled in front of Cathy's, and Mirella May came out in red spangles and white tights, shedding her kimono as she went.

"Ladies and gentlemen, the management wishes to apologize. . . . Ladies and gentlemen, the miraculous Miss Mirella May!" In the orchestra pit, an all-girl orchestra was taking its place in a flurry of sheet music, while the regular orchestra beat a retreat.

"Damn you!" Swanson grabbed Cathy by the arm and yanked her into the wings, his fist raised. The music started up, but the patrons were still shouting. "You told me you could sing. I'm gonna bust your lying face open!"

She tried to tell him that she could sing, that it was Eddie's waiting backstage, about to prey on her, that had terrified her so; but Swanson wouldn't care.

"Get her out of here, Swanny," the stage manager hissed. "They hear you in front!"

Swanson started to drag her down the passageway when Eddie Gamble grabbed her other arm and pushed Swanson away. "Oh, no, you don't. You let her alone."

Cathy cringed between the two of them, knowing that this was no rescue. Eddie's next words confirmed it. "It's a shame you were such a flop, kid, but you're still a hit in my book. And you don't have to sing to pay what you owe *me*."

"Let me go!" She gathered her courage to struggle furiously, but Eddie just laughed. He had hold of her by both forearms. "I'll let you go in a while. When we're square." He turned her around and pushed her down the passage toward the stage door. The other performers gave her blank stares, unwilling to interfere. He dragged her out into the alleyway, and she saw with horror that he had a cab waiting in the darkness.

Cathy began to fight him again, and Eddie gave her a backhanded slap across the face that sent her reeling. He jerked the cab door open. The driver looked in the other direction.

"My name's not really Salton," she wailed. "You don't understand!"

"I don't care what your name is. If you're on the lam, that's not my problem. Now get in!"

She clung to the outside of the vehicle, sobbing, and Eddie's grip loosened just for an instant as the sound of running feet came down the alley. Cathy jerked her head around, afraid that it was Swanson or some friend of Eddie's.

With incredulous disbelief, she saw that it was Sam Brentwood. Sukie, the chorus girl he had been romancing, was stumbling after him in her high-heeled shoes.

Sam hauled Eddie off Cathy and swung an expert punch at his jaw. Cathy leaned against the cab, unable to catch her breath.

Eddie and Sam were rolling in the dirt, swinging at each other in fury as Cathy watched, her hands to her mouth.

"C'mon, Sam," Sukie cheered. "Hit him good." Then she turned to Cathy. "We were out front," she explained. "You got rocks in your head, coming here, you know that? And with a guy like Eddie."

"I didn't know," Cathy whispered.

Sukie shook her head. "Jeez, you're green."

Sam twisted away from Eddie and stumbled to his feet. As Eddie got up too, Sam hit him again. Eddie staggered backward and dropped with a thud.

Sam, backhanding blood from his mouth, stalked over to the cab and looked up at the driver. "You get paid to abduct women often?"

"I get paid to drive," the man said. "I don't stick my fool nose in where it ain't wanted."

"Well, you can drive," Sam wheezed. He marched around to face Cathy. "Get in." He pushed her into the cab and got in, too. "The Waldorf," he told the driver.

"What about me?" Sukie demanded as Sam slammed the door shut.

"Oh, Lord, I forgot about you." Sam opened the door again and pulled her in. "Twenty-ninth Street," he yelled at the driver.

"I've never been to the Waldorf," Sukie sounded wistful.

"Well, you aren't going tonight," Sam said.

The cab lurched down the alley. Inside, Sam leaned back and ran a hand through his hair. He had lost his hat, and his dark hair hung limply in his filthy face. His shirtfront was torn to ribbons, and his knuckles were bleeding.

"All right, you putty head," he said when he had gotten his breath back, "what the hell were you doing in that dump?"

"I wanted to sing," Cathy said, sniffling. "And don't you swear at me, Sam Brentwood."

"You could have been raped," Sam said grimly.

Cathy gasped. That wasn't a word she had ever in her life heard spoken aloud.

"All right, he could have taken liberties with your person," Sam said sarcastically. "After what you've been up to, I didn't bother to mince words."

Now that she was in the safety of the vehicle, Cathy was beginning to get some of her spirit back. "What *I've* been up to?" she asked indignantly, with a look at Sukie. "You're calling *me* on the carpet?"

"I wasn't going to be raped," Sam said, chuckling.

"I think you're just horrible!"

"You're lucky I was there."

"Oh? Well, I'll be sure to tell that to Annie!"

"What are you gonna tell your folks?" Sukie asked, interested. "Your aunt's gonna have a fit."

"You stay out of this," Sam and Cathy said together.

The cab rolled to a stop outside the house on Twenty-ninth Street where Sukie had a room, and Sam left her on the sidewalk with a minimum of ceremony.

"It's not your fault, kid," he muttered, "but I don't think I'll be coming around again."

"Naw," Sukie said sadly. "I guess not. Well, it's been fun."

"Look, do you think you could keep quiet about this?" Sam put some money in her hand.

"Sure," Sukie said. "I don't talk." She stashed the currency in her bodice.

"Buy yourself a present," Sam urged. "Consider it from me." He looked up at the driver. "The Waldorf. And see if you can keep quiet too."

When the cab deposited them at the hotel, Sam added another bribe as an aid to silence and handed Cathy down. She quailed a little at the brightly lit street. She had torn the rest of the tapes loose from her dress so that the hemline reached her shoes, but she knew what she—and Sam—looked like.

He pulled her into the shadows and repinned her hair as well as he could. He threw the plumes into a potted tree with a gesture of disgust.

"All right, walk fast and keep your mouth shut." He guided her through the lobby and into the elevator. Its operator goggled at them, but the elevator was quicker than the stairs. Sam slipped him a bill, too. "Sixth floor, and the young lady is not feeling well, so please don't stop for anyone else."

As they got out, Sam took Cathy by the arm. "You're going to have to confess, so you might as well do it right away."

"What about you?" Cathy demanded. "Are you going to confess?"

"Grateful, aren't you?" Sam snapped.

"I like Annie," Cathy defended. "I think you treat her disgracefully."

"Oh, you do? Well, *I* think I should have left you in the alley."

Sam pushed open Claudia's door and they confronted a stunned tableau of Claudia, Annie, and Claudia's beau, Howard Locke.

"She was singing at a dump on West Thirty-fourth Street," Sam announced. "They threw sausages at her."

"*Oh!* Oh, I wish you *had* just left me there and gone home with that—that harlot!" Cathy screamed at him. She burst into tears and ran from the room. They heard her bedroom door slam.

Before anyone could say anything else, Annie snatched up a vase from Claudia's sideboard and hurled it wildly at Sam. He ducked, and it smashed into the wall behind him in shards of china and sodden flowers. Annie picked up her skirts and ran through the mess, tears streaming down her face, too. Her flying footsteps echoed down the hall, and another door slammed.

Howard Locke took up his hat. "Claudia, my dear, I would stay and help sort things out, but I expect you would rather do without me just now." He bent gallantly over her hand.

"Thank you," she said faintly. "I—it has been a most enjoyable evening, up until this moment. I do hope you will call again."

There was a faint twinkle in Mr. Locke's eyes. "Gracious lady, constantly, if you will let me. When one is my age, one has seen far too much of the world to worry about trifles." He departed with a tip of his hat.

"*That* is a gentleman," Claudia announced to Sam. She pinned him to the wall with her eyes as if he had been a butterfly in a box. "I am furious with you. By the looks of you I gather that you got Cathy out of a scrape, but you have entirely negated it with your boorish behavior. You are *not* a gentleman, and I am ashamed of you!"

"Gran—"

His grandmother's violet eyes bored right through him. "Don't talk to me. I am too angry with you. When a man marries, he makes certain vows, and it is despicable not to honor them. To say nothing of throwing it in your wife's face."

"I didn't throw it," Sam protested. "That little devil in there did."

"I'll deal with her," Claudia said grimly. "My advice to you is to go and make your peace with your wife—if she will let you in. If she won't, you may sleep in the hall." She pointed at the door until he went through it.

Claudia decided to ring for the housekeeping sta[ff]
later; she could hear Cathy hysterically sobbing behin[d]
her closed door.

Now or in the morning? Claudia wondered. *Now,* sh[e]
determined. In the morning the family would be in [a]
flurry with Eden's party. It was a mercy, she thought [as]
she passed Eden's silent door, that the child slept s[o]
well. At least Claudia hoped she did.

She tapped on Cathy's door, and when Cathy sniffle[d]
"Go away," she went in anyway.

★ WAGONS WEST ★

This continuing, magnificent saga recounts the adventures of a brave
band of settlers, all of different backgrounds, all sharing one dream—
to find a new and better life.

☐	26822	**INDEPENDENCE! #1**	$4.50
☐	26162	**NEBRASKA! #2**	$4.50
☐	26242	**WYOMING! #3**	$4.50
☐	26072	**OREGON! #4**	$4.50
☐	26070	**TEXAS! #5**	$4.50
☐	26377	**CALIFORNIA! #6**	$4.50
☐	26546	**COLORADO! #7**	$4.50
☐	26069	**NEVADA! #8**	$4.50
☐	26163	**WASHINGTON! #9**	$4.50
☐	26073	**MONTANA! #10**	$4.50
☐	26184	**DAKOTA! #11**	$4.50
☐	26521	**UTAH! #12**	$4.50
☐	26071	**IDAHO! #13**	$4.50
☐	26367	**MISSOURI! #14**	$4.50
☐	27141	**MISSISSIPPI! #15**	$4.50
☐	25247	**LOUISIANA! #16**	$4.50
☐	25622	**TENNESSEE! #17**	$4.50
☐	26022	**ILLINOIS! #18**	$4.50
☐	26533	**WISCONSIN! #19**	$4.50
☐	26849	**KENTUCKY! #20**	$4.50
☐	27065	**ARIZONA! #21**	$4.50
☐	27458	**NEW MEXICO! #22**	$4.50
☐	27703	**OKLAHOMA! #23**	$4.50

- - - - - - - - - - - - - - - -

Special Offer
Buy a Bantam Book
for only 50¢.

Now you can have Bantam's catalog filled with hundreds of titles plus take advantage of our unique and exciting bonus book offer. A special offer which gives you the opportunity to purchase a Bantam book for only 50¢. Here's how!

By ordering any five books at the regular price per order, you can also choose any other single book listed (up to a $5.95 value) for just 50¢. Some restrictions do apply, but for further details why not send for Bantam's catalog of titles today!

Just send us your name and address and we will send you a catalog!